# Sarah's Psalm

*a novel*

## Florence Ladd

SCRIBNER

*To Michael and Halstead*

SCRIBNER
1230 Avenue of the Americas
New York, NY 10020

SCRIBNER and design are trademarks of
Simon & Schuster Inc.

Set in Stempel Garamond
Designed by Brooke Zimmer

Manufactured in the United States of America

1 3 5 7 9 10 8 6 4 2

Library of Congress Cataloging-in-Publication Data
is available.

ISBN 0-684-80410-7

## Acknowledgments

I am forever grateful to my agent, Faith Hampton Childs, and editor, Leigh Haber. I am indebted also to Jorgene Chartier, Greer Kessel, and Lori Pope.

# Prologue

The letter "A" appeared and faded into a woman wearing a white A-shaped caftan. Her face, the mirror image of my own though more mature, was kind. On her lips, the bud of a smile. She beckoned and said, "Follow me," then stepped back into ripples of the sea. Splashing waves and squawking seagulls surrounded us. Gradually gliding toward a distant shore, still beckoning, she was joined by my seafaring Uncle George. She took his hand. They vanished in the sands of an island shaded by palm trees. Still I could hear her voice, her mezzo-soprano aria of one word, *SENEGAL.* Her song was joined by the music of a flute. In a slow diminuendo, her voice slipped away. The solo flute continued playing. I swallowed hard and heard my voice say, *"I will cast mine eyes upon the ocean from whence cometh my help. My help cometh from Senegal, which is heaven and earth."*

# 1

**1** CHANGED MY MIND IN MIDAIR, SOMEWHERE between Paris and Dakar. Had I been driving overland in the notorious Paris-Dakar race, I would have stopped the car in the desert, dropped out of the race. I had the urge to signal the steward on the Air France flight and demand that the pilot turn back. I heard my mother's plea: "Sarah, please don't go. Don't meddle in that marriage. Don't do something that you'll regret." And my father's question: "I'd really like to know why you have to move to Dakar?" Antonia Dale, my friend and colleague at Boston University, had said adamantly, "I wouldn't go. I'd send a cable—ask him for more information about the circumstances. But I definitely wouldn't go."

Although I had tried to persuade everyone that Dakar was a place where I could do my best work and assist Ibrahim Mangane with his projects, I had convinced no one, not even myself. Still, I had bought a one-way ticket to an uncertain future and had left Ibrahim's post office box number as my forwarding address.

I closed my eyes. The gyration of the plane rocked me to sleep. Startled by the grinding of the landing gear, I woke up, looked down and saw the beckoning finger of a peninsula in the Atlantic. Dakar. I reached into the seat pocket for an airsickness bag and emptied my ambivalent stomach.

Born in a country and social set that seemed alien to me, I knew at an early age that I was meant to exist elsewhere. Juvenile fantasies about a Senegalese girlhood evolved into a fascination with Senegal and my future study of Senegal's major writer,

Ibrahim Mangane. I fell in love with his books, his characters, and their lives in Senegal's cities and villages. His works invaded my dreams, evoked my prayers.

I was not religious, but devoutly I prayed to go to Senegal. I was neither unstable nor possessed, but Senegal was constantly on my mind. I closed my eyes and imagined myself a character in a Mangane novel amid throngs of women, draped in cloth of many colors, ambling through crowded markets where women farmers and their children sold mangoes and coconuts, red peppers and peanuts, sacks of rice and beans yielded by their sometimes meager, sometimes abundant harvests. A flock of pelicans in flight flapped overhead. I heard a griot whisper tales about an ancient village in a language I did not understand to a circle of children, mesmerized by his words, squatting in the sand.

I daydreamed about walking at night with Ibrahim Mangane along endless beaches lit by a forever full moon. Scenes from his novels flashed continuously on the screen of my mind. Ideas from his works invaded my imagination. Ibrahim Mangane, a man I had never met, made a place I had never seen more vivid than the everyday reality of my life in Cambridge, Massachusetts, and more engaging than my marriage to Abraham Lincoln Thompson.

Lincoln and I had been married two years when he began to view my study of African novels and films as an obsession, and I began to question the nature of our marriage. I was a graduate student in comparative literature at Harvard. He was studying engineering at MIT. We lived on Trowbridge Street in a second-story studio apartment with an alcove for a kitchen and an ancient bathroom.

Furnishings were bought at thrift shops or gathered the night before trash collection on prosperous Francis Avenue. Selected from heaps of tastefully worn, discarded household items: a mustard-colored convertible sofabed, a mud-brown overstuffed chair, a red metal kitchen table, four kitchen chairs—each with a different design and provenance, a desk with the initials of previous owners scratched in a drawer.

Lincoln bought a hi-fi set. We stacked our records and books on shelves of boards and cinder bricks that stood on a dirt cheap, cocoa-colored carpet. The apartment looked like a stage set for a drama about a drab student marriage in a university town.

Schedules of classes and seminars, reading assignments, and examinations regulated the rhythm of our lives. Up early on weekday mornings, scanning our notebooks over cornflakes and coffee, we had few words for each other. "Pass the milk." "Your turn to do the laundry this week." "Please turn off the radio—I can't concentrate." At eight o'clock, Lincoln left for MIT. I read at the kitchen table until it was time to go to a seminar from ten until noon on Mondays. On Tuesday and Thursday mornings, I attended lectures on non-Western literature; and on Fridays, I met with undergraduates to discuss the lectures and readings. Friday afternoons found me engaged in sherry hour repartee about Camus, Sartre, and Wittgenstein in Brattle Street book-lined living rooms of uncommonly homely professors. Saturday mornings were for errands, and Sunday mornings for the *New York Times*. Most evenings Lincoln was at his MIT laboratory and I was in Widener Library.

Our marriage was like many student marriages. The apartment that we called "home" was a place to store books and papers, share an occasional meal, play chess, scan the newspapers, watch television, make love in haste and detachment, then fitfully fall asleep.

In the fantasies of our parents, whose mortgaged Washington, D.C., rooftops sheltered wall-to-wall carpets, china closets, Duncan Phyfe copies of chairs and tables, and black bourgeois dreams, Lincoln and I floated in the air against a star-studded Cambridge sky like a Chagall-painted bride and groom. They thought of us as the ideally matched couple living happily ever after in the perfect college town. Our marriage had made our parents' favorite dreams come true.

We had known each other since childhood. The Stewarts and the Thompsons lived in the same neighborhood, shopped in the same stores, worshipped at Calvary AME Zion Church. Lincoln and I had attended the same high school where he was two years my senior. I knew him from a distance, not as a classmate, but rather as an older boy whom I very much admired. He was tall, handsome, athletic, intelligent, and well mannered. He stood when adults entered a room, opened doors for girls, and tipped his snap-brim tweed cap to my father when they passed on the street. When he walked me home, he insisted on carrying my books and tennis racquet. He asked me out on my first date—a Saturday afternoon movie at the Booker T. Washington Theater. We ate a jumbo box of buttered popcorn, held greasy hands in the steamy dark balcony, stole glances at each other, and looked occasionally at the screen illuminated by Audrey Hepburn's amble through *Breakfast at Tiffany's*.

When I was a Wellesley College freshman, Lincoln was a junior at Dartmouth. Parties, football games, tennis matches, and holiday festivities brought us together at black college student events in Boston, New York, and Washington.

I enjoyed being seen with stately, handsome Lincoln Thompson. His features had irregularities: one eye slightly larger than the other and a slightly crooked mustache, which accentuated the near perfection in his six-foot-two model of lean masculinity. We reveled in the company and conversation that whirled about us when we entered parties—I in my ruby velvet strapless sheath and Lincoln in a tuxedo with a ruby bow tie and cummerbund. That people fell in love with the image of us made us feel that we had fallen in love with each other.

Our wedding, an important social benchmark for our families, afforded public recognition of their accomplishments and ours. In the wedding album, our parents, Lincoln, and I were Kodachromed in the traditional poses of the grinning wedding party. Between plastic leaves in the back of the album we kept clippings from *Jet* and *The Washington Afro-American*.

*Sarah Marie Stewart and Abraham Lincoln Thompson III were married on Saturday, June 20, in Rankin Memorial Chapel at Howard University. Mrs. Thompson, a graduate of Wellesley College in Massachusetts, is the daughter of Mr. and Mrs. Henry B. Stewart who are teachers in Wash-*

*ington, D.C., schools. The bride is a graduate student at
Harvard University. The groom, a graduate of Dartmouth
College, is a graduate student at the Massachusetts Insti-
tute of Technology. He is the son of Atty. and Mrs. Abra-
ham Lincoln Thompson, Jr., of Washington, D.C. and
Highland Beach, Maryland. The couple will reside in
Cambridge after a Bermuda honeymoon.*

It took only a few months after our wedding for me to realize
that Lincoln and I were living with a different sense of geography. His was a small world of familiar places, faces, and rituals.
Our apartment was within walking distance of MIT and the
NAACP headquarters where he attended civil rights meetings.
The apartment of his best friend, Sam Higgins, their preferred
tennis court, and their favorite hangout, Cronin's bar, were
nearby. The geography of my imagination, however, had been
stretched by my childhood fantasies about foreign places and
tales of distant lands told by my Uncle George, whose story
about a girl exactly like me in Dakar was rooted deeply in my
mind. The idea of another self—an alter ego—in Senegal had
stirred my curiosity about the country and the rest of Africa. In
the quiet, dark hours before falling asleep, when girls enter the
vestibules of dreams, I was joined by my Senegalese twin. While
other girls cut out paper dolls, I clipped African scenes from
*Life* and *National Geographic*. In the photos of girls, I searched
for her, for myself—for my shining, dark eyes, my button-of-a-
nose, the dimple in my chin, my willowy body with the slight
bulge of emerging breasts. In college, I attended lectures on
African politics and scanned newspapers and magazines,
libraries and bookstores, for anything on Africa. I was
entranced by African art. Percussive rhythms of magical African
music drummed quietly in my mind.

Black Africa was news. Presidents and prime ministers from
Africa appeared on television and the front pages of the *Washington Post* and the *New York Times*. Scholars, writers, and
political figures from Nigeria, Ghana, Senegal, Kenya, and Tan-
zania were invited to lecture at universities in Cambridge and

Boston. Their crisp analyses of black and white relations in richly accented English, their attire and proud carriage fascinated me. With confidence, they spoke of commanding their continent's destiny. They stirred in me an allegiance to Africa that I had never felt for my own continent.

Whether colored or Negro or black or Afro-American, the prospects for our civil rights struggle were uncertain. News of bus boycotts, freedom rides, sit-ins, and the desegregation of southern universities made for moments of hope, while the backlash—hostile crowds of white people hurling epithets and rocks at brave black children—made me weep. I knew there must be a more civil place for the life I wanted to lead.

At a Boston University conference on African literature, I was introduced to the works of Senegal's Ibrahim Mangane. Although Ibrahim was invited to the conference, he was not granted a U.S. visa and could not attend. Instead, he sent a film he had produced and directed, *The Chains of Gorée*. The audience was gripped by the film: the capture of an African family— a couple with three young sons—and the abuses they experienced in the slave house on Gorée Island where they were held, then herded onto a ship for the voyage to American bondage. As I watched, I ached with the agony of the actors in that slave-trade horror show. Their faces radiated resistance. I saw myself in the countenance of a minor character in the film. Was it she—my twin?

When the film ended, at first no one spoke. Then heated discussions erupted among the conferees. A strident debate between black and white scholars resulted in the formation of a black caucus. Within the caucus, Africans and African-Americans disagreed on interpretations of the film. African-Americans found it insulting and offensive; Africans hailed it as cinema verité. I quelled the argument when I said that both sides had defensible positions readily understood in light of their respective sociopolitical histories.

"A very sound observation!" said the chairman of the caucus. "Let's form a committee to study interpretations of Mangane's ideas. And I suggest that Mrs. Thompson review Ibrahim Mangane's novels and films for the committee." I was thrilled that he chose me for the assignment.

Guided by Peter Martin, a Harvard history professor with an interest in African literature, I had read the Nigerians and the Ghanaians, southern Africans and east Africans. On my own, I had found the Francophone writers. I had studied Senghor's poetry and essays. Reading Senghor was the necessary preparation for understanding Mangane's works, the most compelling fiction I had ever encountered. I read and reread Ibrahim Mangane's novels.

In cryptic allegories, Mangane assailed France's impoverishment of Senegal in the colonial past and warned independent Senegal to guard against the French propensity for appropriation. In starkly realistic fiction, he explored the circumstances of Senegalese peasants in plots that challenged traditions. His novel, *Adieu Fatima,* about the abandonment of Senegalese girls and women in the poorest of villages, was banned throughout Africa. My article, "Political Surrealism in *Adieu Fatima,*" appeared in the *Journal of Comparative Literature;* the editors noted that never before had they published criticism by a graduate student.

At some point, I realized that I had to meet Ibrahim Mangane. I needed to make my way into the interior of his world—to feel, see, hear from his perspective the issues of contemporary Africa, to understand the order of his creative process, to watch him progress from a spark to the flame of a work of art.

Ibrahim Mangane and his works became material for conversation and the subject of my dissertation. I thought that I was merely engaged in a scholarly exercise, in learning about the man as a literary figure. At the time, I did not understand that the inquiry had as much to do with me—my own identity and destiny—as with him.

A few weeks before Thanksgiving, I told Lincoln that I had to go to Senegal to study with Mangane. To be sure, my announcement did not surprise him. For weeks I had talked about Mangane over breakfast and dinner, about Mangane's characters, Mangane's ideology, Mangane's style.

"I'm worried about this preoccupation—this obsession you have with Senegal and an unknown Senegalese novelist. You're completely obsessed—no, maybe even worse—possessed. You seem possessed, Sarah, possessed by some African juju." With the resignation of a bewildered husband who thinks his wife may be mentally ill, he said, "So go to Africa—go and find out what's taken hold of you. Find out if your Ibrahim Mangane really exists. Go and get it—get him—out of your system."

Possessed? Perhaps I was possessed.

# 2

AT THANKSGIVING DINNER WITH MY PARENTS and Lincoln, I announced that I planned to spend the following summer—the summer of 1963—in Senegal. The four of us were seated at the dining room table with bowls of pumpkin soup steaming at each place.

"So you want to go to Senegal," said Dad, beaming his approval.

"Please, let's sit down, say grace, eat dinner first," Mom said. She began with "God is great" and our voices—Dad's, Lincoln's and mine—joined hers with "God is good, and we thank Him for this food. By His hands we all are fed. Give us, Lord, our daily bread. Amen."

"Special thanks, Lord, for bringing Sarah and Lincoln safely home for this Thanksgiving," Dad added. "And for this abundant table. It looks wonderful, just wonderful!"

"Well, begin while the soup's hot. It's your Grandma Stewart's recipe, Sarah."

"Mmmm. Delicious, Mom. You know, I'd love to have a collection of her recipes."

"Why?" Lincoln asked. "You don't like to cook."

"Well, Lincoln, I hope you're not too disappointed," said Mom. "Sarah never took an interest in the kitchen as a little girl. She was always reading or building things in the basement workshop with Henry or outside playing ball with the boys. But she'll learn. I only learned when I got married. I'm sure, in no time at all, she'll be a fine cook."

"We'll see," he said skeptically.

Mom said, "Lincoln, we'd hoped your parents and the twins could've joined us for dinner."

"They went to Richmond to be with my grandmother."

"I know. I'll bet they're having a fine dinner. Would you like more soup?"

"No, thanks, Harriet." Dad declined for all of us. "We're eager to get into that bird."

Dad was on his feet at the sideboard slicing the turkey. Mom and I shuttled back and forth between the table and the kitchen, removing the soup tureen and empty soup bowls and bringing dishes of celery sticks, corn relish, olives and pickles, bowls of peas, mashed sweet potatoes, brussels sprouts, oyster stuffing, gravy, and cranberry sauce.

Lincoln studied the Chinese willow pattern on the blue-and-white plate before him. I returned to my place, opposite Lincoln, and surveyed the scene where I had holiday dinners for nearly a quarter of a century—my entire life: chartreuse wallpaper with flecks of gold, flame-shaped bulbs in glass lanterns, a mahogany-framed oversize mirror that distorted the shape and size of the room. At each end of the sideboard were chairs with chartreuse padding that matched the wallpaper and draperies. On the white damask tablecloth, blue Willow bowls were laden with the Thanksgiving feast. In a corner, a turn-of-the-century breakfront cabinet gleamed with crystal and china reserved for very special occasions—more special than Thanksgiving.

Mom liked chartreuse. She wore her chartreuse knit suit, still fitting her trim figure perfectly, on autumn Sundays and holidays. With it, she always wore a robin's egg blue blouse. The combination complemented her nutmeg coloring. Silver strands of hair, brushed up from her temples, glistened in the twist of braids that crowned her like a tiara. Tidy to her marrow, she was proud of maintaining an orderly, carefully managed home.

In the presence of my mother, my resentment of her reverence for structure and form surged. The order and ordinariness of it all evoked my impulse for disorderly possibilities. I had always resisted her imperative to be a proper daughter; and it seemed that I would not be a proper wife. I did not want to repeat the traditional steps in the minuet of marriage that my parents danced. I did not wish to someday inherit the special-occasion china and crystal, the gleaming silver, and their pattern of circumspect conversation. I looked across at Lincoln, who wanted a marriage like theirs and his parents' marriage, a marriage of conventional and commonplace transactions.

Mom filled stemmed glasses with a chilled California rosé, then stood at the sideboard next to Dad who, with dexterity, dissected the turkey. She smiled and said, as she had each time he carved, "You should've become a surgeon instead of a biology teacher." Word for word, I knew the exchange that followed.

" 'Cause you'd rather be a doctor's wife," was his invariable response.

Mom always replied coyly, "Only if you were the doctor, Henry."

Dad handed her the platter of turkey, returned to his place at the head of the table and, with some effort—he was rounder than ever—settled into the chair which creaked under his weight. Spoons tinkled against the platters and bowls that were passed. Dad and I murmured our appreciation of the aroma of sage and rosemary on brussels sprouts, cinnamon and cloves wafting from the sweet potatoes.

Lifting his wine glass for a toast, Dad's thick brown fingers quivered. A slight tremor in his hand had made its first appearance; but there was no tremor in his voice. In a tone for toasting heads of state, he said, "To the wife who graces my life and the daughter and son-in-law who have journeyed here to be with us." Then turning toward me he said, "Tell us about your plans for going to Senegal and your purpose."

"I want to go to Dakar next summer to study with Ibrahim Mangane. He is a writer—a novelist—and a filmmaker. My advisor, Professor Martin, has approved my proposal for a travel grant, and I expect—"

"You know, President Kennedy has announced that one of the first Peace Corps groups is going to Senegal, Sarah. Peace Corps pays for your travel, pays a salary, too. You ought to apply for one of their assignments," Dad said.

"I'm interested in Senegalese literature. I want to do literary research. The Peace Corps is not the corps for me."

Mom said, "Well, I assume you'd go with her, wouldn't you, Lincoln?"

Lincoln furrowed his brow and looked up from his untouched plate. He sounded troubled. "For weeks now Sarah's talked about going to Senegal. She's obsessed with Senegal, with an obscure Senegalese writer. She forgets to go to the laundromat. Doesn't get the groceries, hasn't time to prepare dinner. There's always a lecture on Africa or she's at a reception for somebody from Senegal or she's meeting somebody who might have heard of this writer."

Poised on the edge of my chair, to counter Lincoln's undermining my plan, I shook my head in rebuttal.

"Who's the writer?" asked Dad.

"His name is Ibrahim Mangane," I said.

"How do you spell that?"

"I-b-r-a-h-i-m M-a-n-g-a-n-e. You don't pronounce the final 'e,' " I said.

"Mangane?" Dad said it correctly. "Never heard of him."

Lincoln said, "No one has ever heard of him. Her letters to him haven't been answered. He may even be dead for all we know."

"Is that true? You've written to him and received no answer?" Mom sounded alarmed.

I said, "The mail to and from Africa is slow. And Mangane is very busy—occupied with—"

"You see, she wants to go to see somebody who may not even exist! Some kind of African juju has possessed her." His characteristic reserve fell away. He grew agitated. "Will I go with her? No, ma'am. I'm not crazy or crazy about Africa."

"Calm down, Link, and eat your dinner," Dad said.

"What Sarah may need is a trip to a psychiatrist, not a trip to Senegal," Lincoln murmured. He lifted his fork, but did not eat. Perhaps he thought the food was seasoned with foreign obsessions.

"Lincoln, it's you who needs help," I said. "You need someone to open your eyes, to see the world around you, to see me.

You don't have a clue about my interest in Senegal. You're never interested in hearing about my courses or my dissertation. Luckily, I have an advisor who cares about what I'm reading, what I'm writing, what I might contribute to—"

"Yeah, that Peter Martin. He's part of your problem."

"Sarah, Lincoln, please! Please don't quarrel at the table, over a Thanksgiving dinner we've just blessed," pleaded Mom, her eyes on Lincoln. As she nibbled at the turkey and Lincoln sulked, Dad continued his inquiry.

"Do you know anyone who has actually met the man?" he asked.

"Peter Martin met Mangane at a conference in Paris. He said Mangane is a visionary whose works are going to be tremendously influential."

"And what does Professor Martin think of your plan?"

"He suggested that I spend some time at the University of Dakar reading the critiques of Mangane's works. I could see his films there—films available only in Senegal. And I'll try to arrange to interview him."

"Senegal. Your uncle, my brother, George, was in Senegal once. French colony then. Is Senegal a free country yet?"

"Yes, it was declared independent two years ago—in 1960. Dakar is the capital."

"The political situation—is it stable? Is there an American Embassy in operation?"

"Quite stable. Peter Martin has a friend, a William Nelson, in the Foreign Service at the U.S. Embassy in Dakar. Relations with the U.S. are good. The transition to Senegalese authority has been peaceful—successful."

"I wonder how they treat American Negroes now—how you'll be received? Your Uncle George didn't get a friendly reception, I can tell you that."

"I suppose I should write to Mr. Nelson—he's black—and ask about attitudes, ask him if . . ."

"Be sure to ask him about the cost of living—how much money are you likely to need."

"I've applied for a travel grant. Professor Martin said that it's nearly certain that I'll get it. The grant would cover airfare, living expenses, books, everything."

Mom, who had been listening intently, said to Lincoln, "Sarah's always been interested in places overseas, exotic places. When she was a little girl, the bulletin board in her bedroom was covered with African scenes. And she kept every postcard George sent us from Africa. When you married her, you must have known she was interested in Africa. You knew she'd been studying Africa, didn't you?"

Lincoln did not answer immediately. His arms folded, eyes raised toward the ceiling, lips puckered to pronounce his silence, he pondered his response.

"I married her thinking she'd become a teacher—not an adventurer, a gadabout. I'd hoped we'd build on the foundation that you and my folks have made—a stable, solid home life." For a while no one spoke.

Mom began to clear the table. Helping her, I added to the commotion of moving dishes from the dining room to the kitchen to cover the silence. In the kitchen, Mom whispered, "You shouldn't go unless you can get Lincoln to go with you. Africa seems so dangerous. You'd be a lot safer with him along."

As an after-dinner treat, Dad, between puffs on a redolent cigar, recalled a story about his brother's sojourn in Senegal. It was a story Dad loved to tell and I loved to hear—Uncle George's story for me, about me. It was the story that had aroused my childhood curiosity about Dakar, stirred intriguing fantasies about my being a twin—perhaps having another self, another persona who lived in Dakar.

Uncle George, my Sinbad-of-an-uncle, was a favorite figure in family lore. George the sailor. George the rover. He'd joined the navy at the outset of World War II, Dad often said, "because posters invited young men to join up and see the world." Whenever Uncle George came home on leave, the entire family—four uncles, two aunts, their wives, husbands, and children—all gathered in the parlor of my grandparents' house to hear tales of his travels. Mystery and mischief danced in his gray-brown eyes as he entertained us with stories about his adventures overseas. I was spellbound by his performances and by the grownups' reactions. His foul language, his reenactment of sailors' pranks, and reveling in illicit exploits made my grandfather smile, my father and uncles howl, while my grandmother, mother, and aunts tried to concentrate on their embroidery or crocheting and pretended to blush.

"Lincoln, has Sarah told you about the Uncle George's adventures in Senegal?"

"She's told me—and you've told me many times."

"Well, long after the war ended, my brother, George, finally returned from an extended tour-of-duty with the navy. He sailed everywhere, spoke several languages—Portuguese, French, Arabic, Spanish. His postcards gave us clues as to—"

"He said he's heard that story many times," Mom reminded him.

"Sent us cards from Panama, Singapore, Rio, Bombay, Casablanca, Cape Town, Accra, Dakar—all kinds of foreign places. And, you know, he came back with the damnedest stories.

"He had a story for Sarah. Remember, Sarah?"

"We all remember. Don't keep telling the same old stories," Mom pleaded.

"Well, one day when his ship called at Senegal, at Dakar, he went for a walk in the section of the city called 'the Medina'— poor section—where he saw a little girl who looked exactly like Sarah. A carbon copy, a double. A twin but closer—truly identical. He taught us the French word for it—*le sosie*, remember? First French word she knew. He said that she looked so much like Sarah that, you know, he began to follow her through the alleys of the Medina."

"He was probably drunk. He drank so much that his perspiration smelled like whisky," Mom said.

"Well, though he was walking behind her at some distance, the girl sensed she was being followed. George said when he approached her, offered her a chocolate bar—the currency of the war, you know—she screamed and dashed into a house.

Moments later, George—he was surrounded by maybe a dozen men who seemed to be accusing him of something. Probably thought he'd harm her—molest her, you know. He was scared as hell. Well, one of them had a knife and stabbed George in the back of the neck." Dad struck the table with his fist to reinforce the image. "His blood squirted out and sprayed those guys. They pulled back. Well, George was fast and lucky. He went running through the maze of alleys, somehow got out and made his way back to his ship. Had a scar from the stab wound. Lucky. You know, lucky to live to tell the story. What a story-teller he was! Died telling a story. In the hospital, had his last heart attack, telling the doctor and nurses some story. Ever heard that one, Lincoln?"

"Yes, heard you tell it several times. And Sarah mentions it—she's talked about thinking when she was a kid that she had a twin in Senegal," he said, glancing at me. "Maybe that's why she wants to go. Anyway, I'm sorry, but I'm not planning to go to Africa. And I'm sorry about bringing our problems to you."

"That's all right, son. We need to know about your problems, and help you solve them if we can."

A warm wave of remembrance rippled through me. That story was etched in my memory from the time I was eight or nine. I loved hearing Dad tell the story, each time with slight changes in his gestures, his intonation, his choice of words. I was intrigued by the idea of having *un sosie* in Senegal! An imagined self with a Senegalese identity lived with me.

I have often thought about that Thanksgiving dinner—images of Dad, Mom, and Lincoln, the release I felt when I registered my intentions, and my delight in Dad's ritualistic recitation of Uncle George's story. Exposing the tension in our marriage to my parents that day had felt like a seismic event. It was as if we had revealed a fault just under the surface of our lives.

# 3

DURING THE DRIVE BACK TO CAMBRIDGE, Lincoln and I continued to talk about my going to Senegal.

"Sarah, why do you have to go to Senegal? Can't you do library research here?"

"The books and films I need are in Dakar. Besides it's important to be there—to understand the challenge of establishing a new literature in a climate of independence. I want to witness—"

"Come on! That's the stuff in your proposal. Challenge! Independence! Isn't it sufficiently challenging to deal with our civil rights movement? Must you complicate things by talking about African independence?"

"What you regard as a complication seems essential to my research—and to my life."

"Do you really think it's realistic to plan a life around African literature? It's entertaining, I suppose, to read African writers. But I wonder if any other students and professors—other than you and Peter Martin—are interested in what Africans are writing?"

"The study of African literature is developing. French scholars have been studying the Senegalese writers for decades. French publishers have—"

"So go to France—to Paris. I'm sure you'd find what you need in libraries there."

"I don't want to go to Paris. Besides, it's not likely that I'd meet Mangane in Paris."

"Oh no? Peter Martin saw him there, didn't he? The man's

probably in Paris all the time. If he's so great, he's left Africa—
that's why you haven't heard from him. Hey, now I might go to
Paris with you. MIT has a program in connection with the engineering school in Paris."

"I'm not going to Paris. I am going to Senegal." I closed my
eyes and pretended to sleep.

"Senegal. I suppose you want to go to Senegal because it's
romantic. You like the way African men flirt with you. I've
noticed." Lincoln's vulnerable tone surprised me. Previously he
had seemed indifferent, unconcerned. I assumed he had not
noticed. He was threatened and I felt defensive.

"I suppose I like the way some of them discuss things with
me. They talk about literature, politics, philosophy. *They* speak
to my mind." Eyes closed still, I spoke slowly, as if I were talking in my sleep.

"But they're looking at your body. And don't I speak to your
mind?"

"You and I don't talk about anything really—anything that
matters. We do things—the same things we did when we were
dating—go to movies, play tennis, go to parties, study, go to
coffeehouses, play chess, do crossword puzzles . . ."

"And it's boring. Sure, I'm bored a lot, too. But that's life—
not just married life. That's life. What else is there to do?"

"I can never engage you in talking about ideas or your work
or mine—how our lives, our careers might mesh."

"I'm not sure how they'll mesh if you're away—overseas—
playing the anthropologist. Everybody used to say we were so
right for each other, perfectly matched. I'm beginning to have
my doubts."

"I do, too. But what are you beginning to doubt?" I opened
my eyes, stared straight ahead at the turnpike traffic. I knew I
was leading him on. Aware of my gnawing ambivalence about
our marriage, I wanted Lincoln to declare his.

"Well, I wonder if we're really compatible? You're eager to
explore—to go to Africa. I think that's admirable, courageous
even. But I don't know anybody who's going to Africa just yet.

Delegations are sent. But individuals—students—aren't going. It's too risky."

"And what are the risks?" I demanded.

"Contracting diseases—sleeping sickness, elephantiasis. You'll come back with elephantine legs and you'll be too sleepy to notice!" He chuckled at his joke and turned toward me, waiting for my laughter, a smile at least.

"That's not funny," I said, concealing my amusement. "You're doing it again—joking about something that matters to me."

"You have to admit, you're not prepared for primitive living. Have you thought about where you're going to stay, and about transportation? How exactly do you plan to get around?"

"I'll stay in a hotel at first, then in a university dormitory or a youth hostel."

"You'll stay in a mud hut with a grass roof. And you'll be riding around on donkeys or—"

"Please! You've seen too many Tarzan movies. You're full of stereotypes of Africa. And that's a pity. I'm sorry for you and for all the other—"

"All the others who care about you—your mother, for instance. Going to Africa to locate an unknown writer strikes me as risky—nutty."

"Lincoln, it's merely a three-month trip. The dangers you imagine don't exist. I'll come back with great dissertation material. And then we can get on with it." Leading him on again, I sketched an outline for our future, knowing he would draw over it or erase it. "I'll get a teaching job somewhere. You'll have a terrific job offer from MIT. And once we're settled, we can think about having children."

"I've told you, we're not having any children. I don't want a child of mine exposed to the racial hatred that we're heading into. Race riots are going to break out all over this country. It's no time to think about having kids."

When I was in college, I had visited a Boston tearoom where a gypsy fortune teller had read my palm. She had seen two children in my future and a journey across an ocean. I began to wonder if she had been right about the trip, but wrong about the children.

"Anyway, it's not the time to talk about having kids when you're dying to go to Senegal," he said. "Afterward, when you come back, we'll see . . ."

"I'm not dying to go to Senegal—I'm living to go."

# 4

LINCOLN'S PARENTS, ABE AND GLADYS
Thompson, were proud of their four children. They spared no
expense when there was an occasion to celebrate the achieve-
ments of their offspring. At Christmas we went to their home
where Lincoln's sister, Doris, her boyfriend, Chester Weaver,
and the twins, Lincoln's younger brothers, Mark and Matthew,
had gathered for the holiday. The announcement of Doris's
engagement to Chester at their holiday party, had stirred up a
hurricane of activity in their handsome, commodious house.

Doris and I had been in the same high school class and had
friends in common. She had been a bridesmaid in our wedding,
a prelude to the more elaborate wedding she would have after
her graduation from nursing school. Doris and Chet had met at
Freedmen's Hospital where he was a resident in surgery. In a
receiving line in the foyer, an elated Gladys welcomed guests
who shook hands and exchanged greetings with the future bride
and groom.

The hum of conversation swelled as guests arrived. Couples
paused to take in the setting as they entered the living room.
Candles flickered on the mantel above the fireplace. The
Thompsons' Irish setter, lying near the hearth, was disturbed
from time to time by new arrivals warming themselves by the
fire. The wing chairs, sofas, and loveseats soon were all occupied by the women of the party, who wore cocktail dresses or
full-length gowns of black or white or poinsettia red. They rustled and glittered and chatted in taffeta and sequins. Abe guided
the men, most in black tie, to the dining room where Lincoln

and Mark filled and refilled glasses. Husbands returned with drinks for their wives, then stood around the grand piano, watching Matthew's well-practiced hands render his imitations of Erroll Garner and Oscar Peterson. More guests came. The party had attracted Washington's most prominent doctors, dentists, and lawyers, some affiliated with Abe's firm, and their wives. It was a gathering of friends that felt like a joyous family reunion.

My parents appeared somewhat outclassed, although not uncomfortable, in that company. I made small talk with them for a while, as we circulated among their acquaintances.

Then I joined the younger women—we would have said girls—who had been Doris's friends and mine in high school. Shirley, Barbara, Hazel, and Carolyn had clustered on a sofa.

"The moment I saw Lincoln's bow tie and cummerbund in that ruby velvet, I knew you'd be wearing your ruby velvet gown. You two look just like magazine models," said Barbara.

Examining my hairstyle, Carolyn said, "A french twist! Turn around. How'd you put those pearls in your hair?"

"You're still the prettiest of us all," Hazel said. "When we were in eleventh grade, I used to whisper to the mirror in the gym: 'Mirror, mirror, on the wall, who's the prettiest'—I couldn't make myself say fairest—'of us all.' I could almost hear the mirror say, 'Sarah Stewart, girl, and you'll never even come close.' " Confident in her good looks and famous for her wit, Hazel had us laughing.

Arms folded on the pregnant bulge of her abdomen, Barbara solemnly said, "I'd thought you'd be expecting by now—I thought you and Lincoln . . ."

As I considered an explanation, Shirley chirped, "Lincoln just told me he's not making any babies. Doesn't that bother you?" I let her question hang in the air like flypaper.

"Tell me what's new. What are you doing?" I asked, shifting the focus from my awkward perch on the arm of the sofa. Carolyn said, "I'm finishing dental school next year and we're getting married when Andy finishes med school." She nodded toward Andy in the circle of young men standing in the center of the living room, drinking bourbon and, as the animated twist of his graceful body suggested, talking about football. She extended her left hand with the evidence: a diamond ring.

"Sarah, you're not wearing your wedding ring!" Barbara noticed.

"I've had a rash on this finger—under my ring—some kind of allergy."

"Allergic to gold? I've never heard of *anybody* allergic to gold," said Barbara. "You know you'd better put that ring on, girl. It's bad luck to take off your wedding ring. B-a-a-a-d luck."

I knew that the eczema under my wedding band was an expression of the irritation in our marriage. I wondered if my parents and Lincoln's had noticed that my hands were bare. They wouldn't have mentioned it—would not have tarnished the gleaming festivity of an engagement party with reference to a sign of possible disengagement.

I was itching all over with an impulse that inevitably would be interpreted as betrayal. Virtually everyone present regarded Lincoln and me as paragons of accomplished Negroes poised to excel in a changing society. Abe had made it known that Lincoln was immersed in civil rights activities, and together we were expected to extend our parents' pursuit of access to the mainstream of America and realize their dreams of the next generation's surpassing their own financial and social success. I felt Lincoln's grandparents were glaring down at me from their enlarged turn-of-the-century sepia photographs in the hallowed space above the mantel. Their presence chided me now, only a few generations away from slavery: a promising woman, married to one of their descendants and expected to carry on the noble traditions of their family and race, was harboring dreams of escape.

My musing was interrupted by Shirley, who said she had heard I was going to Senegal.

"Senegal? In Africa?" Barbara gasped. "Why'd you want to do something like that?"

"Now why does that surprise you?" asked Carolyn. "Don't you remember the bulletin board in Sarah's room, the scrapbook she kept—all those pictures of Africa?"

"Uh-huh, and remember her school projects? Always something about Africa," Hazel said. "That's exciting. Go on, girl, and bring back some fine souvenirs—beads and wood sculptures. I'd love something from Africa."

"Sure, I'd love some African trinkets, too, but I wouldn't go over there to get them," said Barbara.

"I hear living conditions are very harsh in Africa. And tribes are always at war. It's terribly dangerous," insisted Shirley.

"The principal at our school wants to go to Africa—to Liberia in fact. He thinks he might have some distant cousins living there," Hazel said.

"Lincoln said you're going this summer. What'll you be doing there?" asked Shirley.

"I'll do more research on the works of Ibrahim Mangane. He's an important—"

"Somebody's opening an African restaurant on Georgia Avenue," Shirley injected.

"Yeah, we can get a taste of Africa without even leaving D.C.," Barbara added.

"You certainly see enough Africans downtown—in the department stores, shopping for their new embassies, and buying appliances to send home," Carolyn said. "And there're a lot of African students in town now."

"Students by day and taxi drivers by night. And are they arrogant!" said Hazel. "They think they're better than us American Negroes."

At the other end of the living room, Gladys, now at the piano, leaned into the keyboard and played the opening bars of "I Got It Bad and That Ain't Good." Barbara got up and moved through the crowd toward her husband, Harold. She took his hand and led him across the room, Standing by the piano, she crooned the lyrics. Harold's mellow baritone caressed her honey-eyed soprano. While they sang, the party, captivated by their duet, was perfectly still.

"Encore, encore!" Abe called as others gathered around the piano. Barbara and Harold, poised to sing another number, signaled Gladys who improvised a treble thunder-roll prelude to their rendition of "Stormy Weather."

I abandoned the discussion of attitudes toward Africans and went to the dining room to find Lincoln surrounded by Chet, Mark, Matthew, Andy, my father, and several other older men. Lincoln was talking about the military occupation of the University of Mississippi where James Meredith had enrolled. He sketched the organization of the black student movement, strategies of the Student Nonviolent Coordinating Committee and CORE (the Congress of Racial Equality), then went on to say that it was in the interest of the Kennedy administration and the nation to advance integration. And as he ended, he said, "In Baldwin's words, "I do not see how one can escape the conclusion that the Negro's status in this country is not only a cruel injustice but a national liability.' "

"Man, you ought to be a politician, run for Congress," somebody said. His audience obviously had been energized by his speech, and I saw that my father was among those who looked on admiringly. The circle broke into small groups of older men who spoke of the work of the Urban League and the NAACP and younger men who talked about the strategies of the Southern Christian Leadership Conference and the Black Muslims. I felt proud of Lincoln's vision and inspiring statement. I moved into the group, stood next to him and listened attentively with the others as he compared the advantages and disadvantages of nonviolent tactics.

Abe called to us, "I'm sorry to break up this confab, but it's time to toast Doris and Chet. Come along." We moved to the living room to join in the toast, Lincoln and I holding hands. Afterward, the entire party, led by Barbara and Harold, sang "Taking a Chance on Love." Lincoln slipped his arm around my waist and led me to the center of the room. We danced while the others stepped back to marvel at the graceful steps of an ideal couple.

# 5

"THERE IS NO BETTER APPROACH TO THE subject matter of one's dissertation than direct contact, personal acquaintance with the figure," said Peter Martin. "Once you meet Mangane, you may change your mind about him, even end up shifting your focus. He may be difficult to interview, being that he's a crusty character, a real curmudgeon. I met him two years ago in Paris and he struck me as very intense, a serious intellectual—he doesn't suffer fools gladly. He's quite handsome, of medium height, thin, wears a beard, graying a bit." He paused and puffed as we climbed the stairs in Widener Library.

Martin continued: "You need to spend at least two or three months in Senegal. Frankly, it would be wiser to go for an entire year. You should interview Mangane in depth, observe him at work, talk to him, to his colleagues, and to the critics of his work. Learn about the sources of his material. Your comprehension of spoken and written French is probably adequate, but you'll need practice—preferably with a Senegalese tutor—in conversational French. And you'll need to learn some Wolof."

"And I'll need that travel grant," I added.

"Don't worry. With your academic record and my recommendation, you'll definitely receive a grant. You have my word." Encouraged by Peter Martin, I wrote another letter to Ibrahim Mangane, enrolled in an intensive French course, and found a Senegalese undergraduate who was able to tutor me in Wolof.

I was pulsing with new energy, an intense energy I had never felt before. It kept me awake and on edge. I wondered whether the energy of religious passion had a similar effect. While Lincoln slept, I lay awake wondering whether the energy of prayer converts dreams into realities. In the dark of a sleepless night, I invented a prayer—a variation on a psalm I had memorized years earlier for a Methodist Sunday school class. *"I will cast mine eyes upon the ocean from whence cometh my help. My help cometh from Senegal, which is heaven and earth."*

I needed the rhythm of praying, the chanting of a mantra to sustain me. There were weeks of preparation shrouded in uncertainty. Would I hear from Ibrahim Mangane? Would help come from Senegal?

In those weeks of waiting, Lincoln and I made a conscious attempt to be more tender and affectionate toward one another. He bought records of West African folk music, music that had us dancing about the living room and laughing at our creative choreography. I accompanied him to Urban League and NAACP meetings and vigorously applauded his speeches on organizing for civil rights demonstrations. On Sunday afternoons, I watched interminable football games on television with him. When Sam Higgins or Lincoln's other MIT friends visited, I baked brownies and made hot chocolate. We went to a Dartmouth-Harvard hockey game, and I cheered for Dartmouth. I read a science fiction novel that he had raved about. I wore his MIT sweatshirt when we went ice skating. He gave me a beaded bracelet made in Kenya and an atlas of Africa. We scanned our photo album with Bermuda honeymoon pictures of us romping on a beach, riding a motor scooter, and dining in the hotel where waiters teased us with erotic references and suggestive gestures. We tried.

As spring approached, my apprehension about the still ill-defined summer in Senegal was palpable. I needed to get away—not just from Lincoln, but from Harvard Square and Widener Library, too. Occasionally I went to Martha's Vineyard to wade in the waves of the Atlantic, waves that had rippled, I imagined, from Senegal's beaches. And I chanted:

*"I will cast my eyes upon the ocean from whence cometh my help. My help cometh from Senegal, which is heaven and earth."*

With the top down on my blue convertible Volkswagen Bee-
tle, I drove from Cambridge to Woods Hole, where I took the
ferry to Martha's Vineyard. Although I tried to avoid the
inquisitive glances and company of other passengers—the
WASPs, the Irish, the Jews, and a few middle-aged black couples on their way to Oak Bluffs—their conversations about the
weather, ferry reservations, the price of lobster, and trendy
restaurants were at times unavoidable.

I was on the same ferry with them, but we clearly were taking
different trips. They were on weekend excursions. I was making
a pilgrimage. They were dressed casually in navy blue blazers,
tan slacks, blue denim skirts, white cable knit sweaters, and tennis shoes. For my pilgrimages I wore scarlet linen slacks with
shirts of purple or orange, tied with a sash of bright blue or
green. My hair was twisted in a bun held with large ornamental
combs. I was intentionally aloof, and kept myself apart from the
other passengers. I wanted privacy, solitude, distance from
whatever seemed ordinary, familiar, and particularly American.

I rather enjoyed being the object of their curious eyes. I read,
watched the gulls, scanned the sky, and wrote in my journal. On
the island, I rented a bike and pedaled hard and fast toward the
ocean on the windward side of the island, where I spent the
afternoon walking along the beach, chanting my psalm, wishing
the wind and waves could carry my words to Senegal.

Exhausted by the emotion those trips evoked, I would return
to our apartment to find Lincoln engrossed in a TV news program or basketball game. He never knew about my pilgrimages.
When he asked how I had spent the day, I simply told him that I
had gone for a drive toward Cape Cod or for a long walk.

"Alone?" he asked.

"Yes, alone."

In late April, I learned that I had been awarded a generous
travel grant. And, finally, I received a brief letter from Ibrahim
Mangane in which he acknowledged my many letters to him
and invited me to Dakar. Peter Martin had written letters of
introduction to colleagues at the University of Dakar and to his
friend, Nelson, who was the U.S. cultural attaché in Senegal.

Help, at last, was coming from many places and I would make it to Senegal!

With little to say to each other, Lincoln and I spent less and less time together. Before I left, an ocean already lay between us. Despite our anxiety about separating, or perhaps because of it, frequently one of us would try to bridge the growing distance in bed. Like couples who cannot face each other in the light of day, we turned face-to-face in the night, adopting postures and passions that somehow relieved the unspeakable tensions driving us apart.

One night, as we lay in bed before falling asleep, Lincoln broke the silence of avoidance. Like the psychotherapy patient who finds his tongue in the last five minutes of the fifty-minute hour, he released a stream of thoughts.

"You're making a mistake—going off to Africa to try to find a man whose work is alien, filled with stuff you probably can't understand. He's an unknown African whose books aren't read. It's unreal. You've become so involved with his fiction that you are fictionalizing your own life."

"What do you mean? My life is real. Mangane and his books are real. Senegal's not a fictional place. You're just trying to demoralize me so that I won't leave. You've said, more than once, that I—"

"That you were obsessed. And I was right. I talked to a psychiatrist about it. He said obsessions grow—result in mental illness. Believe me, baby, I don't want you to go crazy. It's insane to be going to Africa now—avoiding what's going on here." He turned toward me, his hand on my shoulder, his voice strained. "Just think about it. All eyes are on black America, the civil rights movement, what's happening here. And you're going to Africa? Why are you going? What do you think you are going to find there? Your *sosie*—whatever that is? What is this really all about?"

"It's about being in a place where I feel I might belong. I feel alienated here—I've always felt somehow estranged from what is called 'American.' Can you understand how—"

"How alienation feels? Don't you know how I felt at Dartmouth? I was always the outsider. But I didn't give up, I didn't leave. I had to show them I belonged there as much as those third-generation sons of Dartmouth. And you—we—belong here. There's business to take care of here."

"But whose business is it?"

"Baby, it's *our* business. It's our country. As Baldwin said, 'this country is going to be transformed. It will not be transformed by an act of God, but by all of us. . . . We made the world we're living in and we have to make it over.' "

"Just now, what matters most to me is my own work."

"Sarah, we can't afford to be that single-minded, that selfish. Sometimes we have to put aside personal goals for ideals. Our place in this country matters. We've got to reconstruct American attitudes. It's time to care about others, not just about yourself. Instead of going to organizing meetings, I could be at the lab, working on my engineering projects. But right now, I think it's more important to work for a movement that'll help all our people. Don't you care about our people?" he asked quietly.

Our people. He refused to think of Africans as *our people,* or of us as Africa's people. I turned away, but Lincoln reached for me, drew my body back to him, and wrapped his arms around me in an embrace of remembrance of happier times. His sweet breath warmed my brow. I trembled—shuddered at being trapped in his arms and in a marriage that promised security, dignity, and a measure of affection, because I sensed the frustrations that loomed could overtake me. I wiggled out of his embrace and turned my back to him.

Lincoln's weary sigh signaled that he felt the same frustrations. I thought about whether I should postpone the trip. Would it make a difference in Lincoln's opinion of me? I was troubled by his accusation that I didn't care enough about "our people." Africans are our people, too, I said to myself. I cared about African liberation—and I also cared about my own liberation, the freedom to be my authentic self—a self not defined by the conventions and expectations of my parents, friends, or marriage to Lincoln. I wanted to realize a self I was in the process of constructing. To do that I had to go away to Senegal. With a renewed sense of resolution, I fell asleep.

# 6

MY BAGS WERE PACKED A WEEK BEFORE my departure, and the days before my trip seemed to drag on endlessly. Finally, on a sunny afternoon in late May, I was in the car with Lincoln, who was driving like a felon being chased by the police, going to Logan Airport.

"There's no need to speed" I cautioned. I reminded him that I had two hours before flight time.

"I don't want you to miss your plane," he snapped.

Once we emerged from the tunnel and the airport was in view, he spoke again, this time more kindly. "I hope it goes well. I hope you'll find your Mr. Mangane and get the material you want."

"And I hope you'll understand—someday—what this trip means to me." At the terminal, he stopped the car so abruptly that we jolted forward. He was tense. His resentment was palpable. Quickly he unloaded my luggage and summoned a skycap.

"I don't like good-bye scenes," he said. "I'm not going inside. Besides, I've got to get to a meeting. I'm sure you'll be fine. Take care of yourself." With a hug that felt fraternal, and then a quick kiss, he said good-bye. He seemed more eager to get away even than I.

"Wait a second," I said. "I don't want to leave like this. I want to remember this moment—how you look. You—we—are going to be a bit different three months from now." With another hug, a lovers' hug this time, and a long kiss, we were ready to part. We whispered good-bye. At the revolving doors, I turned, just in time to see Lincoln wave as he drove away.

I read and slept and read all the way to Paris. As the plane approached Orly, we were informed that there would be an unexpected delay—six hours or more—before the departure to Dakar because of engine trouble. Vouchers for the bus to Paris were distributed; and passengers were advised to return by bus prior to flight time.

It was my first trip abroad. My seatmate, a robust, middle-aged woman with a throaty Franco-Russian accent, urged me to go into the city. "Don't miss the chance to see the most elegant place in the world, *ma chère*," she said patting my arm with a plump palm. "You are so serious, so studious. *On est toujours gai à Paris.* See Paris and become more lighthearted."

What could I have seen in a few hours? A glimpse of Notre Dame, the Eiffel Tower, the Sorbonne? A whirlwind tour of Paris didn't interest me at all. My fantasies had been focused on Dakar for so long that no other city in the world could have competed with it—not even Paris.

Resigned to the boredom of a long wait, I exchanged a traveler's check for francs, and then bought a croissant, café au lait, a Suchard chocolate bar, a pack of Gauloise, and, in the duty-free shop, a bottle of Chanel No. 22. Chain-smoking cigarettes, I read my notes on Ibrahim Mangane's works:

*Mangane's postcolonialist petty bourgeois civil servants and shopkeepers have colonialists' vocabularies and attitudes although they view themselves as quite different. Their neonationalism is not at all new; rather it is a nationalist variation on the* status quo. *Query: Do civil servants and shopkeepers read Mangane? Have they responded with a critique?*

*His characters, Malick and Demba, acquired vast stretches of farmland owned previously by settlers. Malick redistributed the property among relatives, shared farm equipment, taught them new intensive agricultural methods while Demba, mocking Malick's ways, attempted to manage his farm independently in the style of the settlers. Malick's success and Demba's failure—predictable outcomes. Query: Is there factual evidence of the superiority of collective farming? Reactions to this story?*

*Are his works intended to redirect social and political practices or are they a reflection of what is happening? Can literature change attitudes and practices?*

I put aside my notes, closed my eyes, imagined the possibilities that might await me, and worried. What if Mangane were out of the country—perhaps in Paris? Neither Peter Martin nor I had received any correspondence from him for several weeks. What if he should refuse to see me? What if he *had* died? What, I wondered, in my mother's voice, would become of me?

Finally it was announced that the flight to Dakar was ready for boarding. Restless travelers collected suitcases and parcels and surged toward the gate. The composition of the passenger group was something to behold. Nearly all the other passengers were black—African. I felt a sense of elation, felt my spirits rise. I was in the company of African traveling companions aboard a plane to Dakar at last! I smiled triumphantly.

It was then that I began to understand the emotional meaning of Negritude. Until that moment, my reading of Senghor's essays on Negritude had been merely an intellectual exercise. I looked about me and felt the connection between the spirit of my African fellow travelers and the soul that animates African-American culture. The bearing of the Africans and their mode of conversation had an element of familiarity. Traits transcending national origin infused *l'esprit noir.* I wanted to shout, "*Vive la Diaspora!*"

The plane's approach to the airport at Dakar afforded a view of the finger of a peninsula of Senegal that stretches into the Atlantic Ocean, beckoning passengers on ships and planes to the continent. My pilgrimages to the shores of Martha's Vineyard had been rewarded, my prayerful chant had not been in vain. Suddenly brimming with joy and anticipation, I whispered my psalm once more as I peered through the window to capture my first image of the land that I had loved without seeing. It was stark and bare, with parched red clay and prickly shrubs.

On arrival at Yoff International Airport, I felt simultaneously exhilarated and exhausted. Trailing behind the procession of passengers, I observed relatives and friends welcoming loved ones with embraces and kisses, while porters and taxi drivers bustled about, hustling their services and haggling about prices. Out of the crowd of princely men wearing grand caftans and women regally draped in boubous of turquoise, pimento, azure, and canary stepped an obviously Afro-American man in a tan European-cut suit, extending his hand. "Are you Sarah Thompson?"

"Yes, I am."

"Welcome to Dakar. I'm Bill Nelson, the American cultural attaché. Pete Martin cabled me about your arrival. If you will give me your baggage tickets, Moustapha, my driver, will get your bags. And give me your passport. I'll have it stamped for you." The crisp, officious American took charge.

Peter Martin had told me very little about Bill Nelson. He'd said that Nelson was thirty-seven or thirty-eight, and a real Francophile. They'd been students together at Fisk, but Nelson had spent his junior year in Paris—hanging out at the literary cafés. After college, he had joined the Foreign Service, and had served in Belgium and Morocco before being assigned to Senegal.

Nelson's height and Western attire distinguished him from the throng of other men, shorter and darker than he—men dressed in long robes of blue or sand or white. His tan suit, blue Oxford cloth shirt, striped tie, and air of foreign officialdom signaled that he should not be shoved and jostled by the crowd. People moved aside to make way for us.

Nelson was immediately protective of me. "Don't worry. I'll maneuver you through this mob. Some Americans experience culture shock right here at the airport. Just the sight of this mob makes them want to fly right back to New York." With my elbow in his firm grip, he ushered me through the crowd to an oversized midnight blue Ford with the seal of the United States emblazoned on its doors. He gave the driver the baggage tickets, and then left me in the car while he went back to "deal with the formalities," as Nelson phrased it. Somehow this annoyed me. I did not want someone from the United States in a European business suit and an embassy car to be the first to introduce me to Dakar. When he returned with my passport, I said in an authoritative voice, "Mr. Nelson, I have a reservation at the Hotel Majestic."

"I know," he said. "They had booked you in a room over the entrance, which is rather noisy. I had them switch your reservation to a quieter room in the rear."

Again, his solicitude irritated me, but my heart sank when he said, "I know you're here to study with Ibrahim Mangane. Right now, however, he's in Senegal *oriental* making a film. There is some uncertainty about when he'll return to Dakar."

Had I come here for nothing? I wondered, feeling a flash of panic.

"I spoke with his wife this morning, and told her you would arrive today. She said that Mangane is expected at a conference in Brussels next week, and he has a number of other obligations in Europe after that. You may find that he'll have very little time to spend with you. I have a suggestion: Perhaps, instead of focusing exclusively on Mangane and his works, you should become acquainted with other writers here. There are dozens. I can arrange for you to meet them." He named people I should meet and places I should visit. His litany was lost on me.

The scenes we sped by on the road had captivated me. Women, men, and children on foot carried baskets and burlap bags on their heads. Bicycles pulling makeshift trailers clattered along. Our driver artfully avoided collisions with carts drawn by sluggish beasts. Vans and cars, overloaded with people, accelerated, decelerated, or simply sputtered, as conditions dictated. Nelson noticed that he did not have my attention. He said that he would review the list of other Senegalese writers with me when I seemed "less distracted."

When we reached the Majestic, Nelson helped me check in and then said, "You're very tired. Get some sleep. I'll call for you tomorrow at noon and take you to lunch at the ambassador's residence."

"But it's morning," I said, "and I want to see Dakar." With that, I went up to my room.

# 7

Breathless with the kind of excitement that one feels when meeting a blind date, I prepared to get acquainted with Dakar. I washed my face, changed my blouse, put on lipstick, slipped into sandals. Refreshed, I was ready to explore the city. At the reception desk, I picked up a map, studied it briefly, and then set out for a walk.

Outside the hotel, I inhaled the musky perfume of Dakar—a heavy blend of bougainvillea, overripe fruit, smoked fish, and the sweat of human flesh. I turned left, onto an avenue shaded by colonnades of leafy plane trees and long expanses of stone and stucco walls. Behind the walls, I presumed, were mansions previously inhabited by the families of French colonialists, no longer in Dakar. On the walls were the graffiti of independence: *Vive Sénégal Libre! Indépendance! Liberté!* The avenue led to a stark, sun-drenched plaza, where, in the patches of dappled shade cast by a few trees, lay clusters of sleeping men.

I crossed the plaza and walked along a canopied street admiring the grandeur of its arches and columns. Offices of insurance agents, airlines, and travel agents lined the street. On the walls between the offices and around the columns were posters announcing dance, theater, and film programs. At the corner where the archway ended, I turned left onto a commercial street, its shop windows covered with grills and corrugated steel doors, shut for the afternoon hours when commerce and trade are interrupted by the ritual of the midday meal. At a bustling sidewalk café shaded by an awning, I spotted a vacant table and ordered a Senegalese beer. To avoid the inquiring glances of the men—African and European—seated nearby, I studied my map. I planned a route that would take me to the Sandaga Market. Refreshed by the beer, I resumed my ramble in the direction of the market.

I took the avenue to a vast intersection at the mouth of the market where I was prepared to be swallowed. Stands were vibrant with a vast array of multicolored fabrics; bolts of cloth lining the walls; bright patterned cottons draping the entrances of booths and shops. Brilliantly hued boubous—those loose full-length gowns that billowed in the breeze—and artfully turned turbans adorned the majestic women who paraded through the market examining foods critically, bargaining and buying selectively from vendors. The market scenes I had imagined faded once I was surrounded by the staggering color and vitality of the Sandaga Market.

How many dyes can cotton absorb? Can the human eye discern? There they were, all there, before my incredulous eyes. I was drawn from booth to booth where hand-dyed and embroidered fabrics were rolled out for me to admire and perhaps to buy. "Madame, Madame, look. Only look," a man called out in French. One glance and I was under the spell of market magicians—old and young—who surrounded me with cloth bursting with bright birds, flowers, and patterns that imitated a complex trigonometry. They draped me in material, and exclaimed, "How beautiful! Beautiful, Madame! You must buy!"

Nearby, vibrating with the rapid rhythmic peddling of their sewing machines, were young and middle-aged tailors, who in minutes transformed meters of cloth into handsome boubous. "Madame, we make it for you while you wait. You wear it today. You could be beautiful this evening, even more beautiful, Madame."

Although I was not seduced by the hawkers of cloth, the lure of the jewelry tradesmen proved irresistible. Just as there were fabrics of every imaginable color, so too were there beads of every color, heaped in disorderly profusion. Silversmiths hammered strands of metal into fine filigree pendants and earrings. A pair of earrings caught my eye. I asked the price. The silversmith, wide-eyed with delight when he realized I had only U.S. currency, quickly made the conversion from francs to dollars and, with a shrug that suggested he was selling at a loss, pocketed my five-dollar bill.

Farther along, a stunning display of enameled trays, basins, pots, and pans stopped me. Adjacent to that stood a section where vendors sold hardware and tools for tradesmen of every sort: plumbers, carpenters, electricians, auto mechanics, farmers, coopers, and cobblers. Basket weavers bent over baskets-in-progress in the shade of stacks of baskets; enough, it seemed, for the entire continent.

Then I came upon stands with produce. With the eyes and hands of master painters, women vendors arranged their vegetables and fruits in patterns that shimmered in the shafts of sunlight that illuminated the market—dazzling gardeners' jewels—tomatoes, green peppers, eggplants, scallions, cassava, radishes, and avocados; lemons, mangoes, tangerines, and papayas. Giant baskets and barrels were heaped with mounds of peanuts, rice, corn meal, millet, and flour.

The fish of the Atlantic had been netted and brought to market: red fish, pink fish, monstrous metallic blue fish, rosy prawns, and pale gray squid exuded the salty aroma of the ocean.

In the dimly lit interior stood several stalls with fetishes and charms fashioned from leopard skins, pelican feathers, turtle shells, monkey hair, hippopotamus teeth, buffalo hooves, and rhinoceros horns. Shelves were lined with medicinal powders, oils, spices, and herbs. Their enigmatic purveyors seemed accustomed to the clamor before them. Clusters of high-bosomed, elegantly draped mothers and aunts swished from stand to stand, assessing the advantages and disadvantages of this or that concoction for presumably unmarried or infertile daughters or nieces who tried to appear disinterested, as they observed the transactions from a certain distance.

The faces of the women were familiar. A pout, smirk or smile, a forehead or pair of eyes, the proud tilt of a chin, firm skin, rich brown coloring, folded arms, confident gait reminded me of my grandmothers and great aunts.

I thought of Uncle George's story about my *sosie;* and I began to look for my reflection in the faces and figures of women my age, trailed by two or three children, infants on their backs wrapped in the fabrics of their boubous, and carrying baskets or basins or bundles of goods on their heads. Could I do that, I wondered? They moved through the market with the choreographed glide of dancers, their flowing boubous enhancing their grace. My *sosie,* was she here? Had she swept by me unnoticed?

The faces of the men were also familiar. I saw my father's prominent nose and lips that curved down at the corners when he was in a somber mood, and the elongated face of my grandfather whose features resembled those of Senufo men and their masks. And I saw men with round heads, broad faces, and alert eyes constantly surveying the crowded market's pageantry and celebration of satisfying transactions among people who displayed abundant good cheer and gentility.

Children were everywhere, some hawking goods, others nestling next to their vendor-mothers. A few children wore prim school uniforms and were accompanied by fathers in European suits or mothers wearing chicly cut dresses in bright fabrics, but most were shabbily dressed, barefoot children whose open palms, pained expressions, and plaintive whines begged for francs. As I left the market, three such urchins, two girls and a tiny boy, whom the girls took turns carrying, followed me, poking my hips with their outstretched hands and, in French, pleading for money. "A few centimes, Madame. For food, Madame. You rich, Madame, not hungry. Please, Madame. Is Madame from Paris? From New York? Please, please, Madame." I smiled and said "No." And they became even more persistent, more determined to extract a few coins from me.

When I stopped and examined my map in search of the Medina, they lingered. In the sultry heat of late afternoon along the streets that led to the Medina, they followed. "You going to the Medina, Madame? We know the Medina well. It's our neighborhood. We show you."

Had I been alone, I might have been afraid to enter the maze of tight alleys where countless families huddled cheek-by-jowl in what appeared to be one-room hovels. Even with the escort of street children as guides, I hesitated, remembering Uncle George's story of the Medina.

"Come, come, Madame," chirped the older girl. They picked their way around puddles of sewage and piles of refuse in the narrow passages. I followed their lead, and they watched my every step. I wondered where they were leading me. They wanted me to see a garbage heap where women and children scavenged for food, to smell the gutters where open sewage stood stagnant, to touch the nub of the rotting arm of a leper, to listen to the eerie singing of a blind man. They wanted to see my repulsion, to elicit guilt and money. Soon I had seen enough. I turned back and tried to retrace my steps. The children, amused when I turned into a cul-de-sac, followed me, knowing I could never have found my way out without their direction.

Truly tired by now, I turned toward the center of Dakar, still trailed by the trio, who did not appear at all weary. We reached a broad avenue lined with vendors selling fruits and nuts at stands outside a hospital entrance. There they begged me to buy them some fruit. "Just one orange, Madame, one small orange."

"I don't have any money, any francs."

"You have money, Madame. You come from New York. You must have money, Madame."

"But I don't have any Senegalese money." To make vivid my claim, I drew a dollar from my shoulder bag.

"Doe-lah, doe-lah," they shrieked. "Give us doe-lah."

I refused, wondering what they would do with a dollar, what it was worth in the street children's exchange. We continued along the avenue, following its bend to the Presidential Palace, an exquisite creamy marble structure of perfect proportions, surrounded by a vast lawn watered by rotating sprinklers. I went up to the iron palace gates where a uniformed guard—standing tall in a cardinal red jacket topped off with a cylindrical red cap—smiled flirtatiously. The green, yellow, and red of Senegal's flag fluttered atop the palace and my heart fluttered with respect, and something that felt like patriotism. My three urchins peered between the iron bars. The younger girl whispered, "Madame, it's the president's house. It's beautiful, isn't it?"

At dusk, I began to wend my way toward the hotel. The girls continued to press their appeal. "Madame, please, give us something. Money, bracelet, earrings. Something." At the hotel, I went to the reception desk and exchanged dollars for francs. I returned to the entrance where the children had stationed themselves and put a franc into each outstretched palm. The mockery in their "*Merci*, Madame," and their smirks of satisfaction on being rewarded for persistence, were disquieting.

Exhausted, I went directly to my room, slipped between the sheets and fell into a dream-filled sleep. *In one dream, I was a ragged, hungry urchin living on the streets of Dakar. I begged and badgered passersby. Along came a man—Mangane perhaps. I trailed him, followed him home where he slammed the door in my face. In another dream, I went to an airport to meet Mangane, who never arrived. The letter "A" appeared and faded into a woman wearing a white A-shaped caftan. She whispered, "Be careful."*

# 8

AWAKENED BY THE TELEPHONE, I HEARD
through the white noise of drowsiness a woman speaking
French slowly and carefully.

"Hello? Madame Thompson? Good evening. I am Mariama
Mangane. Bill Nelson telephoned and told me that you arrived
this afternoon. Welcome to Dakar. My husband is away but he
will probably return soon—within a week. Would you like to
stay at our house while you wait for him?"

Disoriented and taken aback by her invitation, there was a
long silence before I found the French for an appropriate reply.
"You are very kind, Madame, too kind."

"Nelson told me that you are a black lady from America and
that you are a student. I would like you to be our guest while
you are here." The musical lilt of her voice, her warmth and sin-
cerity were irresistible, yet I was stunned by her offer. I had read
that tourists in Senegal were received with warm cordiality;
however, I did not expect such a hospitable invitation on the
day of my arrival from the home of Ibrahim Mangane.

"I would like to accept but I have a reservation here and I
don't want to impose—"

"It would not be an imposition, not at all. It would be a pleasure."

Tingling with delight and disbelief, I said, "Thank you, yes, I
would like to stay at your home."

"Good! Mamadou will call for you. Can you be ready to
leave the hotel in an hour?"

"Yes, Madame. I'll be ready. Thank you very much." Ready?

I was more than ready to see the Manganes' home—to be their guest. I was jubilant.

In an instant, I prepared to check out of the hotel. I brushed my hair, retouched my makeup, and, in the full-length mirror, reviewed my attire—a lavender and turquoise striped skirt and a lavender blouse, only slightly wrinkled. Was I really ready to enter the Mangane household? My heart raced. Eagerness and excitement were overtaken by anxiety. Why had she asked me, a total stranger? Was it traditional Senegalese hospitality? Why had I accepted? What would I do in their home? I heard my father's voice and what he had said to diminish my awe—I was ten years old and appropriately awed—the first time he took me into the Library of Congress: "Pull yourself together, girl, we're here to see some fine books."

And so I pulled myself together and summoned a porter who carried my bags to the lobby, where the receptionist was dismayed by my leaving. "If the room is unsatisfactory, Madame, we would be pleased to offer you a larger room," he said. "Our best room at the same rate. Monsieur Nelson said that you would be with us through August."

"The room was fine. However, I've been invited to stay with—a family—in the home of friends."

I tried to imagine Bill Nelson's gestures and expression when he returned and learned that I had checked out of the hotel and left in a car sent by Madame Mangane.

# 9

HALF AN HOUR LATER IN A TINY CITROËN, with Mamadou driving, I was en route to the "home of friends." We rattled along the streets of Dakar and then on to a long stretch of dirt road lit by the car's low-beam headlights. Along the roadside, the flames of lamps and candles lit up the faces of vendors—women, men, and children—selling in the dark of night, peanuts, perfumed oils, and pottery. We passed people on bicycles and motor scooters, and skirted several disabled cars. A herd of goats in the road slowed the traffic. Buses and trucks rumbled by leaving exhaust and dust in their wake. Mamadou peered through the windshield, prepared to avoid the unexpected.

As we shimmied along the rough road, I thought it odd that a writer and filmmaker would have only a matchbox of a car. My notions of lifestyles of celebrities had been influenced by images of homes of musicians, athletes, and Hollywood actors as they revealed themselves to the cameras of *Life* and *Ebony*—extravagant settings studded with sleek, expensive cars and glamorous companions.

Although the car was a disappointment, the house was not. Dramatically perched on the edge of a cliff, it stood alone in the distance. A red clay wall surrounded the immense house, its twin turrets with thatched conical roofs silhouetted against the moonlit sky. Illuminated arched windows in each turret shone like giant's eyes. "That's the house, the Manganes' house," whispered Mamadou as we approached. His pride was evident.

A flick of the headlights signaled an agile figure of a young boy who sprang out of the gatehouse and opened the iron gate.

"Is he the Manganes' son?"

"Ah, no, Madame. He is my son," smiled Mamadou. "He lives with me here to go to school. No school in my village. My wife and younger children live in the village. The Manganes have no child."

The driveway, only a hundred or so meters long, seemed endless that night. It ended at the courtyard where Mamadou stopped at the entrance to the house. Precisely at that moment, the tall carved wooden door opened. A woman, small, slender, and smiling, appeared and stood in an arc of light. Hands on her hips, she looked on with amusement as I bent and stretched to extract myself from the car.

"Madame Thompson, welcome. Sarah Thompson, isn't it? I am Mariama Mangane." I hesitated. I had imagined an older woman as his wife. "Come in, come in. Mamadou will bring your baggage." Her distinct, careful French was paced to accommodate the comprehension of foreign guests.

I stood in the foyer, my eyes drawn to the high walls of the turret where poster-sized portraits of Patrice Lumumba and Fidel Castro were suspended. "Have you had dinner?" she asked.

"I'm much too tired to eat. I walked all afternoon across Dakar." In truth, I felt I couldn't carry on a conversation in French over dinner. I needed to rest.

"Then let me show you to the guest room. It is next to the library where Ibrahim works." I followed Mariama across an enormous sitting room, which she referred to as the great hall. Maghreb carpets, carved stools, cushions and low couches, whitewashed walls adorned with a dozen or more handcarved wooden masks, and two enormous figurative wooden sculptures, gave the room the appearance of a museum gallery. A labyrinth of small rooms and corridors led to another wing of the house where Mariama showed me to a guest room. A Kente cloth spread covered the single bed. At the foot of the bed stood a carved wooden chest. A white goat hair rug covered the stone floor. Overhead, the wooden blades of a ceiling fan whirred lazily. Three antique balafons were mounted on one wall. A long writing table and a chair were against the wall under the balafons. An armoire, the first I had ever seen, was in a corner of the room. Between shuttered windows was a large mirror in a plain bronze frame. I marveled at the handsome simplicity of the room.

Mamadou had placed my baggage beside the table. I was aglow with gratitude. "Thank you for inviting me, Madame Mangane."

"Please call me Mariama and I will call you Sarah. I will bring you some tea."

When Mariama left the room, I opened the shutters, leaned on the wide windowsill, and looked out at a stone patio lit by a full moon. At the edge of the patio was an iron gate; and beyond the gate were giant boulders that appeared about to tumble into the bay. Waves roared and crashed against the sea wall. Enchanted by the sight and sound, I did not hear Mariama return with a glass of mint tea.

"I hope you will be able to sleep. When the tide is high it is rather noisy."

"I expect I'll sleep very soundly. It's wonderful to be here, to see the ocean from this side, actually to be here in the home of . . ." I was tired. My French was faltering. Mariama realized I was drifting into incoherence. She silenced me with a kiss on each cheek and a gentle "good night, beautiful dreams."

Good fortune had kissed me, too. Reverently, I murmured my psalm. After unpacking a few items and slipping on a nightgown, I lay awake, very warm and restless, looking at the night sky brightened by moonlight, listening to the crescendo and decrescendo of the waves washing in and out of the bay, and imagining what I might say to Ibrahim Mangane on meeting him. Would he be as welcoming as Mariama? Would he allow me to stay? Why had Mariama invited me? Was she acting out of traditional hospitality, or was there some other reason for her invitation? I was mystified by her warm reception, but she seemed open and sincere. I liked her immediately. I especially liked the sound of her name. Mariama.

# 10

AWAKENED FROM A DEEP SLEEP BY THE
singing of a woman whose ravishing mezzo-soprano shamed
the chorus of gulls swooping over the bay and by a soft but
steady knock, I opened my eyes, and looked about the room. I
had not been dreaming. I was, indeed, chez Mangane. The sweet
singing was Mariama's; and the gentle knocking at the door, hers
as well.

"Sarah, it is nearly time for lunch. Mamadou is preparing
swordfish. Do you eat fish?"

"Yes and I like swordfish very much! I'm coming."

"Lunch is on the veranda."

The smoke of grilled fish, the clatter of dishes, and the fragrance of ripe bananas and mangoes quickened my appetite. I
went to the window. Waves sparkled under the midday sun. I
was really in Senegal and in the home of Ibrahim Mangane!

In the bathroom across the hall, I showered hurriedly,
dressed in my coral linen sheath dress and sandals, and retraced
the labyrinthine route to the great hall, where I paused to
admire its stately dimensions and the Manganes' magnificent art
collection. I then went outdoors to the veranda where Mariama
was seated at a table covered with an amber tablecloth in the
shade of a palm tree. I felt a twinge of envy as I took in her carefully coifed cornrows of braids, gold earrings, gold bracelets,
and narrow feet in pale orange pumps. A saffron batiked
boubou illuminated her slender aubergine face, sharply pointed
nose, and almond-shaped eyes. I noticed creases at the corners
of her faintly painted lips, lips accustomed to smiling.

"You seemed very tired, so I did not call you for breakfast. But you must not miss lunch. Did you sleep well?"

"Yes. Yes, thank you, I was very comfortable. I slept very soundly, very well."

"Come, sit down. Mamadou has prepared a feast." I sat opposite Mariama at the place set for me at the oblong table. "I am delighted that you have come all the way from America to study with my husband. Some Europeans—mostly French and Belgians—are interested in his work. But he has had very few American inquiries, which is why your arrival from Harvard is an occasion for celebration." I was still tingling with excitement about being there, marveling that I had been delivered swiftly, nearly magically, to the habitat of my hero. Having time to inspect the setting and adjust to its grandeur before meeting him had advantages, too.

Mariama spoke slowly, smiling as she talked. "We have had some American visitors—most of them men. It is usually Bill Nelson who brings them here to meet us and he invites us to Embassy parties where we meet visiting journalists, professors, and artists. They may know of Senghor, Sembéne, or Diop, but they do not know Ibrahim Mangane, the best writer of them all! Nelson, I know, wants you to meet the other writers, but I hope you will concentrate on my husband's works. So you must stay here with us."

Ah-ha, I thought, the calculated hospitality of a wife with ambitions for her husband was the impulse for my being her guest.

She continued, "It is very important to make him well known in America. Americans buy lots of books. Does Harvard know his books, his films?"

"America should know him. And, yes, Harvard, I hope, will recognize him, know his books and films. That's why I have come." At that moment, I realized that the potential for my work extended beyond the dissertation, that it was important to expand his reputation.

"Will you write articles about him? Make him famous in America?"

"I plan to write a dissertation about him, that is to say, about his works. And, yes, I would like to write an article and, eventually, a book—perhaps an intellectual biography." I surprised myself with this bold blueprint of a plan. Mariama, however, did not appear at all surprised.

"Yes, write a book," she said eagerly. "Not a book that only intellectuals will read, but a popular book. Tell the world about him!" She bubbled with excitement.

"What do you want the world to know about him? And about you?"

"Well, I will tell you some things that you should write." Mamadou brought glasses of yogurt with water. "You may serve lunch now," she said.

With the assurance of a renowned chef, Mamadou reappeared with a tray of grilled swordfish encircled with rice, tomatoes, pimento, onions, and parsley. He placed it at the center of the table and then retreated to a corner of the veranda where he awaited our sighs of pleasure. Mariama's slender fingers pressed some rice, bits of fish, and its sauce into a small ball and ate the morsel. I followed her example. Mariama nodded her approval. "Delicious!" I exclaimed. A satisfied Mamadou disappeared into the house.

"Ibrahim works very hard to help politicians, intellectuals, and foreigners understand our people, and to help our people understand themselves." In the monotonous tone of a tired guide at a tourist site, she spoke of him. "He spends weeks listening to people in small villages. Sometimes I travel with him. He listens to their stories about their lives." Her voice deepened. " 'Tell me your story,' he says. They tell him about everything: their family histories, the meanings of their names and their children's names, how they build their huts, everything." Her undulating hands carried me with her on their walks through villages. "They reveal the secret incantations that drive away the locusts, calm the wind, make crops grow, and bring on the rains. He writes their stories, photographs them, and films them while they are talking or just going about their everyday work." She broke for a well-rehearsed pause. Mariama obviously had told countless visitors about her husband's work. "When he comes home, he is at his desk night and day. He turns their simple stories into art. They live beyond their villages now. They live in his books about them. They have been seen in Europe in his films."

"Do they know that their villages, their lives are shown abroad?" Fascinated by her performance, I wanted to hear more, observe further.

"Oh, yes. Ibrahim takes them magazines and his books with their pictures and their own stories. They are astonished when they see their stories in writing!" she said clapping her hands. "Of course, most of them cannot read or write, but it still makes them very happy. He tells them that people in Abidjan, Lomé, Paris, Brussels, and Geneva read the articles and books. In gratitude, the women cook their best yassa—you call it porridge—for him. Weavers give him priceless cloth. Potters load him down with calabashes. Wood carvers imitate his face in their works. In the villages, he is a hero. But abroad, he is relatively unknown. You will make him known." The determination in her tone astonished me.

Mariama was striking a bargain. She had offered hospitality in exchange for the promise of a book that would extend her husband's reputation to readers abroad. And although I was certain I would produce a dissertation and earn a doctorate, I was uncertain about the route from the dissertation to a book. Finding a publisher for a book about a not well-known foreign writer was daunting to say the least. I was in very deep water, well over my head. I needed to shift our focus slightly.

"And you, what would you have me write about you?"

Coyly, her small manicured hands covering her mouth, she said, "Oh, there is little to write about me. I take care of my husband and his house, teach home economics at a girls' school, and tend my garden." She pointed to a clump of prickly succulents in a sunlit corner of the patio.

"There's more to tell, more to your story," I insisted. Mariama's smile faded. She appeared somber.

"Truly, there is little to tell." She was sincere. For a moment, she concentrated on forming a rice ball and the story she would shape. Slowly, as if she were inventing her autobiography, perhaps talking for the first time about her own life, she said, "I am the youngest of five children—three sons, two daughters. Our father was a fisherman. We lived in Kayar. Our mother had come from Mboro. One of our mother's uncles, a fish merchant in Mboro, sent his youngest son, Ibrahim, to visit us. I was very young. I hardly remember his visit. They said I charmed him with my songs and games. My mother decided that Ibrahim and Mariama would marry someday. That is how it happened."

"What happened next?"

"I was nineteen when we were married and Ibrahim was forty. He had done many things. He had left the university to join the French Resistance in World War II. After the war, he lived in Paris, where he worked very hard, very long hours in menial jobs—janitor, porter, construction worker, doorman, dishwasher, taxi driver—and he studied philosophy at the Sorbonne." She hesitated as if she were unaccustomed to relating this passage of his life. "He was engaged to a woman from Martinique who had come to Paris as an au pair. I am told she was very beautiful. She had just become a model when she was killed in a car crash. It was a great sorrow for him. He wrote an account of her life, her struggle to build a life for herself in Paris. And how it was ended. It was the first piece he published and the beginning of his career as a journalist." She paused and called to Mamadou.

"Living among other African students and workers from Senegal, the Congo, Niger, the Ivory Coast, Togo, Dahomey, and Sudan, he wrote articles about the hardships they suffered in France. In the way that he now tells the stories of villagers, he wrote about the life of the African in France. Tragic stories. His articles were published in all the Senegalese newspapers and magazines. While living in France, he became famous in Senegal."

I was intrigued. Whenever she paused, I asked her to tell me more. "Was his family concerned about his remaining in France?"

"The family knew he would return to Senegal someday. He had bought this property." I followed the line of her index finger as she pointed to the road east and drew an arc westward to the bay, indicating that they owned the land beyond the wall that surrounded the compound. "He had lived modestly in Paris, saving his money to build this, his dream house. During one of his visits he arranged to have the gatehouse built, then that cabin was built, and gradually the house itself was built.

"He left the building in Paris where he had lived with several other Africans, and moved in with a French actress with whom he lived for many years." She raised her eyebrows and her chin. "They never married, but their affair did delay his return to Senegal. Finally, talk of Senegal's independence brought him home. We were married seven years ago. Seven years—and still no children. Do you have children?"

"No, we don't. My husband doesn't want to have children—not now."

"I do not understand. What kind of man would not desire children? Ibrahim, I know, wants a son. The miscarriages I have had, all the failed pregnancies have been as painful for him as they have for me. If only I could give him a son, an heir, his happiness would be complete, my life would be complete." Her eyes brimmed with tears of profound sadness. It was my turn to concentrate on fingering the rice and fish.

After a lengthy silence, I inquired about Mariama's family. "Where do your brothers and sister live?"

"They live in Kayar. My sister is married. She has four sons. Recently her husband married again. His second wife, of course, is young. The new wife prefers the company of the sons. A pity. Our brothers are well situated, married, and have children. The eldest is in banking, the next one, a doctor, and the youngest is a businessman who owns a company that processes shark oil. We used to go to Kayar and Mboro frequently, but now it's they who usually come to Dakar, except for my sister who does not leave Kayar. Relatives bring us news of her."

Curious about Senegalese marital customs, I asked, "Is it still common for a man to have more than one wife?"

"It is not uncommon," said Mariama. "Is it not common for a man to have more than one wife in America—perhaps not at the same time, but one after another?"

"It's not uncommon. Touché."

Mariama smiled and continued with the confidence of a mankala tactician whose last play with the stones gave her a certain advantage. "Tell me about your husband who does not want to have children."

I'd scarcely thought of Lincoln since my arrival. Mariama's question evoked images of him, memory's snapshots: Lincoln as a college date, on a tennis court at MIT, bent over a chessboard, in a Dartmouth T-shirt drinking beer from a can and watching a football game on television. Lincoln, surrounded by books, studying for an exam, or smiling with satisfaction during the applause for one of his speeches. And I remembered my last view of him at the airport.

"Lincoln works toward improving conditions for blacks in America. He's very concerned about the future and doesn't want to bring up children in a climate of racial strife," I said defensively.

"Is he a black American or a white American?"

"Black."

"Was he named for your president who ended slavery?"

"Yes, indirectly. That is, his grandfather was named for the president. His father and he, in turn, carry on the name. He's Abraham Lincoln Thompson III."

"Abraham. Ibrahim. The same name! Ah, you are drawn to men with that name. It means father and man devoted to God. And neither has a child." Mariama mused over her insight. A mere coincidence, I thought, of no consequence. For Mariama, however, it was a clue to understanding the mysterious route that had brought me to their home.

"Will he visit you here?"

"No, he is not interested in Africa. Besides, the trip is very expensive."

"Does not want to have children! And a black American who is not interested in Africa. Your Abraham Lincoln is a strange man."

It was Lincoln who had made me feel strange, whose view of me as obsessed or possessed had contributed to our estrangement. Having been accused of being strange myself, I now felt I had been acquitted. I smiled with gratitude at Mariama.

"After lunch I usually work in the garden," she said. "I will introduce you to my plants, my green children."

In rhythm with the routine of her day, Mamadou brought a basket of garden tools and a watering can just as Mariama folded her boubou between her thighs and squatted beside the patch of prickly plants. She scratched the clay at the base of the plants, watered each, as she called its name in Latin or French or Wolof.

The week unfolded slowly, focused as I was on Ibrahim's return. Mariama's mornings were occupied with trips to her school, to shops and markets, and to the hospital to visit sick friends. I usually accompanied her on shopping errands, and observed the way she haggled with preferred vendors and rebuffed others. Lunch always was followed by her prodding the reluctant succulents in her garden; then a nap followed by tea, and later a twilight walk along the rocky shore. We often walked until the light had faded completely and Mamadou's ringing of a giant cowbell summoned us home to dinner.

Mariama was as curious about my world as I was about hers. She wanted to know about women and men, dating and courtship, the meaning of the civil rights movement, the character of New York, Washington, Boston, and Atlanta, how black people live in America, how Senegalese live in America. I wanted to know about schools, family life, arranged marriages, and Moslem traditions; how independence had changed the political climate in Senegal, changes in attitudes toward the French, and the character of the peoples of Senegal—the Wolofs, Lebous, Mandings.

When I asked about Ibrahim—his style of working or his plans, she replied with a litany of concerns about his medical problems, dietary needs, and constant state of overwork. Finally, she dismissed my questions about him by saying, "You must ask Mangane about Mangane."

Toward the end of the week, I ventured into Ibrahim's study for the first time. Books were shelved from floor to ceiling. From the center of the room, I read titles of works, generally arranged by country with identifying labels—Algerian, American, Brazilian, British, Chilean, Egyptian, French, Indian, Japanese, Mexican, Russian, Venezuelan, and more. Shelved on the opposite wall were books by Senegalese authors, Ivorians, Ghanaians, Nigerians, Kenyans, Sudanese, Ugandans, Tanzanians, Angolans, South Africans. His collection of African works was larger by far than I had seen anywhere—larger than the combined collections in Harvard's libraries. I was amazed. On the top shelf were film canisters—films by Eisenstein, Fellini, Ray, Renoir, Rossellini, Sembéne, Truffaut. The systematic arrangement of things surprised me—a librarian's touch. Mariama's work, no doubt.

At the pace of a supplicant approaching an altar, I moved toward his desk. Stacks of folders on each end, a clear space in the center. Did I dare snoop and invade his papers? Yes. I opened a folder with carbon copies of letters to foundations and publishers, letters about film scripts. I scanned his letters in search of clues to his character, examined the curves of his handwriting to discern what a graphologist might learn from his script, studied the framed photographs and awards on the walls, as well as the assortment of pens and pencils in a canister on his desk, sniffed the aroma of his crusty, charred pipes, inhaled the fruity fragrance of his tobacco pouch, and buried my nose in the pillows on his couch in search of his scent. The Ibrahim Mangane that I constructed began to have a certain reality, a phantasmal presence.

Overcome by reverence and reverie, I lay on the couch where Mariama, having returned from her errands, found me. "Our vigil will soon be over," she announced. "Ibrahim is coming home tonight." From the great hall came a blast of brass and drums, the Grand March from *Aïda*, a tape Mariama played over and over again that afternoon. In response to Mariama's stream of instructions, Mamadou dusted and swept, ran errands, and prepared a lamb curry with a pungency that permeated the house. I retreated to the guest room to ready myself for the hero's return—reviewed my notes, jotted down questions to ask him, and polished my nails.

# 11

IT WAS WELL AFTER MIDNIGHT WHEN THE HEAD-
lights of several vehicles, signaling Ibrahim Mangane's arrival,
illuminated the compound. I leapt out of bed and down the hall
to a window with a view of the courtyard. Mamadou was ignit-
ing the torches at the gate. Two vans and a Land Rover crunched
along the gravel road and stopped. Trunks were unloaded.
Doors slammed. Mamadou exchanged greetings with several
people and then Mariama called out her welcome to Ibrahim
and his crew. The uproar of exuberant conversations in French
and Wolof, lavish laughter, the clatter of calabashes, uncorking
of bottles, clinking of glasses—hearty sounds of celebration—
filled the night air like the boisterous bustle at a dock where
sailors are welcomed home after a long voyage.

A rich baritone dominated in the clamor of utterances. It was
Ibrahim's voice that rose above the others, whose voices fell
silent when he spoke. From time to time, I heard Mariama speak
at a higher than usual pitch. Her coquettish conversation punc-
tuated the din of the voices of men. Eventually I heard Ibrahim
ask, "And what has transpired here in my absence?"

"Sarah Thompson has transpired. That is to say, she came
from America a week ago to study with you," Mariama said.

"Ah-ha, a woman to study?" somebody hooted. The crew
chuckled lasciviously.

"Sarah Thompson? Sarah Thomp . . . oh, yes, she is Peter
Martin's student—from Har-vahd. You may be sure, my
friends, that she has come to study—and only to study. I recall

her letters—long, typewritten letters. Letters with footnotes!"
Riotous laughter erupted.

"She is a very nice woman—and she is black."

"Fetch her, fetch Mademoiselle Thompson of Har-vahd," a
mischievous voice demanded.

"No, spare her the view of this intoxicated bedlam," said
Ibrahim. "I'll meet her tomorrow after you rascals have gone."

My anxiety subsided. I was not yet prepared to meet Ibrahim
Mangane. And I certainly did not want an audience at our first
encounter. I tiptoed back to the guest room and into bed where
I strained to hear their rambling conversation, catching only bits
and pieces of stories. Finally, after the gaiety subsided, the vans
rumbled away, and I could hear the roar of the surf again, I
closed my eyes to shut out the glow of the sunlight. I fell asleep
wishing I hadn't included footnotes in my letters.

The glare of the late morning sun aroused me. I got up, showered hurriedly, singing in the shower, *My help cometh from
Senegal, which is heaven and earth."*

The white boubou embroidered with cream silk threads,
bought on a shopping trip with Mariama, was perfect for the
first encounter. Gold earrings. I carefully brushed my hair and
decided to let it hang loose, rather than braid it or twist it into a
chignon. Tangerine lipstick, a brush of blush on each cheek.
Perfume. I rummaged through the contents of my shoulder bag
for the perfume bought at Orly, broke the seal and anointed
temples, ears, neck. Pirouetting slowly before the mirror, I
wondered how my appearance would register in the eyes of
Ibrahim Mangane.

Mamadou's clang of the cowbell was more spirited than
usual. I waited until I heard voices, Ibrahim's and then
Mariama's, before going to the courtyard. Seated at the table,
was a proud Mariama draped in her new blue boubou and
matching blue shoes. Mariama had told me she liked to have
shoes dyed to match her boubous.

Leaning on the wall overlooking the bay was Ibrahim Mangane, dressed in a crisp, white caftan and leather sandals. He
turned and walked toward me, his large black eyes registering

approval. His smile broadened to reach the corners of a thick mustache, animating a lean, oval face with high cheekbones and sunken cheeks, like a living Senufo mask, with the sheen and hue of bittersweet chocolate. His large, deep-set eyes fixed on mine as he walked toward me and extended his hand.

"Madame Thompson, welcome. Welcome to Senegal, to Dakar, and to my home." His bony, callused hand clasped mine in a gentle handshake. We were the same height and both dressed in white, and on meeting we stood motionless, eyes engaged in the recognition of a magical moment. My hand in his began trembling, sending ripples through the soft cotton of my boubou. And I knew he had felt it.

"Come. Sit down. Your letters and Peter Martin's letter about you were intriguing. And here you are." His rich, sonorous French was soothing. I hesitated, then finally responded, "I am pleased to meet you." I should have said "enchanted," because I was.

"So, you crossed the deep blue ocean to meet me? To study me? Well, here I am. Study." Ibrahim stretched wide his arms like one prepared to be crucified. Mariama laughed.

Wishing to be taken seriously, I protested, "I am here to work under your supervision, that is, to study your works, if you will permit me."

"What about working with me, learning with me, studying with me? Let's drink to that." He filled his glass and mine with wine and Mariama's with orangeade.

"To a student from Har-vahd, to your health." He raised his glass. A sip of the white wine made him grimace.

"Why do we allow the Algerians to label this beverage 'wine'? Mamadou, bring us a bottle of French wine—the '61 Fleurie—a wine of feminine grace to grace the company and the occasion." Ibrahim emptied his glass onto the gravel. Mamadou removed the bottle and returned quickly with the more suitable selection. I was surprised by his rejection of a wine from African soil. I had expected him to be anti-French. And shouldn't a man's wine preference follow his political orientation?

"Tell me about yourself—your background, your education."

"I was born in Washington, D.C. I am an only child, as we say. My father and mother are teachers. I attended the elementary school where my mother taught. I graduated from Wellesley College, a college for women in Massachusetts. And since then, I've been a graduate student in comparative literature at Harvard where Peter Martin—"

"Yes, Peter Martin, excellent scholar, a good man. What does he say about my work?"

"He's become better acquainted with your work since I began my dissertation. I believe you're Africa's most important writer, that your works have advanced the continent's political struggle. Your films are breaking new ground and—well, are provocative—that is, they counter anthropological images of African life. Your works are *very* important."

"Ahhh, that is very kind. Are there many like you—black intellectuals—in your university?" he asked.

"Peter Martin is the only black faculty member in the university. There are countless black women and men intellectuals—writers, scholars, researchers—throughout the United States, but very few of us are at Harvard."

"Your civil rights movement and Martin Luther King will change that," Mariama said.

"Universities resist change," said a skeptical Ibrahim. "In any case, Peter Martin is well-regarded and that means his students do exceptional work. One measure of the worth of a professor is the quality of his students' work. You must return to Harvard with a very good report on Senegalese literature and get word out—pull doorbells—about my work."

His voice was rising, the volume increasing. "The world needs to know that there are writers, filmmakers, musicians, painters, sculptors, poets in Africa, that the arts abound in black Africa. It is the artists and intellectuals of the African diaspora who are creating works that the Europeans imitate. Look at what Paris extracted from African art—cubism, for example. The African imagination has enlivened European art. African music has given modern music its dominant cadence, and

African writers have enriched the content of literature. There are few African filmmakers, but we are showing new possibilities for cinema. African artists are atomic!" The force of his declaration shook the table. His air of authority, the crescendo in his spirit, moved me.

"Bravo," whispered Mariama.

Mamadou nodded his agreement as he brought a platter of chicken stew in a tomato and peanut sauce. Ibrahim ate very little. His spare frame needed little nourishment. Instead, he nourished his vision. His large, hungry, acquisitive eyes constantly scanned the cloudless sky, the rippling blue-green waters of the bay, my facial expressions, Mariama's gestures. He had a director's overview, noting the background and light, the tilt of one's head, the exchange of glances, movements of hands—as if cameras were rolling and the scene were being filmed.

After lunch, Mariama turned to her gardening. I gathered my index cards, pens, and notebooks, then joined Ibrahim in his office where he sat at his desk at the far end of the room. I sat on the sofa. Looking over crescent-shaped reading glasses, he said, "Call me Ibrahim. Use *tu* instead of *vous*. After all, you are our guest and I understand you are to be with us for three months. Now let me tell you about what we have here," he said, with a sweep of his right arm.

He listed the titles of films in the canisters on the top shelves. Among them were his films, a few unfinished or not yet ready to be released, he said. He turned to the books mentioning authors whose works he said he cherished: Senghor, Sembéne, Césaire; Wright, Ellison, and Baldwin; Sartre and Camus; Tolstoy and Chekov. He described the organization of the folders in the three wooden file cabinets that occupied a corner. A phonograph, records, and tape recorder were on a shelf near his desk. A tape was spinning out a hypnotic melody on tinkling thumb pianos.

I surveyed the books, then asked, "Who is your favorite author?"

"I am my favorite author!" Ibrahim immediately replied.

Opening a spiral notebook, my pen poised to record whatever would follow, "Which characters in your novels, stories, and films are autobiographical?"

He tilted back in his swivel chair, folded his arms, and glared at me over his glasses. Then he smiled and calmly said, "Your questions are not going to fetch useful answers. Close your notebook. Put away your pen. I do not wish to be interviewed. I don't wish to engage in analyses of my previous works. I want to discuss ideas for future works, explore new possibilities. I need correspondence translated. The galleys of English translations of my short stories need proofreading. I need a collaborator, not a biographer or critic or mere fan. It is no longer flattering to be surrounded by fans. If you think you can be of assistance, then you are invited to remain." So that was how it would be. Ibrahim Mangane had announced his conditions, specified his contractual terms.

Barely containing the flood of embarrassment's feverish tears, I sank between the pillows on the couch feeling sophomoric. Ibrahim swiveled around, his back to me, and occupied himself with the mail for several minutes. Then he spun around and looked at me with compassion.

"Peter Martin sent you. I trust his judgment. I believe you might become a valuable assistant, a valuable colleague, if you wish to remain."

"I want to work with you on your terms. More than anything else in the world, I want to work with you," I whispered and swallowed my tears. I was embarrassed by my presumptions and intimidated by his control of the situation. He extended a hand, a vigorous handshake, and that is how our collaboration—our relationship—began.

# 12

EACH MORNING AT HIS DESK, IBRAHIM WAS occupied with the novel-in-progress. On his right was a stack of a half dozen books—reference books, dictionaries, a thesaurus, and a film directory. On his left, a basket of unopened mail. For a week or more, I sat at a small table to his left opening the mail and sorting letters: reply immediately, next week, eventually. Behind him on another table was his typewriter. On the wheels of his upholstered swivel chair he glided from one end of the desk to the other or spun around to type.

He wrote in French and, generally, wrote only one draft. He was finishing a novel about village women abandoned by their husbands and sons, who had moved to neighboring cities to find work. In the final chapters, for the funeral of a young mother of three, her husband and father return expressing regret and remorse. It was Ibrahim's practice to finish two or three pages, and then pace the room while reading aloud from his impeccable prose.

I knew that I was in the presence of a genuine article, an authentic master craftsman. Doubts that Lincoln had raised about Ibrahim's talents could be dismissed entirely.

Entranced, I listened attentively to his every word. He moved back and forth across the room, changing his voice to fit each character, his tone to match the mood of the episode. When he finished, he stopped pacing, and looked up from the text, over his glasses with a smile of satisfaction.

"Can you visualize the scene?" "Does it strike you as plausible?"

His questions astonished me at first. That he invited my

opinion was daunting. Initially, I merely answered "yes" or "no." Gradually, I realized that he truly wanted to engage me in a discussion of his work; gradually, I became more responsive, asking him to provide more information for readers unacquainted with village customs.

Mamadou brought midmorning tea. The daily pause for tea became a time when Ibrahim delivered what I called his "mini lectures." He offered commentaries on a variety of subjects, for example: differences between French and British colonial structures; Christian missionary influences on Senegalese life; the relevance of Islam to modern forms of social organization; peanut production in Senegal; the French educational system; African Anglophone literature; Scandinavian films; Himalayan geography; the history of chess; the British novel; the Soviet economy; the operation of hot-air balloons; and the rules of cricket. His capacity for information and range of interests were amazing. I was enthralled by his monologues and flattered that he found me a suitable audience. He was an animated lecturer and I, an ardent student. At that stage, it never occurred to me to question his facts or challenge his opinions.

I listened with the expectation of being informed or at least entertained. From time to time, he interrupted himself to ask if I had a different point of view, an alternative interpretation, or a question. As my confidence grew and my awe diminished, I questioned, I challenged, I advanced other opinions. But not at first, only as I came to know him better and trust my own impulses more.

After tea and his mini lectures, we returned to our routine. Invigorated by the sound of his own voice and, to be sure, by my adulation, Ibrahim's words came more quickly; he typed more rapidly. Inspired by his rhythm and intensity, I, too, scribbled furiously, noting his phrases and my observations.

Toward noon, the sound of an approaching car could be heard from some distance. It would be Mariama returning with the mail, newspapers, groceries, and her shopping treasures—fruits, fragrant soaps, a basket, or a bolt of spectacular cloth. The sing-song of her joyful voice announced her arrival, and the midday tumult began. The kitchen resounded with the clatter of kettles. The aroma of Mamadou's cuisine spiced the house. The clang of his cowbell summoned us to lunch.

With the same question at each midday meal, Mariama opened the conversation: "Where did your typewriter take you this morning, my dear?"

"Ahh, from village to village," was Ibrahim's customary reply.

In a lively medley of her morning activities, Mariama related conversations with vendors, shopkeepers, relatives, and friends she had encountered: reports of marriages, pregnancies, births and deaths, updates on land for sale; news of small fortunes made and large fortunes lost.

"Well, my dear, if that is how your morning was wasted, you need a little intellectual sustenance."

Ibrahim always brought a book to the table and would forego the grilled meat or fish or groundnut stew for the chance to read—no, perform—excerpts from the works of Aimé Césaire, Camara Laye, Wole Soyinka, Peter Abrahams, Frantz Fanon, Richard Wright, Lorraine Hansberry, James Baldwin. Or, he would recite poems by Léopold Senghor, Malik Fall, David Diop, Langston Hughes, and Sterling Brown. He paused frequently to sip mint tea, pauses that were filled with our praise and applause—or stunned silence when Ibrahim's renditions so impressed us that we were left speechless.

After lunch, Mariama went to her garden, while Ibrahim and I returned to his office. He dictated correspondence, usually letters to publishers, translators, and university professors. I translated and typed those addressed to Anglophone Africa, the U.S., U.K., and India. After a fortnight of mornings and afternoons working together in Ibrahim's office, the rhythm of our routine became harmonious. We moved around each other like two master weavers at a loom, silently blending the warp and weft of words in tapestries of texts.

Except for an occasional invitation to dinner with the Manganes' friends, my time was occupied by my work with Ibrahim and late-afternoon walks with Mariama. Ibrahim's brothers and nephews occasionally joined us for dinner. In the evenings, the house vibrated with taped music from villages in Senegal or Mali, or fast-paced popular Nigerian and Ghanaian music. After dinner I usually retired to my room where I stayed awake well into the night writing letters, reading, and scribbling in my journal.

Ibrahim's niece, Fatou Kamara, a conscientious university student, came twice a week to type her uncle's French correspondence. We exchanged very few words. Once she asked what I was reading. I said I was reading Mangane. She was amused. I asked what she was reading. Rather smugly she said, "Ralph Ellison—in English."

Since my arrival at the Manganes, Bill Nelson had visited only once to express his dismay about my "running away" from the hotel without informing him; but he telephoned several times to inquire about my progress and to invite me to lunch or tea. I had declined each time. He urged me to attend the Fourth of July festivities at the U.S. Embassy. "They'll serve hot dogs, hamburgers, American ice cream, and Coca-Cola," he said. I hadn't missed those American delicacies, and I wasn't at all interested in going. Another time he called and said, "There'll be news from home—newspapers and magazines. We just received *Ebony* and *The Negro Digest.*" Again he phoned to reiterate his invitation to the July Fourth party: "One of Martin Luther King's associates is in Dakar, and at the party, he'll give a briefing on the civil rights scene. Please come, Sarah." I found his last call persuasive. Bill sounded thrilled when I agreed to attend.

When he called for me, Mamadou announced, "Madame Sarah is not well—not well enough to go out. Didn't eat lunch today. She only smelled the fish and went flying from the table. Malaria, Mr. Nelson. Foreigners always get malaria." Bill insisted on seeing me. He found me dozing in a reclining chair in the great hall. I told him only that I had been very tired. I didn't tell him that I'd had fits of vomiting since breakfast that morning.

His assessment of my condition was the same as Mamadou's. He said, "You probably have malaria. I think you should see a doctor. The Manganes have a friend who is a malaria specialist, Dr. Diouf. I'll ask Mariama to make an appointment for you right away."

When I spoke with Mariama about the symptoms, including the nausea, she asked about my menstruation cycle. I told her I had missed a period or two, not unusual with my history of irregularity.

"It may be malaria, but there are other possibilities," said Mariama suspiciously. She made an appointment for me with Dr. Diouf on the very next day.

After a brief examination and some tests, Dr. Diouf told me that I "appeared to be pregnant"—at least two months pregnant, but he would await the return of the test results before confirming his diagnosis. A few days after the visit, Dr. Diouf telephoned to report the laboratory tests had supported his hunch: I was pregnant.

# 13

INITIALLY, I FELT RATHER PLEASED WITH myself—pleased by the biological affirmation of a willing womb. Then I thought of all the complications: writing a dissertation, life after graduate school, and Lincoln.

How would I deliver the news of my pregnancy—our pregnancy—to what I knew would be a reluctant prospective father? What would he say? And what of my work? I had planned a tight schedule for the dissertation, and there was no time for a baby! I felt the force of a scream rising; I struggled to contain it. Instead of crying out, I chanted, *"My help cometh from Senegal."*

There was some comfort in the sound of my voice and the words that, after all, had lifted me out of a conventional graduate student's existence and brought me to Dakar. Mariama found me by the telephone in the semi-darkness of the great hall chanting and weeping. Warm tears streamed down my cheeks and gathered under my chin.

She sat down and embraced me. "What has happened? What has gone wrong?" The lullaby lilt of her voice made me cry even harder. Finally I stammered, "I'm preg—preg—pregnant. Pregnant!" Fists clenched, I said, "And I'm frightened and angry!"

For Mariama, a woman whose cultural background had prepared her to regard bearing children as a blessing, and as one who had not been so blessed, my emotions were incomprehensible. She raised my shoulders, got me on my feet, and led me to my room where I threw myself onto the bed.

"So Diouf found you pregnant. I wish he had such good news for me again," she said plaintively.

Reminded of Mariama's "failed pregnancies," I tried to regain a measure of composure.

"I'm scared. I guess I'm afraid of Lincoln's reaction. I should tell him soon, but I wish I could wait and tell him in person, see his reaction."

"What do you fear?"

"I don't know whether a baby will bring us closer together or push us further apart. And I'm afraid I won't be able to finish my dissertation. Yesterday my stomach was very upset. Morning sickness they call it, but it lasted all day! I can't complete my work this summer feeling this way. It's a bad time for—"

"If I understand your situation," Mariama said softly, "you must tell your husband immediately. Telephone him or cable him at once. He will probably surprise you—he'll be proud and happy, no doubt. As for your work, let me tell you something, my dear. Your body is preparing itself for work that only women can do—women who are lucky enough to have babies. The work of the mind can be postponed, while you prepare for the work your body must do to bring your baby into the world. This time has been chosen for you to become a mother. We do not choose our time. The time of birth is Allah's choice."

"You're right, I'll cable. He'll need time to get accustomed to the idea. Sending a telegram instead of calling will give us both time to think about it."

"You write the message and I will find Mamadou. He will take it to the post office right away," Mariama said, getting up to inform Mamadou.

Left alone, I got up and moved to the writing table. On a lined yellow pad, soon damp with tears, I scrawled different versions of my message:

*Two months pregnant. Hope you are pleased.*
*Pregnant. Mixed feelings. Due in January.*
*Pregnant. Expecting in January. Should make us happier.*
*Pregnant. Expecting in January. Call or cable.*

The last line would elicit a reply. I wanted to hear from Lincoln. I wanted to know how he felt about becoming a father.

Mamadou rapped on the door. "Madame Sarah, I will take

the message you want to cable. Print it in English. They know English at the PTT." I printed the message, added "Love, Sarah," and surrendered the fateful words to Mamadou along with our Cambridge address.

Mariama returned with chamomile tea. She sat on the bed and I at the writing table silently sipping the comforting brew.

"The baby will make you and your husband very happy."

"Do you know what it takes to write a dissertation and complete graduate school?" I asked woefully. "I have a teaching fellowship for the coming year and I need the fellowship salary. I'd have to give up the fellowship to take care of the baby."

"Relatives will help care for your baby, won't they?"

"You don't understand, Mariama. I don't have sisters, aunts, and cousins in a village a few miles away from Cambridge to help me!" Flushed with frustration, I began to cry again.

"Be thankful that you will not have dozens of opinions about the upbringing of your child."

"But I'll need opinions and help. I'm not ready. I'm neither experienced nor old enough. I need—"

"How old are you?"

"Twenty-four—nearly twenty-five."

"You are certainly old enough to be a mother. You are very mature and sure of yourself. And when your womb is ready to deliver, your head, hands, and heart will be ready to receive." Pleased with her words of intended comfort, she primly sipped her tea.

I strained to imagine myself with an infant in my arms and Lincoln beside me, but I simply couldn't visualize us with a child.

During the days and nights that followed, I was restless and anxious about Lincoln's response. Ethel Waters's "Am I Blue?" hummed inside me.

In the company of Ibrahim, I was uncomfortable and occasionally clumsy. Although I did not speak to him of being pregnant, I knew that Mariama must have told him. He knew that I was distracted; he seemed aware of my fatigue. Instead of continuing our work after lunch, Ibrahim sometimes said that he wanted to work alone and suggested that I relax, perhaps take a nap. He was gentler and more considerate than usual.

During my late-afternoon walks with Mariama on the bluff above the bay, our conversations reached into the far corners of domestic life. We explored the territory of family life in our respective cultures: wedding customs, children, in-laws, mistresses, co-wives, and divorce.

"Have you written to your mother or called her to tell her that you are pregnant?"

"To my mother? No—not yet." After a long silence, I told Mariama that, given the circumstances, I would prefer not to inform my parents until I had heard from Lincoln.

"Won't your mother be happy to know that you are expecting a baby?"

"Of course, it would make her very happy. But my father would understand my conflict, my ambivalence. He'd probably reassure me, suggest that I not worry about the outcome, insist that I write the dissertation, and get on with my life." He had always appealed to my own best judgment and my self-confidence.

Mariama, unable to imagine an exchange between father and daughter on the subject of pregnancy, frowned and shook her head. Perplexed, she did not pursue the subject. She did pursue, however, her worries about her own childless marriage.

"A marriage without a child is like a banana tree without bananas. Could you recognize a banana tree without bananas?" Then, in a more serious tone, she confided, "I worry that if I don't have a baby soon, Ibrahim will take a second wife. In our tradition, it is not uncommon for a man to find another wife if the first one is sterile."

"I don't think I could share a man—a husband. It isn't part of our tradition."

"Not part of your tradition, your fine American tradition?" Mariama, I realized, was capable of sarcasm. "In Africa, we share husbands and households with the support of custom and an understanding community. They say that in America, women share their husbands without knowing it, in secrecy, shame. And then they get a divorce. The man does the same thing with the next wife and the next one. The wives are left with the children and no husband at all. I have read about your marriages. American customs are confusing to me!"

Mariama had a hoard of old wives' tales about pregnancy and a collection of amulets to protect women during "that special time." I selected one and wore it so as not to offend her.

"How are infants given names in America?" she asked. What to name the baby became her preoccupation. She suggested Senegalese names. "Pathé, Yoro, Batele, or Massamba for a boy. If it is a girl, but I'm sure it won't be a girl, call her Anta or Fama." I could not yet give a name to the notion that something—someone—was growing in me. These naming conversations were numbing, and I found Mariama's enthusiasm about my pregnancy depressing. Her righteous remarks and relentless good cheer had the opposite of her intended effect; they left me very, very tired.

# 14

MY TWENTY-FIFTH BIRTHDAY WOULD have passed unnoticed, had it not been for Bill Nelson. A week in advance he telephoned to invite me to lunch.

"Sarah, I understand your birthday is on July eighteenth, and I'd like to take you to lunch to celebrate. How's one o'clock?"

"How on earth do you know my birthday?"

"Access to official documents, you know. Well, how about celebrating with a birthday lunch?"

"I'm not in the mood for a celebration." I thought of other birthdays, happier occasions. My twelfth birthday at summer camp in Vermont with cake and marshmallows around a camp fire. Sixteen was an occasion for a birthday party at Highland Beach. I remembered wearing a rose two-piece bathing suit. We'd played volleyball and gone swimming. They were innocent, carefree birthdays.

"Mariama told me you've been under the weather. All the more reason to come into Dakar for a festive lunch. She and Ibrahim would come along, too. There's a superb new restaurant near the Sandaga Market and—"

"All right. If Ibrahim and Mariama will join us, I'll come. It's very kind of you, very thoughtful."

"Terrific! I look forward to seeing you."

Our arrival caused a stir in the restaurant. Conversations were suspended while we were being seated. Three Senegalese men, two in Western suits and the other in a caftan, stood and bowed to Ibrahim. The man in the caftan embraced Ibrahim and introduced him to the others. They detained him in an animated discussion. Bill, at a round table set for a party of four, immediately was on his feet, greeting Mariama and me with kisses on both cheeks.

"The public man is not permitted a private moment in a public place," Nelson murmured in his impeccable French.

"Ah, how very true," sighed a resigned Mariama.

Bill wished me "happy birthday" in English, French, Wolof, and Arabic—"The languages appropriate for this locale," he remarked. I blushed when he presented me with a dozen birds of paradise, a bouquet of bright apricot and violet plumage of petals on their long stalks.

"Beautiful against your emerald boubou!" exclaimed Mariama. As I thanked him in English, French, and Wolof, Bill placed before me two small boxes wrapped in silver paper and tied with blue ribbon and a stack of U.S. newspapers and magazines.

"Please, go ahead and open them," he urged.

The gifts—a silver bracelet and three white handkerchiefs with the monogram "SST" embroidered in ivory silk thread—were extraordinarily tasteful. I was effervescent with delight. When Ibrahim joined us, Mariama presented their gift, a leather-bound edition of Ibrahim's first novel with this inscription:

*To Sarah—*
*Our sister and our friend for life.*

*Affectionately,*
*Ibrahim and Mariama*
*Dakar 18.7.63*

Lunch, interrupted from time to time by Ibrahim's admirers, began with a platter of pink prawns, followed by a delicious grilled blue marlin and rice. While Ibrahim spoke with visitors, Bill told Mariama and me about news reports on a meeting of civil rights leaders at the White House and the mobilization for a march on Washington.

"I wish I could be in Washington for that march," said Bill. "Wouldn't you like to be there?" he asked me.

"Only if I could be here, too—doing my own work. At the march I'd be only one individual in a throng of thousands. What I'm doing here is work that only I can do. Right now, this is where I should be."

"But don't you want to be a part of an event that might change your country?" Mariama asked.

"Countless people will participate and many reports of the march will be written." Lincoln will be there, I thought. I could have mentioned Lincoln's involvement in the movement and perhaps changed Mariama's opinion of him. Instead, I said, "My friends who participate in the march will tell me all about it."

Bill signaled the maître d'hôtel, who had a waiter bring a pink frosted cake with lighted candles. In their accented English, everyone joined him in singing "Happy Birthday." I was elated.

"Close your eyes, make a wish, and blow out the candles," Bill instructed. With one long breath, I blew out all twenty-six candles, the extra one for good luck.

My high spirits were extinguished with the flames. Nelson asked, "What's changed your mood? We can't have a sad-eyed birthday girl. Waiter! Champagne, please." His directness was disarming. He had made me smile again.

"Thank you for a wonderful birthday. You've made today very special."

"It's Nelson you have to thank for this party," said Mariama. "We would not have known about your birthday if he hadn't told us."

"It's important to observe birthdays. Each birthday is like a border crossing. You step into new territory each year," sighed Ibrahim ruefully.

"You didn't mark you last birthday," chided Mariama.

"No, I am not eager to cross the borders of the late forties, to approach fifty, and the rocky terrain that lies ahead. One begins to wonder how many or how few borders are beyond, how much or how little territory remains," said Ibrahim pensively. I sensed that he would have gone on brooding, but Bill wouldn't allow it.

"To many birthdays and border crossings for all of us,"

toasted Bill. We raised our glasses, and Ibrahim, Bill, and I sipped the fruity champagne. Mariama lifted her glass, but she did not drink.

"To Bill Nelson," I proposed, "who has lifted my spirits."

Afterward in the elongated shadows cast by late afternoon's sun, we parted. Bill returned to the Embassy. I reclined on the backseat of the Ibrahim's ample Peugeot, the birds of paradise across my lap. I felt queasy and slightly intoxicated.

As I dozed off, I overheard Mariama say, "Nelson would make a fine husband for Sarah. She needs a husband like him, a man who appreciates her beauty, her intelligence, her graceful manner. She seems very unhappy about returning to her husband. A child coming and their marriage is unraveling."

"The birth of a child sometimes changes the nature of a marriage," said Ibrahim.

"I wish it were possible for her to remain here until the baby is born."

"So you could vicariously have a baby?" he asked archly. Ibrahim's tone made me wonder about the tension being childless had created in their marriage. "No, she needs to go home. She has unfinished business with her husband and her dissertation. Then the book—I want her to write that book. It would be good for her future and mine. She's a solid researcher, she writes very well, she's ambitious—"

"And beautiful, elegant, chic—you certainly have noticed," Mariama said begrudgingly.

"Who could not notice."

My heart quickened and then moments later I was asleep.

I awoke when the car stopped outside the compound. Mamadou was at the gate to receive us. "Madame Sarah, you had a telephone call from Amer-ree-kha—all the way from Amer-ree-kha! Mr. Lincoln has called you! He will call you again this evening."

I tried to return his call, but the connection crackled and broke down in the relay from operator to operator, from Dakar to Rome to Cambridge. I sat at my writing table where I wrote in my journal.

*July 18, 1963*
  *As Ibrahim suggested, I have crossed a border into new*
*"territory" where I must cope with a dissertation, a baby,*
*and Lincoln. This year will be critical. Typewriter at one*
*hand, a baby in the other—and Lincoln—at just the*
*moment when I was beginning to feel I could direct the*
*course of my life.*
  *Ibrahim has noticed my looks! Or did I dream that?*
*Does he sense my attraction to him?*


The telephone rang. Mamadou padded to my room. With a
vigorous rap on the door, he called, "Telephone call for you,
Madame Sarah. Overseas call from Amer-ree-kha."

At the phone, I heard a series of operators' voices over the
wires, and then Lincoln.

"Hello? Hello, Sarah. Sarah?"

"Hello."

"Happy birthday." Static on the line distorted his voice.

"Did you receive my cable?"

"Yes. How are you?"

"I've been tired, very tired, and I've had morning sickness
from time to time. Normal symptoms at this stage, the doctor
told me."

"I've been worried about you. Do you have a good doctor?
A doctor you trust?"

"Yes, Dr. Diouf who is a friend of the Manganes. He seems
very thorough, capable. I trust him."

"Do you think you can talk with him about the pregnancy?"

"What's there to talk about?"

He spoke slowly, his every word carefully weighed and measured. "I wonder if you could ask him if abortions are legal
there?"

I was silent—stung by his question. I hadn't considered abortion. Adoption had crossed my mind; but not abortion. Abortion was difficult to arrange, dangerous, illegal, taboo.

Firmly I said, "No, Lincoln, I can't ask him that."

"Attitudes about abortion are changing. An American

woman had a legal abortion in Sweden recently, the Fishbein case. Lots of doctors overseas do them. It's a relatively simple procedure, I understand. It might be better if—"

"I don't want to have an abortion," I said, realizing that despite all of my ambivalence about my pregnancy I wanted the baby.

"You know as well as I do that we're not ready to have a child."

I swallowed hard and took a deep breath to contain the nausea and tears that were mounting.

"I know it's difficult to make a decision about this over the phone, Sarah. Think about it for a few days, then we'll talk again. And I need to think more, too. Then we'll decide what to do. I know it must be hard all alone there, so take care of yourself. And try to be of good cheer. Good-bye." With a click, Lincoln was gone.

"Lincoln! Hello?" I stood there weeping into a dead phone.

I hung up and returned to my room where I fell on my bed, and wept for a long time. And I chanted. "*My help cometh from Senegal . . .*" A child, an incomplete degree, and very little money. I wept. Weeping finally gave way to dreaming.

*I dreamed that I had given birth to a son. At the christening, I was dressed in Madonna blue and white with the baby in my arms. Ibrahim, Mariama, and Bill Nelson were there. Bill was the baby's godfather. We named him Ibrahim Lincoln Stewart.*

# 15

AT DAWN THE NEXT MORNING, I PUT ON white slacks, and a tent-shaped turquoise T-shirt, gathered the newspapers and magazines that Bill had given me, and went out to the veranda. As I settled into the wicker chaise longue, Mamadou arrived with a shawl and a glass of tea.

"Good day, Madame. The morning air is cool. You may need this wrap." He did not appear surprised by my early rising. "Too bad you slept through dinner last night. You missed the best fish of the season." Preoccupied with my personal concerns, I didn't bother to respond.

I was imagining a darkened room with a soiled bed, and the muffled voice of a stranger penetrating my cervix with a long, blunt needle. How dare Lincoln suggest an abortion, an assault on my body, on my mind, on my soul? If he loved me, would he have mentioned abortion?

I felt neither loved by Lincoln nor loving toward him. I realized I hadn't missed him. I wondered whether we ever had known the meaning of marital love. The translation of the babble of courtship into the syntax of marriage required an emotional transition we hadn't accomplished. We had been primed for courtship, but we hadn't been prepared for the conflicts that our marriage revealed, or the mutual compassion and compromise that it demanded. I agreed that we weren't ready to have a child. Still, I was expecting.

The chance to observe marriages other than our parents' might have made a difference. Their failure to deal openly and candidly with conflicts perhaps made it more difficult for us to be honest with one another. We only saw the exterior of the bureau drawers of marriage. In our presence, they didn't open the drawers and reveal the disorder of rumpled aspirations, tangled secrets, and the box of lies hidden in the back of the bottom drawer.

Engrossed in such ruminations, I was startled by Ibrahim's throaty, "Good morning, Sarah." I came to know it as his early-morning voice, the congested voice of a pipe smoker before his morning cough. He commented softly, "You're up before the sun," and then came the round of coughing that made his bony chest chatter. He spat in the gravel and cleared his throat. "Come," he said, "I'm going down to the boulders."

Without a word, I was on my feet following his billowing beige caftan. He opened the gate and strode along the path to the giant boulders that protected the bluff against high tides. The air was fresh and warm. Except for our footsteps, the flutter and cries of gulls overhead and the gentle splash of waves against the boulders were the only sounds. I walked behind him, my sandals flapping with each step. Within minutes, I felt lighthearted and younger—perhaps fifteen.

He stood astride two flat boulders, rocks with contours he clearly knew well. I scanned the massive rocks for a secure place to squat, and observe Ibrahim who, with his arms folded, was utterly still as he watched the early morning light change the hue of the rippling water. Then he broke the silence with poetry:

> *Have you already seen the dawn*
> *poaching in night's orchard?*
> *Here she comes homeward from the East*
> *on pathways overgrown with iris.*

"I suppose there were 'pathways overgrown with iris' in Rabéarivelo's Madagascar."

"I don't know those lines, the works of—"

"Jean-Joseph Rabéarivelo, a gifted poet who died tragically in poverty—suicide—poisoned himself." And then Ibrahim recited:

*He who binds to himself a joy*
*Does the winged life destroy;*
*But he who kisses the joy as it flies*
*Lives in eternity's sunrise.*

"You probably know those lines. I'm sure they teach Blake at Har-vahrd."

He leaned over me and pressed his moist lips gently on my forehead. I lifted my chin, inviting his kiss. His lips visited mine with fervor. Afterward, his tobacco-sweet breath whispered, " 'He who kisses the joy as it flies/Lives in eternity's sunrise.' Kissing you is kissing joy and I hope kisses will make you more joyful. You looked very sad up there on the veranda, deep in meditation." Squatting before me, knee to knee, Ibrahim coaxed, "Tell me about your morning meditation."

"I was thinking about love—and life—and marriage."

"What were you thinking?"

"My—our marriage is a loveless marriage. In my last weeks at home with Lincoln, I didn't feel loved or loving. Since I've been here, I've not had a loving thought about him. I really haven't missed him or had the urge to be with him."

"And that troubles you?"

"Yes, because I'm—I'm pregnant and—" I was trembling.

"I know you are pregnant. Mariama told me—and your lovely, drowsy eyes told me."

"When I spoke with Lincoln yesterday, he said that he wants me to—well, Lincoln doesn't want to have a baby."

"Most men do not want the first baby until it comes. When it is born, we are charmed by the resemblance—real or imagined. We feel our mortality has been extended. And then we cannot wait to make the next one, and the next one." His hands were resting on my thighs.

"But he really doesn't want a child."

"Lincoln and I should trade places. It seems that Mariama cannot conceive. The hungry man has an empty calabash, the sated man a full one." Ibrahim rose and lifted me to my feet. "You have grown sad again. Kiss joy as it flies. Choose what will make you happy—even if it is only momentary." And again he kissed my lips. His mouth opened and he kissed me hungrily. I nearly lost my footing. He held me close and steadied me.

Breathlessly I said, "Being here has made me happy—being with you—and Mariama."

"Your being here has made me more than happy. You have been a revitalizing force—your fresh view of things, your energy, ambition, youth. You yourself generate happiness and certainly you deserve happiness. One can have intelligence, beauty, and happiness, too. The mere sight of you excites me, makes me happy. But before I say more than I should," he said taking my hand, "let's go back and plan the day's work."

I wanted him to continue. His expression of what my presence meant to him was the confirmation of his affection I'd yearned for—but I wanted an unmistakable confession of love, as well as a chance to speak of what I felt for him. I knew it was more than a crush. It was love. And although I was unsure whether I loved or had ever loved Lincoln, I had no doubts about my loving Ibrahim with a quiet, humid, interior, secret love.

Without prearrangements, each morning thereafter, Ibrahim and I met at dawn on the boulders. I awoke very early and went out, so that I could be there when he appeared. Awaiting his arrival, I speculated about what he would wear, what verses the morning air would evoke. He came reaching out to me, steadying my foothold on the boulders. We whispered greetings. With each word, each touch, my gaze met his. Our eyes said everything that we could not say to each other.

Creatures of the early morning witnessed our unspoken declarations of love. Mamadou witnessed it, too. From his patch of sacred ground where he lay down his prayer rug outside the compound, Mamadou turned toward Mecca and prostrated himself at sunrise. As he arose from his prayers, he scanned the skyline and occasionally nodded in our direction. Our morning ritual seemed to have his blessings.

An hour or more later Mariama was up and about the house. I assumed that she knew that Ibrahim and I were together at dawn on the wave-splashed boulders beyond the wall. She may have anticipated a flirtation or an episode of indiscretion. She had mentioned that Ibrahim was not immune to affairs. He had had liaisons with a Senegalese starlet and a Lebanese opera singer; and he still received letters from his Parisian companion, the French actress. Mariama said that she had "discouraged the affairs" because she did not "respect those women or deem them suitable for the place of second wife." More than once, she said that Ibrahim needed an intellectual wife, one who could help bring him greater recognition and glory. The fascinating idea of a ménage à trois was material for my fantasies.

If Mariama was jealous, if she questioned Ibrahim's fidelity or, for that matter, mine, she did not make an issue of it. Besides, I wasn't a threat. My sojourn in Senegal would be brief; I had a visa for three months only. And, I was married and pregnant.

I struggled, however, with pangs of guilt. Mariama had offered me hospitality and friendship, had made a place for me in her home. She was aware of Ibrahim's susceptibility to the appeal of other women. And she must have known that a woman attracted to his work would also be attracted to him. The evolution of an affectionate relationship was inevitable, but still I walked in guilt.

Mariama never hinted that she knew Ibrahim and I had begun the day with a celebration of our mutual affection. She must have known, but she was far too intelligent and considerate to suggest that our early-morning meetings were improper. I assumed she regarded the rendezvous as an extension of our work. When I asked Ibrahim if Mariama knew we met on the boulders, he said, "Of course, she knows. If you are asking if it troubles her, I would not know. Mariama keeps her own counsel."

During an evening walk with Mariama I suddenly asked, "What's the policy regarding abortion here?"

"Policy?" She seemed befuddled. "Are you asking if girls have abortions? Or do you mean that you—no, I cannot tell you about abortion. In the market, they sell herbs that bring on abortions. Older women with several children buy them. Sometimes the child is born anyhow, damaged by the herbal potions—born blind, crippled, or deaf and dumb. But why do you ask?"

"I've been wondering about what a woman does when she decides not to have a baby."

"It is not the woman's decision. It is Allah's will." It was evident that I could not talk about it further with Mariama. And if I could not discuss abortion with her, enlisting her help was out of the question. The next day, when I telephoned Dr. Diouf, I lost my nerve, could not broach the subject. Instead, I reported that the nausea had stopped and I felt nearly normal.

A few days later, I announced to Mariama, "My body chemistry, my values, and your advice have helped me with my decision—I'm going through with it."

"What does that mean—'going through with it'?" she asked.

I remembered hearing the phrase used in reference to a high school classmate's unwanted pregnancy. "Is she going through with it?" one girl asked another. I knew that meant carrying to birth, having the child. I explained, "I'll have the baby, with or without further assistance from Lincoln, and I'll make the best of it. I may even find some pleasure in it. Now that the morning sickness has passed, I feel fine—healthy."

"Ah, praise be to Allah. You and your baby will be blessed. You will be guided rightly."

"I suppose I should tell Lincoln that I'm going to have the baby. I'll cable him tomorrow."

The message to Lincoln simply said:

GOING TO HAVE BABY.
RETURNING SEPT. 16

Relieved by my decision, I began to feel clearheaded and calm, with abundant energy for my work. It was a highly productive period. I formulated a topic for the dissertation, *The Genesis of Ibrahim Mangane's Radical Imagination: Politics of Colonialism in the Early Novels*, prepared an outline, and began writing. With a chapter on each of the six early novels, I examined his themes in the context of political and social events. In our discussions, I tried to elicit from him recollections of the incidents that had shaped the works. I began to concentrate on my own work, and on what I needed to extract from Ibrahim and his library before leaving.

From time to time, my concentration was interrupted. I was distracted by Ibrahim's presence. To refocus my attention, I'd ask a question which elicited a mini lecture. I tried to memorize his phrases and cadences. Occasionally he allowed me to tape the sessions. Knowing that I could carry his voice, at least, away with me was a source of solace.

One afternoon, refreshed by a shower, I returned to his study where I found him waiting in his swivel chair. I had put on a new lavender boubou with nothing under it. He reached for my hand, and in slow motion drew me toward him, onto his lap. My arms encircled his shoulders and sweetly I kissed him. His hands glided from my waist to my hips and under the boubou. I felt his feverish tongue around mine. And onto the couch where I slid my hands under his shirt, untied the drawstring of his pants and pushed them from his lean legs, I reclined and opened myself to him, admiring his splendid erection. Then ever so smoothly and tenderly he entered me. With the ebb and flow of small waves at low tide, we made love until I came and he came. And then he kissed me. It was the kiss of life.

# 16

AFTERWARD, IN A HAZE OF GUILT AND PAS-
sion, Ibrahim and I passed each other in the course of doing
customary tasks as if nothing had happened. Except for our
morning salutation on the boulders, I avoided being alone with
him. Instead, I sought out Mariama and spent more time with
her. In her company, I tried to atone for my breach of trust.
With genuine interest, I listened to her anecdotes; and I accompanied her more frequently on outings, which gladdened her.
We attended fashion shows where emaciated models strutted in
dazzling haute couture–styled Senegalese cloth. We were the
guests of honor for tea at the home of one of Mariama's students. At a fashionable boutique, I bought her a silk scarf. She
took me to her hairdresser, who braided my hair in dozens of
dangling and arched braids. This was years before braided hair-
styles became fashionable in the States. Ibrahim admired the
braids and said they enhanced my "Negritude," so I decided to
keep them. Ibrahim, Mariama, and I were invited to preview a
documentary film. In the darkened screening room, he and I
exchanged glances of mutual understanding, as he told Mariama
to sit between us.

From time to time, there were guests at the house, visitors
from the Ivory Coast, Mali, Haiti, and France—scholars, journalists, and politicians who came for lunch or dinner. They
expanded the conversation and relieved the tension that I felt at
the table with only Ibrahim and Mariama. Bill Nelson, a frequent visitor, brought the gossip of the diplomatic circle.
Mariama, eager to escalate my relationship with Bill, encour-

aged his visits. His attention to me amused her. He brought me gifts—U.S. newspapers and magazines, California wines, Vermont maple syrup, and peanut butter. He also arranged a few excursions—a tour of the university, a trip to Rufisque, and a day on Gorée.

Even before my visit, I was intrigued by Ibrahim's film and what I had read about Gorée. Once there, I was captivated by the island's abominable past and the dilapidated grandeur of its architectural treasures. Absorbed in his account of Gorée's history, I walked along with Bill, who knew every cranny of the island, having made fifty or more trips there. We visited the Maritime Museum, and stopped to gaze at an abandoned villa said to be haunted by Mama Couba, the island's guardian spirit. At one of the windows of the villa, I saw a woman, the mirror image of myself, smiling down on us.

"Who is that woman?" I asked Bill.

"Where?"

"At the window above the entrance."

"I don't see anyone. You've been spooked by all the stories about this place."

I knew I hadn't imagined her.

From there we went to the infamous Maison des Esclaves, or "Slave House," where the resident guide described the suffering of the men, women, and children who had been herded into the holding pen, and then chained (at this point, Bill rattled the chains) if they tried to escape. The guide told us that rather than boarding the slave ships, some had climbed the stairs and thrown themselves to certain death in the shark-infested waters.

Ibrahim was enraged when he learned that I had visited Gorée with Bill. Ibrahim exclaimed, "It is scandalous—Nelson's taking you there. Didn't you understand the message of *Chains of Gorée?* Gorée is the Auschwitz of black Americans."

"Gorée is an important point of departure in our history," I countered. "African Americans need to see the Slave House. I now know that our ancestors who endured the crossing on slave ships were heroic. Bill understands Gorée's monumental significance, even if you do not." It was the first time that I had con-

tradicted Ibrahim directly. He was visably agitated by my saying that he didn't understand.

Bill had become my authority on many other aspects of
Senegal as well as my primary source of news about events in
the United States. The delays in newscasts and the infrequent
arrival of newspapers and mail made news reports read like history. Furthermore, what news there was from the U.S. struck
me as intrusive. I did not want to be distracted by it or drawn
into it. The weekly "Mom & Dad" letters—written by my
mother, but signed by them both—brought me news of marriages, births, and deaths in their circle of relatives and friends,
notes about Washington's notorious summer weather, and
warnings against the dangers Mom imagined surrounding me:
"Please don't drink the water; be on guard in the company of
African men; avoid situations and acquaintances that might
expose you to political violence." Cryptic letters and clever
postcards from friends gave me little sense of what was going
on in Cambridge, Boston, New York, Washington, Ann Arbor,
Nashville, Atlanta, Madison, or Berkeley—my academic and
social outposts.

There were also letters from Lincoln, four in all, but only one
that I kept as documentation of his state of mind.

*Cambridge, Massachusetts*
*July 28, 1963*

*Dear Sarah,*

*Belated birthday wishes. Busy here trying to follow the
maneuvers of the various civil rights groups that are mobi-
lizing for a march on Washington next month. I'm a
coordinator for the Boston area. Lots of meetings—
training sessions, strategy planning, writing copy for
leaflets, etc. Meeting wonderful people—genuine grass-
roots people who understand the politics of the movement
much better than the "great minds" in Cambridge. I
spend a lot of time in Roxbury where I ought to be living.
Interesting political possibilities there.*

*It is brave of you to be in Africa now. Everyone asks*

*about you and hopes you are safe. Incidentally, I'm glad*
*that you found the writer you were looking for. I hope*
*that you can get the material you need. Finishing my lab*
*work as soon as possible. MIT is getting me down. It's*
*apolitical, detached, and amoral—except at the top. The*
*president, provost, and some faculty sign statements in*
*support of the movement, but their influence has not*
*touched the students. It's hard to get them interested in*
*civil rights.*

*I hope you will take care of yourself. Try to get good*
*medical help. Be of good cheer.*

*Best wishes always,*
*Link*

That letter evoked a certain sadness about our situation, a
couple lost in the woods of marriage, now taking different paths
to uncertain destinations. At that moment, the problems of our
marriage seemed as distant as Lincoln himself.

A few weeks later, however, as I prepared to leave Senegal,
the reality of life with Lincoln confronted me. Slowly, I assembled books and papers, and carefully packaged the cloth,
bracelets, beads, seashells, pebbles, and other mementos I had
acquired. In my journal, I added details, packing it with memories. With an auditor's inventory of every shelf, every corner of
Ibrahim's study, I took photographs of his books and papers,
the couch, the entire setting.

It was mid-September, the beginning of the rainy season, and
on the day of my departure, rain drenched Dakar. Ibrahim,
Mariama, and Bill Nelson accompanied me to the airport. After
his official send-off remarks, Bill said wistfully, "I'll miss you. I
hope our paths will cross again." Checking the affection in his
voice, he dispatched porters with my baggage and said that he
would wait in the car for Ibrahim and Mariama, who escorted
me into the terminal.

"The heavens are weeping because you are leaving," said
Ibrahim. His sad eyes brought tears to mine. Mariama embraced
me and offered her handkerchief. She wept, too, as she kissed me

several times on both cheeks. Ibrahim kissed one cheek, and his lips intentionally brushed mine as I turned the other. Mariama whispered, "Bring your baby to visit us. He will be a nephew to me."

Smiling through my tears, I boarded the flight to New York feeling like Cinderella at midnight leaving the royal ball and thinking: *"I will cast mine eyes upon the ocean from whence cometh my help. My help cometh from Senegal. . . . Bring me back to Dakar."* As the plane took off, I gazed at the privileged and precious world of Ibrahim Mangane, and realized that I might never return to see again his elegant haven on the bluff, the sturdy boulders and azure waters rippling in the bay. I might never again see him.

# 17

THE PLANE LANDED AT IDLEWILD WHERE I cleared customs and confirmed my reservation on a flight to Boston. Then I telephoned Lincoln. The early-morning call awoke him.

"I'm glad you're back." His sleepy voice touched me in a place that warmed me. I told him that I would arrive in Boston at ten-fifteen on a Pan Am flight.

"I'll be there," he said.

I telephoned my parents. Mom sounded relieved. "Thank the Lord, you're safely back," she sighed. "We've certainly missed you. How's your health?"

"Just fine," I said. I had not told them that I was pregnant; and I assumed that Lincoln hadn't told his parents either. "I feel fine," I repeated, as much to reassure myself as her.

"Your Dad's up and out already. It's Saturday morning, you know. He's doing the marketing. He'll be thrilled to know you're safely home. Lincoln's folks have been asking about you. I'll call and let them know you're back. Call later when you get to Cambridge. You must be eager to see Lincoln. I'll bet you missed each other a lot."

Eager? More apprehensive than eager about a reunion with Lincoln, I didn't want to think about the days ahead. Instead, I summoned images of Ibrahim, his lips brushing mine, his sonorous voice, his touch. In a cloud of memories, I floated through the metallic corridors of the airport toward the Pan Am terminal, my blue batiked boubou undulating, a dozen braids on each shoulder. I was scarcely aware of the stares of early-morning passersby, unaccustomed to the sweep of a gown and a plaited coiffure.

It was nearly ten-thirty when the flight arrived at Logan Airport. Passengers trickled out of the plane, descended the mobile stairs, and walked briskly to the gate. I hesitated for a moment to lift my boubou above my ankles before coming down the steps. Beyond the cluster of faces animated with anticipation, Lincoln impassively studied the scene. As I approached, he stiffened like a soldier about to salute, and extended a limp bouquet of blue asters and yellow chrysanthemums. I stretched up on tiptoe and kissed him on each cheek. Flushed with self-consciousness about a public kiss, even a casual one, he placed his hands on my shoulders and moved an arm's length away to inspect me.

"You've become Africanized. Your gown, your hair, those braids—what have you done to your hair?" He glanced at my protruding abdomen. "And still pregnant," he muttered. Together we collected the baggage and walked to the parking lot. Occasionally I dropped behind to look at Lincoln, to recall what I once had felt, what his brawny body, his proud gait had once stirred in me. Nothing in me quivered now. He might have been a stranger carrying my bags.

In the car on our way toward the tunnel to Boston, Lincoln said, "Tell me about Senegal."

I told him I'd fallen in love with Senegal. He responded sarcastically, "Who's the Senegalese you've fallen for? That writer?" I said dreamily that I'd fallen in love with the people of Senegal. He looked at me with skepticism and asked, "And did they fall for you?" Evading his question, I asked what he'd been doing.

"I suppose you could say that I've fallen in love with life," he solemnly replied. Suggesting abortion, yet falling in love with life! I censored a contemptuous impulse, and instead asked, "Whose life?"

His long sidelong glance let me know that I was close to the center of the target. Something or someone had found the way to his elusive heart. He began to trace the route with a discourse on his civil rights activities.

"It was the call for a March on Washington. I began attending organizers' meetings in Roxbury. They'd have speakers from the Southern Christian Leadership Conference, CORE, SNNC. Some Freedom Riders came and spoke—white guys who had put their lives on the line for us.

"Well, I couldn't see them doing more than I was. So I volunteered—became an organizer, made speeches. On the road a lot, I spoke in Worcester, Springfield, Greenfield, Amherst, Great Barrington—in churches, schools, and community centers. When the time came to sign up groups that were going to the March, I coordinated the transportation for all of Massachusetts.

"I organized busloads of folks, young and old, black and white from all across the state. We rolled into Washington on that 'great gettin' up mornin'.' You should've been here. You have no idea what you missed. You've missed the most important event in this country since the Civil War."

"I saw a television program on the March and I read King's speech. It must have been—"

"TV can't begin to convey the spirit of the March. You had to be there, see the faces, feel the fellowship, the moods that swept through that crowd. And to listen to A. Philip Randolph, Bayard Rustin and John Lewis, to hear Mahalia Jackson sing and Martin Luther King proclaim, 'I have a dream,' . . . well, even men in the crowd were wiping their eyes. I nearly cried myself."

"Yes, I suppose I should have been there," I said with a hint of regret.

Lincoln, imitating King's voice, intoned, " 'I have a dream that one day this nation will rise up and live out the true meaning of its creed.' He was magnificent!"

"And do *you* have a dream?" I asked, puncturing his balloon of celebration.

Defensively, he said, "I've always had dreams, plans. But now I've got some new ones."

I didn't want to hear about his dreams at that moment. Engrossed in my own dreams and perturbed by our circumstances, I looked out at the sailboats on the river and the red brick houses of Boston's Back Bay and MIT's granite campus. In the heavy commercial traffic of late morning, we crossed the Charles River over the Longfellow Bridge and into Cambridge, which appeared, to eyes that had seen Dakar, overbuilt, too dense, and congested. Cars and trucks moved much too fast through Kendall Square and along Broadway. I felt like a foreigner viewing a once-familiar city through alien eyes. At our apartment building on Trowbridge Street, we climbed the stairs to the second floor, where Lincoln unlocked the door.

Welcome to dust and disorder. Beer cans lined the window sills, ash trays were overflowing, leaflets were stacked in a corner, cartons of books and records were near the door. My heart spiraled downward. Cinderella, home from the ball, sank into the mud-brown chair.

"I'm sorry about the appearance of the place. I overslept—didn't have time to clean up. I've had some meetings here—strategy meetings," Lincoln said. Wastebasket in hand, he hurriedly emptied ashtrays and removed the cans. His activity and the dust he stirred up were more unsettling than the disorder.

"Sit down and let's talk. We can clean up this mess later. Tell me about your new interests." He put down the wastebasket and sat cross-legged on the floor facing me. I felt calm and, for the first time, I felt considerably more mature than Lincoln. Despite the pregnancy—or perhaps because of it—I felt I had a certain advantage.

"I think we ought to consider moving to Roxbury. We need to live among our people—not here. We're not needed here. I need to live in a black community, see black faces every day, talk black talk. I've found a place on Walnut Avenue—nice apartment, five rooms for half the rent we're paying. And I've started working for some black political candidates in Roxbury."

"You don't have to *live* in Roxbury to work for candidates there."

"I know. But it does give you credibility, connections, and a better understanding of what the issues really are. It's not just for the campaigns. That's where we—or at least I—should be living."

He stood up and walked toward the bay window that overlooked the street. Looking out, his back to the room, he said, "I'm thinking of quitting MIT. I want to build a political base, run for a seat on the Boston school committee, then run for the city council, and then—well, who knows." He turned away from the window and faced me. "Anyway, I've got some plans. You might say I'm the one who's possessed now."

Crooked smile, eyes twinkling, eyebrows raised, and arms folded, he was prepared for a rebuttal. His plan, however, struck me as rational. His vision of himself in political life seemed valid. I could see the adolescent Lincoln as an ambitious politician, doffing his cap and shaking hands with strangers as he campaigned. I could see the proud expressions of his parents and mine at his swearing-in ceremony. But I couldn't imagine myself in those scenes.

"You'd make an excellent politician. It would be great for you, but what about us?"

His mustache turned down around the corners of his mouth and his brow wrinkled.

"Getting elected to the school committee will take time. I'll have to become acquainted with teachers, union organizers, church people—you'd be bored by their talk. You'd rather talk about—"

"Lincoln, there are a few details we should discuss before you launch your campaign. Remember, we're expecting a baby." At that moment, I began to have sharp pains that felt like menstrual cramps.

"I intend to do my part. I've inquired about medical insurance and your using the MIT Medical Service. I've been thinking about what we ought to do—depending on what's ahead for us." Fumbling for words, he came over, sat beside me on the arm of the chair, and placed his hand on my shoulder.

"I've really felt shitty about the abortion idea. You didn't tell your parents, did you?"

"No, I haven't told them anything. It seemed too uncertain to—"

"Whew! I knew I would've heard from them or from my folks if they knew."

"Having the baby is what I have to do now," I said echoing Mariama. At that moment, I was resolute and clear about my intentions. And I was very uncomfortable. The cramps were persisting.

"Okay, okay. Have the baby. Then we'll see—"

"I don't want you around merely out of a sense of duty and guilt. A fatherless child is better off than one with a reluctant father. I'm very tired, too tired to talk about it now. I'm going to take a nap."

Lifting myself from the chair, burdened more by marriage than impending motherhood, I unfolded the unmade sofa bed. Too tired to undress, I covered myself with the sheet. Wondering who else had slept between those musty sheets while I was away, I fell asleep.

My own shrieking awoke me. I felt a sharp pain pierce my pelvis, the pain of an acute cramp. A warm watery stream trickled out between my thighs. My hips were soaking in a pool of my own fluids. I sprang up. Lincoln was asleep in the chair. I dashed to the bathroom. Just as I sat down, fluid with a form gushed out of my vagina and splashed in the toilet bowl.

"Lincoln! Help me!" Screaming, I slipped off the toilet, knelt, head bent over the toilet bowl, and stared at the sight of the translucent form and bloody membranous sac floating in the toilet. I reached in, my hands in the chilling water, grasping at the slippery fetus. Quivering and moaning, I looked up and saw Lincoln standing over me.

"What is it? Flush it down," he murmured. He leaned over me and clutched my shoulders. "It's dead. Flush it."

"No-o-o," I wailed. "It's my baby, my baby. Get a jar, a pitcher, a pail. I want to save it." Lincoln left the bathroom and returned quickly with a bowl. I scooped the embryo out of the water and watched it slowly slide from my fingers into the bowl. It felt like a giant jellyfish in the warm waters of Chesapeake Bay beaches. I thought of Mom and Dad and summers at the beach. The sting of the jellyfish on my thighs had sent me running to them for help. This time I felt the sting in my head and my heart. I sat on the cold tile floor cradling the bowl in my arms, moaning and rocking back and forth. While I rocked and moaned and prayed to be in Senegal, Lincoln telephoned Cambridge City Hospital.

"I'm taking you to the hospital. You did the right thing—collecting the fetus. They said we should bring it. They want to examine it." He handed me a towel. "Dry yourself. I'll carry it." He reached for the bowl. I hugged it close.

"Is it alive? Did they say they can make it live?" I asked in delirium.

Lincoln got me to my feet and ushered me through the early evening twilight to the car. He seemed composed. My crying eyes stretched wide, I clutched the bowl. In the car, I began to chant: "*My help cometh from Senegal—heaven and earth.*"

"You're still possessed," he said.

Abruptly I fell silent, thinking that it was passion not possession. And I slumped in the seat.

Sometime later, in a cold white-tiled hospital room on a hard, narrow table surrounded by masked white people, I heard a man's voice announce the clinical details, in the staccato of boredom with routine procedures: "Incompetent cervix. Normal fetus, female, one pound, three ounces, dead."

The next morning, alone in a room in the maternity wing, I awoke to the pain of loss and a flowery fragrance—claret roses on the stand to my left and blood red carnations on the right. I felt an inner emptiness. My pelvic region felt gutted. My skull felt hollow. There were no images, no memories, no traces of dreams. My entire being was a *tabula rasa*.

A hubbub of cheerful voices outside my room celebrated the endurance of the women who had labored and the healthy good looks and hearty lungs of their babies. They were admiring other women's babies. Gradually, I reassembled the memories of the day and night before, remembered the moment when the pulp of my womb slipped from me like the core of a mango and splashed into the water of the toilet bowl. I had lost a part of myself.

I tossed from side to side, turning away from the roses sent by my parents to stare at the carnations from Lincoln, his funereal offering for a dead fetus and a woman whose life with him was ending. Moments later, he pushed open the door and looked at me with the glassy stare of a man just released from prison.

# 18

MEDITATIVE WALKS ALONG THE CHARLES River during September's shimmering afternoons healed the scars of my miscarriage. I strolled down the Cambridge bank, crossed the Weeks Bridge to the other side, then walked along the path parallel to Storrow Drive to the Eliot Bridge, where I crossed into Cambridge. The sweep of rowers in sleek shells on the rippling river was soothing. Walking downriver on the Cambridge side, I passed a playground with clusters of mothers and their toddlers. My heart ached at the sight.

During those days of recovery, Lincoln and I scarcely saw each other. He was preoccupied with shifting the focus of his work. He left notes on the kitchen table: *At a meeting in Boston. Returning late. Want to go to a movie Friday? Beer with Sam at Cronin's—today at 5:30. Come if you can.* By the telephone were messages he had taken: *Your mother called. Will you call her tonight? My mother called—she wants you to call her.*

I returned their calls and listened to their advice about my body and their speculations about another pregnancy. There was an undertone of disappointment. They aspired to grand-motherhood and I had failed them. "You'll keep trying, won't you?" they asked.

"But we weren't trying," I insisted.

They never asked directly about how Lincoln and I were getting along. I wanted to tell them that their Chagallesque image of us was vanishing, and that the news of our separation soon would descend on them.

A month or so after the miscarriage I told Lincoln that I

wanted to try a separation. Living separate lives at the same address was awkward. The physical distance between us, I said, ought to correspond to the psychological distance. He agreed. We knew then that the marriage was really over. The moment of recognition had come in a rational discussion, not in the heat of a quarrel. Had we quarreled, we might have felt that the marriage had mattered. Instead, with a sense of relief, we took the initial steps toward permanently ending the relationship. A few days later, Lincoln moved out of our apartment to Sam Higgins's place, where he stayed for a few weeks, then to a Walnut Avenue address in Roxbury.

We met by appointment and with an agenda for each session: what we would tell our parents, how we would divide our possessions—the VW, hi-fi set, records, TV set; silverware, appliances, linens, and other wedding gifts. At the end of each meeting, we embraced, sometimes kissed, and then pulled away in dismay, rethinking the path to our estrangement. Our parents and friends had made us believe we would live happily ever after. However, as a couple, we were dissolving slowly like lumps of sugar in a cup of tea.

With very little common property, no child to fight over, and independent aspirations, the dissolution was peaceful and unremarkable. I noted, with the satisfaction of one claiming new territory, the gradual disappearance of objects that symbolized Lincoln's presence—his clothes, books, television set, tennis racket, hi-fi set, records, a lamp, and posters.

A Senegalese beach scene replaced his poster with students lounging on a grassy Dartmouth quadrangle. I covered the brown chair with a bright blue and amber striped African fabric. And I bought new sheets and blankets, disposing of our conjugal bedding.

At night, however, when the slightest sound disturbed me, I was keenly aware of Lincoln's absence. In the dark, listening to the slam of a car door, footsteps in the street, the wind against the windowpanes, I fretted about being alone. After several sleepless nights, I had bolts installed on the doors and windows.

Thereafter, I slept peacefully. And I stopped wondering where he was sleeping.

Instead, I longed for Ibrahim. I closed my eyes, inhaled deeply, and memories of the aroma of his pipe and perspiration invaded me. Images of Ibrahim kept me awake and put me to sleep—Ibrahim seated at his desk with me at his side, Ibrahim in a Dakar restaurant seated opposite me, Ibrahim squatting on the boulders on the edge of the bay holding my hand. Fantasies about him aroused insatiable sensual desires. When my yearning for him grew unbearable, I often went to Martha's Vineyard where I paced up and down a beach, windswept and desolate in October—paced and chanted and called, "Ibrahim. *Ibrahim!*"

I established a workday routine. Every morning I was in my Widener Library cubicle by nine o'clock, immersed in the task of interpreting the literary innovations of Ibrahim Mangane. ("Mangane." As I looked at my manuscript, I often thought: "How impersonal a way to refer to him!") Consumed by details about the development of his literary career, I retraced the sequence of his publications. I weighed negative reviews of his works against favorable criticism. I read biographies of other literary figures and examined the indulgences of biographers who had been enchanted by their subjects, and criticized for lacking detachment. I struggled with the ethical and scholarly risks associated with writing about Ibrahim and his works.

When I wasn't preoccupied with my dissertation, I was worried about time. How much time would I need to finish it? As weeks passed, I wondered whether Ibrahim would forget me? How could I ever know what might transpire in his life and work during the time we were apart? How long would it take to find a means of returning to Senegal?

I wrote dozens of letters to Ibrahim, several to Mariama, and a few to them both: letters about my marriage and miscarriage, and progress on the dissertation. To Ibrahim I sent book and film reviews, articles about authors, and a list of important books by women "to fill the gaps in his library." I sent clippings about civil rights news. My first letters about the success of the

March on Washington, the energy and vitality in civil rights organizations, were optimistic, only to be followed by letters of anguish and rage after the bombing of the Sixteenth Street Baptist Church in Birmingham where, on a Sunday morning, four black girls all dressed in white were blown to a hollow in high heaven. Mariama replied in her French schoolgirl script.

*Dear Sarah,*

   *I am sorry that your marriage is ending. You must be very unhappy about it and about the miscarriage. And also about the terrible bombing of the church. I hope your work is a source of satisfaction. As your civil rights song says, you shall overcome.*

   *The weather here is the subject of every conversation. The dry season has been protracted. If the rains do not come soon, the crops will be meager. Villagers are moving to Dakar to find work and food. Our household has increased. Two nephews have come to live with us and to find work. There are no jobs for men from the bush. They help with errands and home repairs. Water is in short supply. Times like these test our endurance. But, like you, we will endure.*

*Affectionately,*
*Mariama*

Autumn's days grew shorter and bleaker. On the afternoon of November 22, when President Kennedy was assassinated in Dallas, I was in my carrel in the stacks of Widener Library where the silence was broken by a librarian's announcement of the tragedy. I left the library and went across the Yard to Peter Martin's office, where I joined a distraught circle of students listening to radio commentaries on the events. I wondered how the news of the assassination was received in Senegal, what Ibrahim had said when he heard about it. I wanted to leave the country, to get away, to settle in Senegal—a place that felt secure, civilized, and sane.

In the weeks that followed Kennedy's assassination, I wrote

to Ibrahim almost daily, sending him my views on conspiracy, wiretaps, the position of Malcolm X, the FBI, the CIA, the role of Martin Luther King, and consequences for the civil rights movement. Years later in his files I found a few of those letters:

*14 December 1963*
*Since Kennedy's assassination, some commentators have suggested that government may turn away from commitment to justice, equality, respect for diversity, and hope for improved conditions. His administration symbolized possibilities for dramatic changes in ideologies and attitudes. Since his death, the country seems to be turning toward an acceptance of injustice and inequality, secrecy and concealment; people are fearful about the implications of integrating blacks and whites. While the activists are likely to remain idealistic, courageous, and engaged in social change, it seems that government, politicians, and political analysts will grow increasingly conservative, cynical, cowardly. The latter exercise the power that will shape the destiny of the United States. I am fearful of the consequences for minorities in the U.S.*

*18 December 1963*
*When one has experienced minority status in the U.S., it is refreshing—indeed, liberating—to live in a country in which one is part of a racial majority. Even better and healthier is the chance to live in a situation in which one's race does not matter, where people are accorded respect and opportunities on the basis of their abilities and potential contributions.*

*23 Dec. 1963*
*I am drawn to Senegal because I feel I can find myself there—and perhaps become my best self, realize my full potential. In Senegal, I did not experience the hindrance of social history. In Senegal, my social history seemed irrelevant; my arguments and ideas were what mattered.*

*Perhaps that is what one experiences outside one's own country. I wonder if I would find the same degree of acceptance in any foreign country—elsewhere in Africa or in Asia, Latin America, or Europe. I doubt it. For me, Senegal has had a special appeal because of the acceptance I felt.*

December for me was the cruelest month. I avoided holiday parties, convinced my parents that my dissertation schedule would not permit a Christmas vacation, and immersed myself in my work. And I waited for mail from Dakar. In January, finally, a letter from Ibrahim arrived.

2.1.64

*My dear, dear Sarah,*

*Happy New Year. Your magnificent letters have reached me. Your analysis of nationality and identity is profound. You have become a political correspondent. Because of your letters, I am reading American newspapers, magazines, and American writers—especially Baldwin, the spellbinder, a superb writer. I plan to read a few books by the women on your list.*

*Like Africa, America is in an era of dramatic change. I sometimes regret that my leftist orientation has rendered me persona non grata in the files of your State Department. I would like to visit America. One needs to travel across America to assess the directions of change and determine how those might influence the direction of events elsewhere. Your literary talents, however, should not be diverted into political channels. You should concentrate on completing the dissertation and finding a publisher. I am relying on you and Peter Martin. Please give him my regards.*

*It is heartening to know that you are drawn to Senegal. I hope you will return and travel throughout the country. You need to see the villages to understand the challenges that confront the president and "gentle poet" who leads* this country. You need to hear the frustrations of Senegalese intellectuals and politicians. You must be here for a longer period in order to understand the struggle of this fledgling nation.

So return as soon as your circumstances permit—return for my sake. The moment you left, my world grew gloomy. A protracted eclipse with my sun—my source of energy—gone. I did not write for several weeks. O, my Muse, how I miss you!

With affection and best wishes,
I.M.

# 19

1 WORKED FEVERISHLY ON THE DISSERTATION. David Adams, whose library cubicle was next to mine, was on the same schedule and in similar circumstances. We had entered graduate school in comparative literature in the same year. His dissertation was on a Turkish journalist and novelist who, also, was a reformer. David was in love with a woman named Susan, a "blonde, freckled odalisque," his epithet for her. She was teaching at the American College for Girls in Istanbul.

David and I stayed at the library until closing time nearly every night. After library hours, night after night we sat glumly over coffee at the Harvard Square Hayes-Bickford cafeteria, stirring each other's anxieties about footnotes, deadlines, and letters lost in overseas mail. We exchanged complaints about international postal rates and the irregularity of foreign postal services. We were an improbable pair. Gold-rimmed eyeglasses, along with his cherubic face and tousled auburn hair, gave David the aura of a precociously intelligent child—an impression he cultivated. He wore the same gray tweed jacket he had worn since his last year in prep school at Deerfield. He had a jaunty spring in his step and mock innocence in his voice. Nothing pleased him more than being mistaken for a freshman. People always did a double take when they saw us. Their quizzical expressions asked, "What is that exotically dressed black woman doing with that preppie white boy?"

One evening in late February after a monumental blizzard followed by days of sunshine that thawed the snow and filled the streets with pools of slush, David and I were splashed by muck thrown up by a passing truck. I screamed obscenities at the driver.

David said, "Hey, you're growing very testy. That's out of character for you."

"I know. I've been in a foul mood lately."

"I've noticed. Why don't you get away for a while. A place for house-sitting on Martha's Vineyard was advertised in *The Crimson* yesterday. I clipped it for you." He lifted the clipping from the leaves of his wallet. "*Handsome historical Edgartown house available rent free for 3 wks. in March in exchange for care of pets (2 dogs, 3 cats) and minor maintenance.*" A telephone number was given.

The following morning I telephoned and secured the house-sitting arrangement. A few days later, I packed my car with the drafts of my dissertation, typewriter, colorful slacks and sweaters, and my batiked boubous and left for three weeks on Martha's Vineyard.

James Lowell Weston and his wife, Abigail, white-haired, earnest New Englanders, greeted me with a crisp litany of civil rights organizations they had supported and boycotts observed. It was their way of saying "welcome," announcing their liberalism, their familiarity with "matters that concern blacks—and decent whites, too," James Weston said. They introduced me to the pets, gave me lists of emergency phone numbers and instructions for the operation of the sauna. They assured me that they wanted me to "feel at home in their home" while they vacationed in Acapulco.

Abigail Weston asked, "What are you studying at Harvard?"

"Comparative literature. My dissertation is based on the works of Ibrahim Mangane, an African author, Senegalese. He is the leading—"

"How very interesting. We have a neighbor, a weekend and summer neighbor, who is in comparative literature at Boston University. His name is Henry Boudreau. Do you know him?" she asked.

I told her I'd heard him speak at a conference last year, but I'd not met him.

"Abby, why don't you leave a note for Henry? He'll be here next weekend. Tell him the young lady's here."

"I'll do that. He'll invite you in for a cup of espresso. His house is charming, and you can be sure that he won't flirt with you. Henry's perfectly safe—we think he's—well, we know you'll be safe with him."

When the Westons left, I explored the house, then went for a walk about the neighborhood—a mix of houses and shops-in-houses. An east wind lifted the salty scent of the sea into the air. I walked toward the waterfront, to the end of the long dock, sat on the edge, bare feet nearly touching the high tide. Early the next morning I began writing. At the round oak dining table I wrote until midafternoon, then at the end of the day went for a stroll along the beach. In the pale sunset, I whispered my sacramental chant to the chilly air. Except for brief exchanges in the grocery store, post office, bookstore, and gas station, I talked to no one, save myself, for several days.

While I was browsing in the bookstore on a Saturday afternoon, a middle-aged, dark haired, pear-shaped man wearing sunglasses approached me and introduced himself as Henry Boudreau. As the Westons had predicted, he invited me to his house for a cup of espresso after dinner. I accepted. In the course of our getting acquainted in his small but elegant living room amid a handsome collection of antiques or, as he insisted, "copies of copies of fine French antiques," Henry said, "I've heard about your intervention at the conference. I was told that you stopped their feuding, which had turned very ugly, that it was you who made them see that both sides had valid arguments and that they weren't contradictory. Very clever!" We talked until nearly midnight about the conference, about his work on Gide, and, finally, about my dissertation.

"Tell me, what do you find appealing about Mangane's works?"

"He has a liberated cultural consciousness. His portrayals of indigenous ethnic traditions and relationships are rendered with intelligence, dignity, and authenticity. He encourages readers to value their African heritage. He doesn't use European characters or material in his scenarios. Nor does he follow European conventions about narrative in his novels and films. He's a liberating literary influence. And, as you know, he's produced a significant body of work, enough material for several dissertations."

"It seems you're on to something—material of interest to students in French literature, African studies, and comparative literature. Would teaching at Boston University interest you if there's ever a vacancy?"

I hesitated. "I really want to teach at the University of Dakar where—"

"And I want to teach at the Sorbonne!" Throwing an arm into the air, he snapped his fingers and said, "If I were a magician, you'd be in Dakar and I'd be in Paris. But here we are. Send me your résumé and let me know when your dissertation is finished and approved. It sounds very promising. And when you've had that last sip of espresso, go back to the Westons and write, write, write!"

I worked long hours, typed furiously, driven to finish the work. In my journal, I wrote:

*14 March 1964*
*The magic of Martha's Vineyard! It is not accidental*
*that I am drawn to this island. Meeting the Westons and*
*Henry Boudreau—not random encounters. Is it positive*
*paranoia? People are plotting for me. A teaching job at*
*B.U. would be a good place to start.*

When it was time to leave the Vineyard, I had completed a very respectable final draft with only the bibliography to be assembled. I left a note for the Westons, ample feedings for the pets, and a handful of exquisite seashells in Henry's mailbox. Exhilarated, I returned to Cambridge, compiled the bibliography and delivered the draft to Peter Martin's office. He was out of town. His secretary understood my reluctance to leave the work, so she placed it in a metal file cabinet, locked the drawer, and wrote a note to Peter Martin.

At my apartment, I was met by Mrs. O'Hara, the wife of the

building superintendent. A conscientious, vigilant woman, she lived vicariously through the comings and goings of tenants and the postage stamps and return addresses on their mail. She presented a handful of letters and three magazines, the accumulation of three weeks of mail. From the pocket of her crisp apron, she produced another letter.

She said, "You've got this official-lookin' letter from Middlesex County Court, dearie. Came by certified mail. I signed for it m'self. Needs readin' and answerin' right away, I'd say." She lingered expectantly for a moment, no doubt hoping I would open the letter and reveal its contents. Instead, I slipped it into the pocket of my raincoat and thanked her. Disappointed, she shuffled downstairs and resumed her watch at the basement window that afforded her a view of shoes, ankles, and trouser cuffs of passing pedestrians.

In the envelope was a summons to appear in Middlesex County Court on Wednesday, May 6, 1964, as a party in the case of *Sarah Stewart Thompson v. Abraham Lincoln Thompson*. The charge: incompatibility. Lincoln and I had agreed to the terms; however, seeing it in print was disturbing.

# 20

IMMEDIATELY AFTER RECEIVING THE COMMUNI-
cation about divorce proceedings, I called my lawyer, Tim Harris, who said that it would be a routine hearing since it was an
uncontested divorce with neither children nor property to
divide. Lincoln and I, however, needed witnesses who could
offer evidence of our incompatibility. I knew that Sam Higgins
would be Lincoln's witness. He could honestly swear that we
could not live harmoniously given the divergent paths we were
taking. But who would be my witness? Who could stand by me
and validate the claim of incompatibility. David? He was aware
of our incompatibility; but David was not the right choice.
He'd be an incompatible witness. A woman witness. If I could
have afforded bringing Mariama over, she at least would have
added drama to the scene. The women I had come to know at
Harvard were also graduate students or students' wives, librari-
ans, and department secretaries. Our acquaintance was only
occasional and superficial—coffee together, an exchange of
comments about a film or lecture or the weather. They knew
nothing of my personal circumstances. Marriage and the
intense isolation of graduate study made for an insular existence, which I felt even more keenly when I wondered who
could be my witness.

The close friends of my college years had scattered. None
was in the Boston area. I decided that Joan Brown, my room-
mate at Wellesley and the maid of honor in our wedding, was
the witness I wanted at the scene of the divorce. Joan had had
serious doubts about our compatibility from the beginning. She

lived in Philadelphia, however, and I wasn't sure that she would come. I telephoned her.

"Of course, I'll be your witness, girlfriend. Frankly, I'm not surprised that you're splitting up. I never thought Lincoln was right for you. He may have *seemed* right to everybody because of your family connections and all that D.C. stuff." She shifted into her social worker gear. "Sociologically speaking, he was the 'boy next door,' as they say. But I knew the boy next door couldn't hold you for long. You needed someone already established in a profession, somewhat older, and more cosmopolitan than Lincoln."

"I know just the man," I told her. "When I see you, I'll tell you about him."

The divorce hearing was businesslike and functional, lacking the solemn, ceremonial import that I had expected. I can't remember what we wore or what was said. I remember that it was a bright, balmy May day. The legal transaction had cleared the air. Our lawyers shook hands with us in the lobby of the courthouse and then rushed away to meet other clients. Outside on the steps, Lincoln and I also shook hands.

"Best wishes for a better marriage next time," I said.

"Good luck to you, Sarah. Good luck with getting your degree and going back to Senegal." And as he and Sam backed away, Lincoln called, "No hard feelings!" But, in truth, there were hard feelings on my part. I had wasted time on what had turned out to be an empty marriage. Rumbling with exasperation and irritation about the upheaval in my life, I felt like a volcano on the brink of eruption.

"Nobody in our family has ever been divorced," Mom had whimpered over the phone. "And now I'll never be a grandmother." She was heartbroken. Dad wrote a long letter that said he was sorry it had happened; there was no need for guilt and shame; and that I would be "strengthened by the ordeal." And he had enclosed a check for the legal fees.

I drove Joan to Harvard Square where we parked and walked to the Henri IV Restaurant on Winthrop Street for a lunch of quiche, a salad, and a bottle of Pouilly-Fuissé. Acquainted with the Philadelphia courts to which she occasionally accompanied her clients, Joan assured me that our exchange with the judge and the lawyers was typical: a flat, unemotional, matter-of-fact routine for them. I had wanted a divorce ceremony with solemn ritual and symbolic acts to provide a sense of closure. Perhaps the family members and friends who had congregated for our wedding should have been invited to witness the conclusion of our marriage as well. And an elegiac percussion composition should have been performed by Babatunde Olatunji drumming Lincoln out of my life. The hurried exchange of legal language did not satisfy my need to end our relationship emphatically.

"Well, a chapter in your life is finished." Joan said. "My advice to you would be to take your time before you begin the next one."

I knew that the next chapter already had begun. To Joan I confessed my passionate interest in Ibrahim. Even after we had finished the wine, drunk several cups of coffee, and smoked nearly all of my cigarettes, I was still talking about him. In her expert professional style of probing, Joan asked for evidence of his interest in me: "How did he show he cared for you? How did he respond to you when his wife was around? Did he give you any tokens of his affection? Does he write to you? What makes you think he loves you?"

Ibrahim had never spoken of love; nor had I said I loved him. Collapsing all that I had felt for him into a four-letter word was like reducing the majesty of an ocean to the chemical formula of its contents. And contemplating the meaning of love for Ibrahim on the day of reckoning the value of a marriage was decidedly unsettling. Joan reached for a Gauloise and, with a clinician's patience, waited. Finally, I said, "I know he cares for me," lighting her cigarette with my lighter.

"But you more than care for him. You're in love with him, right?"

"Yes, I'm in love with him."

"Or in love with his world? I mean the world of his books and films, as well as the house, his servants, his fans—that whole scene."

"How can I separate him from his context? Yes, I'm in love with the entire scene—the pageant of his life."

"Is there really a role for you in his pageant?" Irritated by her line of questioning, I was reminded of her college byline: Joan Brown, Wise Woman about Town. A regular feature in the college newspaper was her column on managing relationships with men, tips vicariously derived from confessional chats with girls who told her about ups and downs with their dates or steady boyfriends. Joan was still giving advice.

"Don't waste your time on fantasies about a Senegalese man who is twice your age. You might see him again, even have an affair, but there's no permanent place for you in his life." She composed a compassionate facial expression and patted my hand. I withdrew from her touch and felt myself withdrawing, not wanting any more of her consultation talk.

"You've got the chance to start over. I'm sure there's a man in Cambridge or Boston who'll be head over heels about you before you know it. Someone with a romantic nature that matches yours. Somebody who's interested in Africa." I wanted to tell her that only Ibrahim, and no one else, could win me now. But she wouldn't have understood. She continued, "None of the guys you used to know would be right for you now," and began a roll call of men I had dated. Tallying the results of the friendships and affairs of our college days, she rattled off who had married whom, had had children, which marriages were in difficulty, and who we'd be unlikely to hear from again. The report trailed off into her own lament about being single.

On the way to drop her off at the airport, Joan offered more advice. "Don't do anything on the rebound, girlfriend. Concentrate on your preparation for your oral exam. And after the exam, treat yourself to something snazzy—buy a gorgeous dress. Be good to yourself."

# 21

"APPLAUSE! I COULDN'T BELIEVE MY EARS," sputtered David who was waiting outside the seminar room. "Your committee applauded your exam performance! Hastings, old Woolrich, Shapiro, and even Dumont all came out smiling. She must have been sensational," he said to Peter Martin who had remained to congratulate me.

"She was. She gave a clear, concise overview of Mangane's works in a way that made us focus on genre issues. Woolrich, of course, asked the first question—asked her to compare the Francophone and the Anglophone African novel, a question, mind you, he couldn't have answered." Turning toward me, he said, "That's when you showed them what you know. You gave a stunning historical comparison. And did you see Dumont's expression when he asked about the influence of Balzac and Flaubert on Mangane, and you said their works had had no influence whatsoever, that Mangane is *sui generis*—and illustrated it. Well, he was bowled over."

"What was Shapiro's question?" David asked.

"He didn't ask a question," I said. "He made a statement about critics who don't understand modernism. Hastings, of course, responded defensively and they began to quarrel."

"Your intervention—your implying that modernism wasn't at all relevant to the discussion—startled them. And then you summarized the entire discussion eloquently and acknowledged how their comments on your draft refined the work. Everybody applauded. It was masterful—your control of the examination. Very well done."

I telephoned Ibrahim at once, forgetting that it was after midnight in Dakar. At first slowly, "Sarah? Yes, it is you." I told him that I had defended my dissertation successfully, that the committee had applauded my performance. "Magnificent! Congratulations! The next step then is to find a publisher, I suppose. Ah, but just now you are celebrating. Congratulations." His response was pragmatic and, therefore, disquieting. On to the next stage—the book. He seemed more interested in the future of the work than in the immediate accomplishment or, for that matter, in me. He sounded older than I had remembered. Tired—perhaps it was the hour. Perhaps I shouldn't have called.

On the mid-June afternoon of commencement day, the degrees awarded, the speeches over, gowned graduates grouped for photographs, groundskeepers folded and stacked wooden chairs. Friends embraced and promised to keep in touch. Relatives looked on, admiring their graduating kin and perhaps hoping another graduation might bring them back again.

My parents and I strolled across Harvard Yard enjoying the afterglow of the commencement's heady events.

"We're really proud of you, girl. Dr. Sarah Stewart with a Harvard doctorate! You've done everything we'd hoped you'd do," Dad said.

"Except getting divorced," amended Mom sympathetically. "It must have been awfully hard, handling everything—finishing the degree and getting divorced at the same time. Lord, I don't know how you did it."

"Tell us more about your Boston University job offer," said Dad.

"Your father thinks you ought to take the Boston University position, but I hope you'll come and teach at Howard. There are some fine young men on the faculty there—fine looking, too. And you ought to live at home—live with us. Then you wouldn't be lonely."

"Sarah may not want to come back to Washington, and if she does, she probably wouldn't want to live with us. She has her own life to live, sweetheart, her own way of doing things."

There was a pause in their dialogue, a familiar pause that

interrupted their conversation when an argument was brewing. The pause was my cue for intervention. As a child, I usually asked an irrelevant question or offered a distracting observation at such moments. My childhood voice had relieved the tension and redirected their focus to my corner. This time I summoned my womanly voice to end their debate about what I should or should not do.

"I must shape a life for myself that will make me feel whole, complete—a life that is true to who I am and am becoming." I pointed to the chairs on the lawn near Appleton Chapel where we sat down. "Boston University has offered me an assistant professorship with a three-year contract. I'll begin teaching in their summer session. I need to prepare my dissertation for publication, write a few articles, and save some money for my move to Dakar. My work with Ibrahim Mangane is—"

"Just what is the nature of your relationship with this man?" asked Dad.

"I admire his work and I'm very fond of him."

"Fond of him? He's married, isn't he? Are you going after a married man? Help us, sweet Jesus!" Mom sighed and rolled her eyes heavenward.

"I want to live in Dakar—find a teaching position there," I said matter-of-factly.

Dad leaned toward me and asked, "Is that realistic—is it probable?"

"No, it's not at all realistic," Mom interjected. "It's so far away. What if something should happen to us? You'd be thousands of miles away." Then, in the condescending tone that she used when speaking to her third-grade pupils, she asked, "Sarah, dear, have you thought of seeing someone—a psychiatrist perhaps—about your plans and your—your Senegal problem?"

It was the word "problem"—the idea that Mom viewed my plans as irrational, indeed, pathological, that made me erupt. Like Lincoln, my own mother assumed that I must have been mad, and that was infuriating. I sprang out of my chair and reeled like a dervish around my parents, my crimson gown billowing, two dozen braids flailing about my shoulders. I drew away from them, off the green and on to the paved path. They were surprised and confused. I hissed, "I must go to Senegal! *My help cometh from Senegal!*" My parents seemed frozen in their positions for a few interminable minutes, so stunned were they by my outburst.

I stood on solid ground, safely on my own ground. They looked as if quicksand had eddied under them. They were dazed. I had spiraled away from them—freeing myself from their orbit of influence, moving into my own. At that moment, I felt very strong—capable of doing whatever I chose to do.

The informal procession of graduates and relatives who were passing through Harvard Yard slowed their steps. A few tarried to watch. Not wanting to be part of a scene, my parents gathered themselves up, programs, purse, Mom's navy blue straw hat, collected their dignity, reassembled their commencement expressions, and rose. Dad stooped to pick up the mortar board which I had flung on the grass. They then flanked me, each taking an arm, and turned their steps and mine toward Trowbridge Street. Eager to become indistinguishable from the rest, they guided me as we joined the procession of other family groups and moved away from the site of our scene and into the crowd.

When they linked arms with me, I felt certain that they were going to take me to a mental hospital—that they would walk beyond Trowbridge Street toward Cambridge City Hospital, where they would deposit me for safekeeping at the hospital's psychiatric ward until I "returned to my senses," as Mom would say. Returning to my senses in that instance meant relinquishing my dreams of Ibrahim Mangane and Senegal.

For several minutes we walked in silence. Then Dad initiated the idle conversation that always had hushed the sounds of our domestic discord. They spoke as if nothing had happened. They spoke only to each other. They spoke across me, pretending to ignore me. Between them, taller than my mother by five inches, and nearly as tall as my father, I somehow felt smaller and much younger. I had a distinct recollection of having walked between them when I was five or six years old and having heard the same conversation over my head. Many painful moments had been eased with their empty phrases. My parents continued their intentionally didactic dialogue, showing me how people "should" talk to each other—in banalities, superficialities, in calm, colorless exchanges of random nothingness.

Finally, back at Trowbridge Street and inside my apartment, I apologized. "I'm sorry for my outburst, Mom and Dad. Sorry to have upset you and spoiled the day. But I want you to understand that I must find a way of living in Senegal. Being near Ibrahim Mangane is very important to me."

"You need to get some rest," Mom said. "And you may need to get some help. Maybe Lincoln wasn't right for you, but you ought to be with a man from your own background, someone familiar. I'll be praying for you. God will help you."

"We want you to be happy, don't you know? You ought to do what's in your best interest, and certainly your studies shouldn't be wasted. You've prepared for college teaching, and if you can export your training, and by that I mean, if you can get a job teaching in Senegal, then that may be a reason to go. Frankly, I don't think it's wise to go back just because of this man," my father said.

"You must know that all this talk about Ibrahim Mangane is premature. After all, I plan to stay in this area for a while. I'll begin teaching in the summer session at Boston University in just a few weeks. I've found an apartment in Boston. I have to pack, move, and prepare for classes. I'm going to be very busy with—"

"Glory be! You've decided it all, haven't you? You're staying in Boston. Well! Well, best wishes, and God help you," Mom said with an air of dismissal.

"We love you, girl," Dad added. We want only the best for you, what'll make you happy—only the best."

It was time for them to settle into their silver Chrysler for the drive to Washington, an eight-hour trip during which they would probably talk about the academic procession, the weather, the traffic, the cost of highway tolls, license plates from faraway states, and place names of towns in Connecticut, New York, New Jersey, and Delaware, where distant cousins lived.

And I was certain that they would not speak of me, my immediate plans, my dreams of Senegal.

Relieved by their departure and emotionally spent, I needed a nap before going to the party David Adams was hosting at his Eliot House suite. From my radio, Miles Davis's trumpet whined "Sketches of Spain," and soon I was asleep. David called twice to remind me that I was expected at the party, but I slept through the party time anyway. It was after midnight when I awoke again, covered myself with the crimson gown, and slipped into a dream-filled sleep.

*I dreamed that Ibrahim and I, both dressed in white, were standing before an altar. My father, smiling his approval, had given me into marriage. In the background, my mother and Mariama, both sobbing, comforted each other. Lifted out of the chapel with a sense of flight, Ibrahim and I were suspended momentarily in a Chagall-like wedding pose against a field of blue. When the field began to move, it became an ocean, the ocean that separated us. I was terrified. Then Ibrahim and I appeared cradled in a giant white cloth held in the beak of an enormous stork that flew across the ocean and delivered us safely, gently, to the boulders below Ibrahim's house, where, at last, we were alone.*

# 22

MY CHANGE-OF-ADDRESS CARD WITH "Sarah Stewart, 180 Beacon Street, Boston, Mass., USA" made it known to my family and friends that I had reclaimed my maiden name and acquired a Boston apartment and an element of internationalism. My Beacon Street landlord protested when I requested that the white walls be painted coral. "Lady, what if the next tenant hates the color? Then I'll have to paint it all over again!" Finally, he relented, and soon I found myself surrounded by coral walls, a sapphire blue sofa and chairs, and draperies with coral, magenta, and sapphire stripes. I searched for color-compatible lamps, vases, bookcases, prints, and plants—African violets, of course.

The transition from the status of student to that of faculty member had its advantages and disadvantages. Satisfying as it was to have a respectable income, there were social expectations that went along with it; for example, a suitable wardrobe for the classroom, university receptions, occasional dinner parties, and other occasions that increased the cost of living. After the initial outlay of money for clothes, furnishings, and a housewarming party, I budgeted expenses—rent, utilities, insurance, books, records, subscriptions, clothing, entertainment—and I scrupulously saved the balance in what I called my Senegal account.

Moving from the company of graduate students into the company of faculty was sometimes awkward. Luckily, I was "discovered" by Antonia Dale, the only other black woman on the arts and sciences faculty. An Oberlin graduate with an Oxford doctorate, she was a renowned historian. To be sure, I had known that she taught at Boston University; but at a large urban campus, it was unlikely that I would meet her. And so it was an agreeable surprise to find in my English Department mailbox an invitation from her.

> *Dear Sarah Stewart,*
> *Welcome to B.U.! I understand your summer course was excellent. Please join me for sherry at my office on Friday at 4:30.*
>
> *Antonia Stockwell Dale*

From the moment we toasted each other on the tufted brown leather sofa in Antonia's book-lined office, I knew that I would turn up there faithfully every Friday afternoon to drink to our having endured another week in the university and to summon the courage to face the coming week. The climate of the university was inhospitable. It was widely known that one's colleagues were rarely one's advocates and never one's friends, but Antonia's cordial overture made me feel accepted.

"You're going to need a few friends—powerful friends—in this university if you expect to remain here, and I intend to be among them," announced Antonia. "I was isolated, totally ignored here for fifteen years—until Oxford published my *History of Slavery in the Western World*. Only then did I gain the attention of my department—and tenure." She paused and frowned. Bitter memories, I assumed, deepened the furrows in her wrinkled brow. "I'm going to make certain that you are introduced to the deans, assigned to important committees, invited to official receptions and parties, and so on. They're going to know who you are, Sarah Stewart, know that you are a significant addition to the faculty, and that you're building a career here. You have a three-year appointment as an assistant professor, I understand. You may want to have it extended to five years to give yourself time to publish more before you're reviewed.

"You'll need to cultivate the senior faculty in literature—beginning with Melvin Levinson and Shirley Quincy. They're widely respected scholars, influential with the administration, and they have a sense of fair play—which can't be said of anyone else in that department, certainly not of Eleanor Tanner and her entourage. By the way, has Eleanor invited you to her annual literary potluck supper? Her invitation asks that you bring a dish described in a literary work and, after dining, you read the passage in which the dish is mentioned."

"Yes, I did receive an invitation, but I've another engagement that evening."

"Postpone your other engagement and go to Eleanor's house with an esoteric quotation from English literature and a casserole—something baked to British blandness. That's the way to impress that crowd."

Antonia drew the smoke of a Camel cigarette through a mother-of-pearl cigarette holder and exhaled. "I'm afraid you will have make an effort to impress them. They have no knowledge of African literature. They won't care to know about what you are reading, writing, or teaching. You'll have to show them that you are well acquainted with their beloved English authors. Then they'll take notice."

As she refilled our glasses, Antonia surveyed my attire. "You're going to need a more conservative style of dress. You'll want to stand out because of your scholarship, not because your dresses are scarlet or turquoise or orange and that you wear those African beads, bracelets halfway up your arm, and your hair in those braids."

I merely smiled as I took in her image, from her thin, gray, carefully coiffed curls to her gray stockings and gray suede pumps. Her classically fashionable and unfashionable slate gray suit was adorned only with a silver circle brooch and the limp bow of her oyster gray blouse. A dusting of off-white powder gave her rich brown complexion a certain pallor. For Antonia Dale, wearing shades of gray was a way of demonstrating that her intellect was vivid and lively—that she herself was brilliant. I smoothed the pleats of my scarlet skirt and sipped her sherry.

Antonia offered abundant advice: where to sit in faculty meetings, when to schedule classes, how to announce forthcoming publications, whom to inform about participation in conferences, the type of graduate student one should advise and the type one should avoid. Her interest in my career was both flattering and disconcerting, but I found myself returning every Friday afternoon, listening to Antonia's litany of academic do's and don'ts, while quietly drinking her sherry. I admit I valued her company more than her counsel. I didn't tell her at the outset that my aspirations did not center around a future at the university. Only later, when she pursued the idea of an extension of my appointment, did I tell her of my intentions.

Antonia had read my dissertation and suggested some revisions. Curious about Ibrahim and his works, her questions gave me permission to talk about him. She asked about his position on Negritude and his ideas about the influence of French culture on Senegalese culture.

His writings, I said, affirmed the validity and coherence of black African culture and reinforced the idea of Negritude. I explained that he acknowledged the influence of French culture; after all, much of his work was written originally in French. He seemed to value the interaction of Senegalese and French intellectuals.

Aside from the sherry hours with Antonia, I had few contacts of a personal nature at the university. Occasionally I had coffee with Franco Verdi, a lecturer in the Italian department. His irreverent comments on academic politics made me convulse with laughter. Phyllis Warner, the chaplain's wife, and I had a weekly ice skating engagement from November through February, after which I rarely saw her. Now and then I met colleagues and students for lunch or dinner in restaurants on Beacon Hill or in Back Bay or Harvard Square. On one such occasion, I was with a party leaving Cronin's in the Square when I saw Lincoln bent over a beer at the bar.

"Waiting for someone?" I asked.

"Sarah! Please join me. No, I'm not waiting for anyone—that is, anyone else." He seemed genuinely happy to see me, and I felt an unexpected surge of warmth and affection for him. He looked at his watch—it was nearly ten o'clock—and said,

"You'd probably like cognac at this hour." I nodded and he ordered a glass. We exchanged news about our parents. He told me about raising funds to start a newspaper, *The Black Boston Banner,* and to launch his campaign for a seat on the school committee. As I told him about the courses I was teaching, his attention began to wander to the football game on the TV screen above the bar or glance toward the flow of customers through the door. It was obvious that he wasn't interested, but it didn't matter. I told Lincoln that I had to go home to review my lecture material. He offered to walk me to my car, but I declined. I didn't wish to be in his company any longer. It definitely was over.

My nights were filled with preparation for classes, hours in libraries, or in my office at the university. By day, I delivered lectures, had conferences with students, and graded their papers. I loved the rush of entering the classroom, the excitement of opening a lecture with prepared notes, then continuing extemporaneously on the topic of the day: Traditional Poetry in Francophone Africa, An Analysis of the Poems of Léopold Senghor, A Comparison of the Anglophone and Francophone African Novel, and What Is Lost and Gained in Translation.

The classroom was my theater, each class an occasion for performance. My attire sometimes was a costume related to the lecture. I usually entered the lecture hall a few minutes after the hour, by which time almost all the 120 seats were occupied. Some latecomers scanned the hall for vacant seats in the center of a row under a pile of book bags and jackets, while others sat in the aisles. After surveying the rows of faces, I placed my typewritten notes on the lectern and a tumbler of water nearby, and began with a battery of questions about the topic of the lecture. I cited references, with critical appraisals of each, then related the references to the development of my argument.

When I lectured on Ibrahim's works, I explained that the purpose of my research was to increase interest in Francophone African literature through an analysis of the fiction of a major Senegalese author. I presented a concise synopsis of three of his novels and the repetition of themes in each. For example, the consequences of colonial exploitation was a frequent theme. Looking around the room, I made eye contact with a few students whose expressions, postures, and note taking indicated their level of engagement and comprehension. Knowing when I had made a point effectively, I then picked up the pace and moved on to the next topic. I announced the topic and repeated the question related to it. Jotting unfamiliar terms or names on the blackboard, I paused to allow students time to note them. When I spoke too rapidly or skipped stages in the analysis, I repeated the material and filled in the blanks. Finally, I summarized the major points of the lecture and suggested the issues future studies should address. Then I invited questions or comments. Especially attentive students grew inquisitive. How did you pick Mangane as the subject of your study? What is the most difficult personal challenge for a biographer? Is there any evidence that anticolonial literature influences political attitudes and actions? I explained that I had selected an articulate, self-critical, versatile writer whose works had had a significant influence on younger writers throughout Francophone Africa. The most difficult personal challenge was maintaining a sense of balance in the appraisal of the individual who is the subject of a biography or critical study. As for the influence of literature on political attitudes—well, that is difficult to assess. I struggled to answer some questions that required a deeper knowledge of African literature than I had acquired.

Although there were more women than men in the classes, women students rarely initiated questions. I tried to elicit questions and comments from the women, urged them to speak out over the interjections of male voices. The dynamics of the classroom fascinated me. Each session had its rewards—the gaggle of students who remained after the lecture for further discussion, the students who thanked me for my comments on their papers, and the standing ovation after my last lecture of the semester.

On weekends, in my office at the university, I poured over revisions of my manuscript. I had written to a dozen or more publishing houses to explore interest in the work. And I had a collection of letters with essentially the same message: "Unfortunately, it is difficult to market the publication you have proposed." Finally, a new press in New Jersey offered a contract. I accepted. With a deadline for submission, again I was immersed in Ibrahim's works. And I was writing a paper for the meetings of the Comparative Literature Association.

There also were letters to write to relatives and friends—to Joan in Philadelphia, David in Istanbul, and Bill Nelson, then in Abidjan—and to Ibrahim and Mariama. Mariama's brief letters described the weather, her garden, and products making their first appearance in Dakar's markets. Ibrahim occasionally sent a cryptic message on a postcard or an ambiguous note: "Continue with your important writing. Our futures—yours and mine—depend on it." "Courage, dearest, the ocean between us will become a river, then a stream, then a trickle." "I would rather share a page of fine writing than share a pillow." His messages aroused pleasures and pains that sent me to Martha's Vineyard to chant and splash in the icy waves that refreshed me and reinforced my resolve.

# 23

On a chilly afternoon in late February, several students lingered after class to ask what I thought about the assassination of Malcolm X. I told them that the tragedy of Malcolm X's death magnified the meaning of his life, and that we should recognize his contributions. We discussed the campus controversy about whether to hold a memorial program in his memory. I had signed a petition in favor of it. After talking with the students, I went to Antonia's office where I found her on the telephone conducting business as usual. She was in the midst of a conversation about my appointment.

"Mel, I know you'll do what you can to have her appointment extended. I think Sarah should request it herself. Wait a moment. She's just arrived. I'll ask her."

Turning away from the phone, she said, "There's a meeting of the Committee on Appointments and Promotions next Thursday. Would you be willing to draft a request for an extension of your appointment from three to five years? Mel Levinson is on the phone."

"Antonia, I'm grateful for your efforts, but right now I want to talk about a memorial program for Malcolm X."

Returning to the telephone, Antonia said brusquely, "Mel, Sarah and I need to talk. I'll get back to you." She hung up and turned to me with a stern gaze.

"We're not going to discuss Malcolm X or that petition. We need to discuss your plans. Have a seat, and tell me about them." I sat at one end of the sofa. She moved from her desk and sat at the other end. I took a long breath and began to describe what I knew Antonia would regard as a foolhardy scheme.

"Perhaps I should have told you that I intend to leave for Senegal at the end of my appointment. Malcolm X's assassination is another incident that's made me want to leave this country. After all, I belong in Senegal. I expect to finish my manuscript in a few months and when my book is published, I will settle in Dakar and work with Ibrahim."

Without a word, Antonia got up and went over to the file cabinet for the Dry Sack sherry and fluted glasses. She poured us each a glass. We lifted them in a silent toast. "Tell me more about your plans," she said.

"There's hardly more to tell. I envision a future in Dakar, where I'll do research, write, learn about filmmaking, and be—"

"Be Mangane's 'girl Friday,' his acolyte, his lackey!" she exploded. "Do you think that is a good use of your talent? You may have the chance to get a tenured appointment here or somewhere else—Berkeley, Northwestern, or, with some luck, at Yale. Do you have any idea how well-situated you are? Don't tell me that you are going to abandon a very promising career to work as a clerk for an African writer."

"That is what I'm telling you, except that I will not be his clerk, but his collaborator, colleague, and—"

"And lover? That's really what it's about. Another young woman who's head over heels about an older man with some claim to fame. Well, it's a cliché in relationships, my dear. And he's married, isn't he?"

"Yes, but . . ."

"You young women certainly know how to complicate your lives. Maybe life's been too easy for you. You've attended good schools, had the support of your parents, had the luck of beginning your career at a good university. You seem never to have experienced the difficulties that I've encountered as a black woman struggling up the academic ladder. Never having known adversity, I suppose, makes you feel you should take some risks, for example, risk destroying your career. You're one of our silver-spoon-and-four-leaf-clover Negroes. You've been every-where, had everything, every opportunity. And now you're going to spit in the eye of Lady Luck." She drained her glass and hastened to refill it.

"I'm aware of the advantages I've had, but I also know that my future is in Senegal with Ibrahim Mangane. And if doing what my heart dictates is risky, you're right, I'm taking a risk."

"I've always done what my intellect dictated—and my life has improved through my hard work. And I have no regrets. You'd be foolish to abandon your career here. I hope you'll reconsider. Your chances for advancement are excellent. But you must be careful. Don't get involved with the Malcolm X memorial business. And for heaven's sake, don't tell anybody that you would give all this up for Senegal."

My affection for Antonia and respect for her dedication to the scholarly life stilled my tongue. I didn't tell her I was sched-uled already to speak at the Malcolm X memorial service. For a while we sat in silence sipping sherry. Antonia knew that my thoughts had flown to Senegal.

"Forget him, my dear girl. You've already been married. You know what that's like. Now get on with your work and your life here." She patted my cheek as if the matter were settled, and we parted. As I closed the door, I felt I would not return soon to open it.

# 24

*Dakar*
*4 May 1965*

*Dear Sarah,*
*I have some news for you! The time has been chosen for*
*me to become a mother, for Ibrahim and me to become*
*parents. The baby is due in September. It will bring happi-*
*ness to our home.*
*At first I actually thought I had an abdominal tumor. I*
*was relieved and overjoyed when the doctor found that I*
*was pregnant. I have thought about the time you were*
*pregnant while you were with us. Permit me to say again*
*that we were very sorry that you lost your baby.*
*I hope, dear Sarah, that our news will give you some*
*pleasure. I know that you will have such news for us one*
*day, a baby of your own. For now, share our happy news.*
*You must visit us after the baby is born.*
*Ibrahim sends his regards and best wishes in your work.*
*Affectionately,*
*Mariama*


I read the letter again and again—perhaps a dozen times. The
page rustled in my tremulous hand. Smoldering jealousy and
anger took me by surprise. I was angry with myself about the
extent of my involvement in their lives and in my fantasies
about my future with Ibrahim. I was angry with Ibrahim and
Mariama for entrapping me in the web of their marriage. They
were held together by a mesh of tribal affiliations, bloodlines

that linked them and bound them together. I had become entangled in a web of relationships that had little to do with the reality of my life.

The letter revived memories of my pregnancy, the upheaval in my life, my sense of loss. I had filled the void in my pelvis and my mind with fantasies about living in Dakar—with Ibrahim. Devastated by this unexpected news, I went to bed and dreamed a nightmare.

*At Mariama's bedside at the moment of birth, I was wearing a nurse's uniform. My fingers slid into the birth canal and eased out the head and shoulders of the infant. Mariama screamed from the bowels of her arched body. I held the baby, a boy, above Mariama with the bloody umbilical cord linking mother to son. He was a slimy thing. He slipped and I clutched him with one hand about the neck and strangled him. The purple brown infant became a transparent fetal membrane of a baby in my hand. Mariama screamed again. Her scream became my scream.*

I awoke in a sweat, my palms wet with perspiration that felt like mucous. Frightened by my act in the nightmare, I rolled out of bed and onto my knees, in the prayerful pose of my girlhood's nightly prayers. But no words came. I could not say my psalm.

Heart racing and feverish, I showered and dressed. Then at my desk, I tried to compose a reply to Mariama and a letter to Ibrahim. A wastebasket full of crumpled paper was evidence of several false starts.

I telephoned Antonia. I wanted to view my situation from her perspective. She was expecting guests for Sunday brunch. "I've invited the Steins and the Slaters. You should meet them anyway. Come right away and we'll have time to talk before they arrive."

I walked along Beacon Street and turned onto Charles Street where I glanced occasionally at my reflection in shop windows, imagining Ibrahim beside me, walking hand in hand, his white caftan beside my plum-colored dress with its red sash. I smiled at the reflection in the window of an antique shop. My smile slipped away as the image of a pregnant Mariama emerged.

Mariama pregnant. Why was this news from Mariama the cause of such anguish? The fact was that nothing had changed in my own situation. I was still four thousand miles from Ibrahim with only fantasies about ever seeing him again.

From a dazzling display of florist's flowers, I selected a bouquet of red and purple anemones for Antonia. "Perfect with your dress," the florist observed as he wrapped the flowers. At the corner, I turned right and climbed cobblestoned Chestnut Street to a narrow brick house with a green enameled door and bronze lion's head knocker. I tapped with the knocker and pushed the buzzer. Antonia greeted me heartily, "Welcome, Sarah." I extended the anemones. Antonia, on her tiptoes, stretched and kissed me on the cheek.

"What's on your mind, dear? Having difficulties with your department?"

"No, Antonia, it's not my work. It's my life that I need to discuss."

"You've come with beautiful anemones and existential issues. Would you like a drink—a Bloody Mary or champagne with or without orange juice?" I chose only orange juice and followed Antonia into the kitchen, where she arranged the flowers and filled our glasses. Antonia raised her glass, "To your wonderful life and grand future."

"My future is in Dakar," I said with tears welling.

"Come, let's sit in the living room." Antonia's living room resembled her office: a wall of bookshelves, gray and burgundy paisley patterned draperies, a burgundy leather tufted sofa, and four overstuffed chairs recently upholstered in gray velvet that matched the gray carpet. Her long gray silk dress, cut like a shirt, touched her burgundy velvet slippers. Her somber presentation of herself and my plum and red were contrasting expressions of our approaches to life.

Between the shelves of books and journals were handsomely framed prints of Civil War scenes. There was nothing personal in her living room—no photographs of relatives, evidence of pets, knitting or needlework, no playing cards, puzzles, or games, only a stack of back issues of the *New York Times* suggested that something other than scholarship claimed Antonia's time. I sat in the center seat of the sofa; Antonia chose the opposite chair.

"I'm here because of Ibrahim Mangane. Yesterday I received a letter from his wife, Mariama. She's expecting a baby in September. The news has undone me. She already has him, his company—his voice, his touch. And now she'll have his baby, too. When I read the letter I realized how much I've envied Mariama. She befriended me and now I resent her."

"What did you expect might happen?"

"I suppose I'd hoped that he would find his way out of the marriage. Now with a child, there's little possibility—little hope for . . ." Tears brimming, I closed my eyes and swallowed. Antonia handed me a handkerchief. "I didn't tell you that I was pregnant by Lincoln the summer I was in Dakar. When I came home, I miscarried in the fifth month, and perhaps lost the chance of being a mother—ever." I wiped away the warm tears streaming down my cheeks.

Kindly and with compassion, she said, "Some time ago, I realized that you're driven by an unusual combination of intellect and emotion, and that I may not be able to comprehend fully the energy and aspirations that motivate you. I know that your work—that is, an academic career alone—may not sustain you. The life to which you aspire extends well beyond the boundaries of my experience.

"A fascination with Mangane has claimed you. You're his captive. But you haven't claimed him, it seems. You are in for years, perhaps a lifetime, of frustration and agony, my dear, unless you either can free yourself of him or somehow claim him for your own."

The buzzer sounded and interrupted a rare moment of intimacy between us. Antonia went to the door to greet the guests. The chatter of pleasantries and laughter in the foyer abruptly changed the mood. Returning to the living room with Philip and Nora Stein, Antonia introduced us and left us to become acquainted while she fetched drinks.

Nora, a sociologist, began her inquiry into my origins by

speculating about my accent. "Is it Philadelphia or perhaps Baltimore I detect in your speech?" she asked, smiling.

"I'm from Washington."

"Ah, one of Washington's famous black bourgeoisie, no doubt."

I smiled and reached for my purse. With an aversion to her kind of inquisitiveness and condescension, I decided to leave before Nora interviewed me further.

Phil Stein was surveying Antonia's bookshelves, exclaiming from shelf to shelf about her rare volumes. The buzzer sounded again. Jane and Eliot Slater greeted the Steins affectionately and then were introduced to me. At that point, I announced that I had only dropped in for a brief visit with Antonia and that I had to leave to prepare a lecture, an excuse they readily accepted. At the door, I kissed Antonia good-bye. My parting words to her were, "Despite Mariama, I need to claim a part of Ibrahim for my own." I went away thinking of Mariama's generosity and wondering if she were generous enough to share Ibrahim with me.

*Boston*
*May 15, 1965*

*Dearest Ibrahim,*

*Mariama's letter about expecting a child has made me confront what you mean to me. I confess that I have hoped that you would invite me to share your work and your life. Months have passed with little encouragement from you, little evidence of what our time together meant to you. Yet you still hold my attention as the focus of my work and my love. You have engaged me in your life. You have possessed me.*

*I need to know what I mean to you. With an ocean between us and your becoming a father, any prospect of being with you is fading. Still I love you, Ibrahim. And I want to claim you for my own.*

*Ever yours,*
*Sarah*

I read the letter only once, sealed it in an airmail envelope marked "personal," and affixed more than enough postage. I dashed out to the mailbox and dropped the letter in the slot before the courage to file my claim vanished.

# 25

ALTHOUGH I COULD NOT HAVE ANTICIPATED
it, the summer of 1965 was ideal for a course on "Revolution in
the Francophone and Anglophone African Novel." Journalists,
activists, and politicians were forecasting a long, hot summer.
Lyndon Johnson's domestic "war on poverty" appeared to be
ending in the surrender of impoverished, defeated women, men,
and children throughout the nation. The war against distressed,
war-weary women, men, and children in Vietnam had become
demoralizing and embarrassing. Annihilation and assassination,
reform and revolution were the themes of books, conferences,
television programs, university courses, and cafeteria discussions. University towns were centers of political activity.
Leaflets printed in Berkeley were distributed in Ann Arbor,
Madison, Cambridge, and Boston within hours. At Boston
University's plaza, there were picket lines, placards, and speakers enlisting support for demonstrations, collecting signatures
for petitions, selling buttons and bumper stickers for important
causes.

The registrar's staff, projecting an enrollment of approxi-
mately twenty students for the course, was shocked and sheep-
ish (I had told them I expected a large enrollment) when 174
students arrived for the first lecture, at a classroom with seating
for twenty-eight. After an hour of bedlam, we were shifted to a
lecture hall with ample seating. My practice was to prepare for
every lecture as if it were a revolutionary act. The students'
interest and intensity matched my own, and I made sure they
were never disappointed. After each class clusters of students,

buzzing with comments and afterthoughts, surrounded me. Two or three typically followed me to my office and invited me to a coffee shop where I enjoyed expanding on the lecture and rehearsing material for lectures to follow. The success of the course, Antonia pointed out, "guarantees you security in the university—even if that doesn't matter to you."

Although preoccupied with the course, conferences with students, and protest politics, still I found time to brood about Ibrahim's reaction to my letter. At night, I lay awake imagining his response. Finally, his letter arrived.

> *Bamako*
> *29.7.65*
>
> *My dear, dear Sarah,*
> *Your letter was forwarded to me in Togo and from there to Mali where, at last, it found me. And so the delay. So bold a letter invites a bold reply. Would that the situation permitted my declaring my sentiments. Indeed, your revelation has deranged me. I cannot say that it was unwelcomed or unwanted. I cherish the notion that you, a gifted, young, beautiful woman find me lovable. Could it be only my books and films that you love?*
> *If ever there is an episode when we can test whether it is the reputation or the reality that intrigues you, let us test it. For my part, the reality of you is endlessly intriguing. At the first chance to demonstrate that the fascination is mutual, please come and be with me and let me show you.*
> *Your own,*
> *Ibrahim*

Finally! In his own inimitable style, eloquent French, and graceful calligraphic handwriting, I had proof that my fascination with him was reciprocated. I called Joan and read my translation of the letter to her. Showing it to Antonia was a mistake. She said it was merely the kind of romantic lyricism that literary men practice in their correspondence. Still I cherished it. His words heightened my enticement.

The summer school term over, I decided to join my parents at a Chesapeake Bay cottage they had rented. As a child, I had spent carefree summer days building sand castles with other girls whose parents had sacrificed some essentials for the luxury of a few weeks at Highland Beach. Mom and Dad were happy that I wanted to vacation with them. Each morning Dad proposed a walk along the beach. Preferring another hour in bed, Mom invariably refused to join us. So Dad and I went alone, as we had when I was a little girl. In the silence of our morning walks my thoughts stretched to the realm of Ibrahim and Mariama, spanning the nautical miles between Chesapeake Bay and Cap Vert. Imagining him fondling her pregnant abdomen, kissing her, having intercourse with her—imagining their intimacy took me into the torture chamber of my heart.

"You seem deep in thought. What are you thinking 'bout, Sarah?"

"Family life" or "old friends" or "African households," I replied evasively.

"Well, if you want to talk about it, I'm here to listen," he said.

Every evening, Dad and I went to the hotel bar where to friends and acquaintances he introduced me—his daughter, Dr. Stewart—and listed my degrees, awards, and other accomplishments with palpable pride. Afterward, we sat in silence over our nightcaps—cognac for me, bourbon for Dad, who was there to listen.

Mom arranged an evening of bridge to which she invited the five families with "bachelor sons" whose credentials were suitable.

"A different hairstyle would improve your appearance and your chances of attracting a new man," Mom suggested. I shrugged, shaking my head and my braids vigorously. She no longer seemed disturbed by my resistance; indeed, she seemed resigned to the point of acceptance.

The bridge party guests all knew one another. As they arrived, they resumed conversations begun at the beach earlier in the day. They talked about the rioting in the Watts area of Los Angeles, reports of white backlash, and prospects for the civil rights movement.

One of the eligible prospects asked, "How did you like Africa?" I said that I was only in Senegal and described some scenes I had observed. He turned to Dad and asked what he thought of my "African adventure." Dad said, "It's in her genes," and related Uncle George's adventure in Dakar. Someone asked me about Senegal's politics. In response, I delivered a lively overview of Senegal's colonial past and post-Independence political climate to a party of unconcerned, uninterested individuals who had come only for bridge and bourbon. My lecture did not engage them in the least.

With two card tables in the living room and two on the lantern-lit cottage porch, partners distributed themselves and began their respective games. Between analyses of hands—whether one should have opened with three clubs or ruffed high or led with a trump—I overheard the pointed comments of Mom's friends.

"She looks like a Medusa with all those plaits," clucked one matron to another.

"Does she always wear that type of costume? Is it a tribal dress?"

"African braids and that batiked gown are supposed to make her look revolutionary," said another.

"I understand she'd rather play chess than bridge."

"She's too bookish for my boy."

"And too highfalutin for her own good."

"But isn't she beautiful? She's dark—got her father's color—but she's a beauty."

Their sons would not be encouraged to court me by those conventional mothers. I wasn't the daughter-in-law of their dreams. I was not at all suitable for a doctor from Baltimore, an Annapolis pharmacist, or two lawyers and a dentist from Washington.

The morning after the bridge party, Mom and I talked above the clatter of our cleaning up. She said, "I must admit that those young men were something of a disappointment. They talked about the civil rights movement, but they don't know any more than I do about it, which is what I read in the papers. Now Lincoln, if he'd been here, would have had first-hand reports of sit-ins and demonstrations. And you'd think that educated people would be more curious about Africa and African independence. I must say, you've helped educate your father and me on the subject. And last night, you tried to give them a geography lesson and a history lesson. You're a born teacher, Sarah. But it's a pity they weren't really listening."

I was surprised that my mother hadn't jumped to the defense of her guests. "Mom, do you know how much that means to me? That you care about my interest in Senegal means more than I can say. I want to share my passion for . . ." I hesitated before adding, "for Senegal with you."

"Of course I care about you and your interest in Africa. But I have to be honest with you and tell you that we're still worried about you and that Mr. Mangane. We don't want you mixed up in an affair with a married man, and a married African man at that. And we certainly don't want you living over there. We genuinely care about your happiness and what's best for you."

"Mom, I care about my happiness, too, and by now I know what's best for me." I spoke to her in my woman's voice, not my girl's voice. She recognized the difference.

# 26

IN LATE AUGUST, I WENT BACK TO BOSTON TO resume my routine of research and writing. The day after my return, I received a cable from Ibrahim:

SARAH: COME IMMEDIATELY. PREGNANCY COMPLICATED. MARIAMA'S CONDITION SERIOUS. I NEED YOU HERE.
                              LOVE, IBRAHIM

Despite the curtness of Ibrahim's message, despite my ambivalence, despite all the unknowns in the situation, I knew immediately that I would go to Dakar. I recalled Mariama's attempts to console me when I discovered I was pregnant. I would go to comfort her. And that Ibrahim had said that he needed me aroused fantasies of comforting him, too. With those fantasies came a surge of guilt about my real motives. But yes, yes, I would go. I decided to suspend further analysis and to organize an orderly departure. I inquired about flights to Dakar and quickly made a reservation.

"One way or round trip?" the travel agent asked.

"One way, please." My passport was valid. I would need a tourist visa. The agent said, because it was an emergency, I could obtain a visa in forty-eight hours and soon be on my way to Dakar. "You may need inoculations," he advised. I winced as I recalled the recommended shots—cholera, yellow fever, typhoid, typhus. When I decided not to bother with inoculations, I realized that indeed I was relocating, not merely going for a visit. I had interpreted Ibrahim's cable—his summons—as an invitation to return to Dakar and remain there.

I telephoned Antonia. "Antonia, I am moving to Dakar. Whom should I inform in the university?"

"Begin at the beginning. Tell me just what has happened."

"Let me read Ibrahim's cable to you." Breathlessly, I raced through the message.

After a long pause, Antonia said, "Come over here immediately. We need to talk face-to-face about this."

I took a taxi to Antonia's place. In a burgundy velour dressing gown and velvet slippers, she was at the door when I arrived. She had brewed a pot of tea and was prepared with a formula for my situation.

"If I were you, I wouldn't just go. I'd telephone, send a cable, ask him for more information about the circumstances. But I definitely wouldn't go over there now. September is just a few days away and classes will be starting. You're committed to teaching a full course load. Leaving at this stage would wreck your career. Go later—perhaps during the Christmas vacation. Then you may see him and his situation in an altogether different light. Remember that when you were there before, you were a student, engrossed in his works. Now you're more mature, you're a better judge of character, and you have an academic career."

"A life with Ibrahim Mangane is the only career I'm planning at the moment. If I don't move, and move toward it now, I will next year, or the year after. It's simply inevitable. I'm going to live in Dakar. It is as if Dakar were in my astrological chart. It has become more than a destination; it is my destiny. I'm going now that Ibrahim at last has asked me."

"He hasn't asked you to move there. He's only asked you to come in an emergency. Are you afraid that you may not be asked again? If you don't go now, are you afraid of not hearing from him again?"

"Perhaps. But I know this isn't just a cry for help in an emergency. It's a cry for love from a man who needs me. And I need him. I've a reservation on a flight that leaves on Friday evening. I intend to resign from the university."

"Oh, whatever you do, don't resign! If you must go, request a leave of absence for a semester. Write a letter to the dean. You can honestly say that there is a crisis in Mangane's life and that you have to obtain documents from him before they're confiscated. Get someone at the American Embassy in Dakar to write to the dean on your behalf. It should appear to be a professional mission, not merely a personal matter."

"I am moving to Dakar," I said firmly.

"My dear, you must be practical. You know you shouldn't move abroad precipitously," she said sounding exasperated. "Perhaps you should go, see them, find out what his intentions are regarding his family and you. Then return, carry out your teaching duties, and finish your book about him. He needs to have that book published more than he needs you. And for your sake, you should complete it and get it published. You have a great deal invested in that book project. Protect your investment," pleaded Antonia.

"Look, I know you think I don't understand what I'm giving up, but, believe me, I do. I am drawn to Ibrahim and to Senegal in a way I cannot resist. You may not be able to understand it, but I know it feels right. In any case, the practical thing to do is to complete the manuscript in Dakar and have it published simultaneously here and in Senegal."

"You think you're going to arrive in Dakar entitled to a place in the world of Ibrahim Mangane? That sort of thing happens only in European fairy tales, dear, and not in African fairy tales. Leave if you must—but leave doors open so you can return. And whatever you do, don't resign from the university."

I thanked Antonia for her advice, embraced her affectionately, and returned to my apartment as determined as before to go ahead with my plans. I drafted a letter of resignation to the dean with a copy to my department chairman.

*August 27, 1965*

*Dear Dean Northcross:*
*I have been invited to pursue important work in*
*Senegal where, as you know, I studied with Ibrahim*

*Mangane a few years ago. I wish to resign from the*
*university as of this date in order to move to Senegal and*
*assume my new responsibilities.*

*In view of the interest in my field as indicated by class*
*enrollments, I hope you will find a replacement in the near*
*future. I regret the timing of my resignation; however, I*
*trust you will understand.*

*Sincerely,*
*Sarah M. Stewart, Ph.D.*

At the mailbox with the letter, I paused and waited for a rush
of misgivings. None surfaced. I mailed it.

Laura Livingston, a graduate student, had inquired about
vacancies in my apartment building. When I called and offered
her my apartment with its coral walls and all my furnishings,
Laura was ecstatic. She and her scholarly taxi driver companion,
Ben Weinstock, came over right away and helped me. We sorted
and packed books, papers, records, clothing, jewelry, and other
possessions. There was a colorful heap of woolen caps, mittens,
sweaters, parkas, and boots—clothing I wouldn't need in Dakar,
items to offer friends or to discard. They would ship books and
records to me later. Franco Verdi bought my Volkswagen. I canceled newspaper and journal subscriptions, paid all my bills,
withdrew my savings, and closed my bank accounts. I filled out
a change of address card at the post office, leaving Ibrahim's
post office box number in Dakar as my forwarding address. I
cabled Ibrahim the date and arrival time of my Air France flight.
With the decision made, details dealt with, and the cable dispatched, I then had only to inform my parents. It was late afternoon when I telephoned.

My mother answered the phone. "Hello, Mom. I have wonderful news. I'm leaving for Dakar tomorrow."

"Oh? Dakar? When are you going to be back?"

"I'm not certain of when I'll return. I may be there for a long
time. I am going to work there, live there."

"Live there? Where? What kind of work is there for you in
Dakar?"

"I expect that I'll be able to get a job at the university. I can teach English if nothing else."

"Why are you going if you don't have a job there?"

"Well, I don't have a job, but I have a role, a mission."

"A mission? It's not the kind of missionary work I'm used to hearing about. I know what you're going for. How long have you been planning this?"

"Mom, honestly, it's a very recent decision."

"Did you know that you were going the whole time you were with us at the beach?"

"No, it wasn't until after vacation that I received a cable inviting me to come and—"

"Oh, Lord, from that writer! Don't tell me you're going because of that writer! You're bent on breaking up that marriage, aren't you? Listen, for God's sake. You've always been strong-willed, determined to have your way, to get what you want. And up to now, I've admired that quality in you—even when I didn't agree with you. But now you're going too far. You don't like to hear my advice, and you'll probably just ignore it, but if I didn't tell you what I think, I'd be less than a mother to you. Sarah, please don't go. Don't meddle in that marriage. You'll get over there and find yourself in a lot of trouble. Don't do something that you'll regret."

"Mom, I understand what you're saying and it's good advice. If I were in your position, I would probably tell my daughter just what you are telling me."

"All I'm asking is that you take a little time to think about it. Talk to your university pastor and to your friend, Antonia. Ask their opinions. Your father's out, but the second he gets back, I'll have him call you. Talk it over with him. You didn't really say you're going tomorrow?"

"Yes, tomorrow."

"So you've made all the arrangements and your bags are probably all packed. You're not asking us, you're just telling us. You're going to Dakar and you're going tomorrow. Well!" she sighed.

"Mom, please just accept that I'm going and let me give you a mailing address."

"We'll call you, Sarah, early this evening—as soon as your father comes home. We'll get all the details then. I need to let this news sink in, to talk it over with your father, and you need to talk with him, too. Promise you'll be at home? We'll be able to reach you?"

"Yes, I'll be here, packing and waiting for your call. Bye, Mom."

"Good-bye and God help you, Sarah."

When I finished packing, I checked and double-checked drawers and shelves. There were notes to write, utilities to have disconnected, and the other chores of dismantling an apartment and moving on. I telephoned Joan, who promised to visit once I was settled, and I promised to write in the meantime. A teary Antonia lingered on the line repeating a mixture of warnings and good wishes. Finally, Dad called. "Well, I understand you're going to Dakar, girl?"

"Yes, Dad, I am leaving tomorrow."

"You've got a desire for adventure—like your Uncle George. I know there's no stopping people bound for adventures. I just hope this is the right thing for you, that you know what you're doing. I'd really like to know why you have to move to Dakar."

"Why? It's a matter of commitment to my work," I told him, only half truthfully. "Ibrahim Mangane's works, as you know, are important to me, too. And I'm drawn to the place. I feel clearer about who I am in Senegal than I do here. The spirit of the place seems akin to my spirit. I am beyond wanting to go, I must go."

"You know yourself, what you're capable of. Go ahead, go with our blessings and best wishes. But go only for a couple of months. And then come back and look at the situation from a distance. Come home, spend Christmas with us, and look at the whole picture from here, from our angle."

I didn't promise to come home for Christmas. Instead, I said, "Perhaps you'll come to visit me there. Come and see the Dakar of Uncle George's story and search for my *sosie*."

"Well, keep in close touch with us. Let us know if you need money or anything else. And take good care of yourself." I gave Dad Ibrahim's address and telephone number, and then asked to speak to Mom. Her voice was tired and withdrawn. She didn't want to prolong the conversation this time. And so I merely said, "I'll write often. I'll miss you."

For them, I suppose my leaving for a life abroad was proof that our relationship had failed. An only child, I knew that my parents felt I was abandoning them. Amid baggage and boxes, I moped. I tried to chant, but I couldn't recall the psalm; the words were jumbled. I began humming and then singing the spiritual, "Sometimes I Feel Like a Motherless Child."

I wanted to sleep through the night and into the next afternoon, sleep until it was time to go. Instead, I spent that night awake in my Boston bed anxiously imagining what might happen in Dakar. I envisioned troublesome possibilities: Ibrahim would ignore me; an angry, jealous Mariama would turn against me; their friends and family would despise me. In the early morning light, I got up and made my final preparations for leaving. I put on the beige batik boubou I had bought in Dakar. I would return in Senegalese dress, a sign of my determination to become Senegalese.

Several times I checked the contents of my purse to be reassured by the sight of my ticket and passport. I sat by the door with my bags, awaiting Laura and Ben, who eventually arrived and took me in Ben's taxi to Logan Airport. Before long, I was on a plane and en route to Dakar.

# 27

CAP VERT, THE FINGER-SHAPED PENINSULA OF Senegal that stretches into the Atlantic, beckoned again. I peered through the window of the plane as it descended over the edge of the ocean toward the landing strip. And the words came:

"*I will cast mine eyes upon the ocean from whence cometh my help. My help cometh from Senegal, which is heaven and earth.*"

The steward, over the speaker system, welcomed passengers to Dakar and wished us pleasant sojourns.

Dakar! The nausea of nervousness filled my throat. Panic-stricken, I rippled with tremors. I reached into the seat pocket for an airsickness bag. Only then did I know that I was not entirely prepared for the destiny I was seeking.

My fingers trembled as I took my compact from my purse, powdered my brow, and brushed my cheeks with a rosy blush. Opening my flask of Channel No. 22, I nervously scented myself behind the ears, and I tried to arrange a smile of confidence, assume a posture of composure.

The choice, after all, was mine. I had not taken the advice of others. I had chosen to move to Dakar. But I wasn't quite ready to be here. What was expected of me? What did I expect? I wondered about Mariama's condition and Ibrahim's mood. I whispered, "Please, Ibrahim, be ready for me. Be at the airport to greet me."

I steadied myself before walking down the aisle and stepping from the plane. Once I was on the ground, the warm sunshine felt welcoming. I hesitated at the terminal entrance and surveyed the throng of passengers and porters, relatives, friends, taxi drivers, vendors, and airport hustlers. Searching for Ibrahim, I scanned the crowd.

Just at that moment, I felt his touch, his hands on my shoulders. He turned me toward him, looked with sorrowful eyes into my eyes, and kissed me—four times—once and once again on both cheeks.

"You have come. I did not invent the cabled message. Thank you for coming immediately."

"Ibrahim." First with the satisfaction of seeing him, then, "Ibrahim!" with alarm about his appearance, I spoke his name. Face drawn taut, the whites of his eyes laced with bloody veins, the strain of his ordeal was evident.

"This way, through the entrance for dignitaries," he said. "I told the chief customs officer that there was some urgency. He will stamp your passport and clear your baggage, and then Mamadou will collect it later and take it to the hotel where I made a reservation for you. The house is not—well, you will be more comfortable at a hotel for now. Come, we must hurry to the hospital."

There was a rapid exchange with the customs officer who stamped my passport and swiftly, with a well-practiced hand, pocketed the franc note that Ibrahim gave him. We were on our way to the car where Mamadou was waiting with the motor running.

"Good day, Madame. Welcome. Now we return to the hospital, Monsieur?"

"Yes, as quickly as possible." Seated with me in the backseat of a new Citroën sedan, Ibrahim stretched his arm along the back of the seat and turned to me. "We drove here directly from the hospital. Mariama is gravely ill. She is only occasionally conscious. She asked that I have you come. Three times she has said that there is something she must tell Sarah. I asked her what it is. She said, 'I must tell Sarah myself.' Her sister believes that when Mariama speaks to you, she then will begin to recover. I hope your presence will revive her."

"Oh, Ibrahim, I'm truly sorry she is ill." Compassion had triumphed over passion. "The baby—what of the baby?"

"He is going to be fine. He is small—two kilos—but vigor-

ous. He arrived early, by six weeks. A wet nurse is feeding him.
She says he has a strong spirit. He nurses avidly, and his prognosis is good," Ibrahim said confidently. He exhaled the rich
aroma of his pipe tobacco and I took a deep breath to inhale it.
"He will need to be strong," he said. "He has incurred the wrath
of Mariama's relatives already. They have accused the little one
of nearly costing his mother her life. If she lives, they will forgive him. In any case, they will forgive a boy."

"Tell me what happened. What went wrong?"

"Mariama, in the fourth or fifth month, had some swelling in
her feet and ankles, then in her arms and legs. It was edema, not
uncommon in pregnancy," he said authoritatively. "It was not
diminished markedly by medication. Toward the end of the
sixth month, she began bleeding. 'A bad sign,' the doctor said.
Since then, things have been at a standstill. It has been almost
impossible for me to work for three months. When labor began,
we took her to the hospital, where they detected an infection—
toxemia. Immediately after the delivery, she fell unconscious
and has been declining ever since."

Ibrahim's mustache and the corners of his beautiful mouth
were turned down, his brow furrowed with new lines, and
under his eyes were wrinkles that I did not remember. I wanted
to touch every furrow, kiss every wrinkle, but I sat motionless,
listening intently.

"She has received the best attention. Dr. Diouf—you remember seeing him—has been at her side. He summoned a specialist
from Abidjan, Dr. Patrice Sylla. They have tried everything.
They admitted a village medicine man sent by Kaya, Mariama's
sister. Her aunts and cousins with their herbs and fetishes are
with her, humming their incantations." His shrug suggested that
their performance was in vain.

"Everyone knows what the baby means to Mariama, and no
one better than I. She assumed my ego was damaged by child-
lessness, that it reflected unfavorably on my virility. But that's
another matter. In any case, she tried, we tried, and here we are,
in the midst of a crisis." With the back of his hand, he wiped
tears from his eyes.

Feeling overwhelmed by his sorrow and my own anxiety about my role in this crisis, I was searching for ideas about how I might be useful. And so I asked, "What can I do that will be of help?"

Ibrahim said, "Your being here seems essential to my sanity. I have been terribly distraught recently. Events have been set in motion that I cannot control. I have had to abandon my work. And when I cannot work, I feel life is hardly worth living."

So, he had summoned me, I thought, not merely to witness a moment of crisis in Mariama's life. It was also a crucial moment for him, his work, and his future. Was my presence required to chronicle the nature of an upheaval in his life and an interruption in his work? I began to have misgivings about my interpretation of his cabled message and my decision to move to Senegal.

As if he sensed my doubts and confusion, he said, "You have a unique role in our lives. For Mariama, you are the one person who might write about her contribution to my work. She mentioned, more than once, that you had inquired about her life—her biography—which pleased her enormously. And, to be sure, my indebtedness to you already seems immeasurable. We need you here. I am only sorry that we waited until now." With tears creeping down his long, gaunt cheeks, he said, "With an infant in my life, however, I must summon some enthusiasm for a new beginning."

I squeezed his hand and simply said, "You're right," while pondering how I would embark on my new venture. At that moment, Mamadou swerved around a corner and stopped the car at the gate of the hospital.

Along the sidewalk and flanking the hospital gate were stands heaped with fruits—oranges, mangoes, peaches—and carts with grains and nuts. There were vendors selling flowers, gnarled roots, herbs, powders, and fetishes—contorted dolls, snakeskins, horsehair whisks, and zebra hides. A cloud of pungent odors hung in the sultry air.

Ignoring the vendors' cries, Ibrahim and I hurried past the

guard at the gate and up the steps into the gloom of the hospital. Beyond the foyer, we turned right onto a dimly lit corridor with gray-green walls. Efficient-looking nurses and nuns, walking even faster than we were, passed us in both directions. None of them spoke.

"Here come Diouf and Sylla," said Ibrahim. The doctors' steps slowed and stopped as we approached.

Diouf shook my hand, reached for Ibrahim's, and said, "The inevitable has happened. Mariama died fifteen minutes ago quietly, without regaining consciousness. Her sister, her aunts, and the other women were with her."

Ibrahim's shoulders slumped, his face sagged. Suddenly, he looked ten years older. Although he must have anticipated her death, he obviously was stunned. Diouf took his arm and led him along the corridor. Dr. Sylla walked in silence with me. We stopped at a room where a cluster of women—each consoling the other—was gathered.

On the bed in the darkened room lay a form covered with a sheet from head to toe. Huddled around her bed were a dozen women lost in lamentation. Upon noticing us, one of them hushed their moaning. They looked up and turned their eyes toward us. The mournful eyes of one of the younger women were fixed on me. Her expression of instant recognition told me that she, too, was struck by our mutual resemblance. As the women shuffled out of the room, she stopped before me, reached for my right hand, and placed in my palm the okra-shaped gold pendant on the gold chain that Mariama had worn constantly. "Mariama said you must have this," she whispered, then joined the other women who lingered just outside the room. The pendant, I recalled, was Ibrahim's wedding gift to Mariama.

Dr. Diouf drew back the sheet. Mariama's cheeks were bloated. Her aubergine face was an ashen grayish purple. Lips that liked to smile were stretched wide open for her last breath.

Ibrahim bent his head toward his upturned palms. In the deathly stillness, his Wolof utterances reverberated about the grim, spare room. I stood behind him. I was shocked by the sight of her body. I had never before seen someone who had just surrendered to death. I felt fearful, guilty, helpless, and strange, a stranger in extreme circumstances and in a foreign place. I clasped my hands in a gesture of prayer and said my psalm for myself. It was too late to pray for Mariama.

# 28

OURNING FOR MARIAMA LASTED EIGHT days. Mamadou had arranged accommodations and prepared food for the days of mourning. Ibrahim told me that the most sacred times were the prayers for the dead on the third day and the eighth day. After prayers on the eighth day, the mourners leave the house of the dead and return to their towns and villages. A few would come for rites for Mariama on the fortieth day.

The flock of wounded egrets—Mariama's aunts, nieces, sisters-in-law, and cousins, the women who had been in the hospital room—had changed their plumage for the funeral. Inside the compound, with sharper claws and curved beaks, they spread their wings and became vultures picking at the remnants of her life. One said that she had been promised Mariama's earrings, another demanded her amber beads; others wanted her boubous, bolts of uncut cloth, underwear, and shoes. They searched for Mariama's gold bracelets and rings which Ibrahim had given to her sister, Kaya.

When the pandemonium of their morose plunder subsided, Ibrahim announced it was necessary to arrange a naming ceremony for the boy, who was then a week old. Finally, "the baby," "the boy," "the new one" would be given a name. Ibrahim's eldest brother, Amadon, said that Anna, the younger of his wives, would nurse and care for the baby for a while. Their child—a girl—had been weaned recently. Anna, whose breasts were bulging with milk, said that she would enjoy caring for a boy.

"And what will he be named?" I asked.

Ibrahim and Amadon exchanged glances. "We have decided he is an Ousmane," said Ibrahim. "We had a great-uncle Ousmane. We admired him very much. He was intelligent, idealistic, and politically ambitious."

"He was also defiant and crafty," added Amadon.

"What was his work? What did he do?" I asked.

Ibrahim said, "He was a farmer and a village leader. We don't know what he might have done. He died at an early age—before his time. He was killed in an accident while on a political mission—a visit related to a tribal feud. He might have become one of our great heroes. He had enormous potential—like this boy."

On the following morning, an imam came to rehearse the ritual of the naming ceremony. He embraced Ibrahim and bowed in my direction. Amadon and Anna arrived with the baby. Later in the day, a host of relatives and friends surged into the courtyard. Dr. Diouf and his wife were in the throng.

The imam intoned the opening prayers in Wolof and Arabic. Although I did not understand a word he uttered, I understood the meaning of his gestures and his anointing the baby. Ibrahim, carrying the baby, walked to the center of a circle of men—Ibrahim's brothers and cousins—who skipped, pranced, and cavorted around them before each leapt into the circle, bent over the baby, and whispered into his ear his name: Ousmane. To all gathered, Ibrahim then proclaimed, "The boy is called Ousmane."

Ibrahim was enthralled by the baby, wrapped in a soft white cloth, cradled in his arms. His eyes, filled with adoration and hope, were fixed on the infant. Streams of intense sunlight beamed around them. Immediately overhead, there was clear blue sky; but afar, in the east, there were menacing clouds and the rumble of distant thunder. Later in the day, Anna told me that thunder is an evil omen.

After the ceremony, Amadon spoke to Ibrahim in French, rather than Wolof, presumably so that I would understand, "Reorder your household without delay. Maybe this woman, Sarah, from across the ocean, has come to be your next wife. You are no longer a young gazelle. You must soon find a new savannah for grazing, if your son is to have brothers." Amadon shook with lecherous laughter. Anna blushed. Ibrahim tried to ignore him, and I, pretending I did not understand, looked blankly at them.

During the days of mourning, Ibrahim and others slept on pallets in the courtyard under the stars. I returned to the hotel where I enjoyed some respite from the interminable prayers and monotonous meals. My journal and a few books were my evening companions. In my journal, after the fourth day, I wrote:

> *The strain of being here at this moment has been almost unbearable. Although I have had scarcely an hour of privacy, I have been extremely lonely. Most of the relatives could or did not speak to me. The women glared, the men stared. Only the children were genuinely warm. Ibrahim's friends—even those I had met before—were aloof. My presence may be an embarrassment to Ibrahim. He is distracted and depressed.*
>
> *I wish I felt drawn to the baby. Tiny, frail thing. I am haunted by the dream of harming a baby. I could not touch him; I did not hold him when he was passed around.*

Ibrahim was undemonstrative and reserved throughout the week. Often he slipped into contemplative silence. He hardly noticed me. The watchful eyes of relatives, however, were upon me. Kaya, who spoke only Wolof, guided me through the rites with gestures and signs. Fatou translated from Wolof to French and explained what the rituals symbolized.

At the end of the eighth day, the mourners' exodus began. As I prepared to leave for the hotel, Ibrahim asked me to remain until the others had left. He said good-bye to the last of the departing mourners. At the gate, he lingered with Amadon and Anna, who carried the infant in a layer of cloth on her back. Anna assured Ibrahim that she would visit from time to time with the baby. The gate clanged shut. Ibrahim remained at the gate to watch their van disappear into the ocher dust.

At last, we were alone. It was only then that the strain of the events registered: arriving in Dakar, viewing Mariama's lifeless body, witnessing her funeral, and, for eight days, observing the actions of strangers whose laments were in dialects I could not understand. Watching Ibrahim from the doorway, I stood numb, scarcely able to feel anything. I was certain that I had behaved incorrectly—had said or done the wrong thing at every turn.

Ibrahim called, "Sarah, come sit with me."

My heart ricocheted beneath my breast. As I walked toward him, he reached out, took my hand, and led me into the early evening shadows in the courtyard. The air was still. The gentle waves of ebb tide washed quietly out of the bay. He pointed to a chair where I sat and he placed his chair directly before me. We sat face-to-face, knees touching.

"Mariama recognized that your presence was a positive influence. Your writing about my work made us aware of its importance as literature. She was very happy about that." He withdrew slightly. Our knees no longer touched. He clasped his hands and looked beyond me, over my shoulder, out at the ocean.

"And she understood how your talents complemented hers. When she knew she was dying, she wanted you to be here with me. She wanted you to help me get on with my work." After a protracted pause, he added, "Mariama maintained a certain order in the household to allow me to work. She created a setting for my work, and she herself became part of the setting. She was reliable, loyal, devoted—devoted to me and to our relatives. Then bearing a son became her *raison d'être*. She realized her ambition and it finished her." Ibrahim choked up. Tears welled in his eyes.

"Perhaps she found some solace in knowing that she had given birth to a son," I ventured. I was reaching for the right pitch, for words that would console him.

"Yes, finally, she had a son. She was aware of him. When they tried to have her nurse him, she came out of the coma and was alert for a few minutes. Producing a son—that's what she had lived for. And died for." Sobbing, he covered his face with his hands. Overcome by his mood, I could not contain my tears. He leaned toward me and held my hands. For an hour or more, we sat without words for our sorrow.

The melodic lilt of Mariama's voice, her sprightly welcome, the warm glow of her face reflecting the yellow and orange boubous she wore, her advising and comforting me, her delight in market excursions, the jangle of her bracelets, her footsteps on the gravel in the courtyard, her coaxing the reluctant garden of cacti—my memories of Mariama passed in review. And my mind's ear heard the comforting power of Verdi's *Requiem.*

"You have witnessed some traditional rites, observed our ethnic customs, seen the interior of our family life. You were a paragon of compassion and grace. You earned the respect of the elders."

"And yours, too, I hope. It was difficult sometimes to know what to do, what was appropriate. I felt you were sometimes embarrassed about my being here. You seemed distant, preoccupied—"

"I was preoccupied—what else in the company of death?" he asked in a weary voice. "But I had asked you to come, hadn't I? I wanted you and still want you here—right here," and he pointed to the space between our knees. "You should not feel embarrassed or compromised. It was important to me—and to Mariama—to have you come, to witness the grieving for her. In a few months, you will see the family in a different attitude.

"You belong with the family—and me. It was not accidental that Mariama invited you to stay with us. Fate made this place your destination. I sensed it when we met. There was an air of mystery about your arrival and about you." His mood had changed. He was smiling broadly. "And then your elegance, your exquisite beauty, your intensity, your intelligence entranced us. Enchantress! Conjure woman!" His quiet, throaty laugh followed the accusation.

"It's you, Ibrahim, who entranced me. Someone once said—in fact, it was Lincoln who said that I was possessed by you, that it was a kind of demonic possession."

"He thought you possessed? Well, I want to possess you—to make you mine." He touched the cloth of my boubou, hands on my thighs. I felt feverish. His touch, his warm hands sent heat rippling through me. "I need you at my side. You are my muse. When we worked together, through your eyes I saw characters and scenes from unaccustomed angles. You enlarged my screen, sharpened images, brought ideas into focus. You lit a lantern in my mind." He paused, sighed deeply, and murmured softly, "I was energetic, agile in your presence. Your vitality rekindled my embers. Your beauty made me feel handsome again. Your sensuality aroused mine."

His nose touched mine. His breath was on my lips. His spicy scent enveloped me. Swaying with passion's intoxication, my mouth quivered as I tried to speak. Instead of words, tears came. He kissed the tears from my cheeks. My palms on his chest, I felt his eager breathing.

"Shouldn't I go back to the hotel? Shouldn't you be alone a while?" I whispered.

"No, I need you. I need to feel alive again. Mariama, I believe, would want us to celebrate life." He lifted me to my feet and held me close. Then he slipped his arms inside the wide sleeves of my boubou and embraced me and caressed my breasts. "I have been deadened by all that has happened. Come, please bring me back to life," he begged. Hand in hand, we floated toward the bedroom.

During the days of mourning, the bedroom had been refurbished. One of Mariama's nieces had admired their bed. Ibrahim gave it to her. In its place stood a sumptuous bed with a wooden headboard sculpted by a Gambian carver, who had chiseled in it the shape of a sprawling baobab tree. Covered with an ivory woven cotton spread that had just arrived from Mali, the bed was the centerpiece of the room. A large bronze plaque with musicians had been installed where a framed Korhogo cloth had hung. Across the room, on the opposite wall, a fine Bakuba cloth with a chevron pattern stretched from ceiling to floor. Mariama's goat hair rugs had been replaced by a handsome Berber carpet that Ibrahim favored. A narrow table with a high-

backed chair stood between the windows that framed views of
the starry night sky.

Ibrahim slowly slipped my boubou over my head, and sat for
a while on the edge of the bed, studying my nude body as if I
were à model he would sculpt. I stood before him pulsating
with anticipation.

He slipped off his caftan and, with the slithering artistry of
striptease, he twisted out of his trousers. And there he was. On
the bed, he began kissing my lips, my neck, my shoulders, my
breasts—where he lingered, nuzzling, nursing; he kissed my
abdomen, my navel, and my other lips where he lingered, thrust
his torrid tongue, and extracted love's secretions. When he had
carried me to the edge of ecstasy, he raised my legs and slipped
my ankles onto his shoulders. And slowly, reverently, he
entered me as a worshiper enters a temple. All through that
night of tender passion, we firmly surged, pressed, clasped,
released, tasted, caressed, whispered, shrieked, confessed, for-
gave, vowed, and promised. For once, that night I did not
dream. My dream lay in my arms. My dream, that night, had
come true.

# 29

IN THE WEEKS THAT FOLLOWED THAT DREAM-come-true night, Ibrahim was occupied with the formalities of ritual and transition. During that time, the women of the family assumed I needed company. They arranged excursions to fishing villages, to a village of wood-carvers and weavers, and to the mosque at Ngor. At the end of the day they returned with me to the hotel where I had a room that I scarcely occupied. Nearly every evening, Ibrahim sent for me. No one expressed disapproval about finding me at home with Ibrahim the following day.

The compound bustled with activity. Men came by appointment for brief transactions with Ibrahim. There were messengers with parcels and vendors with merchandise. They greeted me politely—"Good day, Madame. Good afternoon, Madame. Good-bye, Madame." Briskly, they were in and out.

Older women squatted in the shade of the few trees outside the compound to observe the to-and-fro stream of callers. Younger women, accompanied by their children, peered through the grill of the wrought iron gate. Their curiosity was boundless. They had countless questions about my personal history and preferences: Why did I have no brothers or sisters? Why were my toenails polished? Did I like their music, their mangoes, their men? How long did I plan to stay? Was I going to be Monsieur Mangane's wife?

They showered me with a profusion of predictions: Monsieur Mangane would marry me, then take a Senegalese wife; I looked to be the kind that might have only daughters; the food would soon make me fat; the baby boy, when a man, would turn against his father; Monsieur Mangane would become very famous and want a French wife; I would find the weather unbearable and return to America.

Amadon and Anna visited frequently with the baby. Anna unfolded her arms and there he was at the cleavage of her boubou, sucking her breast. Her firm upturned breasts appeared to be a copious source of nourishment; the infant was no longer skinny and wrinkled. His arms and legs had filled out and his eyes were bright. When there was a pause in his suckling, Anna handed him over to me. He felt warm and substantial. Eventually, I was comfortable with him in the curve of my arm, and ruefully amused when he turned toward my lean breasts. Anna looked on with encouragement, as if she were ready to have me assume his care. Ibrahim and Amadon interrupted their prattle to comment on the boy's growth, chuckle, then resume their exchange about family business.

One day Anna asked quietly, "Is it possible to have a wedding in the near future?"

"Why not?" declared Ibrahim. Embracing me, he said, "We have the bride here and an impatient groom. The griots will delight in inventing incantations for this foreign beauty."

"The relatives and friends are ready for a big celebration," said Anna.

"We expect an abundant harvest. Women will make good stews—a feast to remember," said Amadon, licking his lips and rolling his eyes in anticipation.

I was silent. The idea of again being in the midst of another swirl of confusing rites was unsettling. Flushed with anxiety, I sat motionless at the table in the courtyard. Only after Amadon and Anna had left with the baby, I said, "Isn't it too soon to bring the boy to us? And too soon—too soon after mourning—to marry?"

"Too soon? Five months have passed. No, it is not too soon. Indeed, it is nearly too late to wrench my son from Anna's tits. He and she are settling into the arrangement. In a few months, Anna would regard him as her son and want to rear him. It is not at all too soon to bring my son—our son—home." Ibrahim sat down next to me and held my hand. "And as for marriage, you and I are married—privately. The marriage has been accomplished. Only the wedding is belated. You need not concern yourself with arrangements. Amadon and Anna will visit every friend and relation between here and their village, and soon everyone will know when to come, what to bring, what to sing, what to say, what to do. All you need do is to remain beautiful, stately, elegant, alluring—and devoted to me."

"And I need to inform my parents and my friends."

"Inform them? Invite them! Your parents must attend, of course. I'll take care of the airfare and hotel bills. Telephone them at once."

Eager to tell them, I was not mindful of the hour the call would reach them in Washington. Awakened by the ring, Dad sleepily said, "You sound happy. I'm hoping he'll treat you well. Let me put your mother on the line."

"You're getting married to him?"

"Yes, Mom. It's short notice, I know, but Ibrahim and I would like for you and Dad to come for the wedding."

"But you wrote to us about his wife's funeral only a few months ago. I know customs are different there, but shouldn't you wait a tasteful length of time between—"

"At first I thought it too soon, but Ibrahim and others here have convinced me that enough time has passed. This is the time that's been chosen, Mom. Will you come? We will make all the arrangements for you, Ibrahim has offered to take care of your expenses. Please come."

"I'm sure you really want us to be there, and I wish I could say that we'll come. Sarah, as much as we want to be there, it just seems too long and hard a trip. We'd need a lot more time to plan for a trip all the way to Africa. Anyway, I don't understand why you have to rush into this. He's just been widowed and he's got that baby. Sarah, I'm asking you to take your time. Wait a few months and by that time you'll be sure. Then we'll come if you still plan to go ahead with it." Realizing that I would have a wedding that did not include my parents, I ended our conversation with the promise of photographs and a tape of the ceremony.

Within a day or two, all of Dakar knew that a wedding would be celebrated *chez* Mangane. I was reading in the courtyard and basking in the warmth of the midday sun when Mamadou returned after a morning of shopping, giddy with excitement and burdened with bundles. "Madame Sarah, everyone sends greetings to you and Monsieur. In the market, they are buzzing about you. Women asking about you. I tell them you are smart woman, wise woman, you are queenly, like royalty, the way Monsieur is like a chief. Everywhere, they give me something extra today—extra kilos of meal, two copper kettles—though I ask for one. I buy some eggs. I get eggs and she also want me to take an old hen 'so the baby boy have fresh egg every day.' I say Madame Sarah want no hen in the courtyard, in the house, dropping droppings everywhere, and maybe drop one egg a week. It was an old hen. On the road a shepherd is headed this way driving a ram and three ewes—gifts for the house from Monsieur's oldest cousin, the great chief at Touba. Allah be praised."

I, too, was excited, and more than a little apprehensive about everyone's expectations of me. I put aside my book and went inside to run a hot bath, where, for an hour or more, I could contemplate in solitude the days ahead. I would heed Ibrahim's advice—let others make the arrangements. I sat in the steaming tub with my eyes closed.

There were moments when I wished to be whisked, like Dorothy of Kansas, magically out of Dakar on the winds of a tornado and transported to Cambridge to write about Ibrahim. At that moment, my romanticized fantasies about Ibrahim had more allure than the reality of being with him and his omnipresent entourage of relatives, friends and servants. Senegal, however, is not tornado territory, so instead, I trusted *les Alizés,* the gentle breeze from the Atlantic, to blow away my doubts and bring ideal weather for the wedding.

Three weeks later, on a sparkling day with only an occasional wisp of a cloud, the procession of relatives and friends began to arrive for our wedding. They came bearing gifts of grain, calabashes, and cloth; they brought amulets and fetishes of bone, beads, and hair. Three griots with their musical instruments joined the gathering. The night before the ceremonies, the compound had been surrounded by celebrants who danced to the music of bafalons, tambourines, rattles, and drums. Now the fatty smoke of roasting mutton swirled in the morning air, and expectations of the festive day were mounting.

Ibrahim woke me on the morning of our wedding day with what he called his ceremony of kisses, kisses that began at my brow. His lips traversed my face, my neck, my body, lingered here and there, his mustache and beard tickling me. Whatever fantasies of escape I had harbored in the previous days had vanished. Aroused by his sensuality and the prospect of celebrating our love, I was ecstatic.

Mamadou called to us, "Monsieur and Madame, the imam has arrived—the Grand Imam!"

"I suppose we should not keep the Grand Imam waiting," said Ibrahim lightheartedly. He got up, showered quickly, and dressed in a newly tailored white brocade caftan. I took my time, bathing, brushing, anointing, and admiring myself in the mirror, before slipping into a bridal boubou made of the same white brocade as Ibrahim's caftan, my braids swathed in a turban of the same material. Ibrahim, having greeted the Grand Imam, returned to fetch me.

"You are a beautiful bride," said Ibrahim, placing in my hand a thong with a leather pendant encrusted with an engraved gold leaf seal and three cowrie shells. "In our tradition, there is no exchange of rings and kisses. I am giving you this talisman to mark our wedding day. Wear it in remembrance of the day." As Ibrahim draped it around my neck he kissed away my tears of joy. I noticed that he, too, had been moved to tears. "Come," he whispered to me, "they are eager to see the bride."

He led me to the courtyard where the throng greeted us with applause and shouts. Amadon escorted us to rattan thronelike seats. Then the music began. The eldest griot, a countertenor, sang a lengthy meditative memoir about Ibrahim's genealogy.

He was joined by the other griots whose lugubrious hymn to Ousmane brought Mariama's name to the lips of her still heavy-hearted kin. Changing the mood, a band of drummers vigorously rapped, tapped, and thumped rapid rhythms. A griotte—a venerable holy woman—began chanting and dancing. Nearly all the women encircled her and danced to the edge of exhaustion. A harvest feast was spread on the table before us. Gifts were offered with long speeches and embraces. Cables from my parents, Bill Nelson, and others were read. As Ousmane was passed from the arms of one woman to those of another, he was admired and Anna praised for nursing him. Finally, with a strident ululation, the griotte then presented Ousmane to me. Overwhelmed by the solemnity of the moment, I wept as I cradled him in my trembling arms.

And so Ibrahim and I were married with a son, Ousmane.

The arrival of Ousmane would require, Ibrahim said, an increase in domestic staff. He had asked Mamadou's wife, Awa, to move to the compound and assist with the care of Ousmane and other household tasks. She said she would be honored to help us. She assured us that she was a good mother to her three children and turned to Mamadou, who nodded his endorsement. Awa said that their younger children would remain in the village with her mother, since she and Mamadou would have their hands full with the management of the compound, care of Ousmane, and time for their son as well.

Just as wedding arrangements had been made nearly invisibly, plans were being made for the conduct of household affairs. Ibrahim was consulted, to be sure; but my opinion was rarely sought. Initially, I was offended and a trifle paranoid about being overlooked by the domestic retinue. Ibrahim, however, dispelled my concerns, explaining that he was accorded a position of honor in his family because of his relative affluence. It was the duty of family members to facilitate the smooth operation of his household. In exchange, they expected allowances, salaries, tuitions, and gifts for their services. Ibrahim and his trusted accountant nephew handled all the financial transactions. I then realized that the constellation of kin and other parties in our orbit functioned like a royal court. Once it was clear that I was to be essentially free of household maintenance, I accepted my role with grace.

Anna had told Awa that she would come to nurse Ousmane less and less frequently. I learned later that weaning Ousmane had been a topic of vigorous debate among the women. Finally, Awa had been instructed to discuss the matter with me. Showing me a package of baby bottles, she indicated that a daily delivery of milk would begin immediately. We agreed that it would be better now to feed Ousmane by bottle, and Awa offered to tell Anna of the plan. During our conversation, Awa and I laughed about our language difficulties. Being with us, she said, would improve her French; and I told her that I hoped that she would help me with my Wolof. I was pleased by Awa's candor and competent manner, which completely won my confidence.

We began to develop a daily pattern that was shaped primarily by Ibrahim's work schedule, our meal times, and Ousmane's rhythm of sleep and wakefulness. Mornings found Ousmane in the care of Awa and visiting relatives. He was handed over to us during the interval between work and lunch; but often, just before lunch, clasping Ousmane to his chest, Ibrahim would strut around the courtyard and out to the boulders and back, filling his son's ears with stanzas of poems, lines of exquisite prose, and his ambitions for the boy.

On the days when Ibrahim and I went into Dakar to make the rounds of book shops and cafés, I carried Ousmane on my back, wrapped in a *pagne*—a sling of cotton cloth that matched my boubou. I walked proudly with him through the streets and markets, in a cloud of contentment, his skin next to mine, his warm breath on my arm or shoulder. A lively bundle, often he stretched his neck to see what was about, wiggling to free himself of the confining cloth. I adored rambling about with him, exchanging pleasantries with other mothers bearing babies, bundles, and baskets of vegetables, fruits, and flowers. To my surprise, I quickly came to feel that, indeed, I was his mother and he my son. At home at the end of the day, I found very satisfying the tranquillity of napping with Ousmane nestled next to me or merely watching him sleep.

Visitors arrived in the late afternoon and sometimes stayed for dinner: aspiring writers seeking advice, actors with ideas for films, relatives in need of help, and Ibrahim's friends, who dropped by for their typically intense conversations.

Each night, I fell asleep in the arms of my beloved Ibrahim, grateful for a pleasurable day and eager for the next.

# 30

A JUBILANT IBRAHIM CAME HOME ONE AFTER-
noon with news of a proposed international festival that had
provoked excitement among Senegal's intelligentsia, particularly those in the arts. He was ecstatic about the news that
Dakar would be the host city for a World Festival of Negro
Arts. I was excited, too, but I didn't want Ibrahim's exclamations to awaken the baby. "Shhhh! Ousmane is sleeping over
there." Reclining on the divan with a book and monitoring the
baby's fitful breathing, I nodded toward the cushioned basket in
a corner of the great hall.

"Come into the courtyard where I can tell you about the festival," Ibrahim urged. I followed him and then listened as he
paced back and forth in the afternoon sunlight and talked about
plans for the event.

"African, Caribbean, and black American poets, playwrights,
novelists, filmmakers, painters, sculptors, dancers, actors, scholars—all will be invited. Every major African artist will attend.
There'll be a film program—two of my films will be shown.
And I will read from a work-in-progress."

I asked for more details.

"Finally, it is going to happen! We have been trying to organize a black arts festival on African soil for a decade. It is going
to occur here in Dakar in April, and will last three weeks. My
dear, this is the festival the world has been waiting for!"

"Wonderful—but won't it be costly for Senegal?"

"It has the endorsement of the president, Léopold Senghor

himself. Senghor has said that it will require some financial sacrifices. He has convinced the opposition that it is a cultural investment that is essential to development. He has André Malraux's pledge of France's support. Of course, Senghor is delighted that it will be held in Dakar. Artists will come from forty nations—playwrights and actors from Nigeria, Mali, and Jamaica, painters from Ethiopia and Haiti, the great dancers of Brazil, Sierra Leone, Chad, Haiti, and the United States—the Alvin Ailey dancers. The Ellington Band, Miles Davis, and Thelonious Monk will be invited. Poets and novelists from Martinique, Rhodesia, Niger, Ghana, Somalia, and the Americas will read and discuss their works with the audiences. At last, I will meet Aimé Césaire and the American poets, Langston Hughes and Robert Hayden. We are hoping to reach James Baldwin and Leroi Jones, actors Ossie Davis and Ruby Dee, and that grand diva, Leontyne Price. The ideas, energy, the spirit of the arts of the African diaspora assembled in one place—here in Dakar—will be truly phenomenal!"

For the remainder of the afternoon and into the night, we talked about the festival. I had never seen Ibrahim as excited about anything. His exhilaration was contagious. I was tingling at the prospect of meeting literary luminaries, opera stars, actors, dancers. I realized what the festival might mean for Ibrahim's career and mine. For weeks afterward, there were meetings at our house, at the university, in cafés, and government offices to discuss the organization of the event.

Festival planning quickened the pace of our lives. Messengers arrived hourly with proposals for festival events. Ibrahim often wanted to discuss them with me at once. I sat at my desk, trying to review the galley proof of my manuscript. The festival planning was distracting me from my own work: preparing the manuscript for publication. Ibrahim had objected to the title, *Ibrahim Mangane: Master of the Modern Movement.* He protested, " 'Master' is pretentious—even for me—and there is no 'modern movement'—only cyclical reinventions of what others before have proposed. The original title of the dissertation was better. Insist that the publisher change the title," he demanded.

Change the title? Ibrahim's imperiousness about this bothered me. In any case, I wondered if my publisher would consider changing the title at that stage. But I dutifully sent a cable recommending a different title: *Ibrahim Mangane's Radical Imagination,* and requesting a publication date that coincided with the opening of the festival. I had high hopes that the book would draw attention to my credentials and scholarship; and, of course, I also hoped that it would enhance Ibrahim's reputation among Anglophone readers.

In addition to completing the book and festival planning, there was Ibrahim's ever-expanding work—editing, correspondence, translations, and the rest—work he assumed I would continue to do. And there were social obligations to family, friends, and colleagues that claimed more and more of our time. Ibrahim and I had little time for the leisurely cultivation of the conversation of marriage. Even mealtimes became working sessions.

Early one morning while Ibrahim and I were having breakfast, a messenger arrived with an invitation that, despite my being overworked, I did not wish to refuse. It was a letter from U.S. Ambassador Mercer Cook, inviting me to chair the U.S. planning committee for the festival. While it might have been wise for me to have declined, the potential power of the festival-in-the-making was irresistible.

When I talked about it with Ibrahim, I grew enthusiastic about the prospect of organizing events, making arrangements for the writers, musicians, painters from the States, and later getting acquainted with them. Ibrahim, clearly pleased by my decision to take on the assignment, kissed my hand and smiled. There at the breakfast table, I began listing names of people to contact, drafting cables, and planning symposia. I found that having a role to play in the festival gave me new energy.

Delighted by my hearty involvement in my new tasks, Ibrahim observed, "The ambassador certainly has tapped the right person for this assignment. It needs the intelligence of a

superb strategist—and that's you. You could organize a coup,
lead a revolution, save a continent!"

Having completed the revisions in the galleys and returned
them to the publisher, I concentrated on the festival. I had a
desk in an office at the embassy where I worked, with Ousmane
cuddled in the cloth on my back. Senegalese mothers carried
their children everywhere; and so Ousmane often was with me.
The few times I left him at home, I would telephone Mamadou
frequently to inquire about him. Was Ousmane comfortable?
Was he covered with netting to protect him from the flies? What
had he eaten? Had he slept? Had he cried?

I neglected family visits, Ibrahim's correspondence, afternoon teas with women friends, and previews of films with
Ibrahim. Instead, I devoted myself to recruiting volunteers for
various tasks, settling disputes between the Americans' agents and
the festival organizers, and haggling with hotels and airlines.

I sent letters and cables to Antonia urging her to come. I had
remained in contact with her. A cable to her, which I signed as
"Director of the U.S. Planning Committee" for the festival,
elicited her reply. She would come!

I was rarely at home. When I was at home, I was at my desk
or on the telephone with festival business. I felt confident and
indispensable. I found I needed the work to engage my intellect,
my energy, to remind me of the importance of responsibilities
beyond our marriage and home life.

During a dinner that was interrupted by several urgent telephone calls for me, Ibrahim asked in an agitated tone, "What is
the meaning of all this festival business? What will replace it
when it is over? Will Director Mangane return home and find
happiness as a wife and mother again?" I reminded him that he
had encouraged me to become involved.

"Ibrahim, let's deal with those questions when all this is over.
You know how important the festival is. It will internationalize
African art and artists, and increase the world's awareness of
Africa's contributions. You and I need to be identified with this
festival, conspicuously involved in it. For you, it's an opportu-
nity to gain international prominence. And for me, well, it

means a great deal at many levels." I saw that he was pacified, and we finished our dinner without further intrusions.

When the World Festival of Negro Arts opened in Dakar on April 1, 1966, only Léopold Sédar Senghor could have been more delighted than Ibrahim and I. Throughout April, almost daily, there were symposia, public lectures, poetry readings, exhibition openings, theatrical productions, concerts, and dance programs. Ibrahim and I rejoiced when the participants began to arrive. The African diaspora of intellectuals and artists had come to Dakar.

Ethiopian Emperor Haile Selassie gave a reception for the artists. Forty-three nations were represented. The atmosphere was electric. I had the pleasure of welcoming the Alvin Ailey dancers and conductor Leonard de Paur and his chorus. I had several informal chats with Langston Hughes, who reminded me of my father. Antonia arrived on the same flight with Duke Ellington and his band.

I had invited Antonia to stay at our home. She and Ibrahim, like boxers entering the ring, took each other's measure when they met, and they sparred.

"I've been looking forward to meeting Africa's Renaissance man," Antonia said as they shook hands.

"It's a pleasure to meet the doyenne of black American scholarship," he said.

The day before the opening, cartons arrived with eight hundred copies of my book, *Ibrahim Mangane: Renaissance Man and Reformer.* Ibrahim and I were very pleased about the publication, its title, and its timely arrival. It was the centerpiece in a display at the book bazaar in the National Assembly building, where I autographed copies, expressed my thanks to admirers, and concealed my annoyance when asked, "Are you really the girl who wrote this book?"

I had been looking forward to a literary session, introduced by President Senghor, with sociologist St. Clair Drake as the keynote speaker. The subject was the interpretation of "Negritude." Drake characterized Negritude as "a passion for similar types of music, dance, and graphic and plastic art forms . . . a soft and resilient, rather than hard and mechanical, approach to life . . . [and] a deep resentment . . . over subordination to white people during four hundred years of slave trade." To elaborate on Drake's formulation, I raised my hand during the discussion period indicating that I wished to speak. The chairman recognized men in my vicinity of the auditorium; they were called upon and spoke. He overlooked me. Ibrahim, seated beside me, seeing my annoyance and frustration, tried to calm me by saying, "Your comments might have turned that fatuous exchange into a substantive discussion."

In the next session, the debate focused on whether Negritude was "antiracist racism." Again, I raised my hand to indicate that I wanted to comment. Again, men were invited to speak; women—and there were others with hands raised—were overlooked. Ibrahim, aware of my annoyance, suggested that we leave the auditorium.

"It is masculine ignorance and arrogance, Sarah. Try not to take it personally. The chairman ignored all the women who wanted to speak."

"The only women who are recognized in this festival are the dancers and singers, applauded for their sensuality, gyrating hips, and bare breasts. Women with intellectual prowess and scholarly expertise in the arts have not been acknowledged here!" I was enraged.

It was then that I became an observer at the festival, ceased feeling I was a participant. In the news reports on the festival, only men were quoted. After three weeks of neglect, I announced to Antonia, who had traveled all the way from Boston to be ignored in Dakar, and to a cluster of other women from the U.S., the Caribbean, Brazil, and parts of Africa, "The men here have refused to recognize us. Our ideas have not been heard. We'll have to organize an international festival of our own—women writers and scholars of the African diaspora—so that our voices can be heard." Their shouts of agreement echoed in the foyer. We pledged that we would keep in touch and pursue the possibility.

Antonia and I left the festival and spent the afternoon at our home. She preferred to be indoors, and so instead of having tea in the courtyard where Mamadou had set the table, we moved to the cool semidarkness of the great hall.

"Sarah, you shouldn't be surprised to find that we women are on the periphery of this festival," observed Antonia, always pragmatic. "Men only feel secure when they marginalize us. Not even your 'renaissance man and reformer' is attempting to change that."

"Ibrahim will probably make a statement about it later and register his opposition," I said.

"You needn't be defensive. I only meant that Ibrahim Mangane is behaving like all the others: privately outraged, but publicly silent. What matters to me is how you are faring with him."

"How do I appear to be faring?"

"On the surface, I admit your life seems idyllic. You look wonderful, well-cared for, more beautiful than ever. You have a spectacular home, servants—an enviable lifestyle. You're surrounded by beautiful things." From the divan where she sat, she viewed the masks and musical instruments on the walls. "You're obviously fond of your stepson, and Ibrahim appears to be devoted to you—I hope as devoted to you as you are to him. Still one wonders."

"What are you wondering, Antonia?" I ventured.

"You're devoted to each other's ideas. You're fascinated by what his mind does for yours and vice versa, but do you—can you—how can you love him? The cultural distance, the age difference must make it—"

"Make him all the more interesting and appealing. I love Ibrahim."

"And am I to believe you're truly happy here? Are you finding this domestic stuff satisfying? Don't you sometimes miss the gratification of giving a good lecture, having students gather around you—wanting to hear more? Don't you regret that you've given up teaching?"

"I have no regrets about having left Boston University— none. But I sometimes wish I were a lecturer at the University of Dakar. I've made several inquires and each time I've been told that what I can offer on West African literature is taught best by West Africans. That's been a real disappointment. I can't persuade them that my perspective on their literature might expand the range of interpretation and inject new theoretical approaches. I feel my training and expertise are being wasted."

"It's a terrible waste. So your intellectual base is at home. Are you happy about that?"

"Yes, I'm very happy. Ibrahim's exceeded my expectations as a husband who's occupied with dozens of commitments and responsibilities elsewhere—to his publishers, his film collaborators, his public, his relatives. Despite all the demands on him, I feel I'm at the center of his life. It's all very satisfying." I felt that what I told Antonia was genuine. Still she was skeptical.

"You sound convincing, but somehow I'm not entirely convinced. For your sake, I hope it's true. And you may not miss BU, but I certainly miss you. Your vitality and your visits enlivened my corner of the university. No one has replaced you in my life."

"Your coaching me and encouraging me to build a career at BU—all your efforts meant a great deal to me. Your advice was—"

"Disregarded," she finished the statement with her sardonic smile. "But now I understand the allure of this place. It's more than a romantic attraction to the man—it's his realm that has charmed you."

Antonia's questions had made me uneasy. Even her saying that she finally understood didn't reassure me. Her doubts about my situation had provoked my own. I wondered about the alternatives. What if I had remained at Boston University where I probably would have been promoted and tenured? Would I have had another chance for marriage and a family? What if I hadn't left Lincoln for three months in Senegal— would we still be married? I had chosen a complex, indirect route rather than the straight and narrow path Antonia had prescribed for me. And although I didn't know where it would lead, I was certain that it would continue to take unexpected turns through challenging terrain. And I was quite certain that I had made the more intriguing, if not more practical, choice.

Antonia did not witness Ibrahim's finest hours during her visit. He seemed jealous of her interest in me. He thought that it went beyond an interest in my intellectual life. He insisted that she had a crush on me, and I insisted that there had never been the suggestion of lesbian affection in our relationship. He accused me of being naive.

And Ibrahim did not see Antonia at her best either. She was cautious, restrained, and clearly uncomfortable around him. She observed my exchanges with Ibrahim with the eye of a warden on duty during a conjugal visit. Their distrust of each other's motives was palpable. And that neither trusted my judgment about the other was painful. When I repeated that I found my circumstances very satisfying, she said I had a remarkable capacity for self-deception. Her skepticism about my well-being persisted. Her doubts had unleashed my own about the content of my life.

During the final days of the festival, prizes were awarded. Ibrahim received three: the award for the World's Best Film on African and Afro-American Subjects; Best African Film; and the prize to the Premier African Novelist. He was also mentioned as the subject of a significant biography, although I was not cited as its author.

Reporters surrounded us. Photographers' bulbs flashed. Recent acquaintances embraced Ibrahim as if they were old friends. There were interviews with reporters from Africa, Europe, and the Americas. Ibrahim and I were interviewed by the correspondent from *Paris Match*.

**Paris Match:** Are your novels and films for Africans or for Europeans and Americans?
**Ibrahim Mangane:** *They are for audiences that are interested in exploring the human condition. I have used the landscape and peoples of West Africa in several works because of the rich variety they display in the utilization of their talents and environmental circumstances. From my perspective, landscapes that are*

*familiar, faces and lifestyles that are familiar, enhance the fidelity of the novels and films. I expect African readers and viewers to find them familiar and, I trust, authentic. I expect some Europeans and Americans find the human aspects familiar—that they see beyond skin color, physiognomy, style of dress. I hope they, too, see themselves and their situations from a new point of view.*

**P.M.:** How will the independence of African nations affect the form and content of the African novel?

**I.M.:** *The national, regional, and ethnic character of fiction should become more distinct. You will begin to recognize the Senegalese novel, the Nigerian novel, the Sudanese novel, the Kenyan novel, and so on. You do not speak of the European novel, do you? You say the French novel, or English, or Russian, or Italian.*

**P.M.:** Are there common themes in fiction by Africans and Afro-Americans that link them?

**I.M.:** *The common element is the expression of Negritude. Colonial conditions on both continents contributed to the impulse to reaffirm and reinforce African cultural and conceptual material. Another common theme is the triumph of African and black American humanism over oppression, technology, and militarism.*

**P.M.:** Has the festival been a success in terms of bringing together Africans and Afro-Americans?

**I.M.:** *The festival has provided a forum for an extraordinary dialogue between African and black American men. For the women, however, it was less successful.*

**P.M.:** Madame Mangane, do you agree with your husband's assessment of the position of women in the festival?

**Sarah Mangane:** *The voices and opinions of women have been suppressed. Most of the women have not been permitted to speak. Our perspectives have been underrepresented.*

*There are several distinguished women novelists, poets, playwrights, essayists, and scholars at the festival. Their statements would have enlarged the scope of discussions. African and Afro-American women have intellectual perspectives determined by gender, race, and social expectations. We demonstrate our history and experience of oppression and struggle, resistance and rebellion, in terms that complement the spirit and force of our male counterparts. We want equal time, equal space, in festivals, colloquia, symposia. We may need to create festivals expressly for African women—Afro-American, Afro-Caribbean, Afro-Brazilian—to amplify the voices and ideas of women of the African diaspora.*

The interview was published on the closing day of the festival. Many women sought me out to express their agreement and admiration; they said my statement was a summary of their sentiments. For a few hours, I basked in their approbation. Some gave me their cards, addresses, and souvenirs. They urged me to proceed with the idea of a women's festival.

By the end of the festival, Ibrahim had invitations from universities and cultural ministries of several African and Caribbean nations. Articles about him were proposed by literary journals and film magazines. He was invited to France as a consultant for a major cultural project.

The festival created a watershed in my mind. One stream flowed on the surface; the other was diverted into an underground stream of thought about the creative energy of women. I realized it had been a mistake to make my debut as an author at the festival. In the *Festival Notes,* an influential critic characterized me as Ibrahim's "biographer and his bride—a combination of relationships that renders the work suspect from beginning to end." The timing of the book's publication had contributed to a focus on my relationship to Ibrahim rather than the quality of the book itself. Although the biography subsequently received favorable reviews in literary journals, I had been discredited at a moment when it mattered dearly.

The festival bestowed upon Ibrahim a sense of his potential international influence in arts and letters. The moment had arrived for him to explode with the full power of his ideas. For me, however, there were no specific offers or invitations. Instead, I merely deposited addresses, cards, and notes on the festival in a folder labeled "EVENTUALLY."

# 31

AFTER THE LAST OF THE GUESTS OF THE FES-
tival said their final good-byes, and the postfestival theatrical
productions closed, when the fading festival banners finally
were dismantled, and the frayed posters peeled away, Ibrahim and
I returned to our domestic routine. The tempo of our household
escalated with the more rapid cadence of Ibrahim's work—his
writing, film commitments, appointments, and travel schedules.
We made a few trips to Mali, where he was filming. I accompanied
him, editing his scripts and assisting the camera crew. At home,
we had few planned social occasions, although there were frequent spontaneous events. Friends arrived unexpectedly and
stayed for dinner; and nephews, nieces, and cousins appeared
unannounced and remained for indefinite visits.

Ibrahim and I walked to the boulders each morning, surveyed the bay and the sky, then returned for breakfast and the
work of the day. He was working on a historical novel, entitled
*The Saga of Yacine,* which he described as a lament for Yacine
Boubou, a nineteenth-century Senegalese woman who had sacrificed her life to ensure her husband's political future and royal
ascension. I began to empathize with Ibrahim's heroine. Was her
tragedy my destiny?

Ibrahim and I worked in much the same way as we had in our
first summer together. He would read a few paragraphs from
*Yacine,* and I would respond with suggestions. My critiques had
become bolder and sharper, however. One morning I proposed
a complete revision.

Ibrahim was indignant. He said my suggestions would

involve a rewriting of history, which he would not do. I suggested that he could have Yacine explore the influence of the customs of her time, especially those related to the oppression of women, and then have her speculate about other possibilities, about a time when circumstances might be different for women. Ibrahim resisted; he thought I was reading too much of my own situation into the story. He reached for a pipe, filled it, sucked at the stem as he lit it. "I suppose you need reassurance. You are not Yacine and I am not in politics or of royal lineage."

"And I'm not the type who would take her own life. But I am sacrificing time—months, years."

He tried to placate me. "Don't become resentful now. It's an interesting life. Besides, most women make sacrifices for the men they love."

I began to count the hours of typing, editing, revising manuscripts, answering correspondence, reviewing contracts, and handling telephone conversations with agents, actors, lawyers, and literary figures. My irritation, a residue of the festival treatment, was increasing.

Ibrahim was aware of my frustration, but refused to confront it. And I did not want to slow his progress with an argument over the sacrifices made by women in the interest of their husbands and lovers. And so we went on with "our" work; his work had become mine.

The pace of the work was sometimes slowed, however, by an amorous eruption which sent us back to the bedroom for the luxury of midmorning lovemaking. In those sweet, moist hours, Awa and Mamadou protected our privacy, dealt with callers, and amused Ousmane.

Ousmane began walking at eleven months. Soon, too soon, he refused to be carried, but preferred to walk about, to exercise his little legs and his grand capacity for independence. He was top-heavy, with a large head and adult eyes—a man's face on a baby's body. Although he was thin, he was also quite sturdy and nimble. Ibrahim delighted in strolls with Ousmane who happily trotted beside him.

"Do you remember the fantastic dancer from Bamako—

remember the way he walked? Ousmane walks like that dancer. He'll be a great dancer," proclaimed Ibrahim.

Along the dusty paths beyond the walls of our compound, they collected "treasures"—pebbles, seashells, prickly branches, gulls' feathers. Later Ibrahim entertained me with animated accounts of their promenades and, a year or so later, their "conversations."

Language came to Ousmane slowly. I talked to him in English, Ibrahim spoke French, and Awa and Mamadou used Wolof. Finally, he uttered his first words. "Ousmane is going to be a philosopher!" Ibrahim exclaimed. "He knows three words, that is to say, one word in three languages. His word is why. He asks, 'why?' in Wolof, French, and English. Remarkable! Already a philosopher."

It was true that Ousmane was precocious. He was eager to bypass the hurdles of infancy and advance into childhood, to get ahead on the course he had set for himself. Relatives and friends followed his development and commented on his unusual alertness, energy, and effort. And, in every encounter, they remarked on his appearance. "He is just like Ibrahim." "He is unquestionably his father's son." "You know the tree from which that limb was cut." Never were there references to his resembling Mariama, physically or temperamentally. I searched his features for signs of his maternity; but like everyone else, I saw only Ibrahim in Ousmane.

"It's true, Ousmane is very much like you. It's not merely his resemblance—already he tries to imitate you—your gestures, your voice," I observed.

"The boy who mimics his father later, as a man, may mock him," was Ibrahim's stock remark to those who noticed Ousmane's attempts at copying him. Ousmane watched his father's every move like a young chess player apprenticed to a grand master.

The first time Ousmane uttered, "Mama," his eyes looking deeply into mine, I was transfixed with joy. I called to Ibrahim, "Did you hear him? He called me 'mama.'"

"Of course. You are his mama."

"When should we tell him about Mariama?" I asked in a whisper.

How and when to tell him of Mariama was a worry. Ibrahim thought that we should wait until Ousmane was at least five. I was tormented by what I imagined Anna, Amadon, or his cousins might tell him. As a toddler, it was evident that Ousmane was not one to reach out for an embrace, not inclined to be affectionate. I pondered his reserve—wondered whether, in my touch, I had communicated that I was the surrogate, only the stepmother. But he had a certain reserve with Ibrahim, too. Self-contained, generally even-tempered, except for occasional fiery outbursts of frustration, Ousmane was a rather aloof, introspective child.

My affection for him grew gradually as I became more engaged in his care, his diet, the selection of his clothes: a white sailor suit, striped overalls from Mom, and a miniature version of the school uniform he later would wear—gray shorts, blue shirt, burgundy knee socks and necktie. Despite his being somewhat ungainly, his agile grace and robust intelligence won my heart.

Years later, I would leaf through our photograph album to recapture images of the young Ousmane in Ibrahim's arms under the umbrella in the courtyard; climbing on a boulder with Ibrahim's hand there to steady him; on vacation in Malta where Ousmane splashed with another three-year-old at a beach, Ibrahim watching over them. I recalled that later that same day on the beach, Ibrahim and Ousmane flew a kite together, their eyes turned skyward, following the kite's erratic flight.

When Ibrahim and Ousmane were out walking, I usually spent time scouring literary journals and popular magazines—French, British, and American—for items to discuss with Ibrahim as part of our constant colloquy. Since much of our time was spent together, I needed sources of material beyond my own imagination. I searched for news articles, current reviews, and recently published stories. At dinner or during our walks, I would tell him about Marguerite Duras's portrait of Leontyne Price in *Vogue,* an interview with Jeanne Moreau in

*France-Observateur,* commentary on James Baldwin's works in
*The Guardian,* reviews of a recent production of *Rhinocéros,*
and Robbe-Grillet's latest essay on the new novel. I suppose I
sometimes played the student in the company of the professor
she wished to impress or entertain.

And in his professional style, Ibrahim would tell me about
critical reactions to Aimé Césaire's "Discours sur le colonial-
isme" in *Présence Africaine,* reviews of Kubrick's *2001,* or the
status of the debates on Negritude in the cafés of Dakar. Often
he read aloud from his favorite authors. Evenings ended with
recordings of Mahalia Jackson or Leontyne Price, the drums of
Olatunji, the trumpet of Miles Davis, or sometimes the irresistible beat of Jão Gilberto's bossa nova, which brought us to
our feet in a spirited dance.

I treasured our intimate hours together. I knew that soon the
world beyond our sheltered compound would see him as a rising star. He knew it, too; and so while I was his and he was
mine, we cherished the mood of our marriage.

To be sure, there were uneventful times, days filled with the
inconsequential routines of ordinary life—conversations with
Mamadou and Awa, dental appointments, shopping, playing
tennis with Ibrahim, sweeping up the shards of a bowl Ousmane had broken, pasting photos in albums, having my visa
renewed, driving Ibrahim to the airport, attending a reception, a
family ceremony, a funeral—such things occupied us, too. But
even on the dullest of days, there was the excitement of a letter
from abroad, a breakthrough in Ibrahim's plan for a work-in-
progress, an unexpected gift from Ibrahim—perfume, an
imported soap, or another bracelet or necklace or earrings. Even
the routine days had moments that glistened.

Ibrahim urged me to accept the invitations from the wives of
his colleagues and his nieces—invitations to tea, to visit a dressmaker, to have a manicure, to go to lunch or a fashion show.
And there were excursions to villages for weddings, harvest
spreads, naming ceremonies, and funerals. Through the veils of
formality, I began to recognize those who wished to befriend
me and those who were merely discharging social obligations. I

was irritated when conversations shifted from French to Wolof or Fulani so that I could not readily follow, or when a remark directed my way was deliberately an afterthought. Among my friends, I counted Anna, who had nursed Ousmane, Fatou, whose friendship had become more relevant than her kinship, and the well-educated, cosmopolitan Simone Diouf.

Deeply attached to Ousmane, Anna visited at least twice a week. We talked about children and family life. She guided me through the convoluted kinship map of Ibrahim and Mariama, instructing me in the protocol of the family, and preparing me for participation in its rituals. As mutual trust grew, she informed me of family expectations and told me some family secrets. I confided that I wished to revise the opinions of Ibrahim's relatives, who doubted that I was an able wife and a competent mother.

Fatou refrained altogether from discussions of family matters. When she found Anna and me deep in the bush of family lore, she refused to join us. Instead, she went directly to Ibrahim's office, where research assignments awaited her. Prompt, reliable, and meticulous, she toiled with me over the details in Ibrahim's writing. A conscientious grammarian, Fatou also improved my French and Wolof by correcting my pronunciation or usage. When there was a hiatus in our work, we played chess. Fatou was a tenacious opponent, determined in every match to set me up for checkmate, and often she did.

Simone Diouf was my closest friend and confidante. The wife of Ibrahim's good friend and our doctor, she had become a promising companion soon after the festival where she had witnessed my frustration. She, too, had hoped that her participation—she had sung several arias—would have drawn attention to her captivating soprano voice and presented new possibilities for her. Simone had studied in Paris and Milan, had been in the chorus of a few European opera companies, and then had chosen the security of married life in Dakar, with the doctor who adored her, over the uncertainty of an operatic career abroad. We spent many memorable afternoons in her home listening to tapes of Price's *Tosca* or Callas's *La Traviata*.

After her analyses of their performances, she switched to a comical critique of Dakar society. What an eye for social performance! Simone's witty, irreverent satire of Dakar's *haute bourgeoisie* diminished my concerns about my own performance in their company.

"They see you as an extension of Ibrahim. His detractors will always see your faults, while his devotees will continue to admire you. Don't let it bother you," Simone advised. I was bothered, however, by not being viewed as an individual with my own weaknesses and strengths. My identity was totally immersed in Ibrahim's. Sometimes I felt I was drowning.

# 32

IN REPLY TO MY LENGTHY LETTER ABOUT THE festival with clippings from newspapers and magazines, Mom wrote that she and Dad wanted to meet their "distinguished son-in-law." I urged them to visit us and to see something of Senegal. In preparation for their visit, the construction of a guest house in a corner of the compound was begun. After several months of correspondence about the trip, my parents finally arrived. Ibrahim and I met them at the airport.

Ibrahim and Dad were in the front seat of the car, getting acquainted with ease, making small talk about the weather, airplanes, automobiles, world affairs, and sports. Ibrahim's English was accented and halting. Dad spoke slowly and more loudly than necessary. Mom, in the backseat with me, focused on my appearance. "That's a lovely gown or is it a caftan you're wearing? Anyway, that shade of blue becomes you. You look well, but I see you've gained about ten pounds."

"I've gained about two kilos," I said. "Less than six pounds."

She whispered, "He's quite handsome, better looking than the pictures you sent. And younger looking, too. Some gray hair, a lot of gray in his beard, but he's got a young face, a nice face." She paused and listened for a while. "Nice voice, too, charming accent. Now I understand what attracted you to him, now that I see him." Leaning forward to engage Ibrahim, Mom asked, "How's your little son?"

"Ousmane is in good form, energetic, interested in everything. He is a typical three-year-old. He is looking forward to meeting his only grandparents." In the rearview mirror, Ibrahim inspected my mother's expression and mine. I think we both were smiling.

"The compound is just ahead," I said. "We've built a guest house especially for your visit. I hope you'll find it comfortable."

"Just so it's clean and the bed is firm," said my mother. "It was an awfully long trip. Your father slept on both the flights, but I couldn't sleep at all while we were over the Atlantic. I slept a little on the plane out of the Paris airport, but then they woke us up for lunch—or maybe it was dinner. I had coffee and, of course, couldn't fall back to sleep."

Ibrahim stopped the car and got out to open the gate. "You live here? It's like a mansion," gasped Mom.

"It looks like a mighty fine home to me," Dad said.

Mamadou sprang out of the house. He greeted my parents with a deferential bow and carried their luggage to the guest house. Mamadou had found a hibiscus plant with brilliant orange blossoms for the sitting room. A basket of fruit and bottled water were on the credenza. While I opened the shutters, Mom inspected the bedroom and bathroom.

"What an attractive place!" she exclaimed with surprise.

"Ahhh, we're going to be very comfortable here," said Dad, loosening his tie. He seemed relaxed and ready to settle in. Laden with three cameras, Dad began snapping pictures: Mom and I posed together; Ibrahim seated at the table in the courtyard; Ousmane with Ibrahim and me; Ousmane with Awa; Ousmane kicking a soccer ball; Mamadou stirring a pot in the kitchen.

They had also brought belated wedding gifts: a pewter tray, table linens, and my great grandmother's silver spoons. There were toys for Ousmane; delicate nightgowns and underwear for me; neckties and socks for Ibrahim; tapes of classical music and jazz; and a photo album with pictures of my relatives and childhood friends. It felt like Christmas.

They toured the compound with Ibrahim. Interested in the construction of buildings, Dad spent a good deal of time talking with him and gesturing with Mamadou about the composition of walls, height of ceilings, and material of roofs. Curious about Ousmane, Mom had many questions about his capabilities.

After getting acquainted with the surroundings, it was time to discuss their visit.

"Let me tell you what we have in mind for your visit." I began to outline a plan for their two-week stay.

Ibrahim said, "I suggest we let them rest for the evening. In the morning, we will hear what they would like to do."

"A good idea. A sensible man," Mom said.

The following morning, Ibrahim took my parents on a tour of Dakar. The trip took much longer than I had expected. When they returned, bubbling with conversation, they told me that Ibrahim had taken them to the Medina and to the harbor, as well as around central Dakar. My father had told him Uncle George's story.

"Looked for your *sosie*, but we didn't see her," Dad said.

"You have talked about your Uncle George, but you never told me about *le sosie*. I thought you came here to find me. Alas, *un sosie* you are seeking." Ibrahim was amused, but not interested in exploring the subject.

"I was hoping to see some of your films, Ibrahim. You know, we're not likely to get them back home. And I'd like to visit some small towns and villages, stay in a village for a few days. I want to get the feeling of African life. Get acquainted with some folks by going fishing and doing some bird-watching out in the countryside. I've been reading about the varieties of fish, the birds, the vegetation in different sections of this country. Well, I want to get out and see some of it," Dad said.

"All that can be easily arranged. My brothers would be honored to have you stay with them, to fish with them, to show you the countryside," said Ibrahim.

"I was hoping to stay right here," said Mom, pointing at the floor of the great hall where Mamadou was serving tea. "When you've traveled as far as we have to see your only daughter, you'd like to be with her."

"Of course, you may stay here," said Ibrahim.

"Henry may want to journey about the countryside, but I just want to be with Sarah."

Ibrahim said, "Henry, you and I will become well-

acquainted. I need to visit my village, see my family, and survey
some towns and villages to select some sites for shooting a film.
I will enjoy your company."

Ibrahim and Dad were away for nearly a week on a excursion
that took them from the coast to the bush and back. The
moment they left, Mom began her report on Lincoln.

"I suppose you know that Lincoln has become quite the public figure up in Boston. His parents are very proud of him. They
send us articles about him—I don't know why they think we'd
care to know—but they send them, so I brought them along."
She rummaged through the contents of her tote bag and pulled
out a plump envelope full of clippings. Unfolding a few clippings, I smiled at the photos of Lincoln smiling into the camera.
Mom, seated next to me, studied my face for an expression of
loss or remorse.

"He's the president of the Boston chapter of the NAACP and
he's been elected to the school committee. Moving ahead in public life. And I understand he has a radio program on Sunday
mornings. He always had a voice that would be good on radio."
She paused for a reaction. I said nothing. She asked, "Do you ever
miss him? Are you ever sorry about the way things turned out?"

"Never! And I've no regrets about that marriage or its ending. It was an inevitable marriage, an essential stage in our development. Lincoln and I needed to move through that marriage to
get on to more mature relationships."

"Well, are you satisfied with this life—a long way from your
family and friends? Aren't you lonely here?"

I didn't answer right away. She had tapped the nostalgia vein.
Memories of a few people, cherished places, and nearly forgotten
favorite things began to flow: sherry on Fridays with Antonia, conversations with Peter Martin, phone calls to Joan; a leisurely
walk through the National Gallery, an afternoon of browsing in
Harvard Square bookstores, an evening of jazz in a smoke-filled
nightclub; studying in the stacks of Widener Library, going to an
off-Broadway theater, eating popcorn at a cinema, attending a concert of spirituals and gospel music, walking along Fifth Avenue,
hearing Mahler's *Fourth* in Boston's Symphony Hall, taking the

ferry to Martha's Vineyard, listening to a broadcast of the Metropolitan Opera on a Saturday afternoon, seeing the colors of maple trees in mid-October.

"I like my life here, but I sometimes miss the variety of activities that I treated casually," I admitted.

"So you do have some regrets about leaving America?" She continued to probe my feelings. I suppose my defensiveness elicited a rather didactic response.

"Leaving America heightens one's sense of being American. Everywhere I go, people expect me to explain U.S. policies and actions. They're especially interested in understanding race relations there. Only since I've been here have I begun to develop a U.S. identity. Still, I feel a sense of belonging here that I never felt there."

"So you've become African?"

"We've always been African, Mom."

"You may be African, but I'm American and not ashamed of it." There the discussion ended; but the argument did not end. This issue which separated us, an ocean apart, was never to be examined further or resolved. Mom then shifted her inquiry to our marriage.

"You seem to help Ibrahim a lot. I heard you tell him you'd write some letters for him, call the insurance agent, and make some other calls. And, of course, your book is about him. You're certainly doing a lot to help him along."

"And he does a great deal for me," I retorted.

"Well, obviously, he takes care of you quite nicely. But does he have the energy to do—to help you with a family? After all, he's much older—twice your age—nearly as old as your father."

"He's very energetic, vigorous, and quite active sexually—if that's what you're asking."

"Oh, no, I wouldn't dream of asking about your private relationship." She covered her mouth with both hands, embarrassed by my seeking the meaning of her remark. "But I do hope you'll make us grandparents someday. You may think of Ousmane as our grandchild, but he's not a blood relative. He's not like us. He's very dark—like his father. Very dark."

"He's very handsome—like his father."

"Handsome is as handsome does, they say. I hope he'll be a good child. You seem to be a pretty good stepmother."

"Only pretty good?" I wanted to ask her. The ingredients of her own recipe for motherhood had included a cup of criticism, a large jar of judgment, a dash of cynicism, and a pinch of praise. I wanted enthusiastic approbation for my style of mothering Ousmane. Her opinion mattered. All of my early efforts at growing up, under her critical eye, her mouth shaped by words to wish me ever toward an improved performance, had been rewarded with, "That's pretty good." I was concocting a different recipe for rearing Ousmane—a counter-recipe, with equal measures of recognition, praise, affection, and celebration.

Eventually, Mom's questions and comments subsided. She tried to come to terms with my manner of mothering by observing its every detail. She listened closely to my conversations with Ousmane, to whom I spoke English. She accompanied us when I took him to the pediatrician and to the dentist. She was with us at mealtime, playtime, storytime, and bedtime. She noticed that he was eager to learn and that I enthusiastically rewarded his accomplishments.

She also watched my transactions at the market and in shops, and eavesdropped on telephone conversations in English. In the company of my French-speaking friends, at lunch or tea, Mom sat silently and noticed every expression and gesture we exchanged.

According to Ibrahim, Dad was more a participant than an observer. He went out to sea with fishermen, and he mended nets with them; he helped with the pressing of palm wine, joined in the dancing, and when he was not dancing, he sometimes played the drums. He took lots of photos and asked lots of questions. He appeared comfortable everywhere, even where the accommodations were rudimentary and meals were meager.

As their departure date approached, Mom began a countdown of days to leaving for Paris, where she was anticipating a week of museum tours, shopping, and dining. Dad said he would have preferred another week in Senegal.

On the eve of their departure, we hosted a dinner party in their honor at the Majestic Hotel. Amadon and Anna, the Dioufs, and Fatou joined us. Before dinner and between courses there were toasts and tributes. Amadon addressed Dad as his American brother. Diouf toasted both families and said that we symbolized the new linkage between Senegal and the United States. After dinner, Dad made a speech before his toast to Ibrahim and me.

"Dearly beloved friends, we began this journey with apprehension about our daughter's circumstances, conditions here, and how we'd be received. At every turn, we've been astonished and gratified by what we've found. We now realize that the news we get about Africa is propaganda—ideas spread about Africa to make Americans believe that people here lack civilization, education, motivation, and culture. Well, we've found evidence to the contrary. Never before have I known of a place—mind you, I've not traveled overseas before, but I read a lot—where everybody you meet is eager to learn, to profit from experience, and to be successful.

"We've felt safe here, secure, no fear of danger or harm. And I don't know of a country where one finds people who are as kind to strangers as those we've met here. We've been received with friendliness and generosity and warm hospitality, for which we're most grateful.

"On a personal note, I must confess that we've sometimes worried about our daughter's choice of a country and a husband. Our worries are over. She's chosen well. It's reassuring to find that she's very happy here. I want to propose a toast to Sarah and Ibrahim and wish them everlasting happiness."

Ibrahim thanked Dad for his "faith in his daughter's choices" and then presented a gold bracelet to Mom and an ancient drum to Dad. I gave them a leatherbound copy of my book. "I'm certainly going to read this book now that I know the man," Dad said.

"Writing a book is an important achievement," Mom said. She could not resist adding, "It's almost as important as having baby."

# 33

Y OUR KING IS DEAD," CRIED MAMADOU. "THE radio said King was shot dead."

By radio and telephone calls to the U.S. Embassy, I heard the horrific details of the assassination of Martin Luther King in Memphis and the events that followed—the eruption of protests across the nation, riots and fires in Washington, Baltimore, Boston, Detroit, and Chicago, and the call for federal troops to subdue the resistance. Anxious about their safety, with shops ablaze not far from their neighborhood, I tried several times to telephone Mom and Dad. For hours it was impossible to get through to Washington. I telephoned Joan and Antonia. Calls to Baltimore and Boston were not being transmitted. I was immobilized by fear and tears of despair. I thought about Lincoln, tried to imagine what this catastrophe had aroused in him. Finally, I reached Dad. "We're okay. The shops not far from us on Fourteenth Street were burned out, but homes weren't damaged. Such a pity, a shame. So much progress and now this setback. But don't worry about us. We're okay." His voice was weak and sad. I imagined his glancing toward the window, waiting and watching for signs of trouble in the street. I wanted to be there with him, holding his hand. Ibrahim, at my side during the call, was holding my hand.

"I should be in Washington with Mom and Dad."

"You may not be able to get a flight for days. Besides, the worst of it is over—the demonstrations, the fires. But I suppose you could console your parents. In fact, you should go. See what has happened in your capital city."

I called all the airlines. No seats were available on flights for two weeks. I called Bill Nelson, who was in Paris. He advised me not to go to Washington. "Write an article about how Dakar reacted to news of the assassination and the rioting. Put your anguish into print," he suggested. Instead, I wrote letters to Dad and Mom, Antonia, Joan, and a note to Lincoln at his parents' address.

The airwaves hummed with choirs singing "We Shall Overcome" in French and English, Wolof, Fulani, and Mandinke. Magazines arrived with funereal photos of mourners at the service for King whose widow's veil could not conceal her sorrow. Senegalese newspapers carried articles about the collapse of American civilization, civil rights, and civility. Among our friends, tributes to King and the civil rights movement were mingled with tribulations about the future for American blacks and relations between African nations and the United States.

Weeks later, we were stunned by the report of Robert Kennedy's fatal shooting in California, another U.S. calamity that heightened my despair about a country from which I felt alienated, the place Ibrahim referred to as my "strange, destructive native land."

My "anguish" about my "strange, destructive native land" was elicited constantly. Everywhere, I was asked about the meaning of the assassinations of Martin Luther King and the Kennedys; and I would bring Malcolm X's demise into the discussion. There was a particular urgency in the questions from those with dreams of their American immigration. I suggested that they reconsider the urge to leave Senegal, reminding them of the Kenyan author Bahadur Tejani's experience of "a deep daze of dislocation/from color/and creed/and country."

They inquired about the circumstances that had delivered me to Senegal. Had I experienced racial oppression? Was I escaping racial injustice? Had I come to find love and marriage? I thought of Baldwin as I described the experience of racial oppression in the U.S., which I remembered as feeling trapped and unable to breathe in a smoke-filled house, with a fire raging in the basement. I had come to Senegal to breathe freely and to find myself. I didn't elaborate on finding myself. It would have sounded mystical and perhaps would have been misunderstood. I declared myself a content émigré, more satisfied than ever with Senegal as my permanent residence.

After a while, I turned off the news of the turmoil in the United States and toward my immediate concern: making the most of my hours with Ousmane, who was changing at a rapid pace.

He had his first soccer ball. "Come, Mama. Football practice." Off we went to the sandy playing field outside the compound and vigorously kicked the ball back and forth. "Take off your shoes, Mama. You'll play better with bare feet." I took off my shoes, which scarcely improved my kick. "Goal!" he cried. "Ousmane—one; Mama—zero. Try harder, Mama."

We drew and painted. I collected his works in a portfolio. From time to time, we selected the best of them to hang in the foyer. Proudly, Ousmane showed them to his father, Mamadou, and our guests.

Ousmane enjoyed doing "important projects" with Mamadou; but he also looked forward to Mamadou's days off when I made "American" pancakes for breakfast and southern fried chicken for dinner. "How does northern fried chicken taste, Mama?" His questions amused and amazed us.

Returning from an excursion with Ousmane, Ibrahim crowed, "Ousmane made an astronomical observation today! He pointed to the moon in the afternoon sky and asked, 'Why is the moon here in the afternoon? Doesn't it light the night?' Do you know of any other four-year-old who has noticed the moon by day? Who has remarked that it is unusual to see the moon in the afternoon? Extraordinary! He is truly extraordinary."

In every setting, observant Ousmane's eyes flashed from object to object as if he were cataloging them. Puzzles intrigued him. With deep concentration and persistence, he arranged and rearranged parts until he found solutions. He was particularly curious about mechanical toys, clocks, telephones, and radios, fascinated by their interior works. He disassembled three clocks, scattered their parts on the floor of the great hall where he sat and surveyed them. For days, he sorted the parts into groups with similar features, and then in a vain but valiant effort, tried to reassemble them. He was totally immersed in a puzzle he had created for himself. With exclamations of delight, I rewarded his assemblages as he linked parts and held them up for my inspection. I began speculating about a profession to match his talents.

"He's going to be a sculptor, Ibrahim, or an inventor."

"Or a demolition expert."

Ousmane began to resist the obligatory visits to villages where he had aunts, uncles, and cousins of all ages. He protested to Ibrahim. "I don't want to go. It's boring in the village. I want to stay at home. Mama is teaching me to write. To be a writer, like you, Papa." Sullen and cross when his cousins arrived to take him to the village, Ousmane called to us as they drove off, "I don't want to go. I like your company!"

Another source of company for Ousmane was growing in me. Ibrahim noticed even before I knew that I was pregnant. One morning after especially playful lovemaking, he cupped my breasts and gently squeezed them. "Ah," he exclaimed, "some mother's milk." He licked my nipples, tickling them with the tip of his tongue. "You are pregnant, my love, pregnant! And you're going to have this baby—my baby," he crooned. This was an aphrodisiac. Well into the morning we were still rolling and tumbling and, with each motion, shrieking our mounting pleasure.

After a bath, I examined my naked image in the full-length mirror. My breasts had acquired the fullness that I had felt before in the early stage of pregnancy. I made an appointment with Dr. Diouf, whose examination produced the confirming evidence.

"You and my good friend, Ibrahim, deserve this baby, so you must be sure to take every precaution. You are not to take any medications or drink any alcohol. You must give up smoking, put aside for these few months those wretched Gauloises you are fond of. Reduce your coffee intake; drink milk or juices instead. Eat well and in moderation. After the sixth month, you and Ibrahim must abstain from—well, there ought not be any deep penetration after the sixth month. I want you to come to the clinic every fortnight for a checkup. If all goes well, you should have a baby in early January—a fine way to begin the next decade—a 1970 baby."

He didn't need to offer such detailed advice. I had every intention of managing the pregnancy intelligently, observing all precautions, even heeding superstitions and old wives' tales. I was eager to feel the full stretch of pregnancy and give birth to Ibrahim's child.

Sarah Mangane is expecting! Our news was spread swiftly. Before I returned home from Diouf's office with the confirmation, Ibrahim had received a congratulatory telephone call from a cousin who worked in a medical laboratory. By day's end, we had heard from all our circles—writers, actors, friends at the University of Dakar, acquaintances in the diplomatic corps, and, of course, countless kin, both Ibrahim's and Mariama's. Although I did not wish to raise expectations prematurely, I knew the news would delight my parents.

I stayed up beyond midnight in order to reach the U.S. at the end of the day. The voices of several operators in the trans-Atlantic telephone relay finally made the connection. My mother answered.

"Hello. Hello?"

"Hello, Mom."

"Sarah, I was thinking of you the very moment the phone rang. How are you?"

"I'm fine and I'm pregnant!"

"Pregnant! That's wonderful news. I've been praying for you, praying that you and Ibrahim would get around to making a baby. You've seen a doctor?"

"Yes. Do you remember meeting Dr. Diouf? He's my doctor. I have appointments with him regularly—every two weeks. I'm being very careful."

"Well, you can't be too careful. Watch your weight. You don't want to lose your figure afterward. When are you due?"

"Early January."

"January? Six months away. Have you discussed names for the baby?"

"There are traditions here about naming babies, naming cere-monies where—"

"Here's a suggestion—just a suggestion. If it's a boy, name him Isaac. Please don't give him one of those difficult African names."

"Why Isaac? It's not a family name. I don't recall anyone named Isaac."

"Think about it and read your Bible. You'll find Isaac. And if it's a girl, I hope you'll name her Mary, for your grandmother Stewart and your Aunt Mary."

"Mary, Marie, or Mariama—"

"Or Antonia for your friend, Antonia Dale. She'd love to have your daughter carry her name. She'd feel honored. I can't wait to tell your Aunt Mary and our friends. They'll all be happy to hear this news. I suppose you want to tell your father yourself. Wait a moment. He's in the garage; I'll get—"

"I'd rather that you tell him. I'd be happy to have you tell him." We chatted for a few minutes more.

"I shouldn't hold you any longer. This call will cost you a fortune. I'm going right down and tell Henry about the baby. He'll be thrilled. We're happy for you and Ibrahim. We really are happy about the way your life is going. We love you very much. We'll come over again after the baby's born."

"I love you, Mom." We both were sniffling. I could hear the tears in her voice and I was sure she could hear mine in our exchange of good-byes and promises to write and call more fre-quently.

When I reported our conversation as "a transoceanic embrace" to Ibrahim, he said, "Well, I am delighted that you feel closer to your mother, and she to you. It is a good omen, a God-send. You need to understand your mother's opinions and atti-tudes to enrich your own manner of mothering. You have been the perfect mother for Ousmane—well-matched, you and he. It is a joy to see you together, to observe you, especially when nei-ther of you is aware of being observed." Ibrahim paused and lit his pipe. "And your mother likes the name Isaac? Ah, she takes her Bible seriously, doesn't she?"

"What do you mean? Who was Isaac?"

"Isaac was the son of Sarah and Abraham."

"Of course, that's why."

Ousmane had returned from a village visit the day I chose to tell him that we were expecting a child. It was our late afternoon storytime. I had selected a story book about a the birth of a lamb to prepare him for our talk. We had settled in on the divan in the great hall and I had begun the story. Ousmane interrupted to say that his cousins had told him that I was going to have a baby and that he was not my child. They had told him of Mariama. He had been told that she had died when he was born. He wanted to know if she died *because* he was born. Turning to me, turning on me, Ousmane charged, "You're my pretend mama, not my true mama."

"I am a mother who is true to you. I am Mama, your Mama. Mariama gave birth to you, yes. But I have cared for you and I love you as if you had been born to me."

"Auntie Anna nursed me. Awa cares for me."

I tried to hug him. Ousmane ducked away from my reach, dashed to the nursery, and slammed the door. I followed him. Ibrahim, having heard the commotion, came in, too. Tearful and angry, Ousmane was inconsolable.

"But I have mothered you. I want you to know me as your mama."

"But you're not my mother. Papa, are you my true papa? Or are you pretending, too?"

Ibrahim picked up Ousmane and held him before a mirror, their faces side by side. He detailed the similarities in their features: the same eyes, same nose, same chin, same hairline. "There is no doubt that I am your father. Only I could be your papa." Ousmane then turned and looked in my face with a gaze of nonrecognition. Ever afterward, he exercised a certain reserve in his behavior with me. He was less inclined to use English, and more committed to Wolof. His cousins had scattered seeds of suspicion in the furrows of his fertile imagination. Ousmane's trust in me was shaken.

# 34

THE PREGNANCY, FORTUNATELY, WAS "uneventful" or "unremarkable," as Dr. Diouf commented at the end of every clinic visit. At first I was tired, but I didn't experience the nausea and discomfort that had accompanied my failed pregnancy. In the later months, I had considerably more energy, and used much of it for my own work. I sent an article, "Notes of a Native Daughter," to *The Negro Digest*, wrote a short story about a boy beggar in Dakar, and completed a draft of a paper on women in the African tradition for *Présence Africaine*. It was a fruitful season.

It was a generative period for Ibrahim, too. He gave the keynote address at the Congress of African Mothers in Abidjan, where he urged them to organize for the recognition of their legal rights, reproductive rights, marital rights, and economic security. The text of his speech was carried in the major Francophone newspapers. He called me from Abidjan to thank me for some of the ideas included in the speech. From there, he went to Paris to launch *The Saga of Yacine* and deliver a series of lectures at the Sorbonne, where he was heckled by a mob of young African men. They had read or heard about his speech in Abidjan and had taken issue with his appeal for the rights of women. Ibrahim related the incident with an air of amusement. I was not at all amused. I was alarmed.

A few weeks later, an article in a conservative Islamic journal accused Ibrahim of being unfaithful to Islamic values by advocating changes in the treatment of women. They cited his mar-

riage to "an American Christian woman intellectual and sorceress" as evidence of his infidelity to traditional values; and they
charged that his distance from Senegalese women had rendered
him unaware of their priorities. The article called for the ban-
ning of Ibrahim's books and films. The first wave of attacks
against Ibrahim, his works, and our world had begun.

I found the opposition to his work extremely disturbing, but
Ibrahim seemed to revel in this controversy about his writings.
He relished the sensationalism that surrounded him. His sessions with reporters and photographers usually went on much
longer than anticipated. Ibrahim would expound on the need
for legal reforms that would improve conditions for women; he
advocated improved schooling for girls, changes in marital practices and divorce laws. Of course, I did the background research
for his statements.

Occasionally, I joined him for the press interviews. Ibrahim
was voluble, lively, candid, brilliant; but I was reticent and quite
visibly pregnant. One columnist wrote: "Madame Mangane did
not demonstrate that she is either an intellectual or a sorceress.
She was silent throughout the interview, contemplating her
pregnancy, perhaps. She appeared to be expanding before our
very eyes."

Not only was I expanding; our compound was also expanding. Another building was under construction, an annex for the
children and their nurse. The installation of a swimming pool
was also scheduled. Ibrahim was pleased to tell the builder that
he could afford the best materials this time, that the cost would
not be a problem. Privately he said that the additions to the
compound were "subsidized by conservative Muslims." The
public debate and the call for a ban on Ibrahim's works had
enhanced their popularity. His publisher reported that sales on
all his books had quadrupled; the demand for his films was staggering. His works were enjoying unprecedented acclaim.

Ibrahim and I were in high spirits when we arrived at the residence of the ambassador from the Ivory Coast for New Year's
Eve festivities. When Ibrahim called in advance to confirm that

Florence Ladd

Dr. Diouf and his wife would attend the party, I realized that he was quite concerned about the timing of what he had termed our "New Year's gift."

When we arrived at the party, my fuchsia brocade boubou with silver silk embroidery drew murmurs of approval from the haute couture–conscious hostesses from Abidjan. I settled in a comfortable chair, surrounded by a dazzling circle of other elegantly dressed and coiffed women, who spoke of their children's schools in Geneva, restaurants in Paris, dressmakers in Rome, galleries in New York, hairdressers in Washington, markets in Cairo, hotels in Nairobi, and the Expo in Montreal. Ibrahim was encircled by their husbands, who were eager to hear his reaction to the fundamentalists' recent attacks against his work. The arrival of a troupe of Ivorian musicians enlivened the party. The evening became even more lively when the new life in me made its presence felt with the seismic force of the first contraction.

I groaned and whispered to Simone Diouf, who was nearby, "I just had a contraction." Around that elegant circle of women, shock waves of memories of their own contractions, labors, and deliveries rippled. Grandly gowned women were aflutter about me, getting me to my feet, telling me old wives' tales and midwives' secrets.

Moments later, Ibrahim and Dr. Diouf were at my side. I was calm and confident. With a pat on the arm I reassured Ibrahim, who was breathing heavily and perspiring. Diouf, who accompanied us to the hospital, listed other deliveries that had summoned him from parties.

"Frankly, I'd much rather be at the hospital when the New Year comes in," he said, "holding a healthy infant by the heels than holding a champagne glass."

It was nearly dawn on New Year's Day, 1970, when our son was born. The ordeal of pushing, arching, aching with cramps was truly labor. The delivery process was, indeed, very hard work, the work of bringing into our world a robust 3.8-kilo boy. Exhausted and elated, I then rested. A nurse swaddled the baby and presented the bundle to Ibrahim, who was dazzled by the warmth and weight of his second son. When the infant began to cry, Ibrahim passed him to me.

At first, I was aglow with the joy of a successful birth, then suddenly I was very tired and sleepy. While I slept, Ibrahim cabled the news to my parents, composed a poem about child-birth, wrote a few letters, and outlined a film script contrasting a hospital birth to childbirth in a village.

I stirred. Ibrahim kissed my forehead, and said, "You have produced a phenomenal son, Sarah. He is healthy, well formed, and handsome. *Mashallah!*"

"I want to hold him again," I said with a proud smile. Ibrahim asked a nurse to bring the baby. She nestled the infant in the hollow between my breast and the arm that held the lightly breathing bundle of a boy. With the remembrance of my miscarriage, the memory of Mariama's death in the same hospi-tal, and the overwhelming joy of holding my own child, my smiles soon gave way to tears. Ibrahim wept, too.

"Well, what have we here? The Madonna of Tears? I expected to find you up and dancing for joy," said Dr. Diouf.

"We are dancing. Our hearts are dancing. Our eyes show you how the dancing heart makes us feel," said Ibrahim, wiping his tears.

A week later, we were dancing and singing at the naming cer-emony in the courtyard of our home. At dawn, griots sang praise songs to the household. A sacrificial lamb bleated its way to its ceremonial fate. Cables from the U.S. arrived from my parents, Joan, and Antonia Dale. Bill Nelson, who was in Paris, sent a basket of birds of paradise. With the robust infant in my arms, I greeted relatives and friends, who arrived with foods and gifts. Ousmane, like any displaced four-and-a-half-year-old, grew more irritable with the arrival of each group of guests.

Amadon solemnly whispered the baby's name into his ear: Isaac Lumumba Henry King Mangane. A procession of uncles and honorary uncles followed in Amadon's steps, whispering prayers to Isaac. While Ibrahim's eldest sister, Aimée, shaved

Isaac's head, a chorus of women accompanied by balafon play-
ers intoned a lullaby. After the ceremony, the feasting and dancing began. Later I wrote about Isaac in my diary.

> *9 January 1970*
> *A "phenomenal son"—Ibrahim's words for our son—with*
> *King and Lumumba in his name to remind him that he*
> *must continue the struggle for independence in revolutions*
> *to come. He looks like Ibrahim. He enjoys nursing as much*
> *as I enjoy nursing him. Alert and responsive, he is a joy. We*
> *have been blessed.* Mashallah!

# 35

THE ARRIVAL OF ISAAC DREW ME INTO THE nursery and the kitchen more frequently. Instead of walking to the boulders and working with Ibrahim each morning, I rushed to the nursery to oversee the bathing and feeding of our boys. It was important to remind Ousmane of my attachment to him. I wrote songs and poems about Ousmane which I sang and read him. Ousmane was the superhero in a series of stories I wrote for him about a boy who rescued animals, individuals, and entire villages from impending disaster. I invented puzzles and games for him, made frequent trips with him to a hotel swimming pool where he found playmates, and took him on pirogue excursions with a boatman he liked. When Ousmane developed a fondness for chocolate chip cookies, I contacted an acquaintance who supplied me with chocolate chips, and I baked cookies for him. I responded to his accomplishments with praise and celebration. At every opportunity, I showed him that I could be a very good mother to him. In the process, I tried not to neglect Isaac, whose breast-feeding unexpectedly satisfied some sensual urges. I delighted in his cooing and gurgling. I measured time by Isaac's feedings, bowel movements, and naps, and the number of French words Ousmane could read, spell, and write. The caliper of my life, at that stage, was applied only to increments in their development.

Relying less on Mamadou, often I shopped for fish, meat, and vegetables, and took pride in my preparation of lunch or dinner. Haggling with the vendors who came to the compound with flowers, nuts, and spices was a contest I relished. At the end of the day, I related to Ibrahim events of the day as if they were major international affairs.

Although I thrived on the household bustle, Ibrahim found it distracting. His study was no longer conducive to work. Eventually he rented a studio in a warehouse building on the other side of Dakar and hired an assistant. Occasionally he had breakfast with us, but often we saw him only when he returned at the end of the day for an hour of play with the boys.

"Papa is coming! Papa is here!" Daily, with exaggerated enthusiasm, Ousmane greeted Ibrahim. By the time he was two, Isaac joined Ousmane in the greeting.

At first, Ibrahim was charmed by what he called "my domestic theater." Gradually, however, he came to see it as a problem.

"Sarah, your world has contracted to this compound. Do you think it is wise?"

"No, it probably isn't wise, but this is where I need to be now." I told him it was a time of consolidation, a kind of latency period. There was a strange stillness within me, like the sultry calm in the air before a thunderstorm.

"When you are still, I am disturbed. Where is the Sarah Mangane who is a writer, a critic, who reads the great books, who will organize an international festival for women artists?" he asked.

"There's only one Sarah Mangane. For now, this is the woman I am. I've put aside my other work temporarily. I'll read again, write again, perhaps teach again, when I'm ready. Now I am enjoying my time with the children and some domestic conventions in this unconventional family life of ours."

"Come away with me next week to Mali to scout for film locations and, afterward, a few days in Tunisia," he said seductively. "I am to speak at a conference on the fundamentalists' challenge to education at the university in Tunis. It should be an interesting trip. I want you to come. It would be good for you and for us."

"I adore Mali and I've never been to Tunisia. I'd like to go, but I've promised the boys that I—"

"Whatever you have promised the boys can be rearranged.

We leave on Sunday. You need to get away and I need to be alone with you."

I struggled with the idea of being away from Ousmane and Isaac for nearly two weeks. Once we arrived at the airport in Bamako, however, a motive for a focused sojourn of my own immediately took over. I knew it was important at that time for me to be away from home. It was a necessary separation.

# 36

"**I** WANT TO SEE MALI ON MY OWN," I SAID.

Ibrahim was astounded when I told him that I was hiring a driver with a Land Rover to tour some of the less picturesque, more remote villages. In the past, when traveling in Mali with Ibrahim, I'd been constantly at his side. While Ibrahim directed the filming, deploying cameramen and guiding the action, I edited scripts, unpacked and packed the gear, and arranged for fees or gifts to those who had helped us. On this trip, however, my intentions were different.

"What are you looking for? What do you expect to see 'on your own' that you would not see with me?"

"I want to spend time with village women, with mothers, to gain an understanding of how they rear their children, care for other relatives, feed their families, cope with the arduous work of their daily lives."

"Will you write about them?"

"I don't know yet what I'll do with what I see, but I know I must get closer to the experiences of ordinary women. I need to know more about their circumstances, what women are doing for their families and themselves, hear what they are saying—not through the film crew and you—but what they speak of when only with one another." Although I didn't have a project—an article or a book—in mind, I had a purpose. Under the best of circumstances, being a wife and mother demanded much of my time. What if I also had to gather wood, fetch water, plant and harvest crops, and do the laundry and cooking? I wanted to know what energized and sustained village women in impoverished Mali. And I wanted to view my own life from a different perspective—to look at their lives and my own, without Ibrahim's directing the angle of the camera and the action. The prospect of being released, if only for a few days, from the sequence of scenes determined by his commands and expectations was liberating.

"And how am I to manage the crew without you?"

"You'll manage very well."

At the Hotel Amitié, Ibrahim met with a Bambara-speaking guide while I scouted for a driver. With separate arrangements for our stay in Mali, we made the most of a romantic evening together. We walked about Bamako's streets, amid the bustle of vendors, farmers, shopkeepers, and beggars, until sunset when we returned to the hotel. We dined alone in our suite. With tender kisses, loving caresses, and patient pacing, we lifted each other to a passionate pinnacle.

The morning after, as we parted, Ibrahim teased, "I know you need a solitary adventure, but I trust you are not becoming an anthropologist. The region is amply supplied with them."

We kissed and kissed again, and, with Ibrahim's blessing, I left with my driver, Tamsir.

Ibrahim called to him, "Drive carefully. Bring her back safely!"

Tamsir, an enterprising middle-aged man, understood that I wanted to visit villages where I would not find international development workers or anthropologists. He had a Land Rover and a reputation as a cautious chauffeur. With a blanket roll, a backpack and bottled water, I was equipped for four or five days of bush living.

"It is strangely beautiful," Tamsir said of the stark, deforested, dusty landscape as we bumped along 150 kilometers of rocky road toward an isolated mudbrick-walled enclave. Two young boys, squatting in the shadow of the wall, studied our approach. We startled a feeble goat tethered to a tree—the only tree in sight—as Tamsir parked in its shade. An aged man, thin as his staff, limped out of the compound into the heat of the midmorning sun to greet us and invite us in. Tamsir called him "uncle." Inside the walls, women looked up from their work and nodded their acknowledgment of our presence. The compound hummed with the movement of a dozen women and girls, grinding corn, patting mud and manure into bricks, stirring a thin corn porridge in an iron kettle over a fire in the center of the compound, dragging bundles of branches from a hut toward the fire, or fashioning pots out of red clay.

After a brief exchange with the "uncle," Tamsir advised moving on to another village. He said two children had died of fever last week, two others were sick, and the women were not prepared to welcome outsiders.

Another rough 200 kilometers farther, we came to a large compound with a nearby field where women and children were harvesting corn, beans, and peanuts. A drum beat, the clang of a bell, and the clamor of children who bounded out to the vehicle announced our arrival. They surrounded us as we made our way to the entrance where an ancient "aunt" greeted Tamsir warmly and welcomed me with a confident handshake. Curious about my clothing, she fingered my tan slacks, white shirt, and mud cloth vest. With Tamsir translating for me, I told her that the vest was made in Mali of their mud cloth. She seemed especially pleased about that and took me into the compound to meet her family.

Except for being more prosperous, cheerful, and numerous, Aunt Khady's family, in activities and composition, resembled the village where we had stopped earlier: women, girls, and a few boys were working in their gardens, washing clothes, and tending cauldrons over fires. A few women were nursing infants while they worked. Only very old women and men, depleted of energy by age and a lifetime of labor, appeared idle.

Aunt Khady invited us into a large hut where we sat on straw mats. Tamsir entered into a ceremonial exchange with her about my staying in the village for a few days and the fee for meals and accommodations. When the matter was settled, he summarized their conversation for me in French. I nodded my agreement and shook hands with Aunt Khady. Tamsir said that lunch would be brought to us. After a while, a young girl entered with an enormous wooden bowl of *foufou* with a spicy sauce of gumbo and red beans. Aunt Khady, Tamsir, and I fingered the foufou and ate from the common bowl. Through Tamsir's translation, I learned a little about the history of the village.

"Nearly fifteen years ago, a truckload of the men of the village 'disappeared' into Bamako in search of work. It had not rained for three seasons and the men had given up hope for a harvest. At first we women waited for them to return and resume their village duties. A few—the faithful and the lovelorn—returned from time to time. While we waited for the other men to return, the walls of the compound crumbled, our well went dry, crops were meager, and the women wailed about the extinction of our people."

According to her account, Aunt Khady, knowing that the men would not return, appealed to the women to learn the tasks that their men used to do. At first, it was difficult. They had not dug wells, herded goats, made bricks, or built walls. But they were challenged and energized by Aunt Khady and her tales about their great-great-grandmothers, widowed by tribal wars, who rebuilt villages, planted crops and, with the aid of two or three men, continued to have children. With Aunt Khady as chieftain, the village was thriving.

Our conversation ended when a young woman, with a cherubic baby on her back, asked Tamsir if I would like to join a brigade of firewood gatherers. I was glad to be included. Tamsir and I agreed on a time when he would return for me. I left the compound with a group of eight other women, who strode purposefully in the heat of that deforested plateau. No wood for burning was in sight, only saplings that they themselves had planted and dared not strip. Stumbling upon a branch or twig brought forth cheers. Toward dusk, we retraced our path to the compound with baskets far from full. Despite the modest supply of kindling, the women awaiting our return clapped their hands and sang and rewarded us with a steaming bowl of foufou. Crouched among the wood gatherers in a circle around the bowl, I dipped my fingers into the foufou and ate heartily. After supper, under an amethyst sky with only the fire under the steaming cauldron to light our way, Aunt Khady led me to a hut where I spread my blanket, folded my vest and placed it at one end for a pillow, and lay down and listened to the clatter of pans, the chirp of crickets, and the hum of women's voices. I fell asleep for the night, footsore and weary from the trek of the day, safe in the company of bountiful women.

The next day, I joined in harvesting corn. Reaching, bending, breaking, the tedious rhythm of the work was tiring. The day after, squatting with two other women in mud and manure, we fashioned bricks. On the following day, we dug a latrine trench with the stench of the old latrine wafting about us. The morning after, Tamsir returned to drive me back to Bamako.

Reluctantly, I rolled my blanket and stuffed my belongings in my backpack. I thought of Mom—wished that she could know Aunt Khady. I wondered whether I would have found life in the bush exhilarating if it were my only life, if I were not returning to the comfort of our well-staffed compound. Wearing Aunt Khady's gift, a bracelet of goathair and cowrie shells, I said my good-byes sadly to women who had demonstrated their competence in life-sustaining skills, women whose actions were articulate, although not a syllable of their language could I understand. Through them I had realized that an organized collective of women could be a self-reliant community; I had witnessed the fundamentals of independence. Content in their midst, I have returned to their village from time to time to learn a few other things from them about my own life and to be revitalized.

An agitated Ibrahim awaited me at the hotel. Disturbed because I had not been with him to handle some details (he mentioned noting descriptions of locations, obtaining official documents, and comforting him), he was eager to leave Bamako for Tunis. I was eager to tell him about Aunt Khady and my work with the village women.

"You ought to consider Aunt Khady's village as the setting for a film—a film about the dynamics of building teamwork and solidarity in a village of self-supporting women rather than another film about weak, oppressed, abused women. It would make an important political statement."

"Sarah, audiences are moved by sorrowful scenarios, not by success stories. Anyone can make simplistic documentaries about how a village feeds itself. In an artful way, I want to show how economic, political, and religious forces intersect in the drama of deteriorating village life. I want actors to play out my script, to create cinematic events that will incite protests. I want audiences to stream out of cinemas and storm the ministries, mosques, and churches that are hindering progress, hampering the independence of individuals, villages, nations.

"But people need positive examples, actual accounts of relief from poverty and oppression, inspirational examples—not merely the rhetoric of revolution," I responded. The static of a serious disagreement crackled between us.

"In Tunis, at the university, I hope you will find some inspirational examples of women literary scholars. Give up your romantic ideas about rural life and return to research and writing. We'll discuss this on the plane," he said with finality. I was annoyed by his dismissive attitude.

We didn't discuss anything of consequence during the flight. Instead, Ibrahim slept. While he was sleeping, I was recording everything I could remember of the days and nights in Aunt Khady's village. The everyday chores of those ordinary peasant women were heroic acts that sustained their children, their village, and their traditions. In remote, neglected regions across the continent, village women were contributing to the security of Africa. What I had found beautiful, restorative, and stimulating in the lore, language, and quality of life in my quarter of Dakar, was derived, in part, from the toil of village women. My own leisure was linked in some measure to their work. Somehow this was a vitally important insight. I knew that my life would be changed by my comprehending that the labor of village women was part of the infrastructure that supported the entire continent.

# 37

IN TUNIS, THE UNIVERSITY TEEMED WITH PRO-
fessors and students from the Maghreb and the Middle East,
participants in the conference on Current Trends in the Islamic
World. Ibrahim was invited to comment on films screened at the
conference. He suggested that I take a taxi tour of the Bay of
Tunis or visit Carthage or go to a beach. Instead, I decided to
tour the university. In the courtyard of the university were
tables with brochures, pamphlets, and books. I greeted a woman
who was setting up a display of pamphlets and posters on
divorce, contraception, maternal care, and education for girls. I
told her I was pleased to find the materials and that I wanted
copies to take home to Senegal.

"Let me give you several publications," she said. Gathering
them, she began her spiel in clear, deliberate French. "There
have been progressive efforts to distribute information about
birth control and health care to women throughout Tunisia. We
train women as public health representatives. They travel in
mobile units across the country, take clinics to villages, offer
advice about health and medical care, offer contraceptives, and
give inoculations. I'll give you information about our literacy
campaign and our drive to educate girls. Of all the North
African countries, I believe we have the highest level of education among women. And what is Senegal doing for its girls and
women?" she asked.

Embarrassed that I was not prepared with facts about Senegal's programs and statistics, I hesitated. I could have related
anecdotes about Senegalese friends, relatives, and acquaintances.

I could have reported impressions derived from our film research; but I had little or no reliable information about the condition of the women of Senegal. Instead, I told her about Aunt Khady and the work of women who were sustaining the development of their village. When I told her that I would send her demographic information about Senegalese women, she gave me her card:

AZIZA
L'ALLIANCE DES FEMMES
*TUNIS* 259-111

Aziza asked for my card. Card? At that moment, I realized that since I had been in Senegal, my calling card had never been required. I had circulated in the company of Ibrahim, and was known to acquaintances and strangers as Ibrahim Mangane's wife. I told Aziza that I didn't have any cards with me. I said I would write to her from my office at *l'Alliance des Femmes* in Senegal. Standing there before Aziza, I could see the sign on the door under the arcade on Dakar's Place de l'Indépendence, visualize the furnishings in the office, imagine work being done, and the role I would play in making a contribution to other women's lives. And I would have my card!

During the flight from Tunis to Dakar, I told Ibrahim about my conversation with Aziza. Excitedly, I began to elaborate on the idea of starting an organization for women in Senegal, an equivalent of the Tunisian *l'Alliance des Femmes.*

"I could not comprehend your romance with rural life in Mali. And I do not know why you wish to organize *l'Alliance des Femmes* in Dakar. Leave that to Dakar's *grandes dames* who have little to do. At the moment, I have plans for new work—periods of intense work and travel, filming on location in Mali, lecture tours, conferences in London and Venice, film festivals in Ouagadougou and Cannes. I would like to have you with me. This is not the time for you to step out in a new direction. The boys need you. I need you. I cannot curtail my work, shift my travel schedule to accommodate your incompatible enterprises.

You also need to return to your writing. You understand, don't you?"

"Of course, I understand. I don't expect you to curtail your projects or your travels because of me and the directions my interests are taking. Ousmane and Isaac will need me for a while, but soon they will be away at school. And you need a professional staff for your projects."

"Perhaps I should develop a staff, but I will always need you," he entreated. His eyes widened and his tone was earnest.

I was not persuaded. Something within me had changed. Like a shift in the earth's tectonic plates, levels of consciousness had shifted, and what mattered to the core of my life had moved to a higher level.

# 38

ALTHOUGH I HAD RETURNED FROM TUNIS
with my sights set on announcing an agenda for a collective of
women, instead I found myself again responding to the habitual
expectations of Ibrahim and the children. For three or more
years, my pattern of life changed very little, while Ibrahim was
undergoing a startling metamorphosis.

Ousmane and Isaac, by now at fourteen and nine years old,
were at stages that engaged me completely. Ibrahim's aunts,
nieces, and cousins rejoiced about my involvement with the
boys' schooling, their sports, and their other interests. Fatou
explained that the relatives had feared that I would be entirely
devoted to Ibrahim's work and would neglect our sons. Despite
his gently chiding me about diminishing interest in his projects,
Ibrahim delighted in finding me in the courtyard surrounded by
the boys, their pets, and their toys.

Like many mothers, I turned my energies and aspirations
toward the boys' performance and progress and formed friendships with other women whose sons were at school with Ousmane and Isaac. We compared our sons' traits and their
accomplishments, each mother certain that her sons were supe-
rior in important respects.

Françoise Dia, whose sons were between Ousmane and Isaac
in age, sometimes lamented that she had abandoned her legal
studies. Her consolation: "However, my husband is a lawyer
and our sons will be lawyers."

Aissatou Fall, a political scientist at the university with a son
Isaac's age, had not married. She explained, "There's no hope of

finding a husband who might allow me the independence and time that my profession requires. I have my work, my dear son, and the friendships of colleagues and students." I envied her autonomy.

Like many families of men in public life, ours sometimes was the focus of unwelcome attention. For instance, we were viewed as a model couple by some Senegalese men who had married African-American women. They introduced their wives to me with the expectation that the secrets of our domestic life might be shared with them. They had met at Howard, Oberlin, Cornell, or Purdue and entered into marriage, unaware of the social and emotional tariffs attached to importing their relationships into family life and society in Senegal. I spent countless hours with American brides who felt they had been deceived by their Senegalese husbands who had not prepared them for their obligations to in-laws with whom they lived in rural family compounds. At the end of each session, we agreed that my situation was quite different from theirs, that they lacked the privacy, wealth, and prestige that I enjoyed. Despite our differences, I understood the discontent and deprivation they felt.

As Ibrahim's eminence grew and our private sphere became increasingly public, inquisitive journalists and photographers penetrated our domestic boundaries. They wanted to know about Ibrahim's favorite dishes, the details of our routine with the children, the frequency of my dressmaker's visits, and the value of my jewels. At the beach, making sand castles with the boys, cameras surrounded us. When Ibrahim took Isaac for his first day of school, there was a photographer at the gate to record the moment. *Ebony* magazine sent a crew from the States that hoped to take a picture of our bedroom! At the Cannes Film Festival, Ibrahim and I were trailed by photographers. During our vacation in Greece, a reporter with a video camera followed us from island to island.

Visibly irritated by the presence and persistence of reporters and photographers, I resisted their inquiries, protested the intrusiveness. As I did so, Ibrahim often said, "When cameramen turn their lenses elsewhere, it is then that I am disturbed. When there are no reporters inquiring about my opinion, then I am concerned."

"Why are you hungry for their attention? You've become media hungry."

He protested that he was not hungry for attention. "I am hungry for the truth," Ibrahim corrected. "When people recognize that a book or a film brings them closer to some truths about their society and their moment in history, then they want to know more about the source of it, understand the nature of its authorship. As long as the media are interested in me, I know that what I am delivering has some importance for our times. I know that I have touched truth."

I didn't have an effective rebuttal or counterargument. I was still offended, however, by voyeurs and other strangers who violated our private occasions. I was reminded of my birthday lunch when Mariama, Bill Nelson, and I watched as Ibrahim was greeted by admirers in the restaurant. How would Mariama have managed the public interest that later surrounded Ibrahim's life? Would Ibrahim's work have become controversial and claimed international attention if Mariama had lived? I wondered about my influence and the extent of my responsibility for the turn of events in Ibrahim's career.

At a conference in Paris, reporters shoved me aside to inquire about Ibrahim's views on the position of women. He responded pensively with a statement that was a recitation of strategies that I had formulated just the night before. Some of the ideas were mine. He was quoting me—without acknowledging the source. The following day I read in the news my ideas about strategies for changing the polygamy system. The article appeared under this caption: "Mangane Calls for Deinstitutionalization of Polygamy."

"Ibrahim, do you recall who suggested these proposals?" I asked, waving the newspaper.

"That's partnership, my dear. And that is what sometimes happens with partners." He smiled affectionately, reached for my hand, and kissed my palm. My annoyance was not allayed. I withdrew my hand. He added pompously, "They want the senior partner to deliver the ideas."

My veneration of Ibrahim was the foundation of our partnership and marriage. In the beginning, I was completely dedicated to his artistic vision. I was generous with my opinions and my material. My own objectives, beyond the dissertation and then the publication of the book, were vague. The aggrandizement of Ibrahim's career was my career—at least initially. When his career no longer required my promotion, when his works no longer needed my amplification, the nature of our partnership began to change. Our marriage changed.

We remained loving partners in bed; and we worked steadily at our partnership as parents. "Papa" was the authority, the decision maker, as viewed by Ousmane and Isaac; our decisions about their upbringing were made jointly, however. Together we determined what schools suited them best, which values we wished to instill, and where we would vacation with the children.

In intellectual matters and artistic work, however, our partnership faltered. Ibrahim began to draw inspiration and concepts from other sources. Filmmaking, for several years, became his primary medium.

"Film is the art form and propaganda instrument of the future," he told an audience. "It takes much too long to write novels that are intended to have a political impact. By the time you finish the novel, the conditions that you want to influence have changed. By the time it is read—and understood—the epoch of the novel has passed, and the individuals who inspired the creation of the protagonists are dead."

Ibrahim's film work brought sleek, fashionable young women and men into his circle, slang fresh from Paris, New York, and Los Angeles into his vocabulary, and trendy images onto his screen. Wearing T-shirts and blue jeans rather than his handsome caftans was another symptom of his change. He bought a red Maserati and drove it much too fast. The change in his personal style, I suppose, was essential to his art; however, I found in it another source of tension in our marriage—a marriage that was sagging under the weight of his celebrity.

And then came the situation that made Venice a frequent destination. Initially, Ibrahim was invited to a conference in Venice on cultural cooperation. He had asked me to accompany him. I declined. I didn't want to leave the boys. Besides, we had been there to the film festival earlier in the year.

A month after the conference, Ibrahim returned to Venice for a "follow-up session"; and the following month he made two trips for "report writing." I had become concerned about the frequency of the Venice trips and his aloofness when he returned. I filled the emptiness brought on by his absence with the boys' activities, trips to villages in Senegal with an Oxfam America representative, a meeting with a UNESCO agent, sessions on the advancement of women at the Ministry of Development, and library research on the status of women. Occasionally, I had lunch or dinner with the Dioufs, the Dias, or Aissatou Fall, all of them aware of Ibrahim's trips to Venice.

During his longest absence, Aissatou asked me to meet her for lunch. Waiting for her at a restaurant overlooking the harbor on the Corniche, I lit a Gauloise—I was smoking again—and ordered an apéritif. My mind was on Ibrahim. My head was filled with the music of Billie Holiday, Bessie Smith, Roberta Flack, Aretha Franklin—singing everywoman's blues. Breathlessly, Aissatou arrived with news that confirmed my blues. She handed me a magazine, turned to a page with a photo of Ibrahim dancing cheek to cheek with a blonde in a strapless gown. "Contessa Martellino Dancing Toward Romance?" the caption read.

"European women have a certain appeal for African men and vice versa," Aissatou remarked.

I was stunned like a bird in flight, struck by a hunter's buckshot.

"Well, Sarah, what are you going to say to him? What are you going to do? Now we know why he's been going to Venice. An Italian hussy. We thought Ibrahim was an advocate for women, a feminist. But he's just another philanderer. I suppose you should have expected something like this now that he's a celebrity."

"That's enough. Enough, Aissatou! I don't want to talk about him. What's there to say about a picture in a tawdry magazine? I'm not having lunch. I'm going home. Please excuse me." Clutching the magazine, I dashed to the car where Mamadou was waiting.

*15 November 1979*
*I overreacted to Aissatou's comments about the photo of Ibrahim dancing with an Italian countess. I knew there was a woman in Venice, not a committee! Patience. Understanding. Talk with him. Hear his account. That is the advice I would give to someone in my place. Patience and trust! Can I trust him?*
*"And in the dusk you will be full of regret for the burning voice/that sang once of your dark beauty."*
                                                            *—L. S. Senghor*

That night Ibrahim telephoned from Venice. The connection was poor, the line crackled; his voice was faint. I asked him to shout.

"I've been delayed," he strained.

"Who's delayed you, Ibrahim?"

"There is a great deal of confusion about the report, about translations. I wish you were here to help with—"

"I'll join you. I can get a flight out tomorrow."

"No, no, Sarah, dear. You needn't come. We've nearly finished. I'm flying home tomorrow—yes, tomorrow. I merely called to say that I will return tomorrow on the evening flight via Rome. I love you." He hung up. I sat there, on the edge of our bed, clutching the phone. I was burning with fury and fear. I buried my face in his pillow, biting it, wanting to bite Ibrahim, to hurt him badly. I lay there sobbing.

Tomorrow finally dawned. It was a long day of waiting and searching for words for my fury and fear. Confront him? Curse him? What should I say to him? What should I do?

Toward midnight, the murmur of his Maserati signaled Ibrahim's return. Brandishing the crumpled magazine and fuming with rage, I was waiting for him.

"Disturbed by this photo, are you? Well, you shouldn't be, my dear. Angelica Martellino is happily married and you and I are happily married. Her husband was at the ball—it was a benefit for UNICEF—with her."

"Are you having an affair with the woman, Ibrahim?"

"I had a flirtation with her, not an affair. You know Venice. Ibrahim Mangane having an affair with Pietro Martellino's wife in Venice? Impossible! They would be dragging the Grand Canal for my body. She was on the committee, we saw each other at meetings, had lunch together once or twice, and at the ball, for the photographer, we playfully posed. That's all. There's no more than that to it. Besides, it's over—the work of the committee is finished. I've made my last trip to Venice. It's over, Sarah."

Whether or not it was over scarcely mattered. What troubled me deeply was that it had happened. Was it Mariama's revenge? Had she felt the injury of infidelity as painfully as I? That night, I slept in the guest house. Before I went to sleep, I wept with guilt about Mariama and pity for myself.

# 39

I NEEDED TO GET AWAY. A TRIP ABROAD—A FEW
weeks in Europe and a swing through Boston, New York, and
Washington. I wanted to travel alone. Ousmane and Isaac could
manage very well without me. I felt that, by this time, I was
more dependent on them than they were on me. I needed to
recover my independence. I booked reservations and, afterward, told Ibrahim of my itinerary.

"Alone? Why do you want to go alone?"

"I need to be alone. I need to try to figure out who I now
am—who I've become. Who am I when I'm not identified as
your wife or the mother of Ousmane and Isaac? Who am I outside this compound, your realm, outside Dakar? I need to find
out a few things about myself—what I want to read, when I
want to bathe, what I want to eat, what I will wear—without
thinking about how you, your grand public, or for that matter,
the boys influence what I do and who I am."

"I will go with you. I certainly need a vacation, too. Istanbul,
Rome, Nice, Paris, London, Boston, New York, Washington—
an unusual itinerary. Why go to Istanbul, Nice, London, and
Boston? Nothing is happening in those cities. I'd want to visit
Cannes for the festival, Paris, of course, Berlin, and in the U.S.,
New York, Los Angeles, and San Francisco."

"You've just demonstrated why I need to go alone—to follow my own itinerary—alone! I've made reservations for a
flight from Dakar to Istanbul; another from Istanbul to Rome
where I'll spend a few days, then fly from Rome to Nice, Nice
to Paris, Paris to London. Then to Boston and Cambridge to

see Peter Martin and Antonia, visit some old haunts, to see friends in New York and family in Washington. And it's not a vacation, Ibrahim, it's a pilgrimage."

"Are you going away to get even, Sarah? To meet someone, have a fling or an affair yourself?"

I felt a flush of annoyance at his suggestion, then had a fleeting fantasy about a few hours with a more mature Lincoln, a rendezvous with Bill Nelson, or an erotic encounter with a new acquaintance. But I truly very much wanted to be alone.

"You don't understand. I'm going away to be alone."

"Very well. I will transfer funds for the trip to your account. And money for presents, clothes, and anything else you might find along the way. If you change your mind and decide you want company, I will be happy to join you."

As I made arrangements for accommodations, it became clear to me that I did not wish to be entirely alone. I had planned to visit places where I had friends or acquaintances.

In Istanbul, I stayed with David and Susan Adams in their Bebek house, precariously cantilevered above the rippling waters of the Bosporus. David and I had corresponded from time to time after our Harvard years. His interest in Turkish literature and his pursuit of Susan had taken him to Istanbul, where they had a comfortable income generated by teaching English, translating novels, and buying exquisite Turkish kilims, which David sold to the foreign visitors. Fair-skinned, freckled, with curly red hair, David and Susan looked like twins; and they acted as if they had spent their entire lives together. Through David, Susan and I knew something about each other, but my arrival in Istanbul was our first meeting.

"Whenever we've encountered a brilliant, compassionate, beautiful woman whom I've admired, David has said, 'Yes, she's wonderful, but wait until you meet Sarah!' And here you are."

Curious about his account of my graduate years, I asked, "What else has David told you?"

"He said that in graduate school, whenever anyone was in difficulty—a student, department secretary, a young faculty member, you had a way of doing something or saying something that changed the nature of things. He's often said that you made his days in Cambridge bearable. And you made him feel that his interest in Turkish literature was valid and important when no one else did—not even his professors."

That Susan had bothered to tell me how I was remembered endeared me to her. She was an indefatigable companion for exploring Istanbul's markets. We spent hours in the Grand Bazaar haggling about the price of amber beads, gold bracelets, and silk. I wanted a suit made of Bursa silk. Susan's dressmaker, who required several fittings, turned out an elegant mauve suit.

David and I exchanged the little information we had about acquaintances from our Harvard years. Eventually, he asked about my work.

"I scan the journals and reviews of African literature looking for your name—"

"And you don't find me. I haven't written anything of consequence since the publication of my book."

"It's a pity, Sarah. The vantage point you have on African writing is unique. You're uniquely positioned to analyze African Francophone and Anglophone literature. You're surrounded by it."

"Or submerged under. And under Ibrahim, his interpretations, his literary preferences and critical opinions. I'm too much under his influence, much too dependent on him."

"That's a benefit of marriage. Marriage legitimizes intellectual dependency."

"Husbands are more likely to realize the benefits than wives."

Neither David nor I wished to pursue the topic. His own work was facilitated by Susan's ideas for subject matter, her editorial hand, and proofreader's eye. In the acknowledgments of both his books, he had thanked her for her "conscientious editing and constant encouragement." And I was sure that there was much more to be acknowledged.

David and Susan's relationship was a study in mutual dependence. Each anticipated the other's moods, ideas, and plans. One would begin a sentence and the other complete it. They boasted that they had never spent a night apart since they were married. No need for children, they had each other. They surrounded each other—and anyone else in their midst—with attention and affection. I enjoyed their embrace; however, on the day of my departure, I looked forward to being alone.

In Rome I was alone, but rarely unaccompanied—or not followed. In and out of galleries, book shops, and churches—even at the Vatican—men followed me. "*Bella!*" they murmured. They stared, they leered. Their dark eyes followed me. At the opera, the aggressive interest of the man seated next to me spoiled the last scene of an otherwise fabulous *Aïda*.

"*Bella!*" said an admiring salesman in a shop on Piazza Barberini when I swirled before the mirrors in a magenta taffeta gown. "*Bella!*" chorused the sales staff and customers. "I must have the gown," I said, seduced by their fascination with me.

> *Rome*
> *28 April 1980*
>
> *Finally, I am finding the solitude I have needed. Feeling alone at last, but not at all lonely. I feel revitalized— young. I lingered at Castel Sant'Angelo and watched the scene change with the changing of the light. It made me wish I were a painter—Turner perhaps—at the site that every painter who comes to Rome must attempt. Where are the works of women who have painted the landscape of Rome?*
>
> *Pensione Sistina is perfect. Attentive staff. Being cared for, feeling attended to, feeling that my wants matter—is that what I have been missing? Is that what this trip is about? It's about time—time to listen to my own heartbeat and regain an awareness of my own rhythm.*
>
> *2 May*
>
> *See Rome and live to see Rome again! Spectacular sunset this evening. For the first time, I missed Ibrahim. Wanted to be with him at sunset and beyond. Tried to phone him; could not connect with Dakar. It is just as well.*

*I would rather that he call. Beginning to miss O & I, too. Time for a change of scene. Tomorrow to Nice.*

David had suggested that I stay at the Hotel West-End in Nice instead of the Negresco. "The Negresco is overdecorated and terribly overpriced," he'd said. I canceled my reservation at the Negresco and reserved a room at the West-End, a room tastefully furnished in Provençal style, with floor-to-ceiling windows and a balcony that overlooked the Baie des Anges, sparkling under late-afternoon sun when I arrived.

Drawn to the balcony and the waves on the bay, I whispered, *"I will cast my eyes upon this bay from whence cometh help. My help cometh from Senegal, which is heaven and earth."* I stood gazing at the water, pondering the question: to call him or not to call him. At that moment, the telephone rang.

"Hello."

"Sarah?"

"Ibrahim!"

"You have deviated from your schedule. You're not at the Negresco."

"How did you find me? No matter. I'm very happy that you have. I was thinking of you at the very moment the phone rang."

"Have you had dinner?"

"No, but, Ibrahim, where are you?"

"I'm only an hour away—at Cannes. Will you have dinner with me?"

"Cannes? Wonderful! When? Where should we—"

"I am coming for you. I have a superb suite at the Carlton. You remember the Carlton? I can't wait to see you—to be with you. Tell the front desk you are checking out. I will be there within the hour. Sarah, I love you. I love only you. I've missed you very much."

"I adore you."

Of course, Ibrahim was at Cannes. The festival was opening. And, of course, he would be at the Carlton. I remembered it well. I shivered with delight at the prospect of seeing him. I had

missed him constantly. I returned to the balcony. I sat mesmerized by the view and waited for his ring. While I waited, I tried
to recall a sentence from one of the volumes in Durrell's *Alexan-
dria Quartet:* "To the student of love, separations are painful,
but necessary," is how I remembered it. If the words weren't
accurate, the sentiment certainly was.

Ibrahim had been invited to Cannes to receive the Caméra
d'Or. He was in high spirits. He nearly lifted me off my feet and
danced me out of the lobby of my hotel to the limousine that he
had hired. The bell captain gave us a conspiratorial wink—his
wink for couples involved in illicit affairs. Like illicit lovers, we
cuddled and French-kissed in the commodious backseat of the
limousine that took us to the Carlton, where a bottle of chilled
champagne was waiting and a luxurious bed was turned down
for the night. No need for dinner. We were only hungry for each
other.

Ibrahim asked which films would interest me. We saw those
films. During the films, we held hands, he caressed my thighs,
kissed my neck.

There was a program at which Ibrahim was presented with
the Caméra d'Or. His acceptance speech was magnificent. He
received a standing ovation. I wore the magenta gown from
Rome, a tiara of magenta flowers in my upswept hair, and a
heart-shaped pin studded with rubies and pearls, Ibrahim's gift
for the occasion.

At the banquet that followed, directors, actors, and critics
spoke in praise of Ibrahim's works. It was a grand night for us.
Except for the banquet and an evening in Saint-Paul-de-Vence,
where we had dinner with James Baldwin at La Colombe d'Or,
we dined alone—romantic dinners—at restaurants or in our
suite.

Each morning in Cannes we walked along the Croisette, the
boulevard at the edge of the beach. We spent an exhilarating
afternoon at the Maeght Foundation, where in each painting,
each sculpture, Ibrahim saw traces of African art. "Contemporary European art would be sterile without the influence of
African art," he observed. On the eve of my scheduled depar-

ture, we toured the clubs and danced until dawn. When we awoke, we lay in bed considering whether I should leave for Paris or stay on with Ibrahim for another week at Cannes.

"Will extending our time together diminish our pleasure? Is that what you are wondering?"

"Yes, precisely. What do you think?"

"You must decide. I would love to have you stay here until the end of the festival. But I know what this trip means to you. It is a hardship for us—for the boys and me—having you abroad for nearly three months. We miss you. Our days are empty without you and my nights are terrible. I don't sleep well when you are not at my side.

"I hadn't planned to come to Cannes merely for an award ceremony. When I realized that I might lie in ambush here, intercept you, court you, renew our love, I decided to come. I didn't come for the Caméra d'Or. No, I came for the grand prize—you! You, my prize, my treasure, my beauty." He kissed my bare shoulders, my neck, my open mouth.

"Now that I am here, they expect me to attend a few sessions and comment on some films. I cannot take the award and run. They would say, 'You see, he is uncultivated. One expects that sort of behavior from an African.' I would like very much to go to Paris with you—not that you've invited me. After the festival, I could join you in Paris, see the Nelsons, Bill and his wife, and—"

"By that time, I'll be in London," I said, staring at the ceiling.

"And you need to continue your odyssey alone. I know that you need some time, some distance from me, and time for yourself. These weeks apart have been good for you. You are clearer about what interests you, what you want to do. It is as if your vision had become blurred and your voice muffled in our years together."

"You're not only a great author and film director, you are becoming a perceptive husband," I said playfully. Then earnestly, "I love you, Ibrahim. I need to be with you, but I also need to be away for just a few weeks more. But I worry about the boys—how they are interpreting my absence. It may be a good idea to have them join me. They'll be out of school when I go to the States. What would you think of their meeting me in New York and going to Washington?"

"Splendid idea! Your parents haven't seen them for years. The boys need to know your family, know where you grew up. At this age, they would appreciate it. Let's phone them now and tell them. They should be at home." After several attempts, the connection to Dakar was made and the telephone rang. Mamadou answered. Ousmane was at his tennis lesson. Isaac, however, was there. Ibrahim spoke in Wolof with Isaac about the trip and then I took the phone. In French, Isaac said, "Mama, we're going to New York and Washington with you! *Formidable!*" He whistled his delight and almost immediately hung up, eager to tell Mamadou, his cousins, and his chums.

I was forever grateful to Ibrahim for intercepting me. At the airport, we had an affectionate parting. We parted with a renewed commitment to our marriage, an understanding of the necessity of our relationship. We had six days together in Cannes—six perfect days. It was the honeymoon that we had never had.

# 40

IN PARIS, I STAYED WITH BILL NELSON AND HIS wife of five years, Elaine, an accomplished painter. Bill, then cultural attaché at the U.S. Embassy in Paris, was proud of Elaine's talents. When they married, Bill sent his bride's résumé along with their wedding announcement. Their sparsely furnished apartment—more a gallery than a home—was on the second floor of a fin-de-siècle building between the Champs-Elysées and Avenue Franklin D. Roosevelt.

It was a very warm afternoon, yet Bill was wearing his usual diplomatic service attire, a three-piece midnight blue pinstriped suit, white shirt, and striped tie. The moment I arrived, he showed me Elaine's paintings, geometric abstract oils on canvas, and announcements of her shows—shows in Oslo, Stockholm, Amsterdam, Vienna, Brussels, and Madrid. She used her own name, Elaine Rivers. Her youthful copper-colored face, Nefertiti features, intense olive-black eyes, close-cropped black hair, and large silver earrings were arresting. She dressed entirely in black—black slacks and shirts adorned with ornate silver pendants or pins. I always wore white in Paris—a white linen suit, white slacks and blouses, white boubous for evenings. The contrast wasn't lost on Parisians who saw us together.

"We just learned that a gallery in the fourth arrondissement wants to exhibit Elaine's latest paintings," boasted Bill.

"It's a first-class gallery. I am ecstatic about it," she said. She spoke rapidly and smoked constantly.

"Do you exhibit in New York?" I asked.

Her face reddening and eyes flashing, she vented her spleen.

"I've sent my slides and announcements of my shows in Europe to museums and galleries in New York and up and down the East Coast—Boston to Miami—and to Chicago, Santa Fe, Denver, San Francisco, Detroit, even to Cleveland, and they've sent them back with their regrets. They regret—damn them—that the work doesn't look like the work of a black artist. If it's not figurative, doesn't represent scenes of black folks, preferably down-and-out black folks, with tenements crumbling in the background, then it's not acceptable from a black painter. Gallery owners and museum curators have decided that they'll control what black artists may and may not show in America. Luckily, galleries here have looked only at my work—not at my race or my color—and they have liked it, and shown it. And I've sold nearly every painting that I've shown."

Elaine wanted me to see her Paris. We spent hours in museums, galleries, and the ateliers of her artist friends and in cafés discussing what we had seen. In the late afternoon, Bill joined us and we made the rounds of bookstores and bookstalls. I bought dozens of books—biographies, autobiographies, letters, novels, literary criticism, poetry, philosophy. Most of them were by women authors—African, Caribbean, European, Latin American, and North American women.

Elaine continued browsing while Bill and I filled out the forms required for shipping the books to Dakar. In the midst of the paperwork, I said, "I'm glad you and Elaine found each other. She seems to be an ideal partner for you."

"I was, of course, looking for you, that is to say, for somebody like you when I met Elaine. Her energy, creativity, and intelligence reminded me of you. She's very capable, very spirited. Like you, she knows how to make things happen."

"I'd like to make some things happen in the lives of some of the village women I've met."

"So that's your new interest. I'm surprised," said Bill. "I'd assumed that you would continue to pursue a career in the arts and cultural affairs."

"The arts became a secondary concern for me when I realized that without food security, clean water, maternal health care, literacy programs, and environmental reclamation campaigns, there may not be artists or audiences for the arts—in Africa or elsewhere—generations from now."

"But you're an excellent organizer and advocate for artists. I remember very well all you did to organize and produce the festival at Dakar. It was your vision, determination, and persuasiveness that made it happen. Everyone in the arts in Paris knows of you. They know about your unheralded work as a producer and what you have done over the years to help African painters, sculptors, artisans, actors, dancers, singers, and writers. Ibrahim hasn't been the sole beneficiary of your altruism. Every Senegalese artist I've met has acknowledged your assistance. You're a legend in the arts. I can't imagine your shifting to development work at this point in your life."

"I can imagine a very satisfying work experience in the company of people who are struggling for survival, especially the women who are trying to maintain customs, social order, and family life."

"What does Ibrahim think of your concern about development projects?"

"He finds it—well, diversionary. He's discouraged it."

"Because it might compete with his work or because it is your initiative?"

"A bit of both."

"You're right about the importance of focusing on women in village work. But I wonder if it is the appropriate focus for you, if development work would be the best use of your education and experience? If I were in Dakar, you, Ibrahim, and I would have some very interesting discussions on this subject. Oh, to be in Dakar with you and Ibrahim Mangane there. That's the place to be!"

Growing nostalgic about Dakar, Bill suggested that we visit "Dakar-sur-Seine" on my last day in Paris. As we strolled through Paris's Senegalese markets, and then to a club where we lingered over Senegalese beer, Bill reviewed memories of a time when our lives were relatively simple. After his second beer, Bill said, "The summer we met, when it was clear that romance wasn't in the cards, I decided I'd become a brother to you. I told Elaine that she should think of you as a sister-in-law. We were meant to be more than friends. We were meant to be family. I want your sons to know me as an uncle and Elaine as an aunt. They should stay with us when they come to Paris." I accepted his including us in his family and his parting fraternal kiss.

# 41

THE SLOANE SQUARE HOME OF PATRICIA
and Geoffrey Mackenzie was my London destination. Patsy
was from Trinidad. We had met at Wellesley College. She had
spent her junior year in Edinburgh, where she met Geoffrey, a
tutor in Nordic history. Twice her age, he was married with
two children, and had the additional burden of being titled
nobility.

When Patsy returned to Wellesley for her senior year, Geoffrey invented invitations to New England universities. Tall, with
broad shoulders, thick blond hair, blond mustache, and silver-
rimmed glasses, he was the center of attention when he called
for "Miss Patsy Williams" at the dormitory. Patsy would
appear, her long, lithe figure under a loose-fitting flowered
frock that only women from the Caribbean somehow rendered
attractive. She was as dark as he was fair. Together they were
stunning.

A few years ago, I'd received a letter from Patricia Williams-
Mackenzie. She had read in the alumnae magazine that I was
married to Ibrahim Mangane and lived in Dakar. She wanted to
"renew contact since we both had chosen lives that spanned the
Atlantic." We began an exchange of Christmas greetings, postcards, and occasional letters.

Patsy had married Geoffrey two years after her graduation.
The marriage precipitated his dismissal from Edinburgh. He
had been employed at the BBC ever since. As a Caribbean specialist for the Commonwealth Secretariat, Patsy spent several
months each year in the islands. During my sojourn with Patsy,

Geoffrey was on assignment in Stockholm. Both their sons were away at school, but their captivating daughter, Miranda, materialized from time to time, usually wearing a leotard, and bending or stretching her way toward a career in ballet.

While Patsy was at her office, I visited the Tate, the Victoria and Albert, the National Portrait Gallery, and the Wallace Collection. I spent hours in Hamley's in search of games and puzzles for Ousmane and Isaac; and I shopped at Harrods for gifts for Ibrahim, Antonia, and my parents. Patsy and I went to see an Old Vic production of *Macbeth*.

On my last evening in London, she suggested an Indian restaurant for dinner. As we scanned the menu, Patsy posed an issue that shaped our dinner conversation.

"Nearly every woman I have known has speculated about the experience of being the wife of a famous man. Tell me what it's really like. How do you manage to have a normal married life with a man who is a public figure? One finds his books and films everywhere. And now there are articles about your private life. How ever do you deal with being married to him?"

"I assume you've read what the tabloids have printed about our marriage: 'The Manganes live a luxurious life in a secluded compound in an exclusive suburb of Dakar. Ibrahim Mangane, despite his Marxist tendencies, has an American capitalist wife. She is a fanatical feminist who has claimed him as a convert. While his earlier writings covered a wide range of subjects, thanks to his wife, he now concentrates on women's liberation and other feminist topics. Because of her Christianity, he has turned away from his Islamic traditions.' This is nearly verbatim what a newspaper carried about us! And it's a myth—journalistic mythology!"

"The true story, then. What's the true story?"

"It is true that we have a comfortable, secluded, exclusive lifestyle. My feminist influence on his work is evident. However, Ibrahim was always dedicated to improving social conditions in general—for women, men, and children. He understands that widening the roads that women travel will afford more space for men, too.

"As for my being Christian, well, that's highly questionable. Certainly, I was brought up in a family that went to church regularly and observed Christian holidays. But prior to our marriage I began to study the Koran. I have profound respect for Islam. I haven't influenced Ibrahim's religious attitudes whatsoever. I'm quite troubled by the fundamentalists who've denounced Ibrahim, blaming me for his interest in reform!"

"Sarah, you sound a bit defensive. What the press writes clearly has agitated you. I suppose that's part of the answer to what it means to be married to someone who is famous. Your marriage is influenced by what is written about it."

"To an extent, yes. But we try to remain faithful to the values and mutual interests that initially united us."

"Faithful to values and to each other?" She asked. I wondered if Patsy had seen a photo of Ibrahim and the Italian. Fortunately, the waiter appeared. I asked about the various tandooris before responding to her increasingly meddlesome questions.

"I've been faithful to Ibrahim. If he has been unfaithful, he has done so discreetly."

"You were married for a while to that handsome chap who dated you at Wellesley—Thompson, that was his name. Do you ever hear from him or wish that the marriage had worked?"

"I hear about him from time to time. I think our marriage ran its course. We were wise to end it, and I'm happier now with my life than I would have been as Lincoln's wife." The waiter interrupted to take our order, but the interruption did not divert Patsy from her inquiry. She then wondered why, if I claimed to be happy with Ibrahim, I was taking a long trip alone. In responding to her, I articulated an interpretation of our relationship which I found clarifying.

"Ibrahim has become larger-than-life. I sometimes feel emotionally and intellectually dwarfed in his presence. With an international reputation come obligations to a vast public audience. Witnessing his progress has been exhilarating. Without a doubt, I've enjoyed his successes, and I've contributed to them.

That's been very satisfying and, for a long time, that was sufficient. Now it's time for me to develop projects of my own."

"What do you have in mind?" Patsy's attentive manner elicited discussion of my new ambition.

"Ibrahim made a documentary in rural Mali. When I went there with him, I spent some time in a village of women. I fetched firewood and harvested corn with them, squatted with them and ate foufou. I slept on a dirt floor in a hut. As I worked with them, I began to understand better their strengths and their courage. I felt that they should be telling their own stories without our intervention, and making their own films. Those women are gifted storytellers. In different circumstances and with training, we'd probably discover that there are filmmakers, painters, sculptors, poets, and philosophers among them. I suppose that my wanting to explore their talents is an expression of my need to exercise my own," I confessed candidly.

"Yes, but what can you really do for them?"

"I'm interested in building an institution—an international center—where women of African descent could work together in a development community. I envision a place where peasant women and educated women could exchange information about reorganizing village labor, experimenting with crops, improving health care, and so on. And there would be space for the arts—weaving, pottery making, painting, sculpting, and creative writing."

"Sarah, that's an exciting concept! A settlement with African women of different classes and nationalities exchanging ideas!"

"At the moment, it's only an idea. I haven't discussed it with anyone else at all."

"It's a grand idea, but it would be bloody expensive. You would need to provide a facility, salaries, travel expenses, allowances, a support staff, maintenance, and so on." Patsy's managerial mind raced on. "It's a magnificent ambition—an international women's center. I've always admired your daring spirit. You should try to do it!"

Patsy's enthusiasm about my idea reinforced my own interest

in what had been only a vague fantasy. Her questions had given the fantasy some definition. After our discussion, I began to consider where the center could be established and how it would change my life.

A waiter brought Kingfisher beer and chapattis and returned with chicken curry, spinach with white cheese, rice, dahl, and chutneys. The aroma of the cuisine shifted our conversation to Patsy's concerns about relations between Indians and West Indians in London's neighborhoods. Toward the end of dinner, our talk turned to our children and our hopes for them.

"Ousmane is curious about religions. He's explored animism and he's excused himself from school on Christian holidays to attend Catholic services. He used to collect rosaries, crucifixes, and miniatures of the Virgin Mary, but now he's studying Islam. He has boasted that his teacher, a rather conservative imam, disapproved of Ibrahim's recent works. I worry about Ousmane, his tendency to oppose Ibrahim. Isaac, on the other hand, is open and curious about everything. He wants to be a journalist. He started a newspaper at his school and declared himself editor of the international page. He's a very enterprising fellow, well suited for journalism." As I spoke of them, I began to miss Ousmane and Isaac, and to look forward to my reunion with them in New York.

On the flight from Heathrow to Boston's Logan Airport, I wrote in my journal:

*I learn more about myself through observations of other women and conversations with them. Purpose and passion are what I now desperately need. At one time, I wanted only a well-balanced relationship with Ibrahim—with each of us sharing the world of the other completely. No more. It is no longer possible. Ibrahim now has a world of his own and I must create mine! I must define my own purpose, realize my own dreams. Perhaps I am no longer possessed.*

# 42

FOR ANYONE WHO HAS RETURNED TO HAR-
vard Square after a long absence, there is a sense of nonrecognition, resentment, and shock. Things are never where you
thought you left them.

Charming three-story buildings with specialty shops had
been replaced by high-rise concrete and glass structures. Except
for the Mandrake bookstore, the other small bookstores had
been forced out of business by book supermarkets. Once a
modest department store, the Harvard Coop now had annexes
and branches at MIT and in Boston. Formerly trusting shopkeepers now required two forms of identification for a purchase
paid by traveler's check. The soul of a town that had been a
scholar's paradise had become a commercial purgatory.

Fortunately, the Sheraton Commander Hotel had resisted
renovation and retained its unpretentious, underdecorated
appearance. I checked in at the Commander, where an aging
porter sagged under the weight of my bags. (In every city, I had
bought gifts—books, clothing, prints, and posters.) When we
reached the room, he said, "Lucky to have a single for you,
ma'am. It's graduation time, you know."

It was early June. Proud parents had come to witness the
Harvard-Radcliffe commencement ceremonies and celebrate
the success of their offspring. My thoughts flashed back to my
own graduation, my parents' visit, and the tension in my life at
that point. In retrospect, I wished that I had been a kinder, more
considerate daughter in the season of my graduation.

I had returned to see Antonia Dale, locate a few other friends, visit Wellesley College, browse in Harvard Square bookstores and Widener Library, tour the Fogg Museum and Boston's Museum of Fine Arts; stroll along Newbury Street and across Boston's Public Garden, find a club with good jazz, and hear a concert in Symphony Hall.

I had written to Peter Martin, who replied that he would be at the Aspen Institute while I was in Cambridge. I phoned his office anyway and left a message for him with my greetings. When I telephoned the history department at Boston University and asked for Antonia Dale, a secretary told me that Antonia had not been to her office for several weeks. She was recovering from a mild stroke. She could be reached by telephone at the home of her friend, the novelist Dorothy West, on Martha's Vineyard. She gave me the number. And so I returned to Martha's Vineyard on a sunny, warm island day. I drove to Woods Hole, where I left my rented car. On the ferry I whispered:

"*I will cast mine eyes upon the ocean from whence cometh my help. My help cometh from Senegal which is heaven and earth.*"

Homesickness for Senegal surged through me like an electric shock that leaves one clearer and more sharply focused on whatever is central to one's existence. Just as it had been important for me to leave Senegal for a journey into old and new territory, it felt essential for me to return to Senegal—to go home.

During the crossing to Oak Bluffs, I asked a few people for directions to Dorothy West's house. Everyone I asked knew of her; a few mentioned that they read her articles in *The Vineyard Gazette,* and finally a couple, a handsome, gray-haired, carefully but casually dressed black couple, told me that they passed her home on the way to theirs. They would be delighted to give me a ride to her door.

Waiting at the door of a tiny Victorian cottage with yellow clapboards and black shutters was an elderly, tobacco brown, elflike woman, with intelligent eyes and a wide, smiling mouth that welcomed me with a rush of words.

"I *knew* you would be on that ferry. You *must* be Sarah Mangane. I'm Dorothy West. Come in, do come in. Antonia has had her nap. She's getting up now. She's eager to see you."

Antonia, limping slightly, crossed the doll-size living room. We fell weeping into each other's arms. Dorothy disappeared into the kitchen where her typewriter began to clatter.

"Dear, dear Sarah, how good of you to come to see me. You look marvelous—unchanged by time. Let's sit on the porch. I want to hear all about the life and times of Sarah Stewart Mangane." Her speech was slurred, each word expelled with effort.

"Antonia, how are you? Tell me about you."

There were two wicker chairs on the narrow porch, on either side of the door. Antonia and I turned them so that we could look at each other. She reached into the pocket of her gray silk Japanese kimono and extracted a cigarette holder and, with a familiar gesture, inserted a Camel cigarette.

"Well, my story is short. I retired a year ago, went on a six-month tour of Asia, returned to write my *magnum opus,* the book I've wanted to write about nineteenth-century American history from a black perspective. Instead, I had a stroke. It's affected my right side." Slowly, around a heavy tongue, she talked. "So I'm not writing just yet. I am reading, though. I seem to be steadily recovering. Soon I hope to be able to write— to use this hand and type again—like Dorothy. She's got a five o'clock deadline. That's what keeps her going."

Antonia's disabilities were disconcerting. With a flurry of energy, as if to compensate for her lassitude, I gave a lively description of the events at Cannes, summarized Ibrahim's speech and his latest film. I told her about Ousmane and Isaac and described the highlights of my European tour. I had talked for nearly an hour before Antonia interrupted me.

"You've not said one word about your writing. What are you working on now?"

I hesitated for some time, then said, "I haven't been very productive recently."

"Just as I predicted, you've become his 'girl Friday.' You've sacrificed the promise of a brilliant career in order to walk in the shadow of that man." Her speech quickened. She sputtered, "Your name is going to be just one more name on the roster of sacrificial gifted women who have suppressed their ambitions in the interest of the success of their husbands. When you're my age, assessing the credits and debits on life's ledger, please enter that, years ago, I advised you to pursue a career in the university where you could have—"

"Antonia, you've been partially right about what I've given up for my life with Ibrahim. My work is at a standstill, but I have some ideas about a project, about establishing a center for women who—"

"Don't establish anything. Believe me, what you write is what matters. You're not going to be remembered for setting up some women's center!"

The rattle of Dorothy West's typewriter was a reminder of their generation's faith in the written word. I suddenly realized there was scarcely time to catch the 4:15 ferry. Rather abruptly, I said good-bye to Antonia, to Dorothy, and to Martha's Vineyard. It was my last visit with Antonia. In November, Dorothy sent me a copy of *The Vineyard Gazette*'s obituary of Antonia Stockwell Dale.

Driving from Woods Hole to Cambridge revived memories of my Vineyard pilgrimages when Lincoln and I were married. I took the same route I'd taken then. Memories led me to Trowbridge Street where we had lived. I saw that our building had been replaced by a honeycomb of buildings with condominiums and a sign proclaiming it "Trowbridge Village." What of Lincoln? He, too, may have disappeared.

At the hotel, I leafed through the telephone directory. Thompson, A. Lincoln, 6 Carver Street, Roxbury, 963-2468. I dialed the number. Two rings, then in Lincoln's voice a recorded message: "Please leave a message after the tone or call the headquarters of Link Thompson for U.S. House of Representatives."

After the tone, I said, "This is Sarah Stewart Mangane of Dakar calling to wish you a successful campaign. Best wishes in Washington."

His voice evoked a rush of bittersweet memories and the warmth of satisfaction about his run for Congress. If I had been living in Massachusetts, I would have worked in his campaign. An intelligent, honest, idealistic man, Lincoln deserved to win.

# 43

ANNOUNCING MY NEW YORK VISIT IN advance, I wrote or telephoned several friends whom I invited to meet me for champagne at the Algonquin on June tenth between 4:30 and 7:00 P.M. I had always found the Algonquin agreeable for conversation.

Excited about seeing my New York friends, I wondered who would join me. They all came: television producer Ellis Haizlip; lawyer Chuck Hamilton; college president Bernie Harleston and his wife, Marie; corporate executive Pam Carlton; columnist Lee Daniels; and the director of New York's service for international visitors, Kate Harris. They were thrilled to be in each other's company, as I knew they would. And they were happy to see me. In a peach linen boubou and peach headband studded with rhinestones, my braids in a tiara twist, I felt like royalty receiving royalty. Our table, bustling with announcements, revelations, confessions, and pure gossip, drew everyone's attention. Afterward, Ellis and I went to dinner at a forgettable French restaurant in the west forties, where he planned my New York agenda.

"You've got to see the new acquisitions at MOMA. Then for fun, you should check out the bathing suits at Saks. I'll meet you at the Plaza at one o'clock, and we'll go to a very WASPy club near there, where I can have breakfast and you can have lunch. And I want you to wear this thing—this boubou—you're wearing. We'll turn that place upside down! Then I'll take you to the airport to meet your sons. Okay, baby?" Okay.

Ousmane and Isaac had slept nearly all the way from Dakar

to New York. They arrived wide-eyed and exuberant. I was tearful and anxious—anxious about how they might have changed, how they would be touched by U.S. racism, whether they would be seduced by material goods, what my parents would think of my sons, and what my sons would think of my dear friend Ellis, who was wearing a copy of a costume for Joan of Arc.

Isaac kissed me and embraced me over and over again. He had grown just above my shoulder. "He's tall for ten years old," Ellis observed. Ousmane, who was my height when I left, seemed no taller; however, his shoulders were firmer, more muscular; and there was the fringe of a future mustache sprouting above his pouting mouth. Ousmane's greeting, a perfunctory peck on each cheek, was reserved. Scrutinizing Ellis and his garb, Ousmane said pointedly, "Papa sends you his regards, Mama."

Aware of Ousmane's aloofness, Ellis tactfully told the boys that he and I had been friends since grammar school; he added that he worked in theater and television, which immediately transformed him in their eyes. Only minutes in New York, and they had met a star.

I asked if they wanted to rest when we arrived at the hotel.

"No, Mama, I'm ready to discover America," Isaac said. He began by discovering all the amenities in the U.N. Plaza Hotel, after which he declared, "I like America."

"You like this hotel," Ousmane said.

They were eager to begin sightseeing, ready for the schedule of events that Ellis and I had arranged. I wanted them to see aspects of New York that had fascinated me on my childhood visits to the city. We went on a tour of the United Nations building, and then went across town to meet an anthropologist I had known at Harvard, who guided us through the American Museum of Natural History. Afterward we went uptown to Sylvia's Restaurant on Lenox Avenue, walked along 125th Street, saw the Apollo Theater and the Studio Museum of Harlem, went along historic Striver's Row and then to Sugar Hill. We drove through the South Bronx, visited the Bronx Zoo, and toured Columbia University; we took the elevator to the top of the Empire State Building, had a hansom ride through Central Park, saw the Alvin Ailey Company at Lincoln Center, and dined at the Russian Tea Room.

Exhausted after several days of sightseeing, Ousmane, Isaac, and I nodded and napped during the train ride from New York through the backyards and industrial dumps of New Jersey, Delaware, and Maryland to Washington. My parents, my cousin Rosemarie, her husband Sam, and son Ronald, were waiting at Union Station. My mother's voice rose above the greetings of the others, above the roar of the Amtrak engines, above the rumble of the arrival and departure of passengers.

"Glory be, there they are, safely home at last," Mom cried. "Isaac! Finally, I get to see my grandson Isaac." She wrapped her arms around him, then stepped back to look at him. "He looks like you, Sarah. He looks like us." I knew that she meant he was not as dark as Ibrahim and Ousmane. His burnt sienna skin color, close to her own, pleased her. Skin color still mattered to her.

"Welcome home, Sarah, Ousmane, Isaac," Dad said in a voice without energy or emotion. His hair had turned white; he was no longer robust and stout, but thin and frail with ashen skin. I knew he had been ailing, but when I saw the ravaging effects of his condition, I realized he was suffering. We held each other in a long embrace, and somehow held back our tears.

"Hi, gorgeous!" called Rosemarie who, although she was three years older than I, had always looked younger and always was dressed like a fashion model. "My goodness, these big boys can't be your sons. We were just looking through the photo album. They looked like babes in the latest pictures—and look at them now. Ronnie, meet your African cousins and help them with their bags."

Ronnie, the age and height of Ousmane, smiled and shook hands.

"How do ya like Ronnie's pendant?" asked Sam, pointing to a copper pendant in the shape of Africa. "Look, they're genuine Africans and they're not wearin' no necklaces with Africa hangin' from it, Ronnie. And they're not wearin' buttons with slogans about Africa either."

Ronnie, flushed with embarrassment, lagged behind. Ousmane, quick to side with someone in conflict with a parent, or to notice a flicker of tension, walked in step with Ronnie.

Isaac moved ahead and walked with Dad, hand in hand, engaged in an animated conversation. I was arm in arm with Mom and Rosemarie.

"We were hoping your husband would come," said Rosemarie.

"How is Ibrahim?" asked Mom. "I'm sure he's busy with some film he's making." It was her way of telling Rosemarie that only important work would keep him away.

Out of cool, cavernous Union Station, we walked into the heat of Washington's mid-June sun.

"How long you stayin' here?" asked Sam.

"We're leaving July first," I said.

"Too bad you can't stay a few days more so your boys could see the fireworks on the fourth of July," he said.

The lyrics of the *Star Spangled Banner* rippled through my memory: "*And the rockets' red glare, the bombs bursting in air . . .*"

I looked over my shoulder, toward the U.S. Capitol, and saw dozens of flags—stars and stripes—aflutter in the wind. A week in Washington was a long time. I felt my unresolved conflicts about identification with the U.S. resurfacing. I carried a U.S. passport, although I preferred to present my passport issued by the Republic of Senegal. The irony of feeling foreign in the city of my birth, the capital of my native land, was very disturbing.

Sam said, "While these kids are here, Sarah, I'm goin' to show them the sights, the Capitol, the Washington Monument, the White House, the State Department, and the FBI Building. Maybe drive to Annapolis to see the Naval Academy. I'll show 'em what makes us a great nation."

Sam had served in the U.S. Marines in the Korean War. A beneficiary of the G.I. Bill, he owned a prosperous construction company. He, Rosemarie, and Ronnie lived in a suburban Maryland rambling ranch house with a pool, drove expensive cars, and kept a boat at a marina on the Chesapeake Bay. Sam, who had realized "the American dream," was proud of being politically conservative.

When we reached the parking area, our party split up, with Ousmane riding with Ronnie in Rosemarie and Sam's car, and Isaac and I riding with Dad and Mom. Isaac sat in the front seat between them, and I sat in the backseat, scrutinizing my parents' skin blotches, thinning hair, and deepening wrinkles. I wondered: who will go first and how will the survivor manage without the other? And what will they expect of me as they grow older?

For Ousmane, the Washington visit was instructive; for Isaac it was fun. With Sam they saw "official" Washington; and with Dad they toured affluent residential areas and the city's shabby neighborhoods. He told them about the changes he had witnessed in his seventy-eight years of growing up and growing old in the city. He spent an entire day with them at the Air and Space Museum. Together, we spent another day at the National Gallery and the Phillips Collection, where Mom and I pointed out our favorite paintings and sculptures to Ousmane and Isaac.

There were visits with relatives and family friends who were eager to show two boys from Africa—and me—some of the comforts of residential life. New gadgets and appliances, home entertainment centers, swimming pools in various shapes, patios with gas barbecue equipment, and cultivated gardens were displayed as a way of saying, and some actually said, "I bet you don't have these things in Senegal"; or "Sarah, see what you're missing by living in Africa"; or simply, "We have a higher standard of living."

"Now I understand why you left America and married Papa," said Ousmane. "These people are greedy for capitalist goods, Mama. They're good people, but they don't know that they are exploited civil servants working for a government that simply uses them."

On Sunday, Mom took us to church, where the pastor prayed during the service for "Sister Stewart's fine daughter and grandsons who journeyed all the way from Africa to worship with us." The choir's soulful harmony filled the church with "Get on Board, L'il Children," and for a moment I felt welcomed and at home.

"I'd like to see the streets where there were riots when King was assassinated," Ousmane requested. "Sam wouldn't take us to the neighborhood where the riots happened."

"I'll take you there, son," Dad said. "I know the area very well. Out of anger and frustration, they burned out a commercial area, not caring about destroying some people's hopes or memories."

Isaac didn't go along to see the riot area. Instead, he stayed at home and watched television with endless fascination. He toured supermarkets and shopping malls as if they were museums, enthralled by the abundance of goods. "Mama, when I grow up, I'm going to live in the States!"

As we were leaving, Isaac said, "I'm coming back to live with you, Grandpa." With tears brimming, Dad embraced him.

# 44

A FEW MONTHS AFTER OUR RETURN FROM the U.S., a police van with its siren blaring arrived at our compound. Out stepped Ousmane escorted by three policemen. The officer in charge said that Ousmane and a friend had made a small bomb, which they had detonated that morning at the entrance of the U.S. Information Agency library, and while no one had been injured, several windows were shattered by the explosion. Later that day an investigator came to issue a warning to Ousmane. In his conversation with us, the investigator treated the incident lightly; he dismissed the episode as merely "an amateurish schoolboy prank."

Ibrahim and I, however, felt the investigator should have been more severe. Certainly, we were alarmed. "What is the meaning of this?" I asked Ousmane angrily. "Surely you can find better things to do with your time and intelligence!"

Ibrahim seethed, "I thought you were interested in religion, but it seems your real interest is in physics. In any case, you need to get away from your bomb-making friends, and begin to prepare for your university studies. You will study abroad for a while. You need to see something of the world, meet a wider range of people, and find yourself."

"Do you realize you could have provoked an international incident," I shouted with irritation at his sullenness.

Ousmane responded venomously, "Your precious American capitalist government doesn't care about what happens in Senegal. It would take more than fireworks and petrol in Coke bottles in Dakar to get its attention."

Ibrahim was exasperated. "It is quite sufficient that it got the attention of the headmaster of your school. You have been expelled. So now we must try to enroll you in a school abroad— a lycée in France or Switzerland, perhaps. Eventually you will go to Paris for university," he said.

"I will not go to a European lycée. And I will go to an African university, not a European university. I am not going to be indoctrinated by Europeans."

"There's a very good lycée in Cairo," I suggested. "Several students from your school are there, and I hear they like it very much."

Ousmane still protested, "But it's an international school, not an African lycée. I know the boys who are there, sons of Senegal's capitalists and civil servants. Of course they like it. They are training to become capitalist lackeys, mercenaries, and spies like their fathers. Everybody knows the school gets CIA money; it's a CIA front. It may be the place for them, but not for me."

"Your mother is right, the international school at Cairo may be just the place for you," pronounced Ibrahim. In the months that followed, while we corresponded with the school, Ibrahim devoted most of his attention to Ousmane, taking him to the newly independent Zimbabwe, where they had an audience with members of the Patriotic Front and Prime Minister Robert Mugabe. This did not impress Ousmane as much as his father had hoped. What did touch him, however, was a chance encounter with an exiled black South African in the mist of Victoria Falls. On returning to Dakar, Ousmane became involved in the movement to free South Africa. Whenever Ibrahim was invited to speak at universities, he insisted that Ousmane accompany him. Together they traveled to conferences throughout Senegal and abroad. Isaac and I saw very little of either during those months. In fact, Isaac began to feel neglected by his father. In the meantime, the debate about where Ousmane should go to school continued. Still immersed in his study of the Koran, he did not appear at all concerned about missing a year of lycée. His Koranic tutor told us that Ousmane was not at all interested in theology; instead, Moslem law and political consciousness exclusively had engaged him.

A year after the bombing episode, I helped Ousmane pack his clothing, books, including several versions of the Koran, a prayer rug, posters, and tennis rackets. He was leaving for the international school in Cairo. I proposed a farewell party, but Ousmane refused. Throughout the year, he had avoided his few friends and shunned the well-wishers who had come to inquire about him. Before leaving for Cairo, he made several trips to villages "to work and worship" with his cousins. He took them food from our kitchen, cooking utensils, and tools. He returned from each visit in a state of rage about the villagers' poverty.

The evening before Ousmane's departure for Cairo, we gathered for a dinner in his honor, which turned out to be a rather gloomy family affair. Mamadou prepared a feast of Ousmane's favorite dishes, but Ousmane only picked at his food. Amadon and Anna came with gifts and tried to lift his spirits and ours with humorous anecdotes about their travels in Egypt, but Ousmane was not amused. Upbeat Isaac asked questions of Ousmane to draw him out: where he would live in Cairo, what courses he would study. Ousmane's replies were terse: "In a dormitory." "A pre-engineering course."

After he left, we sent weekly letters to Ousmane at Cairo, and frequently we attempted to reach him by phone, but three months passed before we heard from him. In a brief letter, he sent a bank account number for deposits and a new address. He wrote that he had moved out of the dormitory, and told us he would spend his holidays and school vacations in Algeria with a classmate. Ibrahim, after visiting him in Cairo, came home with a disturbing report of Ousmane's surliness. At the end of the year, on academic probation for irregular class attendance and marginal performance, Ousmane announced he was leaving school to study independently. He would go to Syria to seek what he termed "a genuine education."

"*Wanderjahre*" said Ibrahim. "Don't worry, Sarah. Young men need to roam about the world before they settle down. He'll come back to us eventually."

Ousmane wrote from Syria that he was "studying the politics of the Arab world." He traveled in Algeria and Tunisia, returned briefly to Senegal, then went to Mali. In all, he traveled for nearly four years before declaring himself ready to pursue his university studies in Paris. Checks sent to him were endorsed, the canceled checks returned with Ibrahim's bank statements. Noting when and where checks were cashed was our only means of tracking Ousmane's whereabouts.

Before leaving for Paris, Ousmane, then twenty years old, came home for a visit. During his stay, he tried to warn Ibrahim that his recent works were offensive to some fundamentalists. Ousmane and his traveling companion, a morose Sudanese youth named Hassan, argued vehemently with Ibrahim about politics. Both wearing paratrooper boots, black jumpsuits, and black-and-white checkered kaffiyehs tied about their heads, they were a formidable twosome. Ousmane accused Ibrahim of being a reformist whose writings and films were a threat to Islam. "Before it is too late, recant, Papa. Issue a statement about your being misguided. Renew your Islamic vows. Make a film about the wholesomeness and honesty of the fundamentalist way of life. Apologize and free yourself of alien influences."

Ousmane rarely spoke to me. When he did, he no longer called me "Mama"; instead, he addressed me as "Sarah." He dismissed my attempts to reason with him. "You can't be expected to understand the fundamentalist movement because you're American." I had been relegated to the category of alien influences.

Ousmane, Isaac, and Hassan took long walks and, we presumed, had intense conversations. They were seen frequently in Dakar's political bookstores and cafés. We wondered what Isaac, at age fifteen, was making of their conversations. Isaac said that Ousmane had told him to travel and study in Syria and Algeria to fortify himself for the racism of France, then join him in Paris. He told Isaac to resist going to a European or American university, where he would find frivolous students, an undisciplined atmosphere, and a colonialist curriculum.

Finally Hassan left for Khartoum and Ousmane prepared to

leave for Paris. He packed his books and the few mementos that mattered, then inventoried the compound as if to note what he had rejected and had elected to leave behind. The moment of parting was painful on both sides. Ousmane, dressed in a camouflage jumpsuit and boots, clasped Isaac in a protracted embrace and whispered to him. He extended his hand to Ibrahim and said, "I pity you, Papa. Your failure to understand this moment in our religious and political struggle is pitiful. Too bad. You might have become a great Moslem."

"I am hopeful, son, that you will become a wise man and a constructive force for whatever purpose you choose."

Ousmane had no words for me, only the perfunctory brush of each cheek.

# 45

A CALL FROM MOM SUMMONED ME BACK TO Washington to be with Dad. He had had surgery for prostate cancer. Initially, the prognosis was good; he appeared to have recovered. Mom had written that he had been on a fishing trip, and was preparing an exhibition of his photographs at a neighborhood center. Until she called, I had hoped that his recovery would be complete.

Isaac wanted to travel with me to Washington. There would be other trips to visit my parents, I told him. Besides, he had a series of important examinations which would determine his college prospects. But Isaac insisted and Ibrahim joined him in making the case for his going.

So together we went in late March, through the show of daffodils and tulips in bloom around the city to the sterile efficiency of a hospital, where, surrounded by tile and stainless steel, Dad lay dying. Mom was at his bedside, veiled in sorrow. When we arrived, he grew more alert. He was interested in news from Senegal and eager to hear Isaac's review of his classes and soccer matches, his descriptions of his teachers and friends, and interpretations of Ousmane's behavior. He and Isaac leafed through magazines and talked about photography. In those last days, he concentrated on conversations with Isaac. Bright and lucid when Isaac was present, Dad fell back on his pillow and closed his eyes when he left the room. He held Mom's hand, and smiled and nodded at me, but moments of clarity were only for his grandson.

After a week of daily visits, Dad ended their dialogue with a

whispered, "Come home to America, Isaac," and then surrendered to a deathly sleep. Isaac, who first tried to shake him back
to life, collapsed on the floor at Dad's bedside. Overcome with
grief, Isaac cried from a deep well within his soul. Between sobs,
Mom recited words that I learned later were from a psalm:
" 'Fearfulness and trembling are come upon me, and horror
hath overwhelmed me. . . . Oh that I had wings like a dove! For
then would I fly away, and be at rest.' Lord, help me." And I
remained still and sorrowful until a doctor and nurses came and
gave us rational language for our loss.

Neighbors and long-forgotten friends filled the house with
their condolences. Cousins arrived from Virginia, Delaware,
and New Jersey for a graveside service. A pastor, who scarcely
had known Dad, solemnly summarized his life and laid him to
rest with eloquence extracted from Ecclesiastes: "It is better to
go to the house of mourning than to the house of feasting. . . .
The heart of the wise is in the house of mourning." After the
service, the cortege returned to our house for an evening of food
and drink prepared by Rosemarie and other cousins.

Lincoln sent flowers to me the day after the funeral with a
letter in which he said he would like to be of help to my family.
He wrote that he was able to assist with obtaining visas and
other documents, and that I should "just say the word" if I had
problems. I considered calling him, but I decided against it. In
truth, I had little to say to him except thanks for the bouquet,
words I sent in a carefully written note.

A few days later, Isaac left for Dakar. I remained for a few
weeks with Mom, who needed help with the paperwork that
filled the hours of the next of kin. It was a tender time. Her tart
tongue was forgiven, my stubbornness forgotten. I felt we were
renegotiating the terms of our relationship. I stayed until she let
me know that she could safely navigate the shoals of widowhood.

# 46

ISAAC PERFORMED WELL IN SECONDARY SCHOOL. Unlike Ousmane, he had been an effective leader and never was in trouble. He completed with highest honors the courses leading to the baccalaureate. The director of his school wrote: "Isaac Mangane is an excellent student of French, English, and American literature. Strong interest in political science. Aspires to be a diplomat. Well-prepared for international studies. Has stronger capabilities as literary scholar. Accepted by Harvard, Yale, Princeton, and Georgetown universities."

In August 1988, Isaac and I packed his clothes, books, including his *Tintin* collection and a Bible my mother had sent him, his flute, a Walkman, cassette tapes, camera, chess set, his lucky soccer ball, and gifts for Mom which he would deliver at his Thanksgiving visit to Washington. And now Isaac was off, via Paris to see Ousmane, then to New Haven and college at Yale in the class of '92.

With new vigor and a renewed commitment to my own ideas, finally I had time to pursue projects of my choice: I wrote several magazine articles about women farmers and an article about attitudes toward women intellectuals. When I traveled in Zaire, Mali, Togo, the Ivory Coast, Kenya, Somalia, Ethiopia, Zimbabwe, South Africa, Namibia—wherever I went in Africa—I sought out women in the poorest sections of cities and the poorest of the rural poor. Using interview material, observations, and statistical data, I developed a series of articles about destitute women—widows, abandoned women, women without families.

Relief and development organizations invited me to participate in international conferences on the status of African women. I was a panelist in a UNESCO session at the University of Dakar on literacy among rural African women and children. Fatou, who had attended the session with me, later told Ibrahim that I had played a very important role in the UNESCO meeting. She said she was astonished by the acceptance of my contributions to the deliberations. "The other panelists were in total agreement with your proposals. It's clear that they viewed you as an insider, an African—not an American," observed Fatou.

"Sarah is quintessentially Senegalese. She has assimilated the unique intelligence, eloquence, entitlement, and grace that we regard as the best of our national character," said Ibrahim proudly. "Her knowledge of our history and customs and her mastery of Wolof are phenomenal. She now corrects my Wolof when she edits!"

"It's important for me to feel accepted here. And I'm beginning to feel useful—beyond this compound and our circle."

"You have always been useful to a wide circle of friends and associates—a source of information, ideas, inspiration. And now you have expanded our circle, moved into a sphere of international organizers with important humanitarian projects. You have stepped into development work in an admirable way," said Ibrahim.

"And I applaud your stepping out of Ibrahim's shadow," said Fatou.

"At first, I needed the cover that shadow provided. It's taken some time to find my niche here—to be allowed to feel that I am doing my own work."

After a long silence, Ibrahim said, "I am pleased that you have found work that is your own." He had come to terms with my departure from his projects. He was genuinely pleased.

At the same time, Ibrahim's literary career continued to soar.

His films were being shown throughout the world. His books were receiving wider critical acclaim abroad. Energized by the international recognition of his fiction and essays, he had returned to writing.

"Personal events have brought me back to my typewriter," he told a reporter. Ibrahim had begun writing his now infamous work, *My Dear Imam,* a long letter to the Islamic world—an appeal for the modernization of Islam. He might have called it *My Dear Ousmane;* for it was an appeal from father to son that centered around their religious differences. It dealt with the domestic life and education of Moslems, international images of Islam, and contributions of Moslems to international politics. It was critical of the conflation of Islam and ethnic religious practices in black Africa. Denounced by sub-Sahara African fundamentalists, the book was acclaimed by Moslem intellectuals in Egypt, Tunisia, Turkey, Iran, Afghanistan, Pakistan, and France.

In 1989, Ibrahim traveled for several months across North Africa, the Persian Gulf, and Central Asia on promotional tours. He gave lectures and held press conferences at universities and Islamic centers. In his telephone calls to me, Ibrahim was intoxicated by the furor the book had provoked. The few invitations he received from institutions in Guinea, Nigeria, Somalia, and the Sudan eventually were canceled. That the book was banned in those countries both annoyed and delighted him. Pirated copies were in circulation. We were inundated with telephone calls, faxes, and correspondence about the book. Newspaper and magazine headlines about the controversy over the book were ferocious: "Mangane Peddles Tensions"; "Burn *My Dear Imam*"; "Mangane—A Peril to the People."

A year after the publication of *My Dear Imam,* it was rumored that Ibrahim had been nominated for the Nobel Prize in literature. It was rumored also that if Ibrahim accepted the prize, fundamentalists had vowed to "eliminate" him. He received a note in a miniature coffin: "You, Ibrahim Mangane, who would destroy Islam will be destroyed."

Early on an October morning, Ibrahim received a call from Stockholm. Having just showered, I was wrapped in a towel when the call came. Ibrahim burst into the steamy bathroom with the news.

"Sarah, the rumors are true. That call was from the Alfred Nobel Foundation! It is true! This year I am to receive the prize." He embraced me. For several moments we held each other, bubbling with joy.

"The Nobel Prize! Congratulations. You've earned it, Ibrahim."

"Finally, the recognition every writer of conscience hopes to achieve. That the work has provoked death threats, I suppose, is a statement about its power and veracity."

"Try to forget the threats for a moment. It's a time for celebration. Your courage and your genius will be celebrated and rewarded. Bravo!" Although I tried to disregard the threats for a time, I was terrified. I knew that the danger would be heightened by the increased visibility the prize would bring.

Before we had finished dressing, the telephone rang again. *Le Monde*'s correspondent in Dakar wished to come immediately with a photographer. His call was followed by a series of others: reporters, writers, and friends from all over Africa, all around the world.

When the Nobel Prize in literature was announced on radio, television, in newspapers and magazines, the commentaries were varied and conflicting. The contrast in the reactions of Ousmane and Isaac mirrored the extremes of statements that the media carried.

Ousmane telexed from Paris:

*Ibrahim:*
  *You may be proud of this moment, but you will live to regret it. Your work is not in the best interest of Islam. Do not accept the Nobel Prize. It is their way of trying to demoralize Moslems. They will not succeed. Allah is great.*
                                            *Ousmane*

Isaac, who immediately telephoned his congratulations, also sent a letter.

> P.O. Box 1036
> Yale Station
> New Haven, CT
> 06521 USA

Dearest Papa and dearest Mama,

Congratulations on the Nobel Prize for your great works, Papa, and your great courage. I am happy for you and very proud. Your brilliance has been deservedly recognized. I am looking forward to being with you in Stockholm for the ceremonies.

I know that many of your ideas, Mama, were of value to Papa. You both deserve prizes for the books, articles, and films. The films are being featured in a festival in New York. Everywhere there are articles about "Mangane's films." This is a proud moment for Africa, for Senegal, and for our family.

> Love always,
> Isaac

Ibrahim received proclamations from the president of Senegal and other heads of state; major writers and filmmakers sent telexes and letters; professors, presidents, and chancellors of universities; ministers of cultural affairs; relatives and friends wrote to him.

A Nigerian Nobel laureate wrote: "*Congratulations. Brace yourself, my dear fellow, for a volley of invitations, honorary degrees, endless celebrations. You may have little time henceforth to write, my friend. Happy to have your company as a laureate.*"

Bill Nelson called from Paris. He said he would go to Stockholm to "witness the blessed event." Other friends, some we had not heard from for years, inquired about attending the ceremonies.

The Nobel Foundation sent detailed information about

travel arrangements, the program of events, and appropriate attire. Wives were instructed to bring dresses for afternoon events and three evening gowns. We would be flown by Scandinavian Airlines to Stockholm. Arrangements would be made to fly our sons from the United States and France, if they wished to attend. Suites in the Grand Hotel, overlooking Lake Mälaren and the Baltic Sea, would be reserved for our family.

On the eve of our departure for Stockholm, festivities were planned in honor of Ibrahim in Dakar. A hundred or more of Senegal's literati and political dignitaries were invited to dinner at the presidential palace. As the guard opened the palace gates, I recalled my first day in Dakar. With three street children as my escort, I had lingered outside the palace. I was again impressed by the formal grace and architectural harmony of the building.

Inside, we were greeted by the president, handsome in his white tie and tails. A sash of ribbons and several medals adorned his narrow chest. He embraced Ibrahim. "Mangane, welcome. You have commanded the attention of the world and brought glory to Senegal," he said, "and I am especially pleased to welcome you, Madame Mangane." He bowed and kissed my hand, then led us to a reception hall that sparkled under a glimmering crystal chandelier. The president's wife greeted us. Her necklace of diamonds and rubies shimmered at the neckline of her cardinal red boubou. I wore a lilac taffeta gown. I knew the women of Dakar would want to see a gown that I would wear in Stockholm. Ibrahim, in white tie and tails, was resplendent.

Dozens of guests had arrived, colleagues, friends, and acquaintances of Ibrahim's. Each greeted him affectionately. One after another embraced him, had a warm, animated moment of conversation, embraced him again, and then moved on to make way for the next in line. The mood was festive. Cabinet ministers and diplomats were in tuxedoes; the other men— journalists, professors, actors, and artists wore their finest caftans. Women in government, the university, and the arts, all brilliantly gowned, rustled about greeting one another.

A distant drummer drew closer. The hum of the kora and whistling flutes joined the drumming. Over the loudspeaker a voice announced a dance group that sprang from the four corners of the hall—from each corner two men and two women—onto a platform. Their torsos painted gold, the women in raffia skirts swished seductively around the male dancers who undulated at center stage. The guests cooed their delight with the performance.

Suddenly, interrupting the program, the palace guards, with rifles hoisted, stormed into the hall. The guard with a gold insignia on his beret, barked: "Gentlemen and ladies, a telephone caller has made a bomb threat. I must ask you to leave the palace immediately. Mr. President, Mr. Mangane, ladies and gentlemen, please follow us out at once."

Ibrahim was near the entrance. I was at the other end of the hall. His arm was in the air beckoning me. In the commotion, everyone was crowding toward the door. Ibrahim managed to grab my hand and we scurried across the tile floor in the foyer to the door and then outdoors into the twilight. We stood at a distance from the palace with the president and his wife while platoons of guards, soldiers, and policemen inspected the grounds and the building for more than an hour. Most of the guests fled to their cars and deserted us. Could Ousmane or an agent provocateur known to him be responsible for this, I wondered? At that moment, Ibrahim said, "Fortunately, Ousmane is in Paris. Otherwise he would be a prime suspect."

The guard with the gold insignia reappeared, saluted and reported, "Mr. President, I am relieved to tell you that it was a hoax. We found no bomb or any evidence of tampering. You may resume the reception, sir."

"Colonel, exactly what did the caller say?"

"Sir, he said that the palace would be blown up in fifteen minutes, that Mr. Mangane was the target of the attack. Mangane, he said, is an enemy of the nation. That Allah is great. The caller then hung up the receiver, Mr. President."

"Do you have any more information?"

"No, sir. We followed the emergency procedures. Your children and household staff were removed immediately, sir. They have been driven to . . . ." He whispered to the president.

"Well, I am sorry, Mangane. I regret that the bomb threat has spoiled the event. When you return, we'll celebrate your prize. We'll invite only close associates, and we'll have tight security. I'll see that you are accompanied to your house tonight. A military team will be stationed at your gate throughout the night and will escort you and Madame Mangane to the airport tomorrow. I expect it's a mere scare tactic. Still, we must pay attention. My sincere apologies."

"It is I who should apologize," said Ibrahim. "I am sorry to have brought the threat of danger into your life." We said our good-byes with firm embraces.

I was trembling all over. I was afraid that a bomb might be planted in our car or that our beloved museum of a home might be bombed. Shaking visibly, I could scarcely walk toward the car. Ibrahim, his arm around my waist, moved me along with him.

With each step, he said, "Be calm, Sarah. Calm."

Mamadou was standing by our car with the door open.

"Was it a bomb, sir?"

"A bomb scare; only a prank, Mamadou."

At that moment, I was looking forward to leaving Dakar, eager to be on our way to Stockholm, where I expected we would be protected by the protocol of ceremony.

# 47

AWAKE BEFORE DAWN THE NEXT MORNING, I packed my bags and was prepared for the trip hours before departure time. When Ibrahim finally stirred, he was surprised to find me in my maroon boubou, dressed for travel.

"You are up and dressed. Eager to venture into the land of the midnight sun?"

"I'm eager to get away, Ibrahim. Having soldiers on guard outside is terribly unsettling."

"The visibility that comes with the Nobel Prize increases the political stakes and the need for protection. I expect their interest in my life—or death—will subside quite rapidly, as soon as the prize is no longer news. We'll not be bothered. I'll no longer be a target." He sounded tired and looked preoccupied.

While he dressed and packed, I spoke with Mamadou about making the compound more secure, reminding him not to admit repairmen or strangers. Mamadou, apprehensive, too, readily understood my concern. He moaned that a bomb meant for us might indeed kill him and his family. We agreed that Awa, their daughter, and grandchildren should move temporarily to their village.

On the way to the airport, motorcycle policemen flanked our car. Mamadou, speaking to the image of Ibrahim framed in the rearview mirror, said, "Sir, maybe you need a younger driver, a man who would know right away if someone plant a bomb in the motor. A man who know motors—who notice tampering."

"No, Mamadou, another driver would never do. Don't worry about that bomb scare. It's the sort of thing they try only once. Somebody just wanted to disrupt the party. There's nothing to fear," he reassured from the backseat.

Mamadou was not comforted. Nor was I. Ibrahim reached for my hand with a squeeze and said gently, "There is no need to worry. Last night's episode must not rob us of the joys that come with this prize." He kissed my palm and I kissed his. We rode on in silence.

In that silence my inner voice prayed, "*Preserve him from all evil; preserve his soul.*"

At the terminal, there were dozens of people—some of the guests at the aborted party—with banners and bouquets ready for a rousing send-off. Soldiers and policemen vigilantly surveyed the crowd.

Mamadou briskly stepped out of the car and opened the rear doors. Silently Ibrahim and I scanned the crowd for signs of trouble. We stepped out of the car and walked toward the gathering of friends and acquaintances. Despite the motions and signals from the policemen, who were pressing us to board the Scandinavian Airlines Learjet on the runway, we stopped to embrace those dear to us. They had brought bouquets of lilies and birds of paradise. With an armful of flowers, I looked back to view the cheering throng as I boarded the plane. Ibrahim, mounting the steps, was waving vigorously and smiling broadly at the well-wishers. Two government agents and a press officer boarded. Moments later we were aloft.

Ibrahim heaved an audible sigh of relief. "At last," he said, "I'm on my way to become a laureate. You will adore Stockholm. And the Swedes will adore you. You are going to feel exotic there. I have had good times in Stockholm, once I appreciated their curiosity about my African looks, my exoticism."

He reached for his briefcase with the program of events. We reviewed the schedule.

"A reception for the other laureates and their family members is scheduled at our hotel an hour or so after our arrival. Isaac should arrive in time for the reception," said Ibrahim, looking at his watch.

"Perhaps Ousmane will have a change of heart and surprise

us with an appearance," I ventured. "I asked that they reserve accommodations for him at the hotel."

"Given his current persuasion, I'd almost prefer that he not come. I'd rather see him afterward—in Paris—where we would not be inhibited or distracted by the festivities. He and I need some uninterrupted time to analyze our beliefs and actions as reasonable men—not as father and son."

"Ibrahim, I must insist that you find him and find time to be with him. In my letters, I've begged him to try to understand the importance of the political and literary dialogue that you've generated. I've sent him clippings of articles that followed the announcement of the prize. And I've begged him to come home and discuss the differences, to resolve the—"

"Let us not speak of Ousmane now. After Stockholm, I will deal with Ousmane. Right now, I want to review my notes. To sound like a laureate, I need to prepare for the interviews and press conferences. One does not become wiser upon receiving the prize, but one has to sound wiser." Ibrahim put on his reading glasses and opened his notebook.

"Reporters will ask you about your plans for the prize money."

"Twelve hundred thousand francs," he said and whistled. "I hope you have thought about the relief organizations that are helping African women and identified the most effective ones. We'll give half of the funds to those organizations. The other half will be deposited in trusts for Ousmane and Isaac."

As Ibrahim turned to the correspondence from the Nobel Prize Committee, I turned toward him, taking in his enduring good looks, the gray of his beard, hairline receding, his hair a fluffy salt-and-pepper, and new crescent-shaped eyeglasses—a more powerful prescription—on the tip of his nose. His face, for a long time familiar to the literary world, now had become an image of international importance. I nestled closer to him, and rested my head on his shoulder.

"Ibrahim," I whispered, "you've earned your place in history." I was proud beyond measure.

Awaiting our arrival in Stockholm was an entourage of Senegalese and Swedish diplomats and reporters, with umbrellas and raincoats under dark gray clouds that had just released an icy drizzle. We were welcomed and then escorted to a Volvo limousine that took us to the Grand Hotel. The street approaching the hotel was lined with children who waved small Swedish flags. The sight of their bright raincoats and the blue and gold of their flags offset the discomfort of the damp, chilly air.

The windows of our hotel suite overlooked the glistening ripples of Lake Mälaren. Across the water stood the Old Town and the palace where the ceremonies would be held. The view was stunning.

"It *is* the Venice of the north, Ibrahim. What a lovely city."

Moments later, there was a knock at the door. A familiar knock. Ibrahim opened the door. An elated Isaac embraced us.

"Papa, Mama, this Nobel scene is fantastic, wonderful, awesome—absolutely awesome. Congratulations. Papa, I am proud of you, proud to be your son, proud to be Senegalese. I arrived this morning on the flight from New York with three Nobel Prize winners and their families. They treated us all like celebrities. First class all the way. My room—no, it's a suite—is down the hall. It's super—not as grand as this, of course," he said, surveying the amenities and the view. "Is Ousmane coming? I have a double room—the reservation was for Ousmane and me. Is he coming?"

"We've not heard from Ousmane lately," I said.

"I spoke to Ousmane last week," Isaac said. "He said emphatically that he would not come to Stockholm which is why I was surprised to find a double room, reservations for us both."

I said that I had hoped Ousmane would reconsider and join us.

"Not a chance," Isaac continued. "He said if we want to see him, we should 'try to find him' in Paris. He was in a nasty mood. I told him I'll see him in Paris, spend the weekend with him. Have you been in touch with him, Papa?"

"I have not talked with him in months. I have written to him—several letters. Not one has been answered or returned. I do intend to find him in Paris. I want to have a long talk with him—to discuss our differences and perhaps resolve them. Is he still at the rue Clauzel address?"

"He's there occasionally. I have three telephone numbers for him. He's on the move. He's become a man of mystery."

"What do you mean by that?" I asked.

"He's suspicious, distrustful, and mysterious. He doesn't even trust me. I think he's become sort of paranoid about political matters. A political paranoia that—"

Ibrahim interrupted, "Political paranoia! Are you studying psychology this semester, son?"

The telephone rang. Ibrahim answered, "Hello. Yes, thank you very much. Yes, immediately." He hung up. "Photographers are in the lobby. They want some informal shots of us. After the photos, we will be taken to a reception. Come along. The photographers want smiling faces. Let us go and look like celebrants."

Flashbulbs crackled. A family portrait. Isaac and I flanked Ibrahim. A portrait of the Nobel laureates and their families. A group picture with the nine laureates, nine smiling men—an economist, two chemists, three physicists, two physiologists, and Ibrahim. Amid the multilingual babble of introductions and greetings, photographers positioned themselves discreetly for informal shots. Afterward, laureates and their relatives were escorted through the crowd of onlookers, who applauded. A few called out, "Bravo, Mangane," as we passed. A driver was waiting to take us to the first of the receptions.

All week, there were receptions. Dozens of candles flickered on tables laden with salmon, smoked ham, sliced venison, Scandinavian cheeses with dill and caraway seeds, and a variety of breads. The laureates were surrounded by clusters of admirers. Their wives, children, and friends chatted about what happened when they received news of the prize.

Between receptions, there were lectures. Each laureate was asked to speak on his subject. Ibrahim's lecture, "Postcolonial Literature: Liberation of Creative Intellectuals," was interrupted several times by bursts of applause. Afterward he read a chapter from *The Imam's Daughters,* his novel-in-progress. I was seated on the front row between Isaac and Bill Nelson. Dead silence at the end of his reading and then thunderous applause. I was ecstatic and Isaac was moved to tears. Bill Nelson shouted bravo louder and longer than anyone else.

"Papa is a giant among giants, Mama. Listen to the response!"

Isaac was transfixed. He stared at Ibrahim as if he were seeing him for the first time.

"If only Ousmane were here. If only he could have heard Papa," Isaac lamented. "What a standard Papa has set for us."

For Isaac, the moment was transformative. To be sure, he had known Ibrahim was a celebrity. But never before had he heard him give a public lecture or read from his works to an immense audience. I put my arm around Isaac and felt his heart pounding. His gaze was fixed on Ibrahim, as if he were trying to memorize every aspect of that instant.

In the days that followed, we heard other lectures, attended a few more receptions, walked along Stockholm's streets and bridges, visited museums, and met an astonishing number of fascinating people. Ibrahim was jovial and generous with the press. Isaac was at his side at every moment, enchanted by his father's intellectual prowess.

"I wish I had listened more closely to you when I was younger, Papa. I should have taken notes on everything you ever said."

"The most important words I have ever said to you, Isaac, are 'I love you. I cherish you. I am proud of you as a son.'"

Over the years, I have been warmed by memories of that scene, which illuminate my soul with a glow like candlelight in the early dark of that December in Stockholm.

The ceremonies ended, but Ibrahim's grand tour was only beginning. He had engagements in Paris and Brussels. He then planned to go to New York before returning to the continent, stopping in Lagos and Abidjan before returning to Dakar. I didn't wish to accompany Ibrahim on the next part of his trip, although he had made it clear that he wanted me with him.

"Sarah, please come with me to Paris. I want you around when I see Ousmane. You are expected at La Défense for the luncheon hosted by PEN and the Association of Francophone Writers with a program to honor both of us. They are calling for a new edition of the biography, so the author should be present, as well as her subject. You must come. I'll need you there."

"Isaac will be with you. And Bill Nelson will be there. You'll have a jolly time. Besides, you need some time with Ousmane to discuss your estrangement, without my hovering in the background. I'm leaving tonight for Dakar as I'd planned." Tenderly, lovingly, and lightheartedly Ibrahim, Isaac, and I parted. They went off to a dinner in Ibrahim's honor at the Senegalese Embassy. Snow flurries danced out of the dark sky as I flew from Stockholm toward Senegal's peninsula, which beckoned me home.

# 48

TWO DAYS AFTER RETURNING FROM STOCK-
holm, I was awakened early in the morning by the sound of a
tree limb exploding, splintering, crashing through the withered
leaves of the lower branches and landing with a thud on the
ground. Moments later another branch splintered and dropped
to the ground. I went to the window. Branches had fallen from
our plum tree. Dry branches and unripe plums, their sweetness
sapped by the savannah heat and the interminable drought, lay
on the ground.

"This morning a big limb fell from the plum tree and then
another limb, a small one fell. An omen, madame, very bad
omen," wailed Mamadou as he brought me yogurt and bananas
for breakfast. I gave little thought to his superstitious wailing. I
was eager to start the day. I began opening the mail that had
accumulated in our absence.

Just before noon, I received a telephone call from the French
Embassy. A secretary told me the ambassador was en route to
our house with a message that he had to deliver personally. It
was only then that I became apprehensive. What could it be?
Ibrahim? An automobile accident? With the Paris traffic it was
quite likely. Or maybe Ibrahim had had a heart attack. Or
something had happened to Isaac? Was Ousmane in some trouble? I worried constantly about Ousmane. Maybe there was no
calamity. It could be an honor for Ibrahim—a plaque or medal.
But, if that were the case, the ambassador would present it personally to him. What then?

Moments later, a car drove up to the gate. I opened the shut-

ters and looked out. It was the ambassador, Jean-Louis Gallimard. Mamadou was there to open the gate. I went to the great
hall to greet the ambassador.

"Madame Mangane, there has been a tragic incident. May we
sit down?"

"What is it? What is it?" I was frantic with worry.

He handed me an envelope. Without waiting for me to open
it, he said, "This is a communiqué about the assassination of
your husband and the death of your son in Paris this afternoon.
A bomb was planted in an elevator at La Défense. Your husband
was the target of the bomb. He was killed instantly. Your son
was severely wounded. He was rushed to the hospital. Every
attempt was made to save him, as he was an essential witness.
Regrettably, madame, he died in the emergency service at the
hospital. There were three other men—two Senegalese officials
and a policeman—in the elevator. There were no survivors,
madame. Three fundamentalist organizations have claimed
responsibility for the incident. We will do everything we can to
assist you and your family. On behalf of the French government, the president, the mayor of Paris, and other officials, I
extend our deepest sympathies. My wife and I offer our personal condolences, Madame Mangane."

While Gallimard talked to me, his chauffeur must have
related his version of the incident to Mamadou, who broke into
a shrill cry that made masks on the walls vibrate and the ancient
instruments hum. At the gate holding the shrieking Mamadou
was the chauffeur. Gallimard kissed my hand, called to his
chauffeur, and left.

I dashed to our bedroom, locked the door, and closed the
shutters. Screaming and sobbing, "Ibrahim! Ibrahim! Isaac! My
sweet Isaac! My baby! And my Ibrahim. Ibrahim assassinated.
Assassinated! Killed, dead."

I must have fainted or fallen asleep. Awakened by the insis-
tent ringing of the telephone, memory struggled with Gallimard's message—the assassination of my husband and the death
of my son. Was it a terrible nightmare? A nightmare. It couldn't
have happened.

The ringing stopped. There was a knock at the bedroom door.

"Madame Mangane, Madame Mangane?"

"Who's there?" My voice was rasping, my throat dry.

"It's Djibril, madame, Ibrahim's cousin, Djibril. Mamadou's gone, left the house, took all his things. I'm taking care, taking good care. Madame, the telephone call is for you—a call from Paris."

With a limp hand, I reached toward the bedside table and gripped the phone. The voice of a Parisian operator said, "I have a call for Madame Mangane."

"I am Madame Mangane."

"Here is your party, sir."

"Hello, Mama, Mama?"

"Isaac? Is it you, Isaac? Isaac! You're alive! Ah, I just had a terrible dream, a nightmare. You are all right?"

"Yes, Mama, but I have terrible news. Papa was killed today, Mama. Papa was killed by a time bomb that went off in an elevator." He began in French, then continued in English. He spoke slowly, his every word carefully chosen. "Ousmane had made the bomb and planted it. He was working with a terrorist group—the Messengers from Khartoum. He knew the Messengers were going to assassinate someone who would be on the elevator at that time. The others did not tell him that Papa was the target of their plot. Only afterward, when it was too late, one of them told him. Ousmane tried to prevent it, Mama. He drove out to La Défense, raced to the elevator, somehow got there moments after they had stepped into the elevator. Ousmane got to the elevator, tried to pull Papa, to snatch him out of the elevator. The door closed. The elevator began to rise. It was too late. The bomb exploded. Papa was killed there in the elevator, Mama. Ousmane was badly wounded. He died later in a hospital. He tried to rescue Papa. He truly did try, Mama."

"It wasn't a nightmare. Assassinated. Assassinated by Ousmane."

"No, Mama. Ousmane wouldn't have—"

"Where were you? Where are you now, Isaac?"

"When it happened? I was at Place du Puits-de-l'Ermite in the tea room of the Grand Mosque. Ousmane was to have met me there. Now I am at a police station where I must sign some papers." He hesitated, then asked, "Is somebody there with you, Mama? Of course, Mamadou is there. He'll help you. You should not be alone. Call Fatou to comfort you. Call Madame Dia, your friend, Françoise Dia. Someone should be with you.

"I am to fly home in two or three days with the—with Papa and Ousmane. Our embassy is making the arrangements. Bill Nelson has been with me to help. The police took me from the mosque to a morgue to see—to identify them. Bill Nelson was there. He'd already identified them. He's here with me. The police are waiting now with some papers. I'll call you again as soon as I can. I'm sorry, Mama. I love you. We only have each other now." His voice cracked, he broke down, crying.

"Isaac, courage Isaac. You will have to handle the affairs there. Steady, now. Courage!"

He cleared his throat and said, "I'm all right, I'll manage. I love you, Mama. Good-bye." Isaac hung up. I dropped the receiver. It fell to the floor. I went out into the courtyard. It was very warm; the air was still, utterly still. To the gate, down the path, to the boulders, to the bay.

*"I will cast mine eyes upon the ocean from whence cometh my help. My help cometh from . . . cometh from . . ."*

I went out to the boulders and called to them. Ibrahim! Ousmane! Ibrahim! At the edge of the boulders, knee-deep in the bay, by falling facedown and breathing deeply, I knew I could join them. And if I were to die, too, what of Isaac? Isaac. Isaac. In a stupor, I awoke with Djibril and Fatou carrying me over the boulders, back to the house. My white boubou was cold and wet. Djibril's hands supported my shoulders, and Fatou's plump, stocky figure at the other end, carried my ankles as if pulling a rickshaw.

During the endless nights and days that followed, I went from room to room, touching objects that Ibrahim had collected and weeping, gazing at photographs of him and weeping, looking at articles about him and weeping, sitting in his closet to inhale the scent in his clothes and weeping, putting his pipe stems between my lips and weeping, brushing my hair with his hair brush and weeping, burying my face in his pillow and weeping. I leafed through photo albums to etch in my memory images of Ibrahim, Ousmane, and Isaac. I kissed their pictures. Roaming through the house, I searched for mementos of Ousmane—his school blazer, a tennis racket, his first camera, a few books, some posters. I was neither sleepwalking nor awake. Numb, dazed, I moved about like a survivor of a terrible shipwreck.

Fatou, Françoise Dia, and Djibril silently came and went. I have no recollection of what they were doing. I know only that they were there.

Mourners, curiosity seekers, and photographers gathered outside the compound to await the return of the bodies of Ibrahim and Ousmane. Djibril said that among them were some who believed that Ibrahim would return alive. Refusing to accept the idea of his death, they had to see his casket, walk behind it in the funeral cortege, witness the entombment. Outside the compound, throughout the days and nights of waiting, a mournful drummer thumped an elegiac largo. From time to time, the shrill countertenor of an ancient griot's lament shattered the air.

Unopened letters and cablegrams were heaped in an enormous calabash in the foyer. Baskets of fruit appeared—mangoes, bananas, and oranges, mounds of oranges—"oranges from Israel sent by the Israeli Embassy," whispered an incredulous Djibril.

Incredible. Inconceivable. Unreal. I was unwilling to believe that my life, our marriage, and family were scattered like shards at a ruin.

I hoped that the mourners at the gate, expecting resurrection, could muster the power to summon Ibrahim and Ousmane back to life.

A hearse arrived with the caskets draped in green flannel mourning cloth. The bleating mob outside pushed against the gate. They fell silent when I walked toward them. I returned the nod of the imam who preceded the caskets, and looked beyond him, beyond the coffins, in search of Isaac. Isaac.

"Isaac!" I cried when he came into view. He moved around the pallbearers and ahead of the imam. His eyelids were swollen, eyes anguished, his weary shoulders sagged under the burden of surviving his father and his brother.

"Isaac, what an ordeal this has been for you. Dear Isaac."

"And what an ordeal—a great loss—for you all alone, Mama." We embraced and, although I knew I had no more tears, again I heaved with sorrow and more tears came.

Bill Nelson, accompanying the cortege, invited the imam into the house. The imam blessed the house, Isaac, and me and announced when he would return to perform the funeral ritual. The president and other dignitaries would accompany him. A burial site, in a place of honor, had been selected for Ibrahim. It would be a state funeral. There would be international guests. Ibrahim Mangane would be honored appropriately. As for Ousmane, well, a different location would be found for him.

There were concerns about political demonstrations and security. Ousmane, of course, would be buried elsewhere—privately—given the circumstances. Isaac should attend the service for his brother along with Amadon. I was not expected to attend. The imam was certain that Isaac and I appreciated the complexities of our situation and he hoped that we would accept the arrangements he had made.

"Madame, you have Isaac. Ousmane was perhaps the sacrifice. Allah is merciful," the imam concluded.

"Merciful? Merciful?" The word rang in my head over and over and over again in the days that followed.

It is impossible for me now to recall what transpired in those days. There is an empty space in my life, a void in my memory. Isaac and I somehow witnessed the rituals and carried out various duties; dignitaries and details filed before us. Perhaps Isaac remembers the eulogies, the rites, the tributes and, one day, will relate them. Perhaps.

# 49

THE IMAM VISITED US A FEW DAYS AFTER the burial.

"Madame Mangane, there is a mourning period of at least forty days. It is one of our sacred customs. Please observe our customs, Madame, and remain at home during your mourning—and, given your situation, perhaps longer, much longer. I hope you will be here with your mother, Isaac."

"Isaac should return to his university."

"Madam Mangane, you will find his assistance essential. There are documents to be processed and transactions that Isaac should handle for you. There will be requests for interviews and statements from you. And there are agitators, provocateurs who will try to cause trouble, to use your remarks to their advantage. You are at the center of an Islamic conflict, Madame. Please be cautious, be careful. You may have visitors, women visitors—women relatives and women friends. Only women. Be reserved even in your conversations with them. Avoid discussing controversial subjects—Islam and politics. Allah is great. May Allah protect you."

His warnings were hardly necessary. I didn't plan to leave the house. I had no interest in receiving visitors, although a procession of women—Ibrahim's nieces and cousins—passed through the house. They brought stories of other widows—always in worse circumstances—widows who had grieved, recovered, and overcome the tragedies of widowhood. They offered fetishes, amulets, and oils to appease the spirits and ward off further harm. In clusters they came, chattered, made pronouncements, presented their parcels, and moved on. In silence, I endured the visitations. I listened, but did not hear. Nor did I speak. Numbed by the reality of tragedy, I had no words.

Only Isaac managed to penetrate my silence. "Decisions have to be made, documents have to be signed, don't they, Mama?"

"Yes, Isaac, but must I do so now?"

"Yes, Mama. It's better to finish the business—get it over."

Stolid and calm, Isaac handled our affairs very competently. He decided that it was too late to return to Yale to complete the semester. He would return in September. Eager to review the accounts and documents related to settling the estate, Isaac met daily with bank representatives and handled a battery of lawyers. He hired a cook and a housekeeper and engaged a maintenance man to attend to household repairs. He traded in the Maserati for a more serviceable Renault. Isaac was busy, very busy. He busied himself so as to postpone probing the depths of his bereavement.

Nearly two months had passed before Isaac was struck by the meaning of the tragedy. Early one morning—just before dawn—I was awakened by a mournful howl that rose to a piercing cry. Isaac was screaming as if he were being attacked.

Terrified, I dashed down the hall and burst into his room where he was writhing on the floor beside his bed. In agony, his lean body was curled in the fetal position. He rolled from side to side shrieking.

"Isaac, what is it? Are you in pain? What hurts?"

I reached for him, touched him. He withdrew, rolled away from me. I knelt and cupped his head in my hands—his head the shape of Ibrahim's, his hair the same texture as his father's. In his profuse perspiration was the scent of Ibrahim's musk. I wrapped my arms around his shoulders. He rolled into my embrace and sobbed, "Papa is gone, he's dead. Killed by Ousmane's bomb. Ousmane took him from me. Ousmane—his favorite. Why? Why did it happen? Why did Ousmane want to destroy him, destroy us? Papa loved Ousmane—he loved him more than he loved me, even more than he loved you. Why,

Mama, why?" We sat there on the floor and cried together into the morning light.

In the following weeks, Isaac grew pensive and somewhat passive. Except for the roar of blustering waves crashing against the boulders, the whine of April's last trade winds, and conversations among the servants, the house was still. At mealtime, I had to urge Isaac to have another bite, and another. Finally, after a dinner that we scarcely touched, I decided to talk with him about his condition and mine.

"Let's go for a walk, Isaac, out to the boulders to watch the sunset."

"I'll get a sweater and bring your cape, Mama."

We walked in silence toward the boulders where Ibrahim and I often had sat in the blush of early evening, watching Ousmane and Isaac skip from rock to rock. Now Isaac and I went to that same spot. I sat cross-legged on what the boys had always called "Mama's rock" and Isaac stepped reverently around "Papa's rock" and knelt just below it.

"What can we do, Isaac, to recover? I walk about the house like a zombie, unable even to speak. And now you have grown silent."

"There's no need to speak, Mama. What has happened is unspeakable. No need to try to say anything about it."

"I miss your bustling about, your interruptions," and to amuse him, "your meddling with my silences."

Isaac smiled. "I've been trying to meditate. I wish I could pray. I wish now that I had had some religious training—Moslem or Christian or animism—something to help me make sense of what has happened. I wish I could believe in an afterlife and imagine Papa and Ousmane together, explaining things to each other. I wish I knew about my ancestors, that I could believe that they're watching over us. But I don't believe in anything, Mama. I wish Papa had taken us to mosques or even mass sometimes, you know, instead of museums. I might have learned to pray. I don't know any prayers!"

"Oh, my dear, yes, we could have taken you to churches or to mosques. We could have sent you to Sunday school or to study with an imam, but we didn't. I could have taught you the Lord's Prayer, bedtime prayers, the psalms I once knew, but I didn't. As a child, I went to a Methodist Sunday school where I learned very little—the Lord's Prayer and a few psalms. When I was young—just a few years older than you—a psalm, that is, my version of a psalm, became my prayer."

"What was it? What psalm was it?"

"The 121st psalm: '*I will lift up mine eyes unto the hills from whence cometh my help. My help cometh from the Lord, who made heaven and earth.*' When I was in graduate school, reading about Ibrahim's works, I paraphrased the psalm which became my chant, my mantra."

"What was it? Say it, Mama."

"*I will cast mine eyes upon the ocean from whence cometh my help. My help cometh from Senegal, which is heaven and earth.*"

"That was your prayer? You actually prayed to come to Senegal. Have you any regrets about it, Mama? Now do you regret it?"

"Regrets? Ibrahim's body returned to me in fragments. Ousmane tormented for years and finally destroyed by a bomb of his own making. I ache with regret. I deeply regret what has happened to us. I don't like breathing the still air of tragedy that now surrounds us." I bit my lip and swallowed my tears.

"But you and I have to remember that the years before were filled with some very proud and happy times. I adored Ibrahim, the projects he pursued, the life of celebration he produced for us. You and Ousmane—until Ousmane turned away from us— were charming and rewarding. And living here—I have loved the world your father created for us and brought home to us."

"What will you do now? You did a lot of things for Papa and with him. What now?"

"What do widows do? How do they manage when death leaves a vast void and renders them empty, surrounded by empty relationships, empty rooms, and enormous silence? I've thought about the public widows—stripped by assassination of husband, purpose, celebrity. Newspaper images of Coretta

King, Jacqueline and Ethel Kennedy, Betty Shabbaz, Sonia Gandhi—all have flashed on and off again and again. And now I know the sensation behind the veil, the gaze, the frozen smile. But I've wondered if they could have felt what I feel—fractured, fragmented, irreparably damaged. You and I are doubly wounded, with two deaths to reconcile. Husband and father, son and brother. It's terrible—it feels like living out a Greek tragedy."

"It's worse. It's an African tragedy, Mama. Africa has been damaged by what has happened—and the way it happened. I listened to Papa and Ousmane debate the causes of extremism, conflicts with modernization, the pros and cons of so-called Westernization. Africans everywhere are debating the same issues. The continent is splintering with tensions about religion and politics. Ousmane said Papa was no longer Moslem. Papa said Ousmane was not a true Moslem, that he was unreasonable, intolerant, going through a fanatical stage. Papa thought that he would grow beyond it. Ousmane was converted, thoroughly converted, though, to a militant way of thinking and living. His so-called brothers—the Messengers—are a destructive band.

"This may sound paranoid, but I fear they may not stop— you may not be safe here. You ought to leave Senegal, move to Washington and live with Granny. Or New York or New Haven. You could teach again. Granny would feel more secure with you in the States. And I would, too."

"Leave Senegal? Live in Washington? New York? No, I can't imagine living there now, at this point in my life. No. Here in Senegal is where I belong. I feel safe here and you should—"

"But, Mama, I know you're not safe, you're not safe here or perhaps anywhere. You'll be a target, too. Don't you read the papers, the magazines? There are two or three articles every week about the 'fall of the house of Mangane' and our being 'doomed due to foreign influences.' Mama, they are blaming you—that's what they mean by 'foreign influences'—you, Mama. They know that you were the source of many of Papa's progressive ideas. I know that you urged Papa to write about the oppression of women—to denounce it. Ousmane and I heard those conversations as you revised his manuscripts, his articles, edited the films. Your magazine articles have the same ideas and similar language. They challenge traditions and sacred customs. The extremists don't like it at all. They might attack you. I think there's an extremist conspiracy against us."

"A few sensational stories do not constitute a conspiracy, Isaac. I am not leaving Senegal—not relocating abroad. We are as safe here as we would be anywhere else."

"What will you do? How will you manage?"

"We should be secure financially. The royalties go directly into trust funds that generate enough income to support us quite comfortably. There are separate educational trusts for you and Ousmane, now both yours. And I'll continue to write my magazine column for *Attention, Femmes!*"

"That's not what I mean. I need to know what you'll do from day to day. Will you be occupied, involved in activities at the university, attend conferences, go to film openings, have an interesting life? I mean, without Papa, I can't imagine what you'll do. I can't imagine you without Papa."

"I am sure I will have a great deal to do in the coming months. There's the business of film releases and contracts, and a constant flow of papers about finances that I must study. Letters to answer—endless correspondence. Ibrahim's agent wants to publish his letters—and I've agreed to assist with that project."

"That's all Papa's work, not your work. When you were young, before you married Papa, even before that—before your first marriage—what kind of life were you planning?"

"I wanted to become a university professor—to teach litera-ture. My first job, my only job, really, was a teaching position at Boston University. If my life—my career—had evolved in a typical fashion, I probably would have continued teaching at BU or somewhere else. I would have never remarried. Instead, I would have followed the progress of my students, written two or three textbooks by now, and had a few colleagues as friends. In retrospect, that seems rather conventional. I'm not at all sorry that I made some unconventional choices, that I followed my heart."

"But you are asking me the questions that I ought to ask of you. What kind of life are you planning? What are you going to do over the next, say, ten or fifteen years?"

With a shift of his gaze toward the sky, Isaac evaded my question.

"Mama, what a fantastic sky! It's gone from rose to purple."

It was a familiar evasion. Ibrahim often drew attention to a moment in nature when he preferred to avoid a subject. Isaac had been a student of his father's style, a faithful observer. The cloudless amethyst sky distracted us for a while. But again I asked, "Isaac, what sort of life are you planning?" He turned toward me with his honest eyes and most earnest expression.

"Mama, I want to live in the States. I've always wanted to live there and be American. Now I know I do. I know I'm afraid to live here. After college, I'd like to study journalism. I want to try for the journalism school at Columbia. And then work for a major newspaper or news magazine—*Newsweek* or *Time.* Live in the east—New York, maybe. Marry. Have some kids—two or three. And have you come and live with us. Can you understand my wanting to live there, Mama?"

"Of course, I understand. Didn't I leave to come here? I understand the importance of finding the place where your soul wants to settle, living in a place where you can live with your true self. Ibrahim used to call you our 'American son.' You were always attracted to things American—clothing, films, magazines, people. You found it all rather exotic, which amused us. Well, Mom will be pleased to learn that you want to live there."

"Oh, Granny already knows. I told her at Thanksgiving when I went to visit her. And, yes, she was very happy to hear it. Well, so now I've told you and it's okay. I didn't know how you and Papa would feel about it. And now with you so alone . . ."

"Isaac, I want you to have plans of your own, to be clear about what you must do, what's in your best interest. I'd hoped that you'd recognize that the U.S. suits you—or, rather, that you seem equipped to cope with life over there."

"I am. I'm ready for it. I feel at home there—more at home there than here. It's getting dark. We'd better go in."

Isaac extended his hand and steadied me as I stood and stepped from the boulders on to the sandy path, now barely discernible in dusk's pale light. We walked in silence. With Isaac's intentions now explicit, I felt the weight of some ill-defined responsibilities fall away.

In late August, Isaac left for New Haven. On his future trips to Dakar, he arrived with the air of a returning tourist, a visitor interested in hearing about new developments in the region, seeing a few relatives, and meeting a few old friends. And he always appeared ready to leave a day or two before his scheduled departure.

# 50

EACH MORNING I WAS UP AT DAYBREAK. I dressed in boubous of storm cloud gray, drab olive, and earth brown, boubous in shades worn by widows. I walked out to the boulders, to Ibrahim's rock and to mine, along the bluff on the trail above the bay, and then back to the compound, braced for the transactions of the day.

My thoughts traveled across the ocean and back again. I wondered about Isaac and worried about Mom. I now understood better the emptiness of her widowhood.

Memories of Ousmane as a bright, inquisitive youngster and as an angry, insolent adolescent haunted me. I reviewed incidents which might have helped me to account for his final horrific act. And I addressed Ibrahim. In daily monologues I asked, "Why did it happen to us, Ibrahim? What should we have done differently?"

The light of each new day was reassuring. The serenity of those morning walks sustained me. I hardly knew how long or how far I had walked. The quantity of ocherous dust in my sandals was the measure of those walks. Waiting at the gate to greet me was Djibril's wife, Dara, with their sons. The younger one was cradled on her back and their older son stood at her side, a four-year-old, whose large, sad eyes and slender face reminded me of Ousmane. "Good morning, madame. Your tea is waiting for you." And so each day began.

On Ibrahim's desk, Dara placed a tray with a pot of tea, a basket of fruit, and bread or a bowl of yogurt, whatever she assumed might please me. My work—Ibrahim's work—lay there before me: letters to be answered, correspondence with film studios, publishers, and agents; unfinished manuscripts, forms for permission to use his works, essays to be edited, memorial notes and obituaries to be filed, scrapbooks to be filled. Widows' work. Daily tasks that were deadening.

There were, of course, other possibilities for work. Other projects, such as appeals for assistance from women's development projects: would I like to organize a session for a conference in Lagos, attend meetings in Dakar or Bamako, teach in Togo, evaluate a project in Botswana, write an article for a U.N. magazine, be a delegate to an international congress? No, I did not have time. I had more important work, the task of memorializing Ibrahim.

I usually had lunch alone in the courtyard, with only the clatter of Dara, Djibril, and the children, who ate the same fare from a common dish in the kitchen as company. When their banter became too distracting, I covered the sound with the music of Orff's *Carmina Burana*, repeatedly playing the chorus—"*Fortuna, imperatrix mundi.*"

Except for Djibril and Dara, faithful Fatou was the only other person who had a key to the gate and unannounced access to the compound. She came and went as her teaching obligations and other commitments permitted. After greeting Djibril or Dara, complimenting them on the grooming of the courtyard or the appearance of the house, she then would come to me. One day, when she found me sitting lifelessly at the desk, Fatou said, "Let's assign priorities to these tasks. What is pressing? What would you feel good about accomplishing? And what can you ignore, discard, forget?"

On another visit, she found me turning over the soil at the base of the giant cactus with a trowel. "Sarah, that cactus has been growing for years without any help. Why are you poking at it now? That's Mariama's chore." With a sweep of her hand toward the sky, "Let Mariama continue to take care of it!"

Fatou sometimes had dinner with me. She reviewed films for a newspaper, and sometimes brought videotapes of recent films. To keep me engaged, she often interrupted the viewing, asking my opinion of the acting or the plot. She scribbled notes, stopped the reel again, offered her interpretation, made more notes. Only when I insisted I was unable to concentrate or too tired to continue watching would she rewind her tape and go home.

Later, when I could summon the energy to entertain, I called Françoise Dia or Suzanne Rémy, a gallery owner who had become a friend. Lunch with one of them frequently extended into the late afternoon—afternoons of conversation about politics, art, books, food, fashions, films, and trips they had taken or were planning. They avoided mentioning their husbands and their children, and, of course, they stayed clear of references to Ibrahim and Ousmane. Only just before leaving would they inquire about Isaac. "And how is Isaac? What have you heard from him?"

Fortunately, Isaac wrote lengthy letters, which I summarized for them: the topic of a term paper, his performance in a soccer match, his excitement about a lecture by Cornel West; or an observation about U.S. students, whom he found to be blissfully unaware of the political affairs of Africa. Invariably, my friends remarked that Isaac soon would be disappointed by America; he would be assaulted by American racism and would come home.

When I didn't have company in the afternoon, I turned to the unfinished business on Ibrahim's desk. My nights were long, dark, and empty. Sleep eluded me. In the episodes of insomnia, I read contracts and other legal documents, which I thought would be sleep-inducing. Instead, they held my interest and kept me awake.

In December, dozens of invitations were in the mail. It was the beginning of the season of cultural and sporting events in Dakar which extended into April. The invitations lay unopened. The trauma of the previous December revisited me. The shock, despair, and depression that I thought I had moved beyond overtook me. I drew the shutters and retreated to the sanctuary of our bedroom. December had become the cruelest month.

"It's the anniversary reaction," Fatou said. "It's normal.

You'll recover. Isaac is coming in a few days. He'll need to find you in good condition. You should go out with him and attend a few events of the season."

Françoise Dia's son was arriving from New York on the flight with Isaac. She met them at the airport and drove Isaac home. In her breezy mood, Françoise announced him. "Your handsome Yale man has returned! And what a political analyst he has become. He explained the U.S. elections brilliantly—better than the journalists."

Isaac and I embraced. My depression was apparent to him. I went limp in his arms. He and Françoise literally carried me to the divan in the great hall, where I lay for hours, sipping tea and listening to Isaac. His presence relieved my depression. He talked about his classes, described the eccentricities of lecturers, and parodied his classmates with mirthful animation.

When we went into town to dine with the Dias and the Dioufs, Isaac appeared lighthearted. He insisted on taking Fatou and me to a new restaurant and to the theater. Dakar was bustling with cultural events and tourists. After a few excursions with him, I chose to stay at home. Isaac, however, went into the city frequently to see films and to rendezvous with his lycée friends. In general, he was very cheerful. I thought his high spirits were exaggerated; he was compensating for my gloomy mood.

At home, he spent the evening hours alone, watching over and over again the videotape of the Nobel Prize proceedings. He asked me to watch it with him. I watched the opening ceremonies. When Ibrahim appeared on the screen, I left the room. I couldn't watch.

Isaac said, "It helps me to see Papa, to remember him as he was at the ceremonies, brilliant, proud, courageous, and celebrated—recognized by the world. The memory of that moment gives me the will to carry on."

On New Year's Eve, Isaac left Dakar on a flight to Paris to join a Yale student who was visiting her family. "Her family lives in Princeton. Her father is a historian—he teaches French history. They're in Paris where he's on sabbatical." Isaac drew from the breast pocket of his blazer a passport photo of the friend, Rebecca. A pleasant smile, wide eyes, high forehead, keen features in an elongated face, close-cropped hair, she resembled Isaac. I didn't comment on the resemblance or suggest that one's first love is often a reflection of oneself. Delighted by her image, I merely said, "She is very, very beautiful. You make an attractive couple, I'm sure." And I thought of Lincoln.

Isaac packed a few of Ibrahim's books, the white caftan that Ibrahim often wore, and a copy of the videotape. And he was off to Paris without a word about how it might feel to return to the city where his father and his brother had been blown to bits only the year before.

# 51

ALTHOUGH I WAS NOT YET READY FOR PUBLIC appearances, I accepted an invitation to attend a rally in Dakar on International Women's Day. Fatou brought an engraved invitation from the Commission on Women's Rights in early January. At first I resisted.

"The commission wishes to honor you. They are making a medal with your name on it, Sarah. They want you to offer brief remarks—only five minutes. You must attend," insisted Fatou.

Finally I agreed. March was weeks away. There would be time to prepare myself for it. On the morning of the eighth of March, I awoke with a queasy stomach and an uneasy feeling about being on a podium in the midst of a crowd. I lay in bed inventing plausible excuses that might release me from the commitment. Upset stomach. Flu. Still grief-stricken. Laryngitis. Somehow I made myself get up, shower, and dress in an indigo boubou with white silk embroidery at the neckline and a band of indigo cloth twisted turbanlike about my head. I drafted a statement and asked Djibril to drive me to the stadium in Dakar.

Along the route, clusters of women, dressed in festive finery, wended their way toward the city. With each kilometer, the throng grew denser. Young women trudged along with infants bundled on their backs, provisions in baskets on their heads, and jugs of water in their hands. Older women and young children were crammed in vans and buses.

By the time the stadium was in view, the streets were clogged with pedestrians and traffic. Dakar teemed with women and children. Some had the solemn expressions of religious pilgrims, some the boisterous air of football fans, and some the militant manner of protesters. They had traversed Senegal to attend the mass meeting. Banners with slogans announced their towns—Thies, Passi, Kaolack, Joal, and Saint Louis—and their objectives: FARMS FOR WOMEN FARMERS!; CLEAN WATER! OUR CHILDREN ARE THIRSTY!; TEACH US TO READ!; SEND SEEDS—NOT ADVISORS! We were inching along the avenue. Traffic ahead appeared to have stalled.

"Djibril, stop the car. I want to be in the crowd. I'll walk from here," I said.

"Madame, in this mob? If you walk, I must walk with you."

"No need to. I'll be fine."

"I will wait for you, Madame, near the entrance of the stadium."

I stepped out of the car into a bedraggled bunch of peasant women from Betani who told me that they had been traveling for three days. Their truck had broken down 85 kilometers away. They had abandoned the truck and walked the remaining distance with their young children and a few provisions, peanuts, and dried fish.

Just ahead, a marching band of uniformed schoolgirls struck up a martial anthem. The music changed the cadence of the Betani women who raised their banner higher and, with pep in their step, paraded proudly along the boulevard.

Inside the stadium, under a searing sun, the program was in progress. A group of women, vigorously dancing their village choreography, tested the stability of the platform in the center of the field. Drumbeats, pounding through the sound system, and the rhythmic hand clapping of the crowd drove their frenzied motions. As their pace escalated, the crowd cheered and clapped more and more vigorously.

In the crush of women and children, I felt a moment of panic. Remembering the VIP badge in my packet, I pinned it on and soon was spotted by an usher, who escorted me to the canopied stand for dignitaries, where the president's wife greeted me.

"Madame Mangane, we are delighted to have you with our party. You are one of the three women who will receive the commission's medal of honor this afternoon. We are looking forward to your remarks."

"I'm delighted to be here. This is a magnificent demonstration—absolutely exhilarating." I took the seat reserved for me. With an excellent view of the proceedings, I surveyed the stadium. The bleachers were nearly filled. Hundreds of women and children were still making their way into the stadium.

There was hearty applause for the dancers when they completed their performance. They were followed by a young poet who recited in Wolof, Fulani, and French a poem that was a tribute to generations of village women who fetched water for their young and their elderly in the dry season. After the poet, a choir of Catholic nuns sang a spirited round about liberation theology and a hymn to the mothers in the audience. The mistress of ceremonies then invited the president's wife and the recipients of the medal of honor to come forward.

As we approached the platform, a trumpet fanfare blared while an honor guard of uniformed Girl Scouts saluted us. The crowd cheered. The president's wife read the proclamations and then draped us with blue sashes on which she pinned silver medals. My citation read as follows: *In recognition of courage, perseverance, and high purpose in the interest of enlightening society and improving the condition of women.*

We were asked to address the audience. I was the last to speak. I thanked the Women's Commission and spoke briefly on the importance of International Women's Day as an occasion when women throughout the world should register their claim for authority, a statement drawn from an article I had written. I said, "We are here to claim our authority as women. It is an authority derived from our participation in campaigns, resistance movements, boycotts, protests, and struggles: struggles against injustices and indignities that affect the lives of women and against the forces—formal and informal—that devalue the contributions of women. We need to encourage women in every sector of society to acknowledge their authority and to actualize their own power. Women must regard other women as sources of authority and power. Women, unite to empower women!"

Scattered applause grew to a crescendo. They roared their agreement. As we were escorted from the platform, hoards of women rushed toward us. In the midst of cheering strangers, Fatou and Françoise appeared.

"You did it! You said what they had come from all over the country to hear. They needed to hear that message from you. They know what you've been through. Now they have seen you return. It was a show of great resilience," said Françoise.

"Overcome tragedy—that's what you've shown them today. These women will draw inspiration from your words for years to come," said Fatou. "I hope you're happy that you came. Now get on with greeting people. Everybody wants to shake your hand. I'll see you tomorrow."

It was an afternoon of passionate expression. With each handshake, I accepted commiseration and heard a story of personal suffering and loss. It was a long afternoon in relentless heat. Gradually the crowd diminished, and their chants and songs receded in the distance. Clusters of weary women and children walked slowly toward the trucks and vans that would carry them onto the dusty roads that led to their towns and villages.

Djibril, who had parked in the shade of a tree, was watching for me. He hurried to escort me to the car.

"You were a great success, Madame! Everybody who came out was talking about what you said. They said it was the best speech of the day."

When Fatou arrived the following day, she found me not at Ibrahim's desk, but in my study at my own desk. I was reading the mail that had accumulated: personal mail, bulletins from women's organizations, brochures, pamphlets, and reports.

"Well, I am pleased to see you at your desk. What happened?" Fatou settled into the rattan chaise lounge.

"The events of yesterday made a difference. It was strangely gratifying to know that other women—complete strangers—understood my experience. Their compassion reduced my sense of isolation. And something else happened: My speech was a challenge to my own exercise of authority. My own words made me look at myself and think about my own potential authority."

"That's progress. You spoke brilliantly. You were very brave. No references to Ibrahim or what happened. You weren't his widow yesterday. You were yourself. I've been very concerned about you, afraid of your turning into a professional widow— what some call an 'action widow'—widows who devote themselves entirely to the promotion of the works of their late husbands at the expense of their own interests and careers."

"An action widow? Perhaps I am. It's difficult to reclaim one's self when more than half of one's life has been in the service of a celebrated partner. There are expectations on the part of others interested in Ibrahim's estate. I have some obligations to them, and an interest in completing his work, perhaps a greater interest than anyone else, except Isaac. And for Isaac, I must reinforce the importance of Ibrahim's contributions and set the record straight."

"Must you do it for Isaac? I wonder. What about you—what must you do for yourself? You speak of obligations, expectations—what are your expectations for yourself? Your obligations to yourself?"

"I'm beginning to think about those questions."

"Well, this isn't the best place to think about them. You need to get away—and I know where! Yesterday, after the program, I ran into Suzanne Rémy. She's going to call you with an offer—a kind of vacation offer—that you ought to accept."

"A vacation? Unthinkable, Fatou."

"Well, think about it, Sarah." Fatou wiggled to the edge of the seat and got to her feet. "Don't call it a vacation—call it whatever you wish. But get out of this house for a while. This place has become a mausoleum of memories and regrets."

# 52

SUZANNE AND CLAUDE RÉMY OFFERED ME THE use of their Gorée house while they scouted for an apartment in Paris. Suzanne and Fatou recognized, before I did, that I needed to leave the compound, at least for a brief time. I needed to escape the books, papers, certificates, trophies, paintings, sculpture, carpets, clothing, pens, and pipes that had been Ibrahim's. I needed to be free of the letters and telephone calls that required replies, inquiries about the use of his films, his published and unpublished works, indeed, sometimes merely the use of his name, the words "Ibrahim Mangane." I needed to install myself in a place where the memory of Ibrahim would have fewer claims on me.

Gorée. Ibrahim and I had never been to Gorée together. After filming *The Chains of Gorée,* Ibrahim had sworn that he never would return to the island and he'd kept his promise. My fascination with Gorée had annoyed him. He was baffled by the appeal of a place that represented atrocity and genocide. I had visited the island several times, first with Bill Nelson; and on occasion, I had accompanied tourists from the U.S. and other countries. Each visit had aroused an odd mixture of emotions. Whenever I was on the ferry to Gorée, I thought of my trips to Martha's Vineyard. When the soft pastels of Gorée's grand tile-roofed houses—slave traders' mansions—came into view, history and reverie collided. I shuddered as I thought of the Slave House, La Maison des Esclaves, where, along with other tourists, I had heard well-rehearsed guides tell the grotesque story of the slave trade that had occupied the house.

They showed the relics of brutality—chains and fetters, pokers and branding irons—and brooded over the tragedy of human suffering, mourned the unknown resisters who threw themselves or were thrown to the sharks, and marveled at the miracle of human determination in that sturdy band of Africans who had survived. Survival was what Gorée symbolized for me. Survival.

Suzanne Rémy had sent me magazine articles about their handsomely furnished house. She said that their household staff would take good care of me. For someone in search of solace and solitude, Gorée and the Rémys' house seemed ideal.

I packed a suitcase with a few essentials: white boubous, white slacks, and white shirts. I filled my jewelry case with gold bracelets, my necklace of gold and lapis lazuli, the heart-shaped pin with rubies and pearls, and other gifts from Ibrahim. What else? Music would be satisfying company: the voices of Leontyne Price, Kathleen Battle, Miriam Makeba, Nina Simone, Aretha Franklin, and Zap Mama; works by Vivaldi, Orff, Kay, Messiaen, Ellington, and T. J. Anderson. From a shelf of my favorite books, I plucked Miriama Ba's *So Long a Letter*, Toni Morrison's *Beloved*, and Deirdre Bair's biography of Simone de Beauvoir.

Djibril drove me to the launch that ferries passengers across the bay from the port of Dakar to Gorée. On the way, I reminded him that I wished to be left alone. "Don't tell anyone where I am. When people inquire, tell them I've gone abroad, away on business, that I'll return next month."

I boarded the launch for the twenty-minute cruise as if I were setting out on a long voyage. Facing the island, I settled into a deck chair and heard myself think: "*I will cast mine eyes upon these waters from whence cometh my help. My help cometh from Gorée!*"

As the launch docked, the gathering of vendors, beggars, and guides awaiting its arrival surged forward. In the crowd was a tall, stately woman who was not a vendor, or a beggar, or a guide. As our eyes met, we exchanged gazes of recognition. The resemblance was arresting. Our features—eyes, nose, mouth—

were nearly identical. We were about the same height. Her fig-ure was leaner; her taut skin stretched over prominent cheek-bones. Our faces were almost identical, although she appeared slightly older.

As I stepped off the launch, she approached me. In a husky contralto, speaking with the cadence of market women, she said in a blend of Wolof and French, "Madame Mangane, I am sent to help you. Give me your suitcase." Without waiting for my response, she reached for it and took command of my arrival. Her deliberate stride led us away from the harbor, across the sandy esplanade baked by the late-morning sun. I followed the flow of her boubou with its shades of batiked green, admired her tight cornrows of braided hair, the regal tilt of her head, the confident rhythm in her stride. I compared our physical similar-ities, wondering whether she, too, had been struck by our resemblance. When she turned onto a palm tree–shaded street, I walked beside her, studying her profile.

"Thank you for meeting me," I said. "It was good of the Rémys to send you. What's your name?"

"Call me Aisha," she answered.

"Are you the Rémys' housekeeper?" I inquired.

"Not the housekeeper," she said. I assumed I soon would ascertain Aisha's role in their household.

At a weathered wooden gate in a high stone wall, Aisha pro-duced an enormous key, unlocked the gate and, with a nod, invited me to enter. Abundant clusters of marguerites and giant yellow marigolds lined a narrow stone path leading to the house. We stepped out of the bright heat into the cool of a darkened sitting room with deep cushioned sofas and armchairs covered with bold African fabrics. A Benin bronze pot with a colossal bouquet of tropical flowers adorned a round oak din-ing table at the end of the room. Aisha opened the shutters. Sunlight poured into the room and illuminated dozens of paint-ings and prints in glistening gold frames on the whitewashed walls.

"Come," she said. I followed her up the narrow, creaking stairs into a blue room—a bedroom in Matisse blue—blue walls, blue carpet, a blue bedspread covered a queen-size bed, a blue enameled desk and chair, and a chaise longue upholstered in a fabric with giant blue and white lilies.

"You to sleep here," Aisha said. My immediate smile expressed my pleasure with the room. I surrendered to its elegance with delight. She seemed pleased by my reaction.

"Where are the others—the other household help?" I asked.

"With their families in the villages. Vacation."

"So we're alone here. Very well." It did not seem well at all. I was uneasy about being with Aisha. She had an air of mystery that was disturbing. "May I tell you how I'd like to spend my days here?" She nodded, but went about the room adjusting curtains and covers. She was not very attentive. "Each morning I will go for a walk, walk around the island. When I return, I'd like to have fruit and tea. I read in the morning. For lunch, I'd like fish or an omelette—vegetables, salad, fruit—whatever you find in the market. After lunch, I may take a nap or read. And I'll probably take a walk at the end of the day, when it's cooler. A salad will be sufficient for dinner. I don't want to receive telephone calls and I don't want visitors. Here are some francs for groceries and other essentials." She slipped the money into the pocket of her boubou and nodded.

Aisha moved unobtrusively through the house and the garden, silently observing me as I unpacked, selected a book and magazines, as I trembled when a snake slithered across the garden path, or gazed at a bowl of strawberries—the first of the season. She recognized what needed to be done, and without speaking simply did it. When I returned from a walk, my eyes swollen and cheeks wet with tears, without a word, Aisha brought handkerchiefs. During my morning bath, she removed the bed linen and soiled clothing; after lunch she returned them crisply laundered.

She seemed to like music. When one side of a cassette tape ended, she was there instantly to reverse it. She herself played a single tune on a long wooden flute. Early in the morning and again at nightfall, the delicate high-pitched tones of her instrument filled the house. Gradually, I became comfortable in her company. Her caring presence and her flute music began to make me feel secure.

After a week of serving in virtual silence, except for the sound of her flute, Aisha expressed her curiosity about me. Stirring slowly, after an afternoon nap in a hammock in the shade of the garden, I lifted my lids to find her looking into my eyes, her face bent close, our noses nearly touching.

"Who is you?" Aisha asked.

"You know who I am. You addressed me by name when you met me at the launch. So what do you want to know about me?" Feeling vulnerable in the hammock, I got up and went into the house where I sat at the table. She followed me inside and sat across from me.

"You've seen me from the moment I've gotten up until I've gone to bed, every day and every night for a week. You know who I am, what I do."

"You read much."

"But you know who I am."

"You are called Madame Mangane. Before you was Madame Mangane, who was you? Mangane's dead. Who you now? And who you going to be?"

I didn't answer immediately. I contemplated her questions. Why was it of interest to her? What was she getting at? At what level should I attempt to answer her? Why bother to talk to her about who I am? I was troubled by her curiosity.

"If you are asking whether I plan to remarry—"

"No, no, no," she interrupted. "Go back to the beginning. Who was you?"

"Who was I? It would take too long to recall—"

"Can't remember who you was?" she whispered with incredulity.

"Well, I was a daughter, a student, a student-wife in my first marriage. To Ibrahim Mangane I was apprentice, lover, wife, homemaker, secretary, editor, clerk, bookkeeper, confidante, adversary, friend—all that a woman married to him needed to be."

"Mangane is no more. Who you now?"

"A mother."

"A son who is adult. A man. No need for mother."

"And I am the executor of Ibrahim Mangane's estate, the keeper of his papers and his memory." I thought about my own accomplishments: I had earned a doctorate, been a university lecturer, promoted an international festival, managed the affairs of a great man. It was a life with ample material for an obituary.

"Who is you, the true you? You read, but you don't write. You listen to music, but you don't sing or play the kora or whistle on the flute. You wear cloth, but you don't weave. You cut flowers, but you don't plant, weed, and water them."

"Aisha, in modern times, in a modern world—"

"I know you a modern woman. But women know who they are through the work they do. Madame Mangane come from America to live in Dakar. Not enough. European women live out their lives through the work of their husbands. Not African women. You are African woman. Or are you African? Do you stay here or go back to America—become American again?"

"I'll remain here. This is my home. I'm African."

"When you married Mangane, you became more African woman. You someone, someone of worth, someone who work. When your day, your time is over and death take you into the dark of night, you must leave something you made to show who you were—garden, cloth, beads, pots, new style of dance, music, picture, masks, canes, something. When you tell what you do, you tell who is you."

"Right now, Aisha, I'm a woman who is going for a walk." And as I hurriedly left, I wondered who is this Aisha who dares to query the interior of my being? Why do I become defensive? Why do I bother to answer her questions or talk with her at all? Who is this strange woman who resembles me?

It was too warm to walk around the island, and I didn't want to be surrounded by tourists' talk at a café. I turned into rue Saint-Germain and went to La Maison des Esclaves. Admission fees were listed on the gate. I patted the pockets of my slacks and realized that I had come out without any francs. The caretaker of the museum smiled and greeted me with a powerful handshake. "Good day, Madame Mangane. Welcome. I had heard that you were on the island. I had hoped that you would come to the museum, that you would honor us with a visit again. Please do come in."

I crossed the courtyard toward the sinister stairs that thousands of slaves once climbed, that thousands of tourists now climb. A guide said in a stage whisper to the tourists clustered around him, "That is Madame Mangane, the widow of Ibrahim Mangane. He wrote *The Chains of Gorée,* made a film based on the book. The film was made here when I was a child. I was in the film. I played the role of an enslaved child." He smiled with pride. The tourists turned to watch as I climbed the stairs.

"Iron rings and chains cemented to terra cotta walls of La Maison des Esclaves hold the evidence of its cruel history. A bleak moment in history," continued the guide.

I found a shady corner, sat on the bare clay platform, and contemplated Aisha's questions. Who was she to confront me, and ask me to examine my personal life? She was curious and quite persistent. She had irritated me, yet I was drawn to her as I had been drawn to the island for reasons that were beyond my ken.

In the splash of waves, I heard the voices of those who had been too strong or too frail, too proud or too humiliated to board slave ships, who had dived into the waves, and swum ashore to be free once more—or who had gone under and drowned.

When grieving for Ibrahim and Ousmane initially had engulfed me, I had contemplated walking into the bay where its waters would ripple just under my nose, breathing deeply, and surrendering to the notion of death by drowning. Had notions of drowning brought me here now? I scanned the expanse of the ocean and the horizon.

"*I will cast mine eyes upon the waters from whence cometh my help. My help cometh from . . . my help cometh from . . . my help cometh from . . . ? My help cometh from—from me— MYSELF.*"

I heard Aisha's questions: "Who is you? And who you going to be?" The sun had made its way to the nook where I sat. Drowsy, I succumbed to its heat and slipped into a slumber of fragmented dreams.

*I traversed the African continent in the company of women—
poor women in tatters. We were showing other women how to
dig wells, where to fish, what crops to plant.*

*Aisha took me to my favorite bookshop in Dakar. It was dif-
ferent, however; the books were different. All the books were by
African and African-American women authors and were about
women. Aisha and I owned a women's bookshop.*

*I was digging a well with a group of village women when
Ibrahim appeared and said, "I am proud of you and the work
you are doing."*

The clang of a bell that signaled closing time roused me. I
made my way down the stairs of La Maison des Esclaves, shook
the caretaker's hand, and thanked him. The sun was leaving, too.
In the soft light of late afternoon, I strolled through the sandy
streets and lanes, contemplating Aisha's questions. Along the
way, I stopped at a house with a plaque: "The house of Mother
Javouhey, founder of the order of sisters of Saint Joseph of
Cluny, a nun who devoted her life to the fight against slavery."
On previous visits to Gorée, I had scarcely noticed the house
and its plaque. This time the reference to Mother Javouhey's
dedication connected with my fragmented dreams.

Returning to the Rémys, on the square near Saint Charles
Church I came upon a house with a rusting FOR SALE sign. A
ruin of an eighteenth-century mansion, instantly it became the
site for my fantasy. I lingered before it, counting the broken
windows, noting the battered or missing shutters, the long-
neglected garden of weeds and litter. I imagined it improved,
refurbished, painted, with a sign: L'ALLIANCE DES FEMMES
AFRICAINES. I had found a place for my purpose and my own
work.

At the Rémys, I pushed opened the gate and stepped swiftly
along the garden path.

The music of Aisha's flute abruptly stopped. She called from
the house, "Madame Mangane, that you?" She appeared at the
door. "It don't sound like your feet. And your face is smiling!"

"I've found a house that interests me. I need to phone a real
estate agent in Dakar." I reached the agent and offered half the

sale price of the house. He needed to contact the owner, who lived in Brussels. In the meantime, I revisited the house, gained entry through an open window, and examined the interior. I made inquiries about carpenters, repairmen, and plumbers on the island. The renovation would require an architect.

With *Carmina Burana* the constant background music for my imagination, I made sketches and scribbled notes, listed organizations to contact, and names of individuals—women like Aunt Khady—with instructive projects that I needed to visit. I was excited by the prospect of women across the continent contributing ideas about a development collective, a pan-African alliance of women who would learn from one another and, in turn, teach other women useful skills. Night and day for nearly a week, I drafted a charter, wrote letters, and outlined proposals. Aisha looked on with intense interest, as if she knew exactly what I was trying to do.

Having planned what needed to be done, I told Aisha that I was leaving for Dakar the next morning on the early ferry. I telephoned the compound and told Djibril that I would return the next day. Up before dawn, I gathered my books, tapes, my clothing, and jewelry. An impassive Aisha accompanied me to the dock.

"You come back, madame, come back to Gorée to stay?"

"I'll be back here to stay." We embraced. Tears were in our eyes. I stepped onto the launch and turned to wave to Aisha. She wasn't there.

Once at home, I telephoned Fatou to test the idea on her litmus of pragmatism.

"A grand idea, Sarah! The place is important to its success. Gorée is a good location. A center with a contemporary purpose should be there—a counterbalance for La Maison des Esclaves. We're tired of it, tired of the tourists, tired of their questions, tired of being reminded. Gorée could have a new life and a new meaning."

"Gorée is associated with slavery, yes, but it's also a symbol of survival. Before I acquire that house on Gorée, however, I need to hire someone very responsible to take over things here, to handle Ibrahim's work, oversee the household, and assist with managing the compound."

"There's a couple at the university who would be delighted to take on Ibrahim's work and the compound. I can arrange that for you. By the way, Bill Nelson has been trying to reach you. He's in Dakar for a few days with a cultural affairs delegation. He's eager to see you. I saw him yesterday at the Teranga Hotel, where the delegation is staying."

"Super! He's just the person I need to consult."

I called the hotel and left a message for Bill. He phoned and we arranged to meet for dinner at his hotel.

I hadn't seen Bill since the funerals. We embraced in the lobby. With an air of surprise, he said, "You look very well. You're thinner, but you look healthy. You're wearing slacks now, I see." As we walked toward the restaurant, he gave his nod of approval to my white tunic and white slacks.

He inquired about how I was coping and how Isaac was getting along. And what did I think of the various memorial proposals under consideration?

"We met with the Minister of Culture who discussed the possibility of establishing a Mangane Prize in literature, naming a film festival for Ibrahim, and converting a section of your compound into a film library and museum."

"I like the idea of a film library at the compound," I said.

"Wouldn't that disrupt your life, having a library open to the public as part of your home?"

"The compound was Ibrahim's home. I've decided to move to Gorée and live in a collective of women who will work toward improving conditions in Africa, an alliance of women who will assist other women with the recovery of their villages and their means of productivity."

"An alliance of women? What could they do that the organizations scattered across the beloved continent aren't already doing?"

"The idea is to draw on our internal resources and expertise and to encourage trust in our way of doing things. Women in Angola, Niger, Ethiopia, Libya, Chad, Uganda, Namibia—village women across the continent—have no means of explaining to others their agricultural innovations, medical remedies, techniques for conserving fuel, sharing equipment, making cloth, pottery, marketing goods. Communications among villages, among countries, are very poor. With film, video, in photographs, the details of successful projects could be documented and disseminated to the poorest villages, villages at risk. Villagers could learn some survival strategies from the examples of other village women. The project would move Africa toward self-reliance." As I talked, the vision grew sharper and I became more excited. "I need to understand the operation of Africa's most successful rural development projects, consult people who run them, seek their advice about exchanging information, sharing their expertise, and—"

"This could be a megaproject—something for the World Bank or the IMF. But what's the purpose of it?"

"The purpose? To strengthen alliances among successful projects and to create a center for exchanging ideas about better ways of planting, harvesting, locating water, healing sick children, raising animals, building housing—techniques that improve chances for survival. Many such projects—especially those in rural areas—are managed by women. A pan-African center for development, expressly for women, is what I have in mind. An international alliance of women of African descent—African women in the Americas would be encouraged to come, too."

"Why should a project of this scope be for women only?"

"Women wouldn't be the only beneficiaries. But it is womanpower that sustains village life, provides much of the food, and cares for the health of the continent. Men have left the villages for work in towns and cities. It's the labor of village women and girls across the continent that's essential to Africa. Village women are the farmers, hunters, gatherers, cooks, and nurses. A pan-African alliance could double their productivity and increase the survival potential of generations."

"You'll need advisors and equipment. You'll need funds, Sarah, more money than you have."

"I know. I can afford to buy the building and renovate it. As for the expense of bringing women to the center, documenting their projects, distributing information, and promoting the work, I'll have to raise money—send out proposals to international organizations, divisions of the United Nations, and nongovernmental organizations."

"It's a very ambitious project, Sarah. But if anybody can pull it off, you can. I'd like to help you if I can. I have some contacts at foundations, and access to government agencies. Send a proposal to my Paris office."

"I'll deliver the proposal to you here, before you leave for Paris."

Purchasing the Gorée house and negotiating the cost of renovations with contractors was a complicated business. When Isaac came home in June, he supervised the refurbishing of the building. He worked steadily until September with roofers and carpenters; and a few of his friends joined him in painting the exterior.

When it was time for Isaac to return to New Haven, he said wistfully, "I've loved working on this house, Mama. Did you know the carpenters called it Mama Sarah's house, and now that's what everybody on Gorée calls it? I only wish I could stay here and finish the work."

"You have work to finish at Yale. You helped a great deal this summer. If you hadn't been here, I wouldn't have accomplished the other work that had to be done—contacting organizations, finding sponsors, getting started."

During the two years that followed, I visited villages renowned for recovery from drought, high infant survival levels, and general prosperity. By jeep, bus, truck, camel, plane, and pirogue, I toured villages in every part of Africa. The production of videotapes and manuals about the projects required months. And there were speaking engagements to promote the work. I flew from Dakar to Paris, Berlin, Oslo, London, New York, Los Angeles, Tokyo, Johannesburg, and Geneva. The potential success of the project was exhilarating! With significant contributions and pledges, I returned to Gorée, called a press conference, and announced the establishment of *l'Alliance des Femmes Africaines.*

A week or so later, in the midst of a workshop on the transfer of information from village to village, I was called to the telephone. An urgent call from New Haven. It was Isaac.

"Mama, I had to call. The major magazines are carrying your picture with articles about your center. It is phenomenal! It's exactly what is needed now to unify people and build confidence. And you're doing it!"

"Tell the women you know about the center. Young women, who need to know what they can do of enduring value, should come and work with African women who are ensuring the future of the continent."

"I'll tell them, Mama. And you should tell them about your life, your journey, and your psalm."